D1287845

AGATHA CHRISTIE

Collected Works

AGATHA CHRISTIE

Crooked House

Passenger to Frankfurt

Published by arrangement with
William Collins Sons & Co. Ltd.

Published & Distributed by
Omniprose Ltd.
94 Crockford Blvd.
Scarborough, Ontario
M1R 3C5

Printed in Canada
by John Deyell Company

ISBN 0-921111-11-8 (SET)
ISBN 0-921111-09-6

13 097 009

Crooked House

CONTENTS

CHAPTER I

I FIRST CAME to know Sophia Leonides in Egypt towards the end of the war. She held a fairly high administrative post in one of the Foreign Office departments out there. I knew her first in an official capacity, and I soon appreciated the efficiency that had brought her to the position she held, in spite of her youth (she was at that time just twenty-two).

Besides being extremely easy to look at, she had a clear mind and a dry sense of humour that I found very delightful. We became friends. She was a person whom it was extraordinarily easy to talk to and we enjoyed our dinners and occasional dances very much.

All this I knew; it was not until I was ordered East at the close of the European war that I knew something else—that I loved Sophia and that I wanted to marry her.

We were dining at Shepheard's when I made this discovery. It did not come to me with any shock of surprise, but more as the recognition of a fact with which I had been long familiar. I looked at her with new eyes—but I saw what I had already known for a long time. I liked everything I saw. The dark crisp hair that sprang up proudly from her forehead, the vivid blue eyes, the small square fighting chin, and the straight nose. I liked the well-cut light-grey tailor-made, and the crisp white shirt. She looked refreshingly English and that appealed to me strongly after three years without seeing my native land. Nobody, I thought, could be more English—and even as I was thinking exactly that, I suddenly wondered if, in fact, she was, or indeed could be, as English as she looked. Does the real thing ever have the perfection of a stage performance?

I realised that much and freely as we had talked together, discussing ideas, our likes and dislikes, the future, our immediate friends and acquaintances—Sophia had never mentioned her home or her family. She knew all about me (she was, as I have indicated, a good listener) but about her I knew nothing. She had, I supposed, the usual background, but she had never talked about it. And until this moment I had never realised the fact.

Sophia asked me what I was thinking about.

I replied truthfully: " You."

" I see," she said. And she sounded as though she did see.

" We may not meet again for a couple of years," I said. " I don't know when I shall get back to England. But as soon as I do get back, the first thing I shall do will be to come and see you and ask you to marry me."

She took it without batting an eyelash. She sat there, smoking, not looking at me.

For a moment or two I was nervous that she might not understand.

" Listen," I said. " The one thing I'm determined *not* to do, is to ask you to marry me now. That wouldn't work out anyway. First you might turn me down, and then I'd go off miserable and probably tie up with some ghastly woman just to restore my vanity. And if you didn't turn me down what could we do about it? Get married and part at once? Get engaged and settled down to a long waiting period? I couldn't stand your doing that. You might meet someone else and feel bound to be ' loyal ' to me. We've been living in a queer hectic get-on-with-it-quickly atmosphere. Marriages and love affairs making and breaking all round us. I'd like to feel you'd gone home, free and independent to look round you and size up the new post-war world and decide what you want out of it. What is between you and me, Sophia, has got to be *permanent*. I've no use for any other kind of marriage."

"No more have I," said Sophia.

"On the other hand," I said, "I think I'm entitled to let you know how I—well—how I feel."

"But without undue lyrical expression?" murmured Sophia.

"Darling—don't you understand? I've tried *not* to say I love you——"

She stopped me.

"I do understand, Charles. And I like your funny way of doing things. And you may come and see me when you come back—if you still want to——"

It was my turn to interrupt.

"There's no doubt about that."

"There's always a doubt about everything, Charles. There may always be some incalculable factor that upsets the apple-cart. For one thing, you don't know much about me, do you?"

"I don't even know where you live in England."

"I live at Swinly Dean."

I nodded at the mention of the well-known outer suburb of London which boasts three excellent golf courses for the city financier.

She added softly in a musing voice: "*In a little crooked house . . .*"

I must have looked slightly startled, for she seemed amused, and explained by elaborating the quotation "'*And they all lived together in a little crooked house.*' That's us.

Not really such a little house either. But definitely crooked —running to gables and half-timbering!"

"Are you one of a large family? Brothers and sisters?"

"One brother, one sister, a mother, a father, an uncle, an aunt by marriage, a grandfather, a great-aunt and a step-grandmother."

"Good gracious!" I exclaimed, slightly overwhelmed.

She laughed.

"Of course we don't normally all live together. The war and blitzes have brought that about—but I don't know"— she frowned reflectively—"perhaps spiritually the family has always lived together—under my grandfather's eye and protection. He's rather a Person, my grandfather. He's over eighty, about four-foot ten, and everybody else looks rather dim beside him."

"He sounds interesting," I said.

"He is interesting. He's a Greek from Smyrna. Aristide Leonides." She added, with a twinkle, "He's extremely rich."

"Will anybody be rich after this is over?"

"My grandfather will," said Sophia with assurance. "No Soak-the-rich tactics would have any effect on him. He'd just soak the soakers.

"I wonder," she added, "if you'll like him?"

"Do you?" I asked.

"Better than anyone in the world," said Sophia.

CHAPTER II

IT WAS over two years before I returned to England. They were not easy years. I wrote to Sophia and heard from her fairly frequently. Her letters, like mine, were not love letters. They were letters written to each other by close friends—they dealt with ideas and thoughts and with comments on the daily trend of life. Yet I know that as far as I was concerned, and I believed as far as Sophia was concerned, too, our feeling for each other grew and strengthened.

I returned to England on a soft grey day in September. The leaves on the trees were golden in the evening light. There were playful gusts of wind. From the airfield I sent a telegram to Sophia.

"*Just arrived back. Will you dine this evening Mario's nine o'clock? Charles.*"

A couple of hours later I was sitting reading *The Times*; and scanning the Births, Marriages and Deaths column my eye was caught by the name Leonides:

> On Sept. 19th, at Three Gables, Swinly Dean, Aristide Leonides, beloved husband of Brenda Leonides, in his eighty-eighth year. Deeply regretted.

There was another announcement immediately below:

> LEONIDES.—Suddenly, at his residence, Three Gables, Swinly Dean, Aristide Leonides. Deeply mourned by his loving children and grandchildren. Flowers to St. Eldred's Church, Swinly Dean.

I found the two announcements rather curious. There seemed to have been some faulty staff work resulting in overlapping. But my main preoccupation was Sophia. I hastily sent her a second telegram:

"*Just seen news of your grandfather's death. Very sorry. Let me know when I can see you. Charles.*"

A telegram from Sophia reached me at six o'clock at my father's house. It said:

"*Will be at Mario's nine o'clock. Sophia.*"

The thought of meeting Sophia again made me both nervous and excited. The time crept by with maddening slowness. I was at Mario's waiting twenty minutes too early. Sophia herself was only five minutes late.

It is always a shock to meet again someone whom you have not seen for a long time but who has been very much present in your mind during that period. When at last Sophia came through the swing doors our meeting seemed completely unreal. She was wearing black, and that, in some curious way, startled me! Most other women were wearing black, but I got it into my head that it was definitely mourning—and it surprised me that Sophia should be the kind of person who did wear black—even for a near relative.

We had cocktails—then went and found our table. We talked rather fast and feverishly—asking after old friends of the Cairo days. It was artificial conversation but it tided us over the first awkwardness. I expressed commiseration for her grandfather's death and Sophia said quietly that it had been "very sudden." Then we started off again reminiscing. I began to feel, uneasily, that something was the matter—something. I mean, other than the first natural awkwardness of meeting again. There was something wrong, definitely wrong, with Sophia herself. Was she, perhaps, going to tell me that she had found some other man whom she cared for more than she did for me? That her feeling for me had been " all a mistake "?

Somehow I didn't think it was that—I didn't know what it was. Meanwhile we continued our artificial talk.

Then, quite suddenly, as the waiter placed coffee on the table and retired, bowing, everything swung into focus. Here were Sophia and I sitting together as so often before at a small table in a restaurant. The years of our separation might never have been.

"*Sophia*," I said.

And immediately she said, " Charles!"

I drew a deep breath of relief.

"Thank goodness that's over," I said. " What's been the matter with us?"

" Probably my fault. I was stupid."

" But it's all right now."

We smiled at each other.

"Darling!" I said. And then: " How soon will you marry me?"

Her smile died. The something, whatever it was, was back.

" I don't know," she said. " I'm not sure, Charles, that I can ever marry you."

"But, Sophia! Why not? Is it because you feel I'm a stranger? Do you want time to get used to me again? Is there someone else? No——" I broke off. " I'm a fool. It's none of those things."

"No, it isn't." She shook her head. I waited. She said in a low voice:

" It's my grandfather's death."

"Your grandfather's death? But why? What earthly difference can that make? You don't mean—surely you can't imagine—is it money? Hasn't he left any? But surely, dearest——"

"It isn't money." She gave a fleeting smile. "I think you'd be quite willing to 'take me in my shift,' as the old saying goes. And grandfather never lost any money in his life."

"Then what is it?"

"It's just his death—you see, I think, Charles, that he didn't just—die. I think he may have been—killed . . ."

I stared at her.

"But—what a fantastic idea. What made you think of it?"

"*I* didn't think of it. The doctor was queer to begin with. He wouldn't sign a certificate. They're going to have a post-mortem. It's quite clear that they suspect something is wrong."

I didn't dispute that with her. Sophia had plenty of brains; any conclusions she had drawn could be relied upon.

Instead I said earnestly:

"Their suspicions may be quite unjustified. But putting that aside, supposing that they are justified, how does that affect you and me?"

"It might under certain circumstances. You're in the Diplomatic Service. They're rather particular about wives. No—please don't say all the things that you're just bursting to say. You're bound to say them—and I believe you really think them—and theoretically I quite agree with them. But I'm proud—I'm devilishly proud. I want our marriage to be a good thing for everyone—I don't want to represent one-half of a sacrifice for love! And, as I say, it *may* be all right . . ."

"You mean the doctor—may have made a mistake?"

" Even if he hasn't made a mistake, it won't matter—so long as the right person killed him."

" What *do* you mean, Sophia?"

" It was a beastly thing to say. But, after all, one might as well be honest."

She forestalled my next words.

" No, Charles, I'm not going to say any more. I've probably said too much already. But I was determined to come and meet you to-night—to see you myself and make you understand. We can't settle anything until this is cleared up."

" At least tell me about it."

She shook her head.

" I don't want to."

" But—Sophia——"

" No, Charles. I don't want you to see us from *my* angle. I want you to see us unbiassed from the outside point of view."

" And how am I to do that?"

She looked at me, a queer light in her brilliant blue eyes.

" You'll get that from your father," she said.

I had told Sophia in Cairo that my father was Assistant Commissioner of Scotland Yard. He still held that office. At her words, I felt a cold weight settling down on me.

" It's as bad as that, then?"

" I think so. Do you see a man sitting at a table by the door all alone—rather a nice-looking stolid ex-Army type?"

" Yes."

" He was on Swinly Dean platform this evening when I got into the train."

" You mean he's followed you here?"

" Yes. I think we're all—how does one put it?—under observation. They more or less hinted that we'd all better not leave the house. But I was determined to see you." Her small square chin shot out pugnaciously. " I got out of the bathroom window and shinned down the water-pipe."

" Darling!"

" But the police are very efficient. And of course there was the telegram I sent you. Well—never mind—we're here—together . . . But from now on, we've both got to play a lone hand."

She paused and then added:

" Unfortunately—there's no doubt—about our loving each other."

" No doubt at all," I said. " And don't say unfortunately. You and I have survived a world war, we've had plenty of near escapes from sudden death—and I don't see why the sudden death of just one old man—how old was he, by the way?"

" Eighty-seven."

" Of course. It was in *The Times*. If you ask me, he just died of old age, and any self-respecting G.P. would accept the fact."

" If you'd known my grandfather," said Sophia, " you'd have been surprised at his dying of *anything*!"

CHAPTER III

I'D ALWAYS taken a certain amount of interest in my father's police work, but nothing had prepared me for the moment when I should come to take a direct and personal interest in it.

I had not yet seen the Old Man. He had been out when I arrived, and after a bath, a shave and a change I had gone out to meet Sophia. When I returned to the house, however, Glover told me that he was in his study.

He was at his desk, frowning over a lot of papers. He jumped up when I came in.

"Charles! Well, well, it's been a long time."

Our meeting, after five years of war, would have disappointed a Frenchman. Actually all the emotion of reunion was there all right. The Old Man and I are very fond of each other, and we understand each other pretty well.

"I've got some whisky," he said. "Say when. Sorry I was out when you got here. I'm up to the ears in work. Hell of a case just unfolding."

I leaned back in my chair and lit a cigarette.

"Aristide Leonides?" I asked.

His brows came down quickly over his eyes. He shot me a quick appraising glance. His voice was polite and steely.

"Now what makes you say that, Charles?"

" I'm right then?"

" How did you know about this?"

" Information received."

The Old Man waited.

" My information," I said, " came from the stable itself."

" Come on, Charles, let's have it."

" You mayn't like it," I said. " I met Sophia Leonides out in Cairo. I fell in love with her. I'm going to marry her. I met her to-night. She dined with me."

" Dined with you? In London? I wonder just how she managed to do that? The family were asked—oh, quite politely—to stay put."

" Quite so. She shinned down a pipe from the bathroom window."

The Old Man's lips twitched for a moment into a smile.

" She seems," he said, " to be a young lady of some resource."

" But your police force is fully efficient," I said. " A nice Army type tracked her to Mario's. I shall figure in the reports you get. Five foot eleven, brown hair, brown eyes, dark-blue pinstripe suit, etc."

The Old Man looked at me hard.

" Is this—serious?" he asked.

" Yes," I said. " It's serious, Dad."

There was a moment's silence.

" Do you mind?" I asked.

" I shouldn't have minded—a week ago. They're a well-established family—the girl will have money—and I know you. You don't lose your head easily. As it is——"

" Yes, Dad?"

" It may be all right, if——"

" If what?"

" If the right person did it."

It was the second time that night I had heard that phrase. I began to be interested.

" Just who *is* the right person?"

He threw a sharp glance at me.

" How much do you know about it all?"

" Nothing."

" Nothing?" He looked surprised. " Didn't the girl tell you?"

" No. She said she'd rather I saw it all—from an outside point of view."

" Now I wonder why that was?"

" Isn't it rather obvious?"

" No, Charles. I don't think it is."

He walked up and down frowning. He had lit a cigar and the cigar had gone out. That showed me just how disturbed the old boy was.

" How much do you know about the family?" he shot at me.

" Damn all! I know there was the old man and a lot of sons and grandchildren and in-laws. I haven't got the ramifications clear." I paused and then said, " You'd better put me in the picture, Dad."

" Yes." He sat down. " Very well then—I'll begin at the beginning—with Aristide Leonides. He arrived in England when he was twenty-four."

" A Greek from Smyrna."

" You do know that much?"

" Yes, but it's about all I do know."

The door opened and Glover came in to say that Chief-Inspector Taverner was here.

" He's in charge of the case," said my father. " We'd better have him in. He's been checking up on the family. Knows more about them than I do."

I asked if the local police had called in the Yard.

"It's in our jurisdiction. Swinly Dean is Greater London."

I nodded as Chief-Inspector Taverner came into the room. I knew Taverner from many years back. He greeted me warmly and congratulated me on my safe return.

"I'm putting Charles in the picture," said the Old Man. "Correct me if I go wrong, Taverner. Leonides came to London in 1884. He started up a little restaurant in Soho. It paid. He started up another. Soon he owned seven or eight of them. They all paid hand over fist."

"Never made any mistakes in anything he handled," said Chief-Inspector Taverner.

"He'd got a natural flair," said my father. "In the end he was behind most of the well-known restaurants in London. Then he went into the catering business in a big way."

"He was behind a lot of other businesses as well," said Taverner. "Second-hand clothes trade, cheap jewellery stores, lots of things. Of course," he added thoughtfully, "he was always a twister."

"You mean he was a crook?" I asked.

Taverner shook his head.

"No, I don't mean that. Crooked, yes—but not a crook. Never anything outside the law. But he was the sort of chap that thought up all the ways you can get round the law. He's cleaned up a packet that way even in this last war, and old as he was. Nothing he did was ever illegal—but as soon as he'd got on to it, you had to have a law about it, if you know what I mean. But by that time he'd gone on to the next thing."

"He doesn't sound a very attractive character," I said.

"Funnily enough, he was attractive. He'd got personality, you know. You could feel it. Nothing much to look at. Just a gnome—ugly little fellow—but magnetic—women always fell for him."

"He made a rather astonishing marriage," said my father. "Married the daughter of a country squire—an M.F.H."

I raised my eyebrows. "Money?"

The Old Man shook his head.

"No, it was a love match. She met him over some catering arrangements for a friend's wedding—and she fell for him. Her parents cut up rough, but she was determined to have him. I tell you, the man had charm—there was something exotic and dynamic about him that appealed to her. She was bored stiff with her own kind."

"And the marriage was happy?"

"It was very happy, oddly enough. Of course their respective friends didn't mix (those were the days before money swept aside all class distinctions) but that didn't seem to worry them. They did without friends. He built a rather preposterous house at Swinly Dean and they lived there and had eight children."

"This is indeed a family chronicle."

"Old Leonides was rather clever to choose Swinly Dean. It was only beginning to be fashionable then. The second and third golf courses hadn't been made. There was a mixture of Old Inhabitants who were passionately fond of their gardens and who liked Mrs. Leonides, and rich City men who wanted to be in with Leonides, so they could take their choice of acquaintances. They were perfectly happy, I believe, until she died of pneumonia in 1905."

"Leaving him with eight children?"

"One died in infancy. Two of the sons were killed in the last war. One daughter married and went to Australia and died there. An unmarried daughter was killed in a motor accident. Another died a year or two ago. There are two still living—the eldest son, Roger, who is married but has no children, and Philip, who married a well-known actress and has three children. Your Sophia, Eustace and Josephine."

"And they are all living at—what is it?—Three Gables?"

"Yes. The Roger Leonides were bombed out early in the war. Philip and his family have lived there since 1937. And there's an elderly aunt, Miss de Haviland, sister of the first Mrs. Leonides. She always loathed her brother-in-law apparently, but when her sister died she considered it her duty to accept her brother-in-law's invitation to live with him and bring up the children."

"She's very hot on duty," said Inspector Taverner. "But she's not the kind that changes her mind about people. She always disapproved of Leonides and his methods——"

"Well," I said, "it seems a pretty good houseful. Who do you think killed him?"

Taverner shook his head.

"Early days," he said, "early days to say that."

"Come on, Taverner," I said. "I bet you think you know who did it. We're not in court, man."

"No," said Taverner gloomily. "And we never may be."

"You mean he may not have been murdered?"

"Oh, he was murdered all right. Poisoned. But you know what these poisoning cases are like. It's very tricky getting the evidence. Very tricky. All the possibilities may point one way——"

"That's what I'm trying to get at. You've got it all taped out in your mind, haven't you?"

"It's a case of very strong probability. It's one of those

obvious things. The perfect set-up. But I don't know, I'm sure. It's tricky."

I looked appealingly at the Old Man.

He said slowly: " In murder cases, as you know, Charles, the obvious is usually the right solution. Old Leonides married again, ten years ago."

" When he was seventy-seven?"

" Yes, he married a young woman of twenty-four."

I whistled.

" What sort of a young woman?"

" A young woman out of a tea-shop. A perfectly respectable young woman—good-looking in an anæmic, apathetic sort of way."

" And she's the strong probability?"

" I ask you, sir," said Taverner. " She's only thirty-four now—and that's a dangerous age. She likes living soft. And there's a young man in the house. Tutor to the grandchildren. Not been in the war—got a bad heart or something. They're as thick as thieves."

I looked at him thoughtfully. It was, certainly, an old and familiar pattern. The mixture as before. And the second Mrs. Leonides was, my father had emphasised, very respectable. In the name of respectability many murders had been committed.

" What was it?" I asked. " Arsenic?"

" No. We haven't got the analyst's report yet—but the doctor thinks it's eserine."

" That's a little unusual, isn't it? Surely easy to trace the purchaser."

" Not this thing. It was his own stuff, you see. Eyedrops."

" Leonides suffered from diabetes," said my father. " He had regular injections of insulin. Insulin is given out in small bottles with a rubber cap. A hypodermic needle is pressed down through the rubber cap and the injection drawn up."

I guessed the next bit.

"And it wasn't insulin in the bottle, but eserine?"

"Exactly."

"And who gave him the injection?" I asked.

"His wife."

I understood now what Sophia meant by the "right person."

I asked: "Does the family get on well with the second Mrs. Leonides?"

"No. I gather they are hardly on speaking terms."

It all seemed clearer and clearer. Nevertheless, Inspector Taverner was clearly not happy about it.

"What don't you like about it?" I asked him.

"If she did it, Mr. Charles, it would have been so easy for her to substitute a bona fide bottle of insulin afterwards. In fact, if she is guilty, I can't imagine why on earth she didn't do just that."

"Yes, it does seem indicated. Plenty of insulin about?"

"Oh yes, full bottles and empty ones. And if she'd done that, ten to one the doctor wouldn't have spotted it. Very little is known of the post-mortem appearances in human poisoning by eserine. But as it was he checked up on the insulin (in case it was the wrong strength or something like that) and so, of course, he soon spotted that it *wasn't* insulin."

"So it seems," I said thoughtfully, "that Mrs. Leonides was either very stupid—or possibly very clever."

"You mean——"

"That she may be gambling on your coming to the conclusion that nobody could have been as stupid as she appears to have been. What are the alternatives? Any other—suspects?"

The Old Man said quietly:

"Practically anyone in the house could have done it. There was always a good store of insulin—at least a fortnight's supply. One of the phials could have been tampered with, and replaced in the knowledge that it would be used in due course."

"And anybody, more or less, had access to them?"

"They weren't locked away. They were kept on a special shelf in the medicine cupboard in the bathroom of his part of the house. Everybody in the house came and went freely."

"Any strong motive?"

My father sighed.

"My dear Charles, Aristide Leonides was enormously rich. He had made over a good deal of his money to his family, it is true, but it may be that somebody wanted more."

"But the one that wanted it most would be the present widow. Has her young man any money?"

"No. Poor as a church mouse."

Something clicked in my brain. I remembered Sophia's quotation. I suddenly remembered the whole verse of the nursery rhyme:

There was a crooked man and he went a crooked mile.
He found a crooked sixpence beside a crooked stile.
He had a crooked cat which caught a crooked mouse,
And they all lived together in a little crooked house.

I said to Taverner:

"How does she strike you—Mrs. Leonides? What do you think of her?"

He replied slowly:

" It's hard to say—very hard to say. She's not easy. Very quiet—so you don't know what she's thinking. But she likes living soft—that I'll swear I'm right about. Puts me in mind, you know, of a cat, a big purring lazy cat . . . Not that I've anything against cats. Cats are all right . . ."

He sighed.

" What we want," he said, " is *evidence*."

Yes, I thought, we *all* wanted evidence that Mrs. Leonides had poisoned her husband. Sophia wanted it, and I wanted it, and Chief-Inspector Taverner wanted it.

Then everything in the garden would be lovely!

But Sophia wasn't sure, and I wasn't sure, and I didn't think Chief-Inspector Taverner was sure either. . . .

CHAPTER IV

ON THE following day I went down to Three Gables with Taverner.

My position was a curious one. It was, to say the least of it, quite unorthodox. But the Old Man has never been highly orthodox.

I had a certain standing. I had worked with the Special Branch at the Yard during the early days of the war.

This, of course, was entirely different—but my earlier performances had given me, so to speak, a certain official standing.

My father said:

" If we're ever going to solve this case, we've got to get some inside dope. We've got to know all about the people in that house. We've got to know them from the *inside*—not the outside. You're the man who can get that for us."

I didn't like that. I threw my cigarette end into the grate as I said:

" I'm a police spy? Is that it? I'm to get the inside dope from Sophia whom I love and who both loves and trusts me, or so I believe."

The Old Man became quite irritable. He said sharply:

" For heaven's sake don't take the commonplace view. To begin with, you don't believe, do you, that your young woman murdered her grandfather?"

" Of course not. The idea's absolutely absurd."

" Very well—we don't think so either. She's been away

for some years, she has always been on perfectly amicable terms with him. She has a very generous income and he would have been, I should say, delighted to hear of her engagement to you and would probably have made a handsome marriage settlement on her. We don't suspect her. Why should we? But you can make quite sure of one thing. If this thing isn't cleared up, that girl won't marry you. From what you've told me I'm fairly sure of that. And mark this, it's the kind of crime that may *never* be cleared up. We may be reasonably sure that the wife and her young man were in cahoots over it—but proving it will be another matter. There's not even a case to put up to the D.P.P. so far. And unless we get definite evidence against her, there'll always be a nasty doubt. You see that, don't you?"

Yes, I saw that.

The Old Man then said quietly:

"Why not put it to her?"

"You mean—ask Sophia if I——" I stopped.

The Old Man was nodding his head vigorously.

"Yes, yes. I'm not asking you to worm your way in without telling the girl what you're up to. See what she has to say about it."

And so it came about that the following day I drove down with Chief-Inspector Taverner and Detective-Sergant Lamb to Swinly Dean.

A little way beyond the golf course, we turned in at a gateway where I imagined that before the war there had been an imposing pair of gates. Patriotism or ruthless requisitioning had swept these away. We drove up a long curving drive flanked with rhododendrons and came out on a gravelled sweep in front of the house.

It was incredible! I wondered why it had been called

Three Gables. Eleven Gables would have been more apposite! The curious thing was that it had a strange air of being distorted—and I thought I knew why. It was the type, really, of a cottage swollen out of all proportion. It was like looking at a country cottage through a gigantic magnifying-glass. The slantwise beams, the half-timbering, the gables—it was a little crooked house that had grown like a mushroom in the night!

Yet I got the idea. It was a Greek restaurateur's idea of something English. It was meant to be an Englishman's home—built the size of a castle! I wondered what the first Mrs. Leonides had thought of it. She had not, I fancied, been consulted or shown the plans. It was, most probably, her exotic husband's little surprise. I wondered if she had shuddered or smiled.

Apparently she had lived there quite happily.

"Bit overwhelming, isn't it?" said Inspector Taverner. "Of course, the old gentleman built on to it a good deal—making it into three separate houses, so to speak, with kitchens and everything. It's all tip-top inside, fitted up like a luxury hotel."

Sophia came out of the front door. She was hatless and wore a green shirt and a tweed skirt.

She stopped dead when she saw me.

"*You*?" she exclaimed.

I said:

"Sophia, I've got to talk to you. Where can we go?"

For a moment I thought she was going to demur, then she turned and said: "This way."

We walked down across the lawn. There was a fine view across Swinly Dean's No. 1 course—away to a clump of pine trees on a hill, and beyond it, to the dimness of hazy countryside.

Sophia led me to a rock-garden, now somewhat neglected, where there was a rustic wooden seat of great discomfort, and we sat down.

"Well?" she said.

Her voice was not encouraging.

I said my piece—all of it.

She listened very attentively. Her face gave little indication of what she was thinking, but when I came at last to a full stop, she sighed. It was a deep sigh.

"Your father," she said, "is a very clever man."

"The Old Man has his points. I think it's a rotten idea myself—but——"

She interrupted me.

"Oh no," she said. "It isn't a rotten idea at all. It's the only thing that might be any good. Your father, Charles, knows exactly what's been going on in my mind. He knows better than you do."

With sudden almost despairing vehemence, she drove one hand into the palm of the other."

"I've *got* to have the truth. I've got to *know.*"

"Because of us? But, dearest——"

"Not only because of us, Charles. I've got to know for my own peace of mind. You see, Charles, I didn't tell you last night—but the truth is—I'm afraid."

"Afraid?"

"Yes—afraid—afraid—afraid. The police think, your father thinks, you think, everybody thinks—that it was Brenda."

"The probabilities——"

"Oh yes, it's quite probable. It's possible. But when I say, 'Brenda probably did it,' I'm quite conscious that it's only wishful thinking. Because, you see, I *don't really think so.*"

"You *don't* think so?" I said slowly.

"I don't *know*. You've heard about it all from the outside as I wanted you to. Now I'll show it you from the inside. I simply don't feel that Brenda is that kind of a person—she's not the sort of person, I feel, who would ever do anything that might involve her in any danger. She's far too careful of herself."

"How about this young man? Laurence Brown."

"Laurence is a complete rabbit. He wouldn't have the guts."

"I wonder."

"Yes, we don't really know, do we? I mean, people are capable of surprising one frightfully. One gets an idea of them into one's head, and sometimes it's absolutely wrong. Not always—but sometimes. But all the same, Brenda"—she shook her head—"she's always acted so completely in character. She's what I call the harem type. Likes sitting about and eating sweets and having nice clothes and jewellery and reading cheap novels and going to the cinema. And its a queer thing to say, when one remembers that he was eighty-seven, but I really think she was rather thrilled by grandfather. He had a power, you know. I should imagine he could make a woman feel—oh—rather like a queen—the Sultan's favourite! I think—I've always thought—that he made Brenda feel as though she was an exciting, romantic person. He's been clever with women all his life—and that kind of thing is a sort of art—you don't lose the knack of it, however old you are."

I left the problem of Brenda for the moment and harked back to a phrase of Sophia's which had disturbed me.

"Why did you say," I asked, "that you were afraid?"

Sophia shivered a little and pressed her hands together.

"Because it's true," she said in a low voice. "It's very

important, Charles, that I should make you understand this. You see, we're a very queer family. . . . There's a lot of *ruthlessness* in us—and—different kinds of ruthlessness. That's what's so disturbing. The different kinds."

She must have seen incomprehension in my face. She went on, speaking energetically.

"I'll try and make what I mean clear. Grandfather, for instance. Once when he was telling us about his boyhood in Smyrna, he mentioned, quite casually, that he had stabbed two men. It was some kind of a brawl—there had been some unforgivable insult—I don't know—but it was just a thing that had happened quite naturally. He'd really practically forgotten about it. But it was, somehow, such a queer thing to hear about, quite casually, in *England*."

I nodded.

"That's one kind of ruthlessness," went on Sophia, "and then there was my grandmother. I only just remember her, but I've heard a good deal about her. I think she might have had the ruthlessness that comes from having no imagination whatever. All those fox-hunting forbears—and the old Generals, the shoot-'em-down type. Full of rectitude and arrogance, and not a bit afraid of taking responsibility in matters of life and death."

"Isn't that a bit far-fetched?"

"Yes, I dare say—but I'm always rather afraid of that type. It's full of rectitude but it *is* ruthless. And then there's my own mother—she's an actress—she's a darling, but she's got absolutely *no* sense of proportion. She's one of those unconscious egoists who can only see things in relation as to how it affects *them*. That's rather frightening, sometimes, you know. And there's Clemency, Uncle Roger's wife. She's a scientist—she's doing some kind of very important research—she's ruthless too, in a kind of cold-blooded impersonal way. Uncle Roger's the exact opposite—he's the kindest and most lovable person in the world, but he's got a really terrific temper. Things make his blood boil and then he hardly knows what he's doing. And there's father——"

She made a long pause.

"Father," she said slowly, "is almost too well controlled. You never know what he's thinking. He never shows any emotion at all. It's probably a kind of unconscious self-defence against mother's absolute orgies of emotion, but sometimes—it worries me a little."

"My dear child," I said, "you're working yourself up unnecessarily. What it comes to in the end is that everybody, perhaps, is capable of murder."

"I suppose that's true. Even me."

"Not you!"

"Oh yes, Charles, you can't make me an exception. I suppose I could murder someone . . ." She was silent a moment or two, then added, "But if so, it would have to be for something really worthwhile!"

I laughed then. I couldn't help it. And Sophia smiled.

"Perhaps I'm a fool," she said, "but we've got to find out the truth about grandfather's death. We've *got* to. If only it *was* Brenda . . ."

I felt suddenly rather sorry for Brenda Leonides.

CHAPTER V

ALONG the path towards us came a tall figure walking briskly. It had on a battered old felt hat, a shapeless skirt, and a rather cumbersome jersey.

"Aunt Edith," said Sophia.

The figure paused once or twice, stooping to the flower borders, then it advanced upon us. I rose to my feet.

"This is Charles Hayward, Aunt Edith. My aunt, Miss de Haviland."

Edith de Haviland was a woman of about seventy. She had a mass of untidy grey hair, a weather-beaten face and a shrewd and piercing glance.

"How d'ye do?" she said. "I've heard about you. Back from the East. How's your father?"

Rather surprised, I said he was very well.

"Knew him when he was a boy," said Miss de Haviland. "Knew his mother very well. You look rather like her. Have you come to help us—or the other thing?"

"I hope to help," I said rather uncomfortably.

She nodded.

"We could do with some help. Place swarming with policemen. Pop out at you all over the place. Don't like some of the types. A boy who's been to a decent school oughtn't to go into the police. Saw Moyra Kinoul's boy the other day holding up the traffic at Marble Arch. Makes you feel you don't know where you are!"

She turned to Sophia.

"Nannie's asking for you, Sophia. Fish."

"Bother," said Sophia. "I'll go and telephone about it."

She walked briskly towards the house. Miss de Haviland turned and walked slowly in the same direction. I fell into step beside her.

"Don't know what we'd all do without Nannies," said Miss de Haviland. "Nearly everybody's got an old Nannie. They come back and wash and iron and cook and do housework. Faithful. Chose this one myself—years ago."

She stooped and pulled viciously at an entangling twining bit of green.

"Hateful stuff—bindweed! Worst weed there is! Choking, entangling—and you can't get at it properly, runs along underground."

With her heel she ground the handful of greenstuff viciously underfoot.

"This is a bad business, Charles Hayward," she said. She was looking towards the house. "What do the police think about it? Suppose I mustn't ask you that. Seems odd to think of Aristide being poisoned. For that matter it seems odd to think of him being dead. I never liked him—never! But I can't get used to the idea of his being dead... Makes the house seem so—empty."

I said nothing. For all her curt way of speech, Edith de Haviland seemed in a reminiscent mood.

"Was thinking this morning—I've lived here a long time. Over forty years. Came here when my sister died. *He* asked me to. Seven children—and the youngest only a year old. . . . Couldn't leave 'em to be brought up by a dago, could I? An impossible marriage, of course. I always felt Marcia must have been—well—bewitched. Ugly common little foreigner! He gave me a free hand—I will say that. Nurses, governesses, schools. And proper wholesome nursery food—not those queer spiced rice dishes *he* used to eat."

" And you've been here ever since?" I murmured.

" Yes. Queer in a way . . . I *could* have left, I suppose, when the children grew up and married . . . I suppose, really, I'd got interested in the garden. And then there was Philip. If a man marries an actress he can't expect to have any home life. Don't know why actresses have children. As soon as a baby's born they rush off and play in Repertory in Edinburgh or somewhere as remote as possible. Philip did the sensible thing—moved in here with his books."

" What does Philip Leonides do?"

" Writes books. Can't think why. Nobody wants to read them. All about obscure historical details. You've never even heard of them, have you?"

I admitted it.

" Too much money, that's what he's had," said Miss de Haviland. " Most people have to stop being cranks and earn a living."

" Don't his books pay?"

" Of course not. He's supposed to be a great authority on certain periods and all that. But he doesn't have to make his books pay—Aristide settled something like a hundred thousand pounds—something quite fantastic—on him! To avoid death duties! Aristide made them all financially independent. Roger runs Associated Catering—Sophia has a very handsome allowance. The children's money is in trust for them."

" So no one gains particularly by his death?"

She threw me a strange glance.

" Yes, they do. They all get more money. But they could probably have had it, if they asked for it, anyway."

" Have you any idea who poisoned him, Miss de Haviland?"

She replied characteristically:

" No, indeed I haven't. It's upset me very much. Not nice to think one has a Borgia sort of person loose about the house. I suppose the police will fasten on poor Brenda."

" You don't think they'll be right in doing so?"

" I simply can't tell. She's always seemed to me a singularly stupid and commonplace young woman—rather conventional. Not my idea of a poisoner. Still, after all, if a young woman of twenty-four marries a man close on eighty, it's fairly obvious that she's marrying him for his money. In the normal course of events she could have expected to become a rich widow fairly soon. But Aristide was a singularly tough old man. His diabetes wasn't getting any worse. He really looked like living to be a hundred. I suppose she got tired of waiting. . . ."

" In that case," I said, and stopped.

" In that case," said Miss de Haviland briskly, " it will be more or less all right. Annoying publicity, of course. But, after all, she isn't one of the family."

" You've no other ideas?" I asked.

" What other ideas should I have?"

I wondered. I had a suspicion that there might be more going on under the battered felt hat than I knew.

Behind the jerky, almost disconnected utterance, there was, I thought, a very shrewd brain at work. Just for a moment I even wondered whether Miss de Haviland had poisoned Aristide Leonides herself. . . .

It did not seem an impossible idea. At the back of my mind was the way she had ground the bindweed into the soil with her heel with a kind of vindictive thoroughness.

I remembered the word Sophia had used. *Ruthlessness.*

I stole a sideways glance at Edith de Haviland.

Given good and sufficient reason . . . But what exactly would seem to Edith de Haviland good and sufficient reason?

To answer that, I should have to know her better.

CHAPTER VI

THE FRONT DOOR was open. We passed through it into a rather surprisingly spacious hall. It was furnished with restraint—well-polished dark oak and gleaming brass. At the back, where the staircase would normally appear, was a white panelled wall with a door in it.

"My brother-in-law's part of the house," said Miss de Haviland. "The ground floor is Philip and Magda's."

We went through a doorway on the left into a large drawing-room. It had pale-blue panelled walls, furniture covered in heavy brocade, and on every available table and on the walls were hung photographs and pictures of actors, dancers and stage scenes and designs. A Degas of ballet dancers hung over the mantelpiece. There were masses of flowers, enormous brown chrysanthemums and great vases of carnations.

"I suppose," said Miss de Haviland, "that you want to see Philip?"

Did I want to see Philip? I had no idea. All I had wanted to do was to see Sophia. That I had done. She had given emphatic encouragement to the Old Man's plan—but she had now receded from the scene and was presumably somewhere telephoning about fish, having given me no indication of how to proceed. Was I to approach Philip Leonides as a young man anxious to marry his daughter, or as a casual friend who had dropped in (surely not at such a moment!) or as an associate of the police?

Miss de Haviland gave me no time to consider her question. It was, indeed, not a question at all, but more an assertion. Miss de Haviland, I judged, was more inclined to assert than to question.

" We'll go to the library," she said.

She led me out of the drawing-room, along a corridor and in through another door.

It was a big room, full of books. The books did not confine themselves to the bookcases that reached up to the ceiling. They were on chairs and tables and even on the floor. And yet there was no sense of disarray about them.

The room was cold. There was some smell absent in it that I was conscious of having expected. It smelt of the mustiness of old books and just a little of bees-wax. In a second or two I realised what I missed. It was the scent of tobacco. Philip Leonides was not a smoker.

He got up from behind his table as we entered—a tall man, aged somewhere around fifty, an extraordinarily handsome man. Everyone had laid so much emphasis on the ugliness of Aristide Leonides, that for some reason I expected his son to be ugly too. Certainly I was not prepared for this perfection of feature—the straight nose, the flawless line of jaw, the fair hair touched with grey that swept back from a well-shaped forehead.

" This is Charles Hayward, Philip," said Edith de Haviland.

" Ah, how do you do?"

I could not tell if he had ever heard of me. The hand he gave me was cold. His face was quite incurious. It made me rather nervous. He stood there, patient and uninterested.

" Where are those awful policemen?" demanded Miss de Haviland. " Have they been in here?"

"I believe Chief-Inspector"—(he glanced down at a card on the desk)—"er—Taverner is coming to talk to me presently."

"Where is he now?"

"I've no idea, Aunt Edith. Upstairs, I suppose."

"With Brenda?"

"I really don't know."

Looking at Philip Leonides, it seemed quite impossible that a murder could have been committed anywhere in his vicinity.

"Is Magda up yet?"

"I don't know. She's not usually up before eleven."

"That sounds like her," said Edith de Haviland.

What sounded like Mrs. Philip Leonides was a high voice talking very rapidly and approaching very fast. The door behind me burst open and a woman came in. I don't know how she managed to give the impression of its being three women rather than one who entered.

She was smoking a cigarette in a long holder and was wearing a peach satin *négligé* which she was holding up with one hand. A cascade of Titian hair rippled down her back. Her face had that almost shocking air of nudity that a woman's has nowadays when it is not made up at all. Her eyes were blue and enormous and she was talking very rapidly in a husky rather attractive voice with a very clear enunciation.

"Darling, I can't stand it—I simply can't stand it—just think of the notices—it isn't in the papers yet, but of course it will be—and I simply can't make up my mind what I ought to wear at the inquest—very, very subdued?—not black though, perhaps dark purple—and I simply haven't got a coupon left—I've lost the address of that dreadful man who sells them to me—you know, the garage somewhere near Shaftesbury Avenue—and if I went up there in the car the police would follow me, and they might ask the most awkward questions, mightn't they? I mean, what could one say? How calm you are, Philip! How can you be so calm? Don't you realise we can leave this awful house now. Freedom—freedom! Oh, how unkind—the poor old Sweetie—of course we'd never have left him while he was alive. He really did dote on us, didn't he—in spite of all the trouble that woman upstairs tried to make between us. I'm quite sure that if we had gone away and left him to her, he'd have cut us right out of everything. Horrible creature! After all, poor old Sweetie Pie was just on ninety—all the family feeling in the world couldn't have stood up against a dreadful woman who was on the spot. You know, Philip, I really believe that this would be a wonderful opportunity to put on the Edith Thompson play. This murder would give us a lot of advance publicity. Bildenstein said he could get the Thespian—that dreary play in verse about miners is coming off any minute—it's a wonderful part—wonderful. I know they say I must always play comedy because of my nose—but you know there's quite a lot of comedy to be got out of Edith Thompson—I don't think the author realised that—comedy always heightens the suspense. I know just how I'd play it—commonplace, silly, make-believe up to the last minute and then——"

She cast out an arm—the cigarette fell out of the holder on to the polished mahogany of Philip's desk and began to burn it. Impassively he reached for it and dropped it into the waste-paper basket.

"And then," whispered Magda Leonides, her eyes suddenly widening, her face stiffening, "just *terror* . . ."

The stark fear stayed on her face for about twenty

seconds, then her face relaxed, crumpled, a bewildered child was about to burst into tears.

Suddenly all emotion was wiped away as though by a sponge and, turning to me, she asked in a businesslike tone:

"Don't you think that would be the way to play Edith Thompson?"

I said I thought that would be exactly the way to play Edith Thompson. At the moment I could only remember very vaguely who Edith Thompson was, but I was anxious to start off well with Sophia's mother.

"Rather like Brenda, really, wasn't she?" said Magda. "D'you know, I never thought of that. It's very interesting. Shall I point that out to the inspector?"

The man behind the desk frowned very slightly.

"There's really no need, Magda," he said, "for you to see him at all. I can tell him anything he wants to know."

"Not see him?" Her voice went up. "But *of course* I must see him! Darling, darling, you're so terribly unimaginative! You don't realise the importance of *details*. He'll want to know exactly how and when everything happened, all the little things one noticed and wondered about at the time——"

"Mother," said Sophia, coming through the open door, "you're not to tell the inspector a lot of lies."

"Sophia—*darling* . . ."

"I know, precious, that you've got it all set and that you're ready to give a most beautiful performance. But you've got it wrong. Quite wrong."

"Nonsense. You don't know——"

"I do know. You've got to play it quite differently, darling. Subdued—saying very little—holding it all back—on your guard—protecting the family."

Magda Leonides' face showed the naïve perplexity of a child.

" Darling," she said, " do you really think——"

" Yes, I do. Throw it away. That's the idea."

Sophia added, as a little pleased smile began to show on her mother's face :

" I've made you some chocolate. It's in the drawing-room."

" Oh—good—I'm starving——"

She paused in the doorway.

" You don't know," she said, and the words appeared to be addressed either to me or to the bookshelf behind my head, " how lovely it is to have a daughter!"

On this exit line she went out.

" God knows," said Miss de Haviland, " what she will say to the police!"

" She'll be all right," said Sophia.

" She might say *anything*."

" Don't worry," said Sophia. " She'll play it the way the producer says. *I'm* the producer!"

She went out after her mother, then wheeled back to say :

" Here's Chief-Inspector Taverner to see you, Father. You don't mind if Charles stays, do you?"

I thought that a very faint air of bewilderment showed on Philip Leonides' face. It well might! But his incurious habit served me in good stead. He murmured :

" Oh certainly—certainly," in a rather vague voice.

Chief-Inspector Taverner came in, solid, dependable, and with an air of businesslike promptitude that was somehow soothing.

" Just a little unpleasantness," his manner seemed to say, " and then we shall be out of the house for good—and nobody will be more pleased than I shall. *We* don't want to hang about, I can assure you. . . ."

I don't know how he managed, without any words at all, but merely by drawing up a chair to the desk, to convey what he did, but it worked. I sat down unobtrusively, a little way off.

"Yes, Chief-Inspector?" said Philip.

Miss de Haviland said abruptly:

"You don't want me, Chief-Inspector?"

"Not just at the moment, Miss de Haviland. Later, if I might have a few words with you——"

"Of course. I shall be upstairs."

She went out, shutting the door behind her.

"Well, Chief-Inspector?" Philip repeated.

"I know you're a very busy gentleman and I don't want to disturb you for long. But I may mention to you in confidence that our suspicions are confirmed. Your father did not die a natural death. His death was the result of an overdose of physostigmine—more usually known as eserine."

Philip bowed his head. He showed no particular emotion.

"I don't know whether that suggests anything to you?" Taverner went on.

"What should it suggest? My own view is that my father must have taken the poison by accident."

"You really think so, Mr. Leonides?"

"Yes, it seems to me perfectly possible. He was close on ninety, remember, and with very imperfect eyesight."

"So he emptied the contents of his eyedrop bottle into an insulin bottle. Does that really seem to you a credible suggestion, Mr. Leonides?"

Philip did not reply. His face became even more impassive.

Taverner went on:

"We have found the eyedrop bottle, empty—in the dustbin, with no fingerprints on it. That in itself is curious. In the normal way there should have been fingerprints. Certainly your father's, possibly his wife's, or the valet . . ."

Philip Leonides looked up.

"What about the valet?" he said. "What about Johnson?"

"You are suggesting Johnson as the possible criminal? He certainly had opportunity. But when we come to motive it is different. It was your father's custom to pay him a bonus every year—each year the bonus was increased. Your father made it clear to him that this was in lieu of any sum that he might otherwise have left him in his will. The bonus now, after seven years' service, has reached a very considerable sum every year and is still rising. It was obviously to Johnson's interest that your father should live as long as possible. Moreover, they were on excellent terms, and Johnson's record of past service is unimpeachable—he is a thoroughly skilled and faithful valet attendant." He paused. "We do not suspect Johnson."

Philip replied tonelessly: "I see."

"Now, Mr. Leonides, perhaps you will give me a detailed account of your own movements on the day of your father's death?"

"Certainly, Chief-Inspector. I was here, in this room, all that day—with the exception of meals, of course."

"Did you see your father at all?"

"I said good morning to him after breakfast as was my custom."

"Were you alone with him then?"

"My—er—stepmother was in the room."

"Did he seem quite as usual?"

With a slight hint of irony, Philip replied:

" He showed no foreknowledge that he was to be murdered that day."

" Is your father's portion of the house entirely separate from this?"

" Yes, the only access to it is through the door in the hall."

" Is that door kept locked?"

" No."

" Never?"

" I have never known it to be so."

" Anyone could go freely between that part of the house and this?"

" Certainly. It was only separate from the point of view of domestic convenience."

" How did you first hear of your father's death?"

" My brother Roger, who occupies the west wing of the floor above, came rushing down to tell me that my father had had a sudden seizure. He had difficulty in breathing and seemed very ill.

" What did you do?"

" I telephoned through to the doctor, which nobody seemed to have thought of doing. The doctor was out—but I left a message for him to come as soon as possible. I then went upstairs."

" And then?"

" My father was clearly very ill. He died before the doctor came."

There was no emotion in Philip's voice. It was a simple statement of fact.

" Where was the rest of the family?"

" My wife was in London. She returned shortly afterwards. Sophia was also absent, I believe. The two younger ones, Eustace and Josephine, were at home."

" I hope you won't misunderstand me, Mr. Leonides, if I ask you exactly how your father's death will affect your financial position."

" I quite appreciate that you want to know all the facts. My father made us financially independent a great many years ago. My brother he made Chairman and principal shareholder of Associated Catering—his largest company, and put the management of it entirely in his hands. He made over to me what he considered an equivalent sum—actually I think it was a hundred and fifty thousand pounds in various bonds and securities—so that I could use the capital as I chose. He also settled very generous amounts on my two sisters, who have since died."

" But he left himself still a very rich man?"

" No, actually he only retained for himself a comparatively modest income. He said it would give him an interest in life. Since that time"—for the first time a faint smile creased Philip's lips—" he has become, as the result of various undertakings, an even richer man than he was before."

" Your brother and yourself came here to live. That was not the result of any financial—difficulties?"

" Certainly not. It was a mere matter of convenience. My father always told us that we were welcome to make a home with him. For various domestic reasons this was a convenient thing for me to do.

" I was also," added Philip deliberately, " extremely fond of my father. I came here with my family in 1937. I pay no rent, but I pay my proportion of the rates."

" And your brother?"

" My brother came here as a result of the blitz, when his house in London was bombed in 1943."

"Now, Mr. Leonides, have you any idea what your father's testamentary dispositions are?"

"A very clear idea. He re-made his will in 1946. My father was not a secretive man. He had a great sense of family. He held a family conclave at which his solicitor was also present and who, at his request, made clear to us the terms of the will. These terms I expect you already know. Mr. Gaitskill will doubtless have informed you. Roughly, a sum of a hundred thousand pounds free of duty was left to my stepmother in addition to her already very generous marriage settlement. The residue of his property was divided into three portions, one to myself, one to my brother, and a third in trust for the three grandchildren. The estate is a large one, but the death duties, of course, will be very heavy."

"Any bequests to servants or to charity?"

"No bequests of any kind. The wages paid to servants were increased annually if they remained in his service."

"You are not—you will excuse my asking—in actual need of money, Mr. Leonides?"

"Income tax, as you know, is somewhat heavy, Chief-Inspector—but my income amply suffices for my needs—and for my wife's. Moreover, my father frequently made us all very generous gifts, and had any emergency arisen, he would have come to the rescue immediately."

Philip added coldly and clearly:

"I can assure you that I had no financial reason for desiring my father's death, Chief-Inspector."

"I am very sorry, Mr. Leonides, if you think I suggested anything of the kind. But we have to get at all the facts. Now I'm afraid I must ask you some rather delicate questions. They refer to the relations between your father and his wife. Were they on happy terms together?"

" As far as I know, perfectly."

" No quarrels?"

" I do not think so."

" There was a—great disparity in age?"

" There was."

" Did you—excuse me—approve of your father's second marriage?"

" My approval was not asked."

" That is not an answer, Mr. Leonides."

" Since you press the point, I will say that I considered the marriage—unwise."

" Did you remonstrate with your father about it?"

" When I heard of it, it was an accomplished fact."

" Rather a shock to you—eh?"

Philip did not reply.

" Was there any bad feeling about the matter?"

" My father was at perfect liberty to do as he pleased."

" Your relations with Mrs. Leonides have been amicable?"

" Perfectly."

" You are on friendly terms with her?"

" We very seldom meet."

Chief-Inspector Taverner shifted his ground.

" Can you tell me something about Mr. Laurence Brown?"

" I'm afraid I can't. He was engaged by my father."

" But he was engaged to teach your children, Mr. Leonides."

" True. My son was a sufferer from infantile paralysis—fortunately a light case—and it was considered not advisable to send him to a public school. My father suggested that he and my young daughter Josephine should have a private tutor—the choice at the time was rather limited—

since the tutor in question must be ineligible for military service. This young man's credentials were satisfactory, my father and my aunt (who has always looked after the children's welfare) were satisfied, and I acquiesced. I may add that I have no fault to find with his teaching, which has been conscientious and adequate."

"His living quarters are in your father's part of the house, not here?"

"There was more room up there."

"Have you ever noticed—I am sorry to ask this—any signs of intimacy between Laurence Brown and your stepmother?"

"I have had no opportunity of observing anything of the kind."

"Have you heard any gossip or tittle-tattle on the subject?"

"I don't listen to gossip or tittle-tattle, Chief-Inspector."

"Very creditable," said Inspector Taverner. "So you've seen no evil, heard no evil, and aren't speaking any evil?"

"If you like to put it that way, Chief-Inspector."

Inspector Taverner got up.

"Well," he said, "thank you very much, Mr. Leonides."

I followed him unobtrusively out of the room.

"Whew," said Taverner, "he's a cold fish!"

CHAPTER VII

"AND NOW," said Taverner, "we'll go and have a word with Mrs. Philip. Magda West, her stage name is."

"Is she any good?" I asked. "I know her name, and I believe I've seen her in various shows, but I can't remember when and where."

"She's one of those Near Successes," said Taverner. "She's starred once or twice in the West End, she's made quite a name for herself in Repertory—she plays a lot for the little high-brow theatres and the Sunday clubs. The truth is, I think, she's been handicapped by not having to earn her living at it. She's been able to pick and choose, and to go where she likes and occasionally to put up the money and finance a show where she's fancied a certain part—usually the last part in the world to suit her. Result is, she's receded a bit into the amateur class rather than the professional. She's good, mind you, especially in comedy—but managers don't like her much—they say she's too independent, and she's a trouble-maker—foments rows and enjoys a bit of mischief-making. I don't know how much of it is true—but she's not too popular amongst her fellow artists."

Sophia came out of the drawing-room and said: "My mother is in here, Chief-Inspector."

I followed Taverner into the big drawing-room. For a

moment I hardly recognised the woman who sat on the brocaded settee.

The Titian hair was piled high on her head in an Edwardian coiffure, and she was dressed in a well-cut dark-grey coat and skirt with a delicately pleated pale-mauve shirt fastened at the neck by a small cameo brooch. For the first time I was aware of the charm of her delightfully tip-tilted nose. I was faintly reminded of Athene Seyler—and it seemed quite impossible to believe that this was the tempestuous creature in the peach *néglige.*

"Inspector Taverner?" she said. "*Do* come in and sit down. Will you smoke? This is a most terrible business. I simply feel at the moment that I just can't take it in."

Her voice was low and emotionless, the voice of a person determined at all costs to display self-control. She went on:

"Please tell me if I can help you in any way."

"Thank you, Mrs. Leonides. Where were you at the time of the tragedy?"

"I suppose I must have been driving down from London. I'd lunched that day at the Ivy with a friend. Then we'd gone to a dress show. We had a drink with some other friends at the Berkeley. Then I started home. When I got here everything was in commotion. It seemed my father-in-law had had a sudden seizure. He was—dead." Her voice trembled just a little.

"You were fond of your father-in-law?"

"I was devoted——"

Her voice rose. Sophia adjusted, very slightly, the angle of the Degas picture. Magda's voice dropped to its former subdued tone.

"I was very fond of him," she said in a quiet voice. "We all were. He was—very good to us."

" Did you get on well with Mrs. Leonides?"

" We didn't see very much of Brenda."

" Why was that?"

" Well, we hadn't much in common. Poor dear Brenda. Life must have been hard for her sometimes."

Again Sophia fiddled with the Degas.

" Indeed? In what way?"

" Oh, I don't know." Magda shook her head, with a sad little smile.

" Was Mrs. Leonides happy with her husband?"

" Oh, I think so."

" No quarrels?"

Again the slight smiling shake of the head.

" I really don't know, Inspector. Their part of the house is quite separate."

" She and Mr. Laurence Brown were very friendly, were they not?"

Magda Leonides stiffened. Her eyes opened reproachfully at Taverner.

" I don't think," she said with dignity, " that you ought to ask me things like that. Brenda was quite friendly to *everyone*. She is really a very amiable sort of person."

" Do you like Mr. Laurence Brown?"

" He's very quiet. Quite nice, but you hardly know he's there. I haven't really seen very much of him."

" Is his teaching satisfactory?"

" I suppose so. I really wouldn't know. Philip seems quite satisfied."

Taverner essayed some shock tactics.

" I'm sorry to ask you this, but in your opinion was there anything in the nature of a love affair between Mr. Brown and Mrs. Brenda Leonides?"

Magda got up. She was very much the *grande dame*.

"I have never seen any evidence of anything of that kind," she said. "I don't think really, Inspector, that that is a question you ought to ask me. She was my father-in-law's wife."

I almost applauded.

The chief-inspector also rose.

"More a question for the servants?" he suggested.

Magda did not answer.

"Thank you, Mrs. Leonides," said the inspector and went out.

"You did that beautifully, darling," said Sophia to her mother warmly.

Magda twisted up a curl reflectively behind her right ear and looked at herself in the glass.

"Ye-es," she said, "I *think* it was the right way to play it?"

Sophia looked at me.

"Oughtn't you," she asked, "to go with the inspector?"

"Look here, Sophia, what am I supposed——"

I stopped. I could not very well ask outright in front of Sophia's mother exactly what my role was supposed to be. Magda Leonides had so far evinced no interest in my presence at all, except as a useful recipient of an exit line on daughters. I might be a reporter, her daughter's fiancé, or an obscure hanger-on of the police force, or even an undertaker—to Magda Leonides they would one and all come under the general heading of audience.

Looking down at her feet, Mrs. Leonides said with dissatisfaction:

"These shoes are wrong. Frivolous."

Obeying Sophia's imperious wave of the head, I hurried after Taverner. I caught him up in the outer hall just going through the door to the stairway.

" Just going up to see the elder brother," he explained.

I put my problem to him without more ado.

" Look here, Taverner, who am I supposed to *be*?"

He looked surprised.

" Who are you supposed to be?"

" Yes, what am I doing here in this house? If anyone asks me, what do I say?"

" Oh I see." He considered a moment. Then he smiled. " Has anybody asked you?"

" Well—no."

" Then why not leave it at that. *Never explain*. That's a very good motto. Especially in a house upset like this house is. Everyone is far too full of their own private worries and fears to be in a questioning mood. They'll take you for granted so long as you just seem sure of yourself. It's a great mistake ever to say anything when you needn't. H'm, now we go through this door and up the stairs. Nothing locked. Of course you realise, I expect, that these questions I'm asking are all a lot of hooey! Doesn't matter a hoot who was in the house and who wasn't, or where they all were on that particular day——"

" Then why——"

He went on: " Because it at least gives me a chance to look at them all, and size them up, and hear what they've got to say, and to hope that, quite by chance, somebody might give me a useful pointer." He was silent a moment and then murmured: " I bet Mrs. Magda Leonides could spill a mouthful if she chose."

" Would it be reliable?" I asked.

" Oh no," said Taverner, " it wouldn't be reliable. But it might start a possible line of inquiry. Everybody in the damned house had means and opportunity. What I want is a motive."

At the top of the stairs, a door barred off the right-hand corridor. There was a brass knocker on it and Inspector Taverner duly knocked.

It was opened with startling suddenness by a man who must have been standing just inside. He was a clumsy giant of a man, with powerful shoulders, dark rumpled hair, and an exceedingly ugly but at the same time rather pleasant face. His eyes looked at us and then quickly away in that furtive, embarrassed manner which shy but honest people often adopt.

" Oh, I say," he said. " Come in. Yes, do. I was going—but it doesn't matter. Come into the sitting-room. I'll get Clemency—oh, you're there, darling. It's Chief-Inspector Taverner. He—are there any cigarettes? Just wait a minute. If you don't mind." He collided with a screen, said " I beg your pardon " to it in a flustered manner, and went out of the room.

It was rather like the exit of a bumble-bee and left a noticeable silence behind it.

Mrs. Roger Leonides was standing up by the window. I was intrigued at once by her personality and by the atmosphere of the room in which we stood.

It was quite definitely *her* room. I was sure of that.

The walls were painted white—really white, not an ivory or a pale cream which is what one usually means when one says " white " in house decoration. They had no pictures on them except one over the mantelpiece, a geometrical fantasia in triangles of dark grey and battleship blue. There was hardly any furniture—only mere utilitarian necessities, three or four chairs, a glass-topped table, one small bookshelf. There were no ornaments. There was light and space and air. It was as different from the big brocaded and flowered drawing-room on the floor below as chalk from cheese. And Mrs. Roger Leonides was as different from Mrs. Philip Leonides as one woman could be from another. Whilst one felt that Magda Leonides could be, and often was, at least half a dozen different women, Clemency Leonides, I was sure, could never be anyone but herself. She was a woman of very sharp and definite personality.

She was about fifty, I suppose; her hair was grey, cut very short in what was almost an Eton crop but which grew so beautifully on her small well-shaped head that it had none of the ugliness I have always associated with that particular cut. She had an intelligent, sensitive face, with light-grey eyes of a peculiar and searching intensity. She had on a simple dark-red woollen frock that fitted her slenderness perfectly.

She was, I felt at once, rather an alarming woman . . . I think, because I judged that the standards by which she lived might not be those of an ordinary woman. I understood at once why Sophia had used the word ruthlessness in connection with her. The room was cold and I shivered a little.

Clemency Leonides said in a quiet, well-bred voice:

"Do sit down, Chief-Inspector. Is there any further news?"

"Death was due to eserine, Mrs. Leonides."

She said thoughtfully:

"So that makes it murder. It couldn't have been an acccident of any kind, could it?"

"No, Mrs. Leonides."

"Please be very gentle with my husband, Chief-Inspector. This will affect him very much. He worshipped his father and he feels things very acutely. He is an emotional person."

"You were on good terms with your father-in-law, Mrs. Leonides?"

"Yes, on quite good terms." She added quietly: "I did not like him very much."

"Why was that?"

"I disliked his objectives in life—and his methods of attaining them."

"And Mrs. Brenda Leonides?"

"Brenda? I never saw very much of her."

"Do you think it possible that there was anything between her and Mr. Laurence Brown?"

"You mean—some kind of a love affair? I shouldn't think so. But I really wouldn't know anything about it."

Her voice sounded completely uninterested.

Roger Leonides came back with a rush, and the same bumble-bee effect.

"I got held up," he said. "Telephone. Well, Inspector? Well? Have you got news? What caused my father's death?"

"Death was due to eserine poisoning."

"It was? My God! Then it was that woman! She couldn't wait! He took her more or less out of the gutter and this is his reward. She murdered him in cold blood! God, it makes my blood boil to think of it."

"Have you any particular reason for thinking that?" Taverner asked.

Roger was pacing up and down, tugging at his hair with both hands.

"Reason? Why, who else could it be? I've never trusted her—never liked her! We've none of us liked her. Philip and I were both appalled when Dad came home one day and told us what he had done! At his age! It was madness—*madness*. My father was an amazing man, Inspector. In intellect he was as young and fresh as a man of forty.

Everything I have in the world I owe to him. He did everything for me—never failed me. It was *I* who failed *him*—when I think of it——"

He dropped heavily on to a chair. His wife came quietly to his side.

"Now, Roger, that's enough. Don't work yourself up."

"I know, dearest—I know." He took her hand. "But how can I keep calm—how can I help feeling——"

"But we must all keep calm, Roger. Chief-Inspector Taverner wants our help."

"That is right, Mrs. Leonides."

Roger cried:

"Do you know what I'd like to do? I'd like to strangle that woman with my own hands. Grudging that dear old man a few extra years of life. If I had her here——" He sprang up. He was shaking with rage. He held out convulsive hands. "Yes, I'd wring her neck, wring her neck . . ."

"Roger!" said Clemency sharply.

He looked at her, abashed.

"Sorry, dearest." He turned to us. "I do apologise. My feelings get the better of me. I—excuse me——"

He went out of the room again. Clemency Leonides said with a very faint smile:

"Really, you know, he wouldn't hurt a fly."

Taverner accepted her remark politely.

Then he started on his so-called routine questions.

Clemency Leonides replied concisely and accurately.

Roger Leonides had been in London on the day of his father's death at Box House, the headquarters of the Associated Catering. He had returned early in the afternoon and had spent some time with his father as was his custom. She herself had been, as usual, at the Lambert Institute on

Gower Street where she worked. She had returned to the house just before six o'clock.

"Did you see your father-in-law?"

"No. The last time I saw him was on the day before. We had coffee with him after dinner."

"But you did not see him on the day of his death?"

"No. I actually went over to his part of the house because Roger thought he had left his pipe there—a very precious pipe, but as it happened he had left it on the hall table there, so I did not need to disturb the old man. He often dozed off about six."

"When did you hear of his illness?"

"Brenda came rushing over. That was just a minute or two after half-past six."

These questions, as I knew, were unimportant, but I was aware how keen was Inspector Taverner's scrutiny of the woman who answered them. He asked her a few questions about the nature of her work in London. She said that it had to do with the radiation effects of atomic disintegration.

"You work on the atom bomb, in fact?"

"The work has nothing destructive about it. The Institute is carrying out experiments on the therapeutic effects."

When Taverner got up, he expressed a wish to look round their part of the house. She seemed a little surprised, but showed him its extent readily enough. The bedroom with its twins beds and white coverlets and its simplified toilet appliances reminded me again of a hospital or some monastic cell. The bathroom, too, was severely plain with no special luxury fitting and no array of cosmetics. The kitchen was bare, spotlessly clean, and well equipped with labour-saving devices of a practical kind. Then we came to a door which Clemency opened, saying: "This is my husband's special room."

" Come in," said Roger. " Come in."

I drew a faint breath of relief. Something in the spotless austerity elsewhere had been getting me down. This was an intensely personal room. There was a large rolltop desk untidily covered with papers, old pipes and tobacco ash. There were big shabby easy-chairs. Persian rugs covered the floor. On the walls were groups, their photography somewhat faded. School groups, cricket groups, military groups. Water-colour sketches of deserts and minarets, and of sailing-boats and sea effects and sunsets. It was, somehow, a pleasant room, the room of a lovable, friendly, companionable man.

Roger, clumsily, was pouring out drinks from a tantalus, sweeping books and papers off one of the chairs.

" Place is in a mess. I was turning out. Clearing up old papers. Say when." The inspector declined a drink. I accepted. " You must forgive me just now," went on Roger. He brought my drink over to me, turning his head to speak to Taverner as he did so. " My feelings ran away with me."

He looked round almost guiltily, but Clemency Leonides had not accompanied us into the room.

" She's so wonderful," he said. " My wife, I mean. All through this, she's been splendid—*splendid*! I can't tell you how I admire that woman. And she's had such a hard time—a terrible time. I'd like to tell you about it. Before we were married, I mean. Her first husband was a fine chap—fine mind, I mean—but terribly delicate—tubercular as a matter of fact. He was doing very valuable research work on crystallography, I believe. Poorly paid and very exacting, but he wouldn't give up. She slaved for him, practically kept him, knowing all the time that he was dying. And never a complaint—never a murmur of weariness.

She always said she was happy. Then he died, and she was terribly cut up. At last she agreed to marry me. I was so glad to be able to give her some rest, some happiness, I wished she would stop working, but of course she felt it her duty in war-time, and she still seems to feel she should go on. But she's been a wonderful wife—the most wonderful wife a man ever had. Gosh, I've been lucky! I'd do anything for her."

Taverner made a suitable rejoinder. Then he embarked once more on the familiar routine questions. When had he first heard of his father's illness?

" Brenda had rushed over to call me. My father was ill—she said he had had a seizure of some sort."

" I'd been sitting with the dear old boy only about half an hour earlier. He'd been perfectly all right then. I rushed over. He was blue in the face, gasping. I dashed down to Philip. He rang up the doctor. I—we couldn't do anything. Of course I never dreamed for a moment then that there had been any funny business. Funny? Did I say funny? God, what a word to use."

With a little difficulty, Taverner and I disentangled ourselves from the emotional atmosphere of Roger Leonides' room and found ourselves outside the door, once more at the top of the stairs.

" Whew!" said Taverner. " What a contrast from the other brother." He added, rather inconsequently: " Curious things, rooms. Tell you quite a lot about the people who live in them."

I agreed and he went on:

" Curious the people who marry each other, too, isn't it?"

I was not quite sure if he was referring to Clemency and Roger, or to Philip and Magda. His words applied equally well to either. Yet it seemed to me that both the marriages might be classed as happy ones. Roger's and Clemency's certainly was.

"I shouldn't say he was a poisoner, would you?" asked Taverner. "Not off-hand, I wouldn't. Of course you never know. Now she's more the type. Remorseless sort of woman. Might be a bit mad."

Again I agreed. "But I don't suppose," I said, "that she'd murder anyone just because she didn't approve of their aims and mode of life. Perhaps, if she really hated the old man—but are any murders committed just out of pure hate?"

"Precious few," said Taverner. "I've never come across one myself. No, I think we're a good deal safer to stick to Mrs. Brenda. But God knows if we'll ever get any evidence."

CHAPTER VIII

A PARLOURMAID opened the door of the opposite wing to us. She looked scared but slightly contemptuous when she saw Taverner.

"You want to see the mistress?"

"Yes, please."

She showed us into a big drawing-room and went out.

Its proportions were the same as the drawing-room on the ground floor below. There were coloured cretonnes, very gay in colour, and striped silk curtains. Over the mantelpiece was a portrait that held my gaze riveted—not only because of the master hand that had painted it, but also because of the arresting face of the subject.

It was the portrait of a little old man with dark, piercing eyes. He wore a black velvet skullcap and his head was sunk down in his shoulders, but the vitality and power of the man radiated forth from the canvas. The twinkling eyes seemed to hold mine.

"That's him," said Chief-Inspector Taverner ungrammatically. "Painted by Augustus John. Got a personality, hasn't he?"

"Yes," I said, and felt the monosyllable was inadequate.

I understood now just what Edith de Haviland had meant when she said the house seemed so empty without him. This was the Original Crooked Little Man who had built the Crooked Little House—and without him the Crooked Little House had lost its meaning.

" That's his first wife over there, painted by Sargent," said Taverner.

I examined the picture on the wall between the windows. It had a certain cruelty like many of Sargent's portraits. The length of the face was exaggerated, I thought—so was the faint suggestion of horsiness—the indisputable correctness. It was a portrait of a typical English Lady—in Country (not Smart) Society. Handsome, but rather lifeless. A most unlikely wife for the grinning, powerful little despot over the mantelpiece.

The door opened and Sergeant Lamb stepped in.

" I've done what I could with the servants, sir," he said. " Didn't get anything."

Taverner sighed.

Sergeant Lamb took out his notebook and retreated to the far end of the room, where he seated himself unobtrusively.

The door opened again and Aristide Leonides' second wife came into the room.

She wore black—very expensive black and a good deal of it. It swathed her up to the neck and down to the wrists. She moved easily and indolently, and black certainly suited her. Her face was mildly pretty, and she had rather nice brown hair arranged in somewhat too elaborate a style. Her face was well powdered and she had on lipstick and rouge, but she had clearly been crying. She was wearing a string of very large pearls and she had a big emerald ring on one hand and an enormous ruby on the other.

There was one other thing I noticed about her. She looked frightened.

" Good morning, Mrs. Leonides," said Taverner easily. " I'm sorry to have to trouble you again."

She said in a flat voice :

" I suppose it can't be helped."

" You understand, don't you, Mrs. Leonides, that if you wish your solicitor to be present, that is perfectly in order?"

I wondered if she did understand the significance of those words. Apparently not. She merely said rather sulkily:

" I don't like Mr. Gaitskill. I don't want him."

" You could have your own solicitor, Mrs. Leonides."

" Must I? I don't like solicitors. They confuse me."

" It's entirely for you to decide," said Taverner, producing an automatic smile. " Shall we go on, then?"

Sergeant Lamb licked his pencil. Brenda Leonides sat down on a sofa facing Taverner.

" Have you found out anything?" she asked.

I noticed her fingers nervously twisting and untwisting a pleat of the chiffon of her dress.

" We can state definitely now that your husband died as a result of eserine poisoning."

" You mean those eyedrops killed him?"

" It seems quite certain that when you gave Mr. Leonides that last injection, it was eserine that you injected and not insulin."

" But I didn't know that. I didn't have anything to do with it. Really I didn't, Inspector."

" Then somebody must have deliberately replaced the insulin by the eyedrops."

" What a wicked thing to do!"

" Yes, Mrs. Leonides."

" Do you think—someone did it on purpose? Or by accident? It couldn't have been a—a joke, could it?"

Taverner said smoothly:

" We don't think it was a joke, Mrs. Leonides."

" It must have been one of the servants."

Taverner did not answer.

"It must. I don't see who else could have done it."

"Are you sure? Think, Mrs. Leonides. Haven't you any ideas at all? There's been no ill-feeling anywhere? No quarrel? No grudge?"

She still stared at him with large defiant eyes.

"I've no idea at all," she said.

"You had been at the cinema that afternoon, you said?"

"Yes—I came in at half-past six—it was time for the insulin—I—I—gave him the injection just the same as usual and then he—he went all queer. I was terrified—I rushed over to Roger—I've told you all this before. Have I got to go over it again and again?" Her voice rose hysterically.

"I'm so sorry, Mrs. Leonides. Now can I speak to Mr. Brown?"

"To Laurence? Why? He doesn't know anything about it."

"I'd like to speak to him all the same."

She stared at him suspiciously.

"Eustace is doing Latin with him in the schoolroom. Do you want him to come here?"

"No—we'll go to him."

Taverner went quickly out of the room. The sergeant and I followed.

"You've put the wind up her, sir," said Sergeant Lamb.

Taverner grunted. He led the way up a short flight of steps and along a passage into a big room looking over the garden. There a fair-haired young man of about thirty and a handsome, dark boy of sixteen were sitting at a table.

They looked up at our entrance. Sophia's brother Eustace looked at me, Laurence Brown fixed an agonised gaze on Chief-Inspector Taverner.

I have never seen a man look so completely paralysed

with fright. He stood up, then sat down again. He said, and his voice was almost a squeak:

"Oh—er—good morning, Inspector."

"Good morning," Taverner was curt. "Can I have a word with you?"

"Yes, of course. Only too pleased. At least——"

Eustace got up.

"Do you want me to go away, Chief-Inspector?" His voice was pleasant with a faintly arrogant note.

"We—we can continue our studies later," said the tutor.

Eustace strolled negligently towards the door. He walked rather stiffly. Just as he went through the door he caught my eye, drew a forefinger across the front of his throat and grinned. Then he shut the door behind him.

"Well, Mr. Brown," said Taverner. "The analysis is quite definite. It was eserine that caused Mr. Leonides' death."

"I—you mean—Mr. Leonides was really poisoned? I have been hoping——"

"He was poisoned," said Taverner curtly. "Someone substituted eserine eyedrops for insulin."

"I can't believe it . . . It's incredible."

"The question is, who had a motive?"

"Nobody. Nobody at all!" The young man's voice rose excitedly.

"You wouldn't like to have your solicitor present, would you?" inquired Taverner.

"I haven't got a solicitor. I don't want one. I have nothing to hide—nothing . . ."

"And you quite understand that what you say is about to be taken down?"

"I'm innocent—I assure you, I'm innocent."

"I have not suggested anything else." Taverner paused.

" Mrs. Leonides was a good deal younger than her husband, was she not?"

" I—I suppose so—I mean, well, yes."

" She must have felt lonely sometimes?"

Laurence Brown did not answer. He passed his tongue over his dry lips.

" To have a companion of more or less her own age living here must have been agreeable to her?"

" I—no, not at all—I mean—I don't know."

" It seems to me quite natural that an attachment should have sprung up between you."

The young man protested vehemently.

" It didn't! It wasn't! Nothing of the kind! I know what you're thinking, but it wasn't so! Mrs. Leonides was very kind to me always and I had the greatest—the greatest respect for her—but nothing more—nothing more, I do assure you. It's monstrous to suggest things of that kind! Monstrous! I wouldn't kill *anybody*—or tamper with bottles—or anything like that. I'm very sensitive and highly strung. I—the very idea of killing is a *nightmare* to me—they quite understood that at the tribunal—I have religious objections to killing. I did hospital work instead—stoking boilers—terribly heavy work—I couldn't go on with it—but they let me take up educational work. I have done my best here with Eustace and with Josephine—a very intelligent child, but difficult. And everybody has been most kind to me—Mr. Leonides and Mrs. Leonides and Miss de Haviland. And now this awful thing happens . . . And you suspect me—*me*—of murder!"

Inspector Taverner looked at him with a slow, appraising interest.

" I haven't said so," he remarked.

" But you think so! I know you think so! They all think

so! They look at me. I—I can't go on talking to you. I'm not well."

He hurried out of the room. Taverner turned his head slowly to look at me.

"Well, what do you think of him?"

"He's scared stiff."

"Yes, I know, but is he a murderer?"

"If you ask me," said Sergeant Lamb, "he'd never have had the nerve."

"He'd never have bashed anyone on the head, or shot off a pistol," agreed the chief-inspector. "But in this particular crime what is there to do? Just monkey about with a couple of bottles. . . . Just help a very old man out of the world in a comparatively painless manner."

"Practically euthanasia," said the sergeant.

"And then, perhaps, after a decent interval, marriage with a woman who inherits a hundred thousand pounds free of legacy duty, who already has about the same amount settled upon her, and who has in addition pearls and rubies and emeralds the size of what's-its-name eggs!"

"Ah, well——" Taverner sighed. "It's all theory and conjecture! I managed to scare him all right, but that doesn't prove anything. He's just as likely to be scared if he's innocent. And anyway, I rather doubt if he *was* the one actually to do it. More likely to have been the woman—only why on earth didn't she throw away the insulin bottle, or rinse it out?" He turned to the sergeant. "No evidence from the servants about any goings on?"

"The parlourmaid says they're sweet on each other."

"What grounds?"

"The way he looks at her when she pours out his coffee."

"Fat lot of good that would be in a court of law! Definitely no carryings on?"

" Not that anybody's seen."

" I bet they would have seen, too, if there had been anything to see. You know I'm beginning to believe there really is nothing between them." He looked at me. " Go back and talk to her. I'd like your impression of her."

I went, half-reluctantly, yet I was interested.

CHAPTER IX

I FOUND Brenda Leonides sitting exactly where I had left her. She looked up sharply as I entered.

"Where's Inspector Taverner? Is he coming back?"

"Not just yet."

"Who are you?"

At last I had been asked the question that I had been expecting all the morning.

I answered it with reasonable truth.

"I'm connected with the police, but I'm also a friend of the family."

"The family! Beasts! I hate them all."

She looked at me, her mouth working. She looked sullen and frightened and angry.

"They've been beastly to me always—always. From the very first. Why shouldn't I marry their precious father? What did it matter to *them*? They'd all got loads of money. *He* gave it to them. They wouldn't have had the brains to make any for themselves!"

She went on:

"Why shouldn't a man marry again—even if he is a bit old? And he wasn't really old at all—not in himself. I was very fond of him. I *was* fond of him." She looked at me defiantly.

"I see," I said. "I see."

"I suppose you don't believe that—but it's true. I was

sick of men. I wanted to have a home—I wanted someone to make a fuss of me and say nice things to me. Aristide said lovely things to me—and he could make you laugh—and he was clever. He thought up all sorts of smart ways to get round all these silly regulations. He was very, very clever. I'm not glad he's dead. I'm sorry."

She leaned back on the sofa. She had rather a wide mouth; it curled up sideways in a queer, sleepy smile.

"I've been happy here. I've been safe. I went to all those posh dressmakers—the ones I'd read about. I was as good as anybody. And Aristide gave me lovely things." She stretched out a hand, looking at the ruby on it.

Just for a moment I saw the hand and arm like an outstretched cat's claw, and heard her voice as a purr. She was still smiling to herself.

"What's wrong with that?" she demanded. "I was nice to him. I made him happy." She leaned forward. "Do you know how I met him?"

She went on without waiting for an answer.

"It was in the Gay Shamrock. He'd ordered scrambled eggs on toast and when I brought them to him I was crying. 'Sit down,' he said, 'and tell me what's the matter.' 'Oh, I couldn't,' I said. 'I'd get the sack if I did a thing like that.' 'No, you won't,' he said, 'I own this place.' I looked at him then. Such an odd little man he was, I thought at first—but he'd got a sort of power. I told him all about it. . . . You'll have heard about it all from *them*, I expect—making out I was a regular bad lot—but I wasn't. I was brought up very carefully. We had a shop—a very high-class shop—art needlework. I was never the sort of girl who had a lot of boy friends or made herself cheap. But Terry was different. He was Irish—and he was going overseas. . . . He never wrote or anything—I suppose

I was a fool. So there it was, you see. I was in trouble—just like some dreadful little servant girl. . . ."

Her voice was disdainful in its snobbery.

"Aristide was wonderful. He said everything would be all right. He said he was lonely. We'd be married at once, he said. It was like a dream. And then I found out he was the great Mr. Leonides. He owned masses of shops and restaurants and night clubs. It was quite like a fairy tale, wasn't it?"

"One kind of a fairy tale," I said dryly.

"We were married at a little church in the City—and then we went abroad."

"And the child?"

She looked at me with eyes that came back from a long distance.

"There wasn't a child after all. It was all a mistake."

She smiled, the curled-up sideways, crooked smile.

"I vowed to myself that I'd be a really good wife to him, and I *was*. I ordered all the kinds of food he liked, and wore the colours he fancied and I did all I could to please him. And he was happy. But we never got rid of that family of his. Always coming and sponging and living in his pocket. Old Miss de Haviland—I think she ought to have gone away when he got married. I said so. But Aristide said, 'She's been here so long. It's her home now.' The truth is he liked to have them all about and underfoot. They were beastly to *me*, but he never seemed to notice that or to mind about it. Roger hates me—have you seen Roger? He's always hated me. He's jealous. And Philip's so stuck up he never speaks to me. And now they're trying to pretend I murdered him—and I didn't—I *didn't*!" She leaned towards me. "Please believe I didn't!"

I found her very pathetic. The contemptuous way the

Leonides family had spoken of her, their eagerness to believe that she had committed the crime—now, at this moment, it all seemed positively inhuman conduct. She was alone, defenceless, hunted down.

"And if it's not me, they think it's Laurence," she went on.

"What about Laurence?" I asked.

"I'm terribly sorry for Laurence. He's delicate and he couldn't go and fight. It's not because he was a coward. It's because he's sensitive. I've tried to cheer him up and to make him feel happy. He has to teach those horrible children. Eustace is always sneering at him, and Josephine—well, you've seen Josephine. You know what she's like."

I said I hadn't met Josephine yet.

"Sometimes I think that child isn't right in her head. She has horrible sneaky ways, and she looks queer. . . . She gives me the shivers sometimes."

I didn't want to talk about Josephine. I harked back to Laurence Brown.

"Who is he?" I asked. "Where does he come from?"

I had phrased it clumsily. She flushed.

"He isn't anybody particular. He's just like me. . . . What chance have we got against all of *them*?"

"Don't you think you're being a little hysterical?"

"No, I don't. They want to make out that Laurence did it—or that I did. They've got that policeman on their side. What chance have I got?"

"You mustn't work yourself up," I said.

"Why shouldn't it be one of them who killed him? Or someone from outside? Or one of the servants?"

"There's a certain lack of motive."

"Oh, *motive*! What motive had *I* got? Or Laurence?"

I felt rather uncomfortable as I said:

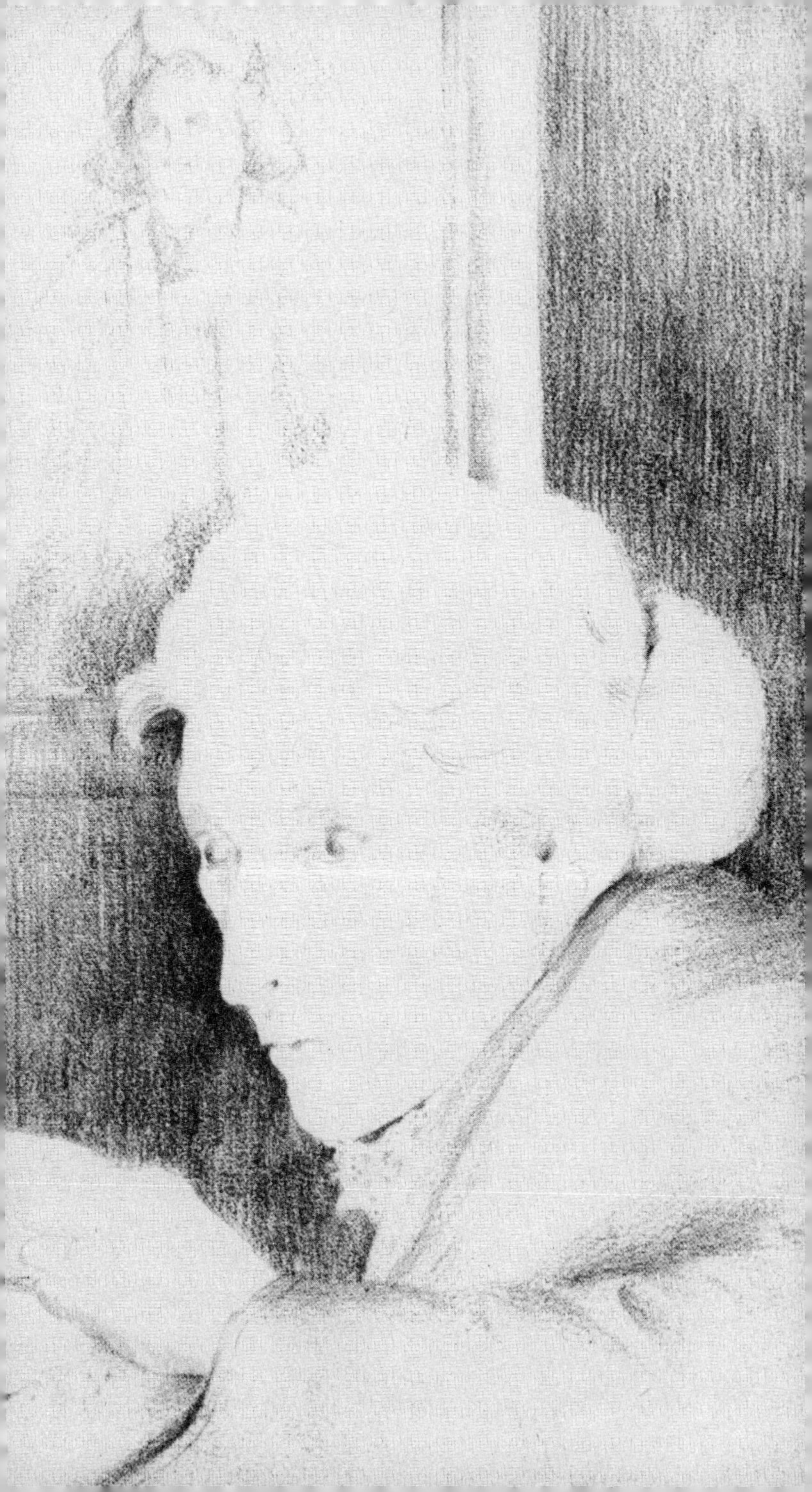

"They might think, I suppose, that you and—er—Laurence—are in love with each other—that you wanted to marry."

She sat bolt upright.

"That's a wicked thing to suggest! And it's not true! We've never said a word of that kind to each other. I've just been sorry for him and tried to cheer him up. We've been friends, that's all. You do believe me, don't you?"

I did believe her. That is, I believed that she and Laurence were, as she put it, only friends. But I also believed that, possibly unknown to herself, she was actually in love with the young man.

It was with that thought in my mind that I went downstairs in search of Sophia.

As I was about to go into the drawing-room, Sophia poked her head out of a door farther along the passage.

"Hallo," she said. "I'm helping Nannie with lunch."

I would have joined her, but she came out into the passage, shut the door behind her, and taking my arm led me into the drawing-room, which was empty.

"Well," she said, "did you see Brenda? What did you think of her?"

"Frankly," I said, "I was sorry for her."

Sophia looked amused.

"I see," she said. "So she got you."

I felt slightly irritated.

"The point is," I said, "that I can see her side of it. Apparently you can't."

"Her side of what?"

"Honestly, Sophia, have any of the family ever been nice to her, or even fairly decent to her, since she came here?"

"No, we haven't been nice to her. Why should we be?"

" Just ordinary Christian kindliness, if nothing else."

" What a very high moral tone you're taking, Charles. Brenda must have done her stuff pretty well."

" Really, Sophia, you seem—I don't know what's come over you."

" I'm just being honest and not pretending. You've seen Brenda's side of it, so you say. Now take a look at my side. I don't like the type of young woman who makes up a hard-luck story and marries a very rich old man on the strength of it. I've a perfect right not to like that type of young woman, and there is no earthly reason why I should pretend I do. And if the facts were written down in cold blood on paper, *you* wouldn't like that young woman either."

" Was it a made-up story?" I asked.

" About the child? I don't know. Personally, I think so."

" And you resent the fact that your grandfather was taken in by it?"

" Oh, grandfather wasn't taken in." Sophia laughed. " Grandfather was never taken in by anybody. He wanted Brenda. He wanted to play Cophetua to her beggar-maid. He knew just what he was doing and it worked out beautifully according to plan. From grandfather's point of view the marriage was a complete success—like all his other operations."

" Was engaging Laurence Brown as tutor another of your grandfather's successes?" I asked ironically.

Sophia frowned.

" Do you know, I'm not sure that it wasn't. He wanted to keep Brenda happy and amused. He may have thought that jewels and clothes weren't enough. He may have thought she wanted a mild romance in her life. He may have calculated that someone like Laurence Brown, somebody really *tame*, if you know what I mean, would just do the trick. A beautiful soulful friendship tinged with melancholy that would stop Brenda from having a real affair with someone outside. I wouldn't put it past grandfather to have worked out something on those lines. He was rather an old devil, you know."

"He must have been," I said.

"He couldn't, of course, have visualised that it would lead to murder. . . . And that," said Sophia, speaking with sudden vehemence, "is really why I don't, much as I would like to, really believe that she did it. If she'd planned to murder him—or if she and Laurence had planned it together—grandfather would have known about it. I dare say that seems a bit far fetched to you——"

"I must confess it does," I said.

"But then you didn't know grandfather. He certainly wouldn't have connived at his own murder! So there you are! Up against a blank wall."

"She's frightened, Sophia," I said. "She's very frightened."

"Chief-Inspector Taverner and his merry, merry men? Yes, I dare say they are rather alarming. Laurence, I suppose, is in hysterics?"

"Practically. He made, I thought, a disgusting exhibition of himself. I don't understand what a woman can see in a man like that."

"Don't you, Charles? Actually Laurence has a lot of sex appeal."

"A weakling like that," I said incredulously.

"Why do men always think that a caveman must necessarily be the only type of person attractive to the opposite sex? Laurence has got sex appeal all right—but I wouldn't expect you to be aware of it." She looked at me. "Brenda got her hooks into you all right."

" Don't be absurd. She's not even really good-looking. And she certainly didn't——"

" Display allure? No, she just made you sorry for her. She's not actually beautiful, she's not in the least clever—but she's got one very outstanding characteristic. She can make trouble. She's made trouble, already, between you and me."

" Sophia!" I cried aghast.

Sophia went to the door.

" Forget it, Charles. I must get on with lunch."

" I'll come and help."

" No, you stay here. It will rattle Nannie to have 'a gentleman in the kitchen.' "

" Sophia," I called as she went out.

" Yes, what is it?"

" Just a servant problem. Why haven't you got any servants down here and upstairs; something in an apron and a cap opened the door to us?"

" Grandfather had a cook, housemaid, parlourmaid and valet-attendant. He liked servants. He paid them the earth, of course, and he got them. Clemency and Roger just have a daily woman who comes in and cleans. They don't like servants—or rather Clemency doesn't. If Roger didn't get a square meal in the City every day, he'd starve. Clemency's idea of a meal is lettuce, tomatoes and raw carrot. We sometimes have servants, and then mother throws one of her temperaments and they leave, and we have dailies for a bit and then start again. We're in the daily period. Nannie is the permanency and copes in emergencies. Now you know."

Sophia went out. I sank down in one of the large brocaded chairs and gave myself up to speculation.

Upstairs I had seen Brenda's side of it. Here and now I

had been shown Sophia's side of it. I realised completely the justice of Sophia's point of view—what might be called the Leonides family's point of view. They resented a stranger within the gates who had obtained admission by what they regarded as ignoble means. They were entirely within their rights. As Sophia had said: on paper it wouldn't look well . . .

But there was the human side of it—the side that I saw and that they didn't. They were, they always had been, rich and well established. They had no conception of the temptations of the underdog. Brenda Leonides had wanted wealth, and pretty things and safety—and a home. She had claimed that in exchange she had made her old husband happy. I had sympathy with her. Certainly, while I was talking with her, I had had sympathy for her. . . . Had I got as much sympathy now?

Two sides to the question—different angles of vision—which was the true angle . . . the true angle. . . .

I had slept very little the night before. I had been up early to accompany Taverner. Now, in the warm, flower-scented atmosphere of Magda Leonides' drawing-room, my body relaxed in the cushioned embrace of the big chair and my eyelids dropped . . .

Thinking of Brenda, of Sophia, of an old man's picture, my thoughts slid together into a pleasant haze.

I slept. . . .

CHAPTER X

I RETURNED to consciousness so gradually that I didn't at first realise that I had been asleep.

The scent of flowers was in my nose. In front of me a round white blob appeared to float in space. It was some few seconds before I realised that it was a human face I was looking at—a face suspended in the air about a foot or two away from me. As my faculties returned, my vision became more precise. The face still had its goblin suggestion—it was round with a bulging brow, combed back hair and small, rather beady, black eyes. But it was definitely attached to a body—a small skinny body. It was regarding me very earnestly.

"Hallo," it said.

"Hallo," I replied, blinking.

"I'm Josephine."

I had already deduced that. Sophia's sister, Josephine, was, I judged, about eleven or twelve years of age. She was a fantastically ugly child with a very distinct likeness to her grandfather. It seemed to me possible that she also had his brains.

"You're Sophia's young man," said Josephine.

I acknowledged the correctness of this remark.

"But you came down here with Chief-Inspector Taverner. Why did you come with Chief-Inspector Taverner?"

"He's a friend of mine."

"Is he? I don't like him. I shan't tell him things."

" What sort of things?"

" The things that I know. I know a lot of things. I like knowing things."

She sat down on the arm of the chair and continued her searching scrutiny of my face. I began to feel quite uncomfortable.

" Grandfather's been murdered. Did you know?"

" Yes," I said. " I knew."

" He was poisoned. With es-er-ine." She pronounced the word very carefully. " It's interesting, isn't it?"

" I suppose it is."

" Eustace and I are very interested. We like detective stories. I've always wanted to be a detective. I'm being one now. I'm collecting clues."

She was, I felt, rather a ghoulish child.

She returned to the charge.

" The man who came with Chief-Inspector Taverner is a detective too, isn't he? In books it says you can always know plain-clothes detectives by their boots. But this detective was wearing suède shoes."

" The old order changeth," I said.

Josephine interpreted this remark according to her own ideas.

" Yes," she said, " there will be a lot of changes here now, I expect. We shall go and live in a house in London on the Embankment. Mother has wanted to for a long time. She'll be very pleased. I don't expect father will mind if his books go, too. He couldn't afford it before. He lost an awful lot of money over *Jezebel*."

" *Jezebel?*" I queried.

" Yes, didn't you see it?"

" Oh, it was a play? No, I didn't. I've been abroad."

" It didn't run very long. Actually it was the most awful

flop. I don't think mother's really the type to play Jezebel, do you?"

I balanced my impressions of Magda. Neither in the peach-coloured *néglige* nor in the tailored suit had she conveyed any suggestion of Jezebel, but I was willing to believe that there were other Magdas that I had not yet seen.

"Perhaps not," I said cautiously.

"Grandfather always said it would be a flop. He said he wouldn't put up any money for one of these historical religious plays. He said it would never be a box-office success. But mother was frightfully keen. I didn't like it much myself. It wasn't really a bit like the story in the Bible. I mean, Jezebel wasn't wicked like she is in the Bible. She was all patriotic and really quite nice. That made it dull. Still, the end was all right. They threw her out of the window. Only no dogs came and ate her. I think that was a pity, don't you? I like the part about the dogs eating her best. Mother says you can't have dogs on the stage but I don't see why. You could have performing dogs." She quoted with gusto: "'*And they ate her all but the palms of her hands.*' Why didn't they eat the palms of her hands?"

"I've really no idea," I said.

"You wouldn't think, would you, that dogs were so particular. Our dogs aren't. They eat simply *anything*."

Josephine brooded on this Biblical mystery for some seconds.

"I'm sorry the play was a flop," I said.

"Yes. Mother was terribly upset. The notices were simply frightful. When she read them, she burst into tears and cried all day and she threw her breakfast tray at Gladys, and Gladys gave notice. It was rather fun."

"I perceive that you like drama, Josephine," I said.

"They did a post-mortem on grandfather," said Josephine. "To find out what he had died of. A P.M., they call it, but I think that's rather confusing, don't you? Because P.M. stands for Prime Minister too. And for afternoon," she added thoughtfully.

"Are you sorry your grandfather is dead?" I asked.

"Not particularly. I didn't like him much. He stopped me learning to be a ballet dancer."

"Did you want to learn ballet dancing?"

"Yes, and mother was willing for me to learn, and father didn't mind, but grandfather said I'd be no good."

She slipped off the arm of the chair, kicked off her shoes and endeavoured to get on to what are called technically, I believe, her points.

"You have to have the proper shoes, of course," she explained, "and even then you get frightful abscesses sometimes on the ends of your toes." She resumed her shoes and inquired casually:

"Do you like this house?"

"I'm not quite sure," I said.

"I suppose it will be sold now. Unless Brenda goes on living in it. And I suppose Uncle Roger and Aunt Clemency won't be going away now."

"Were they going away?" I asked with a faint stirring of interest.

"Yes. They were going on Tuesday. Abroad, somewhere. They were going by air. Aunt Clemency bought one of those new featherweight cases."

"I hadn't heard they were going abroad," I said.

"No," said Josephine. "Nobody knew. It was a secret. They weren't going to tell anyone until after they'd gone. They were going to leave a note behind for grandfather."

She added:

" Not pinned to the pin-cushion. That's only in very old-fashioned books and wives do it when they leave their husbands. But it would be silly now because nobody has pin-cushions any more."

" Of course they don't. Josephine, do you know why your Uncle Roger was—going away?"

She shot me a cunning sideways glance.

" I think I do. It was something to do with Uncle Roger's office in London. I rather think—but I'm not sure—that he'd *embezzled* something."

" What makes you think that?"

Josephine came nearer and breathed heavily in my face.

" The day that grandfather was poisoned Uncle Roger was shut up in his room with him ever so long. They were talking and talking. And Uncle Roger was saying that he'd never been any good, and that he'd let grandfather down—and that it wasn't the money so much— it was the feeling he'd been unworthy of trust. He was in an awful state."

I looked at Josephine with mixed feelings.

" Josephine," I said, " hasn't anybody ever told you that it's not nice to listen at doors?"

Josephine nodded her head vigorously.

" Of course they have. But if you want to find things out, you *have* to listen at doors. I bet Chief-Inspector Taverner does, don't you?"

I considered the point. Josephine went on vehemently:

" And anyway, if *he* doesn't, the other one does, the one with the suède shoes. And they look in people's desks and read all their letters, and find out all their secrets. Only they're stupid! They don't know where to look!"

Josephine spoke with cold superiority. I was stupid enough to let the inference escape me. The unpleasant child went on:

"Eustace and I know lots of things—but I know more than Eustace does. And I shan't tell him. He says women can't ever be great detectives. But I say they can. I'm going to write down everything in a notebook and then, when the police are completely baffled, I shall come forward and say, '*I* can tell you who did it.'"

"Do you read a lot of detective stories, Josephine?"

"Masses."

"I suppose you think you know who killed your grandfather?"

"Well, I *think* so—but I shall have to find a few more clues." She paused and added: "Chief-Inspector Taverner thinks that Brenda did it, doesn't he? Or Brenda and Laurence together because they're in love with each other."

"You shouldn't say things like that, Josephine."

"Why not? They are in love with each other."

"You can't possibly judge."

"Yes, I can. They write to each other. Love letters."

"Josephine! How do you know that?"

"Because I've read them. Awfully soppy letters. But Laurence is soppy. He was too frightened to fight in the war. He went into basements, and stoked boilers. When the flying-bombs went over here, he used to turn green—really green. It made Eustace and me laugh a lot."

What I would have said next I do not know, for at that moment a car drew up outside. In a flash Josephine was at the window, her snub nose pressed to the pane.

"Who is it?" I asked.

"It's Mr. Gaitskill, grandfather's lawyer. I expect he's come about the will."

Breathing excitedly, she hurried from the room, doubtless to resume her sleuthing activities.

Magda Leonides came into the room, and to my surprise came across to me and took my hands in hers.

"My dear," she said, "thank goodness you're still here. One *needs* a man so badly."

She dropped my hands, crossed to a high-backed chair, altered its position a little, glanced at herself in a mirror, then, picking up a small Battersea enamel box from a table, she stood pensively opening and shutting it.

It was an attractive pose.

Sophia put her head in at the door and said in an admonitory whisper, "Gaitskill!"

"I know," said Magda.

A few moments later Sophia entered the room, accompanied by a small elderly man, and Magda put down her enamel box and came forward to meet him.

"Good morning, Mrs. Philip. I'm on my way upstairs. It seems there's some misunderstanding about the will. Your husband wrote to me with the impression that the will was in my keeping. I understood from Mr. Leonides himself that it was at his vault. You don't know anything about it, I suppose?"

"About poor Sweetie's will?" Magda opened astonished eyes. "No, of course not. Don't tell me that wicked woman upstairs has destroyed it?"

"Now, Mrs. Philip;" he shook an admonitory finger at her. "No wild surmises. It's just a question of where your father-in-law kept it."

"But he sent it to you—surely he did—after signing it. He actually told us he had."

"The police, I understand, have been through Mr. Leonides' private papers," said Mr. Gaitskill. "I'll just have a word with Chief-Inspector Taverner."

He left the room.

"Darling," cried Magda. "She *has* destroyed it. I know I'm right."

"Nonsense, mother, she wouldn't do a stupid thing like that."

"It wouldn't be stupid at all. If there's no will she'll get everything."

"Ssh—here's Gaitskill back again."

The lawyer re-entered the room. Chief-Inspector Taverner was with him and behind Taverner came Philip.

"I understood from Mr. Leonides," Gaitskill was saying, "that he had placed his will with the Bank for safe keeping."

Taverner shook his head.

"I've been in communication with the Bank. They have no private papers belonging to Mr. Leonides beyond certain securities which they held for him."

Philip said:

"I wonder if Roger—or Aunt Edith—— Perhaps, Sophia, you'd ask them to come down here."

But Roger Leonides, summoned with the others to the conclave, could give no assistance.

"But it's nonsense—absolute nonsense," he declared. "Father signed the will and said distinctly that he was posting it to Mr. Gaitskill on the following day."

"If my memory serves me," said Mr. Gaitskill, leaning back and half-closing his eyes, "it was on November 24th of last year that I forwarded a draft drawn up according to Mr. Leonides' instructions. He approved the draft, returned it to me, and in due course I sent him the will for signature. After a lapse of a week, I ventured to remind him that I had not yet received the will duly signed and attested, and asking him if there was anything he wished altered. He replied that he was perfectly satisfied, and added that after signing the will he had sent it to his Bank."

"That's quite right," said Roger eagerly. "It was about the end of November last year—you remember, Philip? Father had us all up one evening and read the will to us."

Taverner turned towards Philip Leonides.

"That agrees with your recollection, Mr. Leonides?"

"Yes," said Philip.

"It was rather like the Voysey Inheritance," said Magda. She sighed pleasurably. "I always think there's something so dramatic about a will."

"Miss Sophia?"

"Yes," said Sophia. "I remember perfectly."

"And the provisions of that will?" asked Taverner.

Mr. Gaitskill was about to reply in his precise fashion, but Roger Leonides got ahead of him.

"It was a perfectly simple will. Electra and Joyce had died and their share of the settlements had returned to father. Joyce's son, William, had been killed in action in Burma, and the money he left went to his father. Philip and I and the children were the only relatives left. Father explained that. He left fifty thousand pounds free of duty to Aunt Edith, a hundred thousand pounds free of duty to Brenda, this house to Brenda, or else a suitable house in London to be purchased for her, whichever she preferred. The residue to be divided into three portions, one to myself, one to Philip, the third to be divided between Sophia, Eustace and Josephine, the portions of the last two to be held in trust until they should come of age. I think that's right, isn't it, Mr. Gaitskill?"

"Those are—roughly stated—the provisions of the document I drew up," agreed Mr. Gaitskill, displaying some slight acerbity at not having been allowed to speak for himself.

"Father read it out to us," said Roger. "He asked if there was any comment we might like to make. Of course there was none."

"Brenda made a comment," said Miss de Haviland.

"Yes," said Magda with zest. "She said she couldn't bear her darling old Aristide to talk about death. It 'gave her the creeps,' she said. And after he was dead she didn't want any of the horrid money!"

"That," said Miss de Haviland, "was a conventional protest, typical of her class."

It was a cruel and biting little remark. I realised suddenly how much Edith de Haviland disliked Brenda.

"A very fair and reasonable disposal of his estate," said Mr. Gaitskill.

"And after reading it what happened?" asked Inspector Taverner.

"After reading it," said Roger, "he signed it."

Taverner leaned forward.

"Just how and when did he sign it?"

Roger looked round at his wife in an appealing way. Clemency spoke in answer to that look. The rest of the family seemed content for her to do so.

"You want to know exactly what took place?"

"If you please, Mrs. Roger."

"My father-in-law laid the will down on his desk and requested one of us—Roger, I think—to ring the bell. Roger did so. When Johnson came in answer to the bell, my father-in-law requested him to fetch Janet Woolmer, the parlourmaid. When they were both there, he signed the will and requested them to sign their own names beneath his signature."

"The correct procedure," said Mr. Gaitskill. "A will must be signed by the testator in the presence of two witnesses who must affix their own signatures at the same time and place."

"And after that?" asked Taverner.

"My father-in-law thanked them, and they went out. My father-in-law picked up the will, put it in a long envelope and mentioned that he would send it to Mr. Gaitskill on the following day."

"You all agree," said Inspector Taverner, looking round, "that that is an accurate account of what happened?"

There were murmurs of agreement.

"The will was on the desk, you said. How near were any of you to that desk?"

"Not very near. Five or six yards, perhaps, would be the nearest."

"When Mr. Leonides read you the will was he himself sitting at the desk?"

"Yes."

"Did he get up, or leave the desk, after reading the will and before signing it?"

"No."

"Could the servants read the document when they signed their names?"

"No," said Clemency. "My father-in-law placed a sheet of paper across the upper part of the document."

"Quite properly," said Philip. "The contents of the will were no business of the servants."

"I see," said Taverner. "At least—I don't see."

With a brisk movement he produced a long envelope and leaned forward to hand it to the lawyer.

"Have a look at that," he said. "And tell me what it is."

Mr. Gaitskill drew a folded document out of the envelope. He looked at it with lively astonishment, turning it round and round in his hands.

"This," he said, "is somewhat surprising. I do not understand it at all. Where was this, if I may ask?"

"In the safe, amongst Mr. Leonides' other papers."

"But what is it?" demanded Roger. "What's all the fuss about?"

"This is the will I prepared for your father's signature, Roger—but—I can't understand it after what you have all said—it is not signed."

"What? Well, I suppose it is just a draft."

"No," said the lawyer. "Mr. Leonides returned me the criginal draft. I then drew up the will—*this* will," he tapped it with his finger—"and sent it to him for signature. According to your evidence he signed the will in front of you all—and two witnesses also appended their signatures—and yet this will is unsigned."

"But that's impossible," exclaimed Philip Leonides, speaking with more animation than I had yet heard from him.

Taverner asked: "How good was your father's eyesight?"

"He suffered from glaucoma. He used strong glasses, of course, for reading."

"He had those glasses on that evening?"

"Certainly. He didn't take his glasses off until after he had signed. I think I am right?"

"Quite right," said Clemency.

"And nobody—you are all sure of that—went near the desk before the signing of the will?"

"I wonder now," said Magda, screwing up her eyes. "If one could only visualise it all again."

"Nobody went near the desk," said Sophia. "And grandfather sat at it all the time."

"The desk was in the position it is now? It was not near a door, or a window, or any drapery?"

" It was where it is now."

" I am trying to see how a substitution of some kind could have been effected," said Taverner. " Some kind of substitution there must have been. Mr. Leonides was under the impression that he was signing the document he had just read aloud."

" Couldn't the signatures have been erased?" Roger demanded.

" No, Mr. Leonides. Not without leaving signs of erasion. There is one other possibility. That this is not the document sent to Mr. Leonides by Mr. Gaitskill and which he signed in your presence."

" On the contrary," said Mr. Gaitskill. " I could swear to this being the original document. There is a small flaw in the paper—at the top left-hand corner—it resembles, by a stretch of fancy, an aeroplane. I noticed it at the time."

The family looked blankly at one another.

" A most curious set of circumstances," said Mr. Gaitskill. " Quite without precedent in my experience."

" The whole thing's impossible," said Roger. " We were all there. It simply couldn't have happened."

Miss de Haviland gave a dry cough.

" Never any good wasting breath saying something that has happened couldn't have happened," she remarked. " What's the position now? That's what I'd like to know?"

Gaitskill immediately became the cautious lawyer.

" The position will have to be examined very carefully," he said. " This document, of course, revokes all former wills and testaments. There are a large number of witnesses who saw Mr. Leonides sign what he certainly believed to be this will in perfectly good faith. Hum. Very interesting. Quite a little legal problem."

Taverner glanced at his watch.

" I'm afraid," he said, " I've been keeping you from your lunch."

" Won't you stay and lunch with us, Chief-Inspector?" asked Philip.

" Thank you, Mr. Leonides, but I am meeting Dr. Cray in Swinly Dean."

Philip turned to the lawyer.

" You'll lunch with us, Gaitskill?"

" Thank you, Philip."

Everybody stood up. I edged unobtrusively towards Sophia.

" Do I go or stay?" I murmured. It sounded ridiculously like the title of a Victorian song.

" Go, I think," said Sophia.

I slipped quietly out of the room in pursuit of Taverner. Josephine was swinging to and fro on a baize door leading to the back quarters. She appeared to be highly amused about something.

" The police are stupid," she observed.

Sophia came out of the drawing-room.

" What have you been doing, Josephine?"

" Helping Nannie."

" I believe you've been listening outside the door."

Josephine made a face at her and retreated.

" That child," said Sophia, " is a bit of a problem."

CHAPTER XI

I CAME into the A.C.'s room at the Yard to find Taverner finishing the recital of what had apparently been a tale of woe.

"And there you are," he was saying. "I've turned the lot of them inside out—and what do I get—nothing at all! No motives. None of them hard up. And all that we've got against the wife and her young man is that he made sheep's eyes at her when she poured him out his coffee!"

"Come, come, Taverner," I said. "I can do a little better than that for you."

"You can, can you? Well, Mr. Charles, what did *you* get?"

I sat down, lit a cigarette, leaned back and let them have it.

"Roger Leonides and his wife were planning a getaway abroad next Tuesday. Roger and his father had a stormy interview on the day of the old man's death. Old Leonides had found out something was wrong, and Roger was admitting culpability."

Taverner went purple in the face.

"Where the hell did you get all that from?" he demanded. "If you got it from the servants——"

"I didn't get it from the servants. I got it," I said, "from a private inquiry agent."

"What do you mean?"

"And I must say that, in accordance with the canons of

the best detective stories, he, or rather she—or perhaps I'd better say *it*—has licked the police hollow!

" I also think," I went on, " that my private detective has a few more things up his, her or its sleeve."

Taverner opened his mouth and shut it again. He wanted to ask so many questions at once that he found it hard to begin.

" Roger!" he said. " So Roger's a wrong 'un, is he?"

I felt a slight reluctance as I unburdened myself. I had liked Roger Leonides. Remembering his comfortable, friendly room, and the man's own friendly charm, I disliked setting the hounds of justice on his track. It was possible, of course, that all Josephine's information would be unreliable, but I did not really think so.

" So the kid told you?" said Taverner. " She seems to be wise to everything that goes on in that house."

" Children usually are," said my father dryly.

This information, if true, altered the whole position. If Roger had been, as Josephine had confidently suggested, " embezzling " the funds of Associated Catering and if the old man had found it out, it might have been vital to silence old Leonides and to leave England before the truth came out. Possibly Roger had rendered himself liable to criminal prosecution.

It was agreed that inquiries should be made without delay into the affairs of Associated Catering.

" It will be an almighty crash, if that goes," my father remarked. " It's a huge concern. There are millions involved."

" If it's really in Queer Street, it gives us what we want," said Taverner. " Father summons Roger. Roger breaks down and confesses. Brenda Leonides was out at a cinema. Roger has only to leave his father's room, walk into the bathroom, empty out an insulin phial and replace it with the strong solution of eserine and there you are. Or his wife may have done it. She went over to the other wing after she came home that day—says she went to fetch a pipe Roger had left there. But she could have gone over to switch the stuff before Brenda came home and gave him his injection. She'd be quite cool and capable about it."

I nodded. "Yes, I fancy her as the actual doer of the deed. She's cool enough for anything! And I don't really think that Roger Leonides would think of poison as a means—that trick with the insulin has something feminine about it."

"Plenty of men poisoners," said my father dryly.

"Oh, I know, sir," said Taverner. "Don't I know!" he added with feeling.

"All the same I shouldn't have said Roger was the type."

"Pritchard," the Old Man reminded him, "was a good mixer."

"Let's say they were in it together."

"With the accent on Lady Macbeth," said my father, as Taverner departed. "Is that how she strikes you, Charles?"

I visualised the slight, graceful figure standing by the window in that austere room.

"Not quite," I said. "Lady Macbeth was essentially a greedy woman. I don't think Clemency Leonides is. I don't think she wants or cares for possessions."

"But she might care, desperately, about her husband's safety?"

"That, yes. And she could certainly be—well, ruthless."

"*Different kinds of ruthlessness . . .*" That was what Sophia had said.

I looked up to see the Old Man watching me.

"What's in your mind, Charles?"

But I didn't tell him then.

I was summoned on the following day and found Taverner and my father together.

Taverner was looking pleased with himself and slightly excited.

"Associated Catering is on the rocks," said my father.

"Due to crash at any minute," said Taverner.

"I saw there had been a sharp fall in the shares last night," I said. "But they seem to have recovered this morning."

"We've had to go about it very cautiously," said Taverner. "No direct inquiries. Nothing to cause a panic—or to put the wind up our absconding gentleman. But we've got certain private sources of information and the information there is fairly definite. Associated Catering is on the verge of a crash. It can't possibly meet its commitments. The truth seems to be that it's been grossly mismanaged for years."

"By Roger Leonides?"

"Yes. He's had supreme power, you know."

"And he's helped himself to money——"

"No," said Taverner. "We don't think he has. To put it bluntly, he may be a murderer, but we don't think he's a swindler. Quite frankly he's just been—a fool. He doesn't seem to have had any kind of judgment. He's launched out where he ought to have held in—he's hesitated and retreated where he ought to have launched out. He's delegated power to the last sort of people he ought to have delegated it to. He's a trustful sort of chap, and he's trusted the wrong people. At every time, and on every occasion, he's done the wrong thing."

"There are people like that," said my father. "And

they're not really stupid either. They're bad judges of men, that's all. And they're enthusiastic at the wrong time."

"A man like that oughtn't to be in business at all," said Taverner.

"He probably wouldn't be," said my father, "except for the accident of being Aristide Leonides' son."

"That show was absolutely booming when the old man handed it over to him. It ought to have been a gold mine! You'd think he could have just sat back and let the show run itself."

"No;" my father shook his head. "No show runs itself. There are always decisions to be made—a man sacked here—a man appointed there—small questions of policy. And with Roger Leonides the answer seems to have been always wrong."

"That's right," said Taverner. "He's a loyal sort of chap, for one thing. He kept on the most frightful duds—just because he had affection for them—or because they'd been there a long time. And then he sometimes had wild impractical ideas and insisted on trying them out in spite of the enormous outlay involved."

"But nothing criminal?" my father insisted.

"No, nothing criminal."

"Then why murder?" I asked.

"He may have been a fool and not a knave," said Taverner. "But the result was the same—or nearly the same. The only thing that could save Associated Catering from the smash was a really colossal sum of money by next" (he consulted a notebook) "by next Wednesday at the latest."

"Such a sum as he would inherit, or thought he would have inherited, under his father's will?"

"Exactly."

"But he wouldn't be able to have got that sum in cash."

"No. But he'd have got credit. It's the same thing."

The Old Man nodded.

"Wouldn't it have been simpler to go to old Leonides and ask for help?" he suggested.

"I think he did," said Taverner. "I think that's what the kid overheard. The old boy refused point blank, I should imagine, to throw good money after bad. He would, you know."

I thought that Taverner was right there. Aristide Leonides had refused the backing for Magda's play—he had said that it would not be a box-office success. Events had proved him correct. He was a generous man to his family, but he was not a man to waste money in unprofitable enterprises. And Associated Catering ran to thousands, or probably hundreds of thousands. He had refused point blank, and the only way for Roger to avoid financial ruin was for his father to die.

Yes, there was certainly a motive there all right.

My father looked at his watch.

"I've asked him to come here," he said. "He'll be here any minute now."

"Roger?"

"Yes."

"Will you walk into my parlour said the spider to the fly?" I murmured.

Taverner looked at me in a shocked way.

"We shall give him all the proper cautions," he said severely.

The stage was set, the shorthand writer established. Presently the buzzer sounded, and a few minutes later Roger Leonides entered the room.

He came in eagerly—and rather clumsily—he stumbled over a chair. I was reminded as before of a large friendly dog. At the same time I decided quite definitely that it was not he who had carried out the actual process of transferring eserine to an insulin bottle. He would have broken it, spilled it, or muffed the operation in some way or the other. No, Clemency's, I decided, had been the actual hand, though Roger had been privy to the deed.

Words rushed from him.

"You wanted to see me? You've found out something? Hallo, Charles, I didn't see you. Nice of you to come along. But please tell me, Sir Arthur——"

Such a nice fellow—really such a nice fellow. But lots of murderers had been nice fellows—so their astonished friends had said afterwards. Feeling rather like Judas, I smiled a greeting.

My father was deliberate, coldly official. The glib phrases were uttered. Statement . . . taken down . . . no compulsion . . . solicitor . . .

Roger Leonides brushed them all aside with the same characteristic eager impatience.

I saw the faint sardonic smile on Chief-Inspector Taverner's face, and read from it the thought in his mind.

"*Always sure of themselves, these chaps. They* can't make a mistake. They're far too clever!"

I sat down unobtrusively in a corner and listened.

"I have asked you to come here, Mr. Leonides," my father said, "not to give you fresh information, but to ask for some information from you—information that you have previously withheld."

Roger Leonides looked bewildered.

"Withheld? But I've told you everything—absolutely everything!"

"I think not. You had a conversation with the deceased on the afternoon of his death?"

" Yes, yes, I had tea with him. I told you so."

" You told us that, yes, but you did not tell us about your conversation."

" We—just—talked."

" What about?"

" Daily happenings, the house, Sophia——"

" What about Associated Catering? Was that mentioned?"

I think I had hoped up to then that Josephine had been inventing the whole story; but if so, that hope was quickly quenched.

Roger's face changed. It changed in a moment from eagerness to something that was recognisably close to despair.

" Oh, my God," he said. He dropped into a chair and buried his face in his hands.

Taverner smiled like a contented cat.

" You admit, Mr. Leonides, that you have not been frank with us?"

" How did you get to know about that? I thought nobody knew—I don't see how anybody *could* know."

" We have means of finding out these things, Mr. Leonides." There was a majestic pause. " I think you will see now that you had better tell us the truth."

" Yes, yes, of course. I'll tell you. What do you want to know?"

" Is it true that Associated Catering is on the verge of collapse?"

" Yes. It can't be staved off now. The crash is bound to come. If only my father could have died without ever knowing. I feel so ashamed—so disgraced——"

" There is a possibility of criminal prosecution?"

Roger sat up sharply.

" No, indeed. It will be bankruptcy—but an honourable

bankruptcy. Creditors will be paid twenty shillings in the pound if I throw in my personal assets, which I shall do. No, the disgrace I feel is to have failed my father. He trusted me. He made over to me this, his largest concern—and his pet concern. He never interfered, he never asked what I was doing. He just—trusted me . . . And I let him down."

My father said dryly:

"You say there was no likelihood of criminal prosecution? Why then had you and your wife planned to go abroad without telling anybody of your intention?"

"You know that too?"

"Yes, Mr. Leonides."

"But don't you see?" He leaned forward eagerly. "I couldn't face him with the truth. It would have looked, you see, as if I was asking for money. As though I wanted him to set me on my feet again. He—he was very fond of me. He would have wanted to help. But I couldn't—I couldn't go on—it would have meant making a mess of things all over again—I'm no good. I haven't got the ability. I'm not the man my father was. I've always known it. I've tried. But it's no good. I've been so miserable—God! you don't know how miserable I've been! Trying to get out of the muddle, hoping I'd just get square, hoping the dear old man would never need to hear about it. And then it came—no more hope of avoiding the crash. Clemency—my wife—she understood, she agreed with me. We thought out this plan. Say nothing to anyone. Go away. And then let the storm break. I'd leave a letter for my father, telling him all about it—telling him how ashamed I was and begging him to forgive me. He's been so good to me always—you don't know! But it would be too late then for him to do anything. That's what I wanted. Not to ask him—or even to seem to ask him for help. Start again on my own somewhere. Live simply and humbly. Grow things. Coffee—fruit. Just have the bare necessities of life—hard on Clemency, but she swore she didn't mind. She's wonderful—absolutely wonderful."

"I see." My father's voice was dry. "And what made you change your mind?"

"Change my mind?"

"Yes. What made you decide to go to your father and ask for financial help after all?"

Roger stared at him.

"But I didn't!"

"Come now, Mr. Leonides."

"You've got it all wrong. I didn't go to him. *He* sent for *me*. He'd heard, somehow, in the City. A rumour, I suppose. But he always knew things. Someone had told him. He tackled me with it. Then, of course, I broke down . . . I told him everything. I said it wasn't so much the money—it was the feeling I'd let him down after he'd trusted me."

Roger swallowed convulsively.

"The dear old man," he said. "You can't imagine how good he was to me. No reproaches. Just kindness. I told him I didn't want help, that I preferred not to have it—that I'd rather go away as I'd planned to do. But he wouldn't listen. He insisted on coming to the rescue—on putting Associated Catering on its legs again."

Taverner said sharply:

"You are asking us to believe that your father intended to come to your assistance financially?"

"Certainly he did. He wrote to his brokers then and there, giving them instructions."

I suppose he saw the incredulity on the two men's faces. He flushed.

" Look here," he said, " I've still got the letter. I was to post it. But of course later—with—with the shock and confusion, I forgot. I've probably got it in my pocket now."

He drew out his wallet and started hunting through it. Finally he found what he wanted. It was a creased envelope with a stamp on it. It was addressed, as I saw by leaning forward, to Messrs. Greatorex and Hanbury.

" Read it for yourselves," he said, " if you don't believe me."

My father tore open the letter. Taverner went round behind him. I did not see the letter then, but I saw it later. It instructed Messrs. Greatorex and Hanbury to realise certain investments and asked for a member of the firm to be sent down on the following day to take certain instructions *re* the affairs of Associated Catering. Some of it was unintelligible to me but its purport was clear enough. Aristide Leonides was preparing to put Associated Catering on its feet again.

Taverner said:

" We will give you a receipt for this, Mr. Leonides."

Roger took the receipt. He got up and said:

" Is that all? You do see how it all was, don't you?"

Taverner said:

" Mr. Leonides gave you this letter and then you left him? What did you do next?"

" I rushed back to my own part of the house. My wife had just come in. I told her what my father proposed to do. How wonderful he had been! I—really, I hardly knew what I was doing."

" And your father was taken ill—how long after that?"

" Let me see—half an hour, perhaps, or an hour. Brenda

came rushing in. She was frightened. She said he looked queer. I—I rushed over with her. But I've told you all this before."

" During your former visit, did you go into the bathroom adjoining your father's room at all?"

" I don't think so. No—no, I am sure I didn't. Why, you can't possibly think that *I*——"

My father quelled the sudden indignation. He got up and shook hands.

" Thank you, Mr. Leonides," he said. " You have been very helpful. But you should have told us all this before."

The door closed behind Roger. I got up and came to look at the letter lying on my father's table.

" It *could* be a forgery," said Taverner hopefully.

" It could be," said my father, " but I don't think it is. I think we'll have to accept it exactly as it stands. Old Leonides was prepared to get his son out of this mess. It could have been done more efficiently by him alive than it could by Roger after his death—especially as it now transpires that no will is to be found and that in consequence Roger's actual amount of inheritance is open to question. That means delays—and difficulties. As things now stand, the crash is bound to come. No, Taverner, Roger Leonides and his wife had no motive for getting the old man out of the way. On the contrary——"

He stopped and repeated thoughtfully as though a sudden thought had occurred to him : " On the contrary . . ."

" What's on your mind, sir?" Taverner asked.

The Old Man said slowly :

" If Aristide Leonides had lived only another twenty-four hours, Roger would have been all right. But he didn't live twenty-four hours. He died suddenly and dramatically within little more than an hour."

" H'm," said Taverner. " Do you think somebody in the house *wanted* Roger to go broke? Someone who had an opposing financial interest? Doesn't seem likely."

" What's the position as regards the will?" my father asked. " Who actually gets old Leonides' money?"

Taverner heaved an exasperated sigh.

"You know what lawyers are. Can't get a straight answer out of them. There's a former will. Made when he married the second Mrs. Leonides. That leaves the same sum to her, rather less to Miss de Haviland, and the remainder between Philip and Roger. I should have thought that if this will isn't signed, then the old one would operate, but it seems it isn't so simple as that. First the making of the new will revoked the former one and there are witnesses to the signing of it, and the ' testator's intention.' It seems to be a toss up if it turns out that he died intestate. Then the widow apparently gets the lot—or a life interest at any rate."

" So if the will's disappeared Brenda Leonides is the most likely person to profit by it?"

" Yes. If there's been any hocus-pocus, it seems probable that she's at the bottom of it. And there obviously *has* been hocus-pocus, but I'm dashed if I see how it was done."

I didn't see, either. I suppose we were really incredibly stupid. But we were looking at it, of course, from the wrong angle.

CHAPTER XII

THERE WAS a short silence after Taverner had gone out.

Then I said:

"Dad, what are murderers like?"

The Old Man looked up at me thoughtfully. We understand each other so well that he knew exactly what was in my mind when I put that question. And he answered it very seriously.

"Yes," he said. "That's important now—very important, for you . . . Murder's come close to you. You can't go on looking at it from the outside."

I had always been interested, in an amateurish kind of way, in some of the more spectacular "cases" with which the C.I.D. had dealt, but, as my father said, I had been interested from the outside—looking in, as it were, through the shop window. But now, as Sophia had seen much more quickly than I did, murder had become a dominant factor in my life.

The Old Man went on:

"I don't know if I'm the right person to ask. I could put you on to a couple of the tame psychiatrists who do jobs for us. They've got it all cut and dried. Or Taverner could give you all the inside dope. But you want, I take it, to hear what I, personally, as the result of my experience of criminals, think about it?"

"That's what I want," I said gratefully.

My father traced a little circle with his finger on the desk-top.

" What are murderers like? Some of them "—a faint rather melancholy smile showed on his face—" have been thoroughly nice chaps."

I think I looked a little startled.

" Oh yes, they have," he said. " Nice ordinary fellows like you and me—or like that chap who went out just now —Roger Leonides. Murder, you see, is an amateur crime. I'm speaking of course of the kind of murder you have in mind—not gangster stuff. One feels, very often, as though these nice ordinary chaps had been overtaken, as it were, by murder, almost accidentally. They've been in a tight place, or they've wanted something very badly, money or a woman —and they've killed to get it. The brake that operates with most of us doesn't operate with them. A child, you know, translates desire into action without compunction. A child is angry with its kitten, says ' I'll kill you,' and hits it on the head with a hammer—and then breaks its heart because the kitten doesn't come alive again! Lots of kids try to take a baby out of a pram and ' drown it,' because it usurps attention—or interferes with their pleasures. They get—very early—to a stage when they know that that is ' wrong '—that is, that it will be punished. Later, they get to *feel* that it is wrong. But some people, I suspect, remain morally immature. They continue to be aware that murder is wrong, but they do not feel it. I don't think, in my experience, that any murderer has really felt remorse. . . . And that, perhaps, is the mark of Cain. Murderers are set apart, they are ' different '—murder is wrong—but not for *them*—for *them* it is necessary—the victim has ' asked for it,' it was ' the only way.' "

" Do you think," I asked, " that if someone hated old

Leonides, had hated him, say, for a very long time, that that would be a reason?"

"Pure hate? Very unlikely, I should say." My father looked at me curiously. "When you say hate, I presume you mean dislike carried to excess. A jealous hate is different—that rises out of affection and frustration. Constance Kent, everybody said, was very fond of the baby brother she killed. But she wanted, one supposes, the attention and the love that was bestowed on him. I think people more often kill those they love than those they hate. Possibly because only the people you love can really make life unendurable to you.

"But all this doesn't help you much, does it?" he went on. "What you want, if I read you correctly, is some token, some universal sign that will help you to pick out a murderer from a household of apparently normal and pleasant people?"

"Yes, that's it."

"Is there a common denominator? I wonder. You know," he paused in thought, "if there is, I should be inclined to say it is vanity."

"Vanity?"

"Yes, I've never met a murderer who wasn't vain. . . . It's their vanity that leads to their undoing, nine times out of ten. They may be frightened of being caught, but they can't help strutting and boasting and usually they're sure they've been far too clever to be caught." He added: "And here's another thing, a murderer wants to *talk*."

"To talk?"

"Yes; you see, having committed a murder puts you in a position of great loneliness. You'd like to tell someone all about it—and you never can. And that makes you want to all the more. And so—if you can't talk about how you did it, you can at least talk about the murder itself—discuss it, advance theories—go over it.

" If I were you, Charles, I should look out for that. Go down there again, mix with them all, and get them to talk. Of course it won't be plain sailing. Guilty or innocent, they'll be glad of the chance to talk to a stranger, because they can say things to you that they couldn't say to each other. But it's possible, I think, that you might spot a difference. A person who has something to hide can't really afford to talk *at all.* The blokes knew that in Intelligence during the war. If you were captured, your name, rank and unit, but *nothing more.* People who attempt to give false information nearly always slip up. Get that household talking, and watch out for a slip or for some flash of self-revelation."

I told him then what Sophia had said about the ruthlessness in the family—the different kinds of ruthlessness. He was interested.

" Yes," he said. " Your young woman has got something there. Most families have got a defect, a chink in their armour. Most people can deal with one weakness—but they mightn't be able to deal with two weaknesses of a different kind. Interesting thing, heredity. Take the de Haviland ruthlessness, and what we might call the Leonides unscrupulousness—the de Havilands are all right because they're not unscrupulous, and the Leonideses are all right because, though unscrupulous, they are kindly—but get a descendant who inherited both of those traits—see what I mean?"

I had not thought of it quite in those terms. My father said:

" But I shouldn't worry your head about heredity. It's much too tricky and complicated a subject. No, my boy, go down there and *let them talk to you.* Your Sophia is quite right about one thing. Nothing but the truth is going to be any good to her or to you. You've got to *know*."

He added as I went out of the room:

"And be careful of the child."

"Josephine? You mean don't let on to her what I'm up to."

"No, I didn't mean that. I meant—look after her. We don't want anything to happen to her."

I stared at him.

"Come, come, Charles. There's a cold-blooded killer somewhere in that household. The child Josephine appears to know most of what goes on."

"She certainly knew all about Roger—even if she did leap to the conclusion that he was a swindler. Her account of what she overheard seems to have been quite accurate."

"Yes, yes. Child's evidence is always the best evidence there is. I'd rely on it every time. No good in court, of course. Children can't stand being asked direct questions. They mumble or else look idiotic and say they don't know. They're at their best when they're showing off. That's what the child was doing to you. Showing off. You'll get more out of her in the same way. Don't go asking her questions. Pretend you think she doesn't know anything. That'll fetch her."

He added:

"But take care of her. She may know a little too much for somebody's safety."

CHAPTER XIII

I WENT down to the Crooked House (as I called it in my own mind) with a slightly guilty feeling. Though I had repeated to Taverner Josephine's confidences about Roger, I had said nothing about her statement that Brenda and Laurence Brown wrote love letters to each other.

I excused myself by pretending that it was mere romancing, and that there was no reason to believe that it was true: But actually I had felt a strange reluctance to pile up additional evidence against Brenda Leonides. I had been affected by the pathos of her position in the house—surrounded by a hostile family united solidly against her. If such letters existed doubtless Taverner and his myrmidons would find them. I disliked to be the means of bringing fresh suspicion on a woman in a difficult position. Moreover, she had assured me solemnly that there was nothing of that kind between her and Laurence and I felt more inclined to believe her than to believe that malicious gnome Josephine. Had not Brenda said herself that Josephine was " not all there."

I stifled an uneasy certainty that Josephine was very much all there. I remembered the intelligence of her beady black eyes.

I had rung up Sophia and asked if I might come down again.

" Please do, Charles."

" How are things going?"

" I don't know. All right. They keep on searching the house. What are they looking for?"

" I've no idea."

" We're all getting very nervy. Come as soon as you can. I shall go crazy if I can't talk to someone."

I said I would come down straightaway.

There was no one in sight as I drove up to the front door. I paid the taxi and it drove away. I felt uncertain whether to ring the bell or to walk in. The front door was open.

As I stood there, hesitating, I heard a slight sound behind me. I turned my head sharply. Josephine, her face partially obscured by a very large apple, was standing in the opening of the yew hedge looking at me.

As I turned my head, she turned away.

" Hallo, Josephine."

She did not answer, but disappeared behind the hedge. I crossed the drive and followed her. She was seated on the uncomfortable rustic bench by the goldfish pond swinging her legs to and fro and biting into her apple. Above its rosy circumference her eyes regarded me sombrely and with what I could not but feel was hostility.

" I've come down again, Josephine," I said.

It was a feeble opening, but I found Josephine's silence and her unblinking gaze rather unnerving.

With excellent strategic sense, she still did not reply.

" Is that a good apple?" I asked.

This time Josephine did condescend to reply. Her reply consisted of one word.

" Woolly."

" A pity," I said. " I don't like woolly apples."

Josephine replied scornfully:

" Nobody does."

" Why wouldn't you speak to me when I said hallo?"

" I didn't want to."

" Why not?"

Josephine removed the apple from her face to assist in the clearness of her denunciation.

" You went and sneaked to the police," she said.

" Oh!" I was rather taken aback. " You mean—about——"

" About Uncle Roger."

" But it's all right, Josephine," I assured her. " Quite all right. They know he didn't do anything wrong—I mean, he hadn't embezzled any money or anything of that kind."

Josephine threw me an exasperated glance.

" How stupid you are."

" I'm sorry."

" I wasn't worrying about Uncle Roger. It's simply that that's not the way to do detective work. Don't you know that you *never* tell the police until the very end?"

" Oh, I see," I said. " I'm sorry, Josephine. I'm really very sorry."

" So you should be." She added reproachfully: " I trusted you."

I said I was sorry for the third time. Josephine appeared a little mollified. She took another couple of bites of apple.

" But the police would have been bound to find out about all this," I said. " You—I—we couldn't have kept it a secret."

" You mean because he's going bankrupt?"

As usual Josephine was well informed.

" I suppose it will come to that."

" They're going to talk about it to-night," said Josephine. " Father and mother and Uncle Roger and Aunt Edith. Aunt Edith would give him her money—only she hasn't got it yet—but I don't think father will. He says if Roger has got in a jam he's only got himself to blame and what's the good of throwing good money after bad, and mother won't hear of giving him any because she wants father to put up the money for Edith Thompson. Do you know about Edith Thompson? She was married, but she didn't like her husband. She was in love with a young man called Bywaters who came off a ship and he went down a different street after the theatre and stabbed him in the back."

I marvelled once more at the range and completeness of Josephine's knowledge; and also at the dramatic sense which, only slightly obscured by hazy pronouns, had presented all the salient facts in a nutshell.

"It sounds all right," said Josephine, "but I don't suppose the play will be like that at all. It will be like *Jezebel* again." She sighed. "I wish I knew *why* the dogs wouldn't eat the palms of her hands."

"Josephine," I said. "You told me that you were almost sure who the murderer was?"

"Well?"

"Who is it?"

She gave me a look of scorn.

"I see," I said. "Not till the last chapter? Not even if I promise not to tell Inspector Taverner?"

"I want just a few more clues," said Josephine.

"Anyway," she added, throwing the core of the apple into the goldfish pool, "I wouldn't tell *you*. If you're anyone, you're Watson."

I stomached this insult.

"O.K.," I said. "I'm Watson. But even Watson was given the data."

"The what?"

"The facts. And then he made the wrong deductions

from them. Wouldn't it be a lot of fun for you to see me making the wrong deductions?"

For a moment Josephine was tempted. Then she shook her head.

"No," she said, and added: "Anyway, I'm not very keen on Sherlock Holmes. It's awfully old-fashioned. They drive about in dog-carts."

"What about those letters?" I asked.

"What letters?"

"The letters you said Laurence Brown and Brenda wrote to each other."

"I made that up," said Josephine.

"I don't believe you."

"Yes, I did. I often make things up, it amuses me."

I stared at her. She stared back.

"Look here, Josephine. I know a man at the British Museum who knows a lot about the Bible. If I find out from him why the dogs didn't eat the palms of Jezebel's hands, will you tell me about those letters?"

This time Josephine really hesitated.

Somewhere, not very far away, a twig snapped with a sharp cracking noise. Josephine said flatly:

"No, I won't."

I accepted defeat. Rather late in the day, I remembered my father's advice.

"Oh well," I said, "it's only a game. Of course you don't really know anything."

Josephine's eyes snapped, but she resisted the bait.

I got up. "I must go in now," I said, "and find Sophia. Come along."

"I shall stop here," said Josephine.

"No, you won't," I said. "You're coming in with me."

Unceremoniously I yanked her to her feet. She seemed

surprised and inclined to protest, but yielded with a fairly good grace—partly, no doubt, because she wished to observe the reactions of the household to my presence.

Why I was so anxious for her to accompany me I could not at that moment have said. It only came to me as we were passing through the front door.

It was because of the sudden snapping of a twig.

CHAPTER XIV

THERE WAS a murmur of voices from the big drawing-room. I hesitated but did not go in. I wandered down the passage and, led by some impulse, I pushed open a baize door. The passage beyond was dark, but suddenly a door opened showing a big lighted kitchen. In the doorway stood an old woman—a rather bulky old woman. She had a very clean white apron tied round her ample waist and the moment I saw her I knew that everything was all right. It is the feeling that a good Nannie can always give you. I am thirty-five, but I felt just like a reassured little boy of four.

As far as I knew, Nannie had never seen me, but she said at once:

"It's Mr. Charles, isn't it? Come into the kitchen and let me give you a cup of tea."

It was a big happy-feeling kitchen. I sat down by the centre table and Nannie brought me a cup of tea and two sweet biscuits on a plate. I felt more than ever that I was in the nursery again. Everything was all right—and the terrors of the dark and the unknown were no more with me.

"Miss Sophia will be glad you've come," said Nannie. "She's been getting rather over-excited." She added disapprovingly: "They're all over-excited."

I looked over my shoulder.

"Where's Josephine? She came in with me."

Nannie made a disapproving clacking noise with her tongue.

" Listening at doors and writing down things in that silly little book she carries about with her," she said. " She ought to have gone to school and had children of her own age to play with. I've said so to Miss Edith and she agrees —but the master would have it that she was best here in her home."

" I suppose he's very fond of her," I said.

" He was, sir. He was fond of them all."

I looked slightly astonished, wondering why Philip's affection for his offspring was put so definitely in the past. Nannie saw my expression and flushing slightly, she said:

" When I said the master, it was old Mr. Leonides I meant."

Before I could respond to that, the door opened with a rush and Sophia came in.

" Oh, Charles," she said, and then quickly: " Oh, Nannie, I'm so glad he's come."

" I know you are, love."

Nannie gathered up a lot of pots and pans and went off into a scullery with them. She shut the door behind her.

I got up from the table and went over to Sophia. I put my arms round her and held her to me.

" Dearest," I said. " You're trembling. What is it?"

Sophia said:

" I'm frightened, Charles. I'm frightened."

" I love you," I said. " If I could take you away——"

She drew apart and shook her head.

" No, that's impossible. We've got to see this through. But you know, Charles, I don't like it. I don't like the feeling that someone—someone in this house—someone I see and speak to every day is a cold-blooded, calculating poisoner. . . ."

And I didn't know how to answer that. To someone like Sophia one can give no easy meaningless reassurances.

She said: "If only one *knew*——"

"That must be the worst of it," I agreed.

"You know what really frightens me?" she whispered. "It's that we may *never* know...."

I could visualise easily what a nightmare that would be.... And it seemed to me highly probable that it never might be known who had killed old Leonides.

But it also reminded me of a question I had meant to put to Sophia on a point that had interested me.

"Tell me, Sophia," I said. "How many people in this house knew about the eserine eyedrops—I mean (a) that your grandfather had them, and (b) that they were poisonous and what would be a fatal dose?"

"I see what you're getting at, Charles. But it won't work. You see, we all knew."

"Well, yes, vaguely, I suppose, but specifically——"

"We knew specifically. We were all up with grandfather one day for coffee after lunch. He liked all the family round him, you know. And his eyes had been giving him a lot of trouble. And Brenda got the eserine to put a drop in each eye, and Josephine, who always asks questions about everything, said: 'Why does it say "*Eyedrops—not to be taken*" on the bottle? What would happen if you drank all the bottle?' And grandfather smiled and said: 'If Brenda were to make a mistake and inject eyedrops into me one day instead of insulin—I suspect I should give a big gasp, and go rather blue in the face and then die, because, you see, my heart isn't very strong.' And Josephine said: 'Oo,' and grandfather went on: 'So we must be careful that Brenda does not give me an injection of eserine instead of insulin, mustn't we?'" Sophia paused and then said: "We were all there listening. You see? We all heard!"

I did see. I had had some faint idea in my mind that just a little specialised knowledge would have been needed. But now it was borne in upon me that old Leonides had actually supplied the blue-print for his own murder. The murderer had not had to think out a scheme, or to plan or devise anything. A simple easy method of causing death had been supplied by the victim himself.

I drew a deep breath. Sophia, catching my thought, said: "Yes, it's rather horrible, isn't it?"

"You know, Sophia," I said slowly. "There's just one thing does strike me."

"Yes?"

"That you're right, and that it couldn't have been Brenda. She couldn't do it exactly that way—when you'd all listened—when you'd all remember."

"I don't know about that. She is rather dumb in some ways, you know."

"Not as dumb as all that," I said. "No, it couldn't have been Brenda."

Sophia moved away from me.

"You don't want it to be Brenda, do you?" she asked.

And what could I say? I couldn't—no, I couldn't—say flatly: "Yes, I hope it *is* Brenda."

Why couldn't I? Just the feeling that Brenda was all alone on one side, and the concentrated animosity of the powerful Leonides family was arrayed against her on the other side? Chivalry? A feeling for the weaker? For the defenceless? I remembered her sitting on the sofa in her expensive rich mourning, the hopelessness in her voice—the fear in her eyes.

Nannie came back rather opportunely from the scullery.

I don't know whether she sensed a certain strain between myself and Sophia.

She said disapprovingly:

"Talking murders and such-like. Forget about it, that's what I say. Leave it to the police. It's their nasty business, not yours."

"Oh, Nannie—don't you realise that someone in this house is a murderer?"

"Nonsense, Miss Sophia, I've no patience with you. Isn't the front door open all the time—all the doors open, nothing locked—asking for thieves and burglars?"

"But it couldn't have been a burglar, nothing was stolen. Besides, why should a burglar come in and poison somebody?"

"I didn't say it was a burglar, Miss Sophia. I only said all the doors were open. Anyone could have got in. If you ask me it was the Communists."

Nannie nodded her head in a satisfied way.

"Why on earth should Communists want to murder poor grandfather?"

"Well, everyone says that they're at the bottom of everything that goes on. But if it wasn't the Communists, mark my word, it was the Catholics. The Scarlet Woman of Babylon, that's what they are."

With the air of one saying the last word, Nannie disappeared again into the scullery.

Sophia and I laughed.

"A good old Black Protestant," I said.

"Yes, isn't she? Come on, Charles, come into the drawing-room. There's a kind of family conclave going on. It was scheduled for this evening—but it's started prematurely."

"I'd better not butt in, Sophia."

"If you're ever going to marry into the family, you'd

better see just what it's like when it has the gloves off."

"What's it all about?"

"Roger's affairs. You seem to have been mixed up in them already. But you're crazy to think that Roger would ever have killed grandfather. Why, Roger adored him."

"I didn't really think Roger had. I thought Clemency might have."

"Only because I put it into your head. But you're wrong there too. I don't think Clemency will mind a bit if Roger loses all his money. I think she'll actually be rather pleased. She's got a queer kind of passion for *not* having things. Come on."

When Sophia and I entered the drawing-room, the voices that were speaking stopped abruptly. Everybody looked at us.

They were all there. Philip sitting in a big crimson brocaded arm-chair between the windows, his beautiful face set in a cold, stern mask. He looked like a judge about to pronounce sentence. Roger was astride a big pouffé by the fireplace. He had ruffled up his hair between his fingers until it stood up all over his head. His left trouser leg was rucked up and his tie was askew. He looked flushed and argumentative. Clemency sat beyond him; her slight form seemed too slender for the big stuffed chair. She was looking away from the others and seemed to be studying the wall panels with a dispassionate gaze. Edith sat in a grandfather chair, bolt upright. She was knitting with incredible energy, her lips pressed tightly together. The most beautiful thing in the room to look at was Magda and Eustace. They looked like a portrait by Gainsborough. They sat together on the sofa—the dark, handsome boy with a sullen expression on his face, and beside him, one arm thrust out along the back of the sofa, sat Magda, the Duchess of Three Gables in a picture gown of taffetas with one small foot in a brocaded slipper thrust out in front of her.

Philip frowned.

"Sophia," he said, "I'm sorry, but we are discussing family matters which are of a private nature."

Miss de Haviland's needles clicked. I prepared to apologise and retreat. Sophia forestalled me. Her voice was clear and determined.

"Charles and I," she said, "hope to get married. I want Charles to be here."

"And why on earth not?" cried Roger, springing up from his pouffé with explosive energy. "I keep telling you, Philip, there's nothing *private* about this! The whole world is going to know to-morrow or the day after. Anyway, my dear boy," he came and put a friendly hand on my shoulder, "*you* know all about it. You were there this morning."

"Do tell me," cried Magda, leaning forward. "What is it like at Scotland Yard? One always wonders. A table? A desk? Chairs? What kind of curtains? No flowers, I suppose? A dictaphone?"

"Put a sock in it, Mother," said Sophia. "And anyway, you told Vavasour Jones to cut that Scotland Yard scene. You said it was an anti-climax."

"It makes it too like a detective play," said Magda. "Edith Thompson is definitely a psychological drama—or psychological thriller—which do you think sounds best?"

"You were there this morning?" Philip asked me sharply. "Why? Oh, of course—your father——"

He frowned. I realised more clearly than ever that my presence was unwelcome, but Sophia's hand was clenched on my arm.

Clemency moved a chair forward.

" Do sit down," she said.

I gave her a grateful glance and accepted.

" You may say what you like," said Miss de Haviland, apparently going on from where they had all left off, " but I do think we ought to respect Aristide's wishes. When this will business is straightened out, as far as I am concerned, my legacy is entirely at your disposal, Roger."

Roger tugged his hair in a frenzy.

" No, Aunt Edith. *No* !" he cried.

" I wish I could say the same," said Philip, " but one has to take every factor into consideration——"

" Dear old Phil, don't you understand? I'm not going to take a penny from *anyone*."

" Of course he can't !" snapped Clemency.

" Anyway, Edith," said Magda. " *If* the will is straightened out, he'll have his own legacy."

" But it can't possibly be straightened out in time, can it?" asked Eustace.

" You don't know anything about it, Eustace," said Philip.

" The boy's absolutely right," cried Roger. " He's put his finger on the spot. Nothing can avert the crash. Nothing."

He spoke with a kind of relish.

" There is really nothing to discuss," said Clemency.

" Anyway," said Roger, " what does it matter?"

" I should have thought it mattered a good deal," said Philip, pressing his lips together.

" No," said Roger. " *No!* Does anything matter compared with the fact that father is dead? Father is *dead* ! And we sit here discussing mere money matters !"

A faint colour rose in Philip's pale cheeks.

" We are only trying to help," he said stiffly.

" I know, Phil, old boy, I know. But there's nothing anyone can do. So let's call it a day."

" I suppose," said Philip, " that I *could* raise a certain amount of money. Securities have gone down a good deal and some of my capital is tied up in such a way that I can't touch it : Magda's settlement and so on—but——"

Magda said quickly :

" Of course you can't raise the money, darling. It would be absurd to try—and not very fair on the children."

" I tell you I'm not asking anyone for *anything* !" shouted Roger. " I'm *hoarse* with telling you so. I'm quite content that things should take their course."

" It's a question of *prestige*," said Philip. " Father's. Ours."

" It wasn't a family business. It was solely *my* concern."

" Yes," said Philip, looking at him. " It was entirely your concern."

Edith de Haviland got up and said : " I think we've discussed this enough."

There was in her voice that authentic note of authority that never fails to produce its effect.

Philip and Magda got up. Eustace lounged out of the room and I noticed the stiffness of his gait. He was not exactly lame but his walk was a halting one.

Roger linked his arm in Philip's and said :

" You've been a brick, Phil, even to think of such a thing !" The brothers went out together.

Magda murmured, " Such a fuss !" as she followed them, and Sophia said that she must see about my room.

Edith de Haviland stood rolling up her knitting. She looked towards me and I thought she was going to speak to me. There was something almost like appeal in her glance.

However, she changed her mind, sighed and went out after the others.

Clemency had moved over to the window and stood looking out into the garden. I went over and stood beside her. She turned her head slightly towards me.

"Thank goodness that's over," she said—and added with distaste: "What a preposterous room this is!"

"Don't you like it?"

"I can't breathe in it. There's always a smell of half-dead flowers and dust."

I thought she was unjust to the room. But I knew what she meant. It was very definitely an interior.

It was a woman's room, exotic, soft, shut away from the rude blasts of outside weather. It was not a room that a man would be happy in for long. It was not a room where you could relax and read the newspaper and smoke a pipe and put up your feet. Nevertheless I preferred it to Clemency's abstract expression of herself upstairs. On the whole I prefer a boudoir to an operating theatre.

She said, looking round:

"It's just a stage set. A background for Magda to play her scenes against." She looked at me. "You realise, don't you, what we've just been doing? Act II—the family conclave. Magda arranged it. It didn't mean a thing. There was nothing to talk about, nothing to discuss. It's all settled—finished."

There was no sadness in her voice. Rather there was satisfaction. She caught my glance.

"Oh, don't you understand?" she said impatiently. "We're *free*—at last! Don't you understand that Roger's been miserable—absolutely *miserable*—for years? He never had any aptitude for business. He likes things like horses and cows and pottering round in the country. But he adored his father—they all did. That's what's wrong with this house—too much family. I don't mean that the old man was a tyrant, or preyed upon them, or bullied them. He didn't. He gave them money and freedom. He was devoted to them. And they kept on being devoted to him."

"Is there anything wrong in that?"

"I think there is. I think, when your children have grown up, that you should cut away from them, efface yourself, slink away, *force* them to forget you."

"Force them? That's rather drastic, isn't it? Isn't coercion as bad one way as another?"

"If he hadn't made himself such a personality——"

"You can't make yourself a personality," I said. "He *was* a personality."

"He was too much of a personality for Roger. Roger worshipped him. He wanted to do everything his father wanted him to do, he wanted to be the kind of son his father wanted. And he couldn't. His father made over Associated Catering to him—it was the old man's particular joy and pride, and Roger tried hard to carry on in his father's footsteps. But he hadn't got that kind of ability. In business matters Roger is—yes, I'll say it plainly—a fool. And it nearly broke his heart. He's been miserable for years, struggling, seeing the whole thing go down the hill, having sudden wonderful 'ideas' and 'schemes' which always went wrong and made it worse than ever. It's a terrible thing to feel you're a failure year after year. You don't know how unhappy he's been. I do."

Again she turned and faced me.

"You thought, you actually suggested to the police, that Roger would have killed his father—for money! You don't know how—how absolutely *ridiculous* that is!"

"I do know it now," I said humbly.

"When Roger knew he couldn't stave it off any more—that the crash was bound to come, he was actually relieved. Yes, he was. He worried about his father's knowing—but not about anything else. He was looking forward to the new life we were going to live."

Her face quivered a little and her voice softened.

"Where were you going?" I asked.

"To Barbadoes. A distant cousin of mine died a short time ago and left me a tiny estate out there—oh, nothing much. But it was somewhere to go. We'd have been desperately poor, but we'd have scratched a living—it costs very little just to live. We'd have been together—unworried, away from them all."

She sighed.

"Roger is a ridiculous person. He would worry about *me*—about *my* being poor. I suppose he's got the Leonides attitude to money too firmly in his mind. When my first husband was alive, we were terribly poor—and Roger thinks it was so brave and wonderful of me! He doesn't realise that I was *happy*—really happy! I've never been so happy since. And yet—I never loved Richard as I love Roger."

Her eyes half-closed. I was aware of the intensity of her feeling.

She opened her eyes, looked at me and said:

"So you see, I would never have killed anyone for money. I don't *like* money."

I was quite sure that she meant exactly what she said. Clemency Leonides was one of those rare people to whom money does not appeal. They dislike luxury, prefer austerity, and are suspicious of possessions.

Still, there are many to whom money has no personal appeal, but who can be tempted by the power it confers.

I said: "You mightn't want money for yourself—but wisely directed, money can do a lot of interesting things. It can endow research, for example."

I had suspected that Clemency might be a fanatic about her work, but she merely said:

"I doubt if endowments ever do much good. They're usually spent in the wrong way. The things that are worthwhile are usually accomplished by someone with enthusiasm and drive—and with natural vision. Expensive equipment and training and experiment never does what you'd imagine it might do. The spending of it usually gets into the wrong hands."

"Will you mind giving up your work when you go to Barbadoes?" I asked. "You're still going, I presume?"

"Oh, yes, as soon as the police will let us. No, I shan't mind giving up my work at all. Why should I? I wouldn't like to be idle, but I shan't be idle in Barbadoes."

She added impatiently:

"Oh, if only this could all be cleared up *quickly* and we could get away."

"Clemency," I said, "have you any idea at all who did do this? Granting that you and Roger had no hand in it (and really I can't see any reason to think you had), surely, with your intelligence, you must have *some* idea of who did?"

She gave me a rather peculiar look, a darting, sideways glance. When she spoke her voice had lost its spontaneity. It was awkward, rather embarrassed.

"One can't make guesses, it's unscientific," she said. "One can only say that Brenda and Laurence are the obvious suspects."

"So you think they did it?"

Clemency shrugged her shoulders.

She stood for a moment as though listening, then she went out of the room, passing Edith de Haviland in the doorway.

Edith came straight over to me.

" I want to talk to you," she said.

My father's words leapt into my mind. Was this——

But Edith de Haviland was going on :

" I hope you didn't get the wrong impression," she said. " About Philip, I mean. Philip is rather difficult to understand. He may seem to you reserved and cold, but that is not so at all. It's just a manner. He can't help it."

" I really hadn't thought——" I began.

But she swept on :

" Just now—about Roger. It isn't really that he's grudging. He's never been mean about money. And he's really a dear—he's always been a dear—but he needs understanding."

I looked at her with the air, I hope, of one who was willing to understand. She went on :

" It's partly, I think, from having been the second of the family. There's often something about a second child—they start handicapped. He adored his father, you see. Of course, all the children adored Aristide and he adored them. But Roger was his especial pride and joy. Being the eldest—the first. And I think Philip felt it. He drew back right into himself. He began to like books and the past and things that were well divorced from everyday life. I think he suffered—children do suffer . . ."

She paused and went on :

" What I really mean, I suppose, is that he's always been jealous of Roger. I think perhaps he doesn't know it himself. But I think the fact that Roger has come a cropper—oh, it seems an odious thing to say and really I'm sure he doesn't realise it himself—but I think perhaps Philip isn't as sorry about it as he ought to be."

"You mean really that he's rather pleased Roger has made a fool of himself."

"Yes," said Miss de Haviland. "I mean just exactly that."

She added, frowning a little:

"It distressed me, you know, that he didn't at once offer help to his brother."

"Why should he?" I said. "After all, Roger *has* made a muck of things. He's a grown man. There are no children to consider. If he were ill or in real want, of course his family would help—but I've no doubt Roger would really much prefer to start afresh entirely on his own."

"Oh! he would. It's only Clemency he minds about. And Clemency is an extraordinary creature. She really likes being uncomfortable and having only one utility teacup to drink out of. Modern, I suppose. She's no sense of the past, no sense of beauty."

I felt her shrewd eyes looking me up and down.

"This is a dreadful ordeal for Sophia," she said. "I am so sorry her youth should be dimmed by it. I love them all, you know. Roger and Philip, and now Sophia and Eustace and Josephine. All the dear children. Marcia's children. Yes, I love them dearly." She paused and then added sharply: "But, mind you, this side idolatry."

She turned abruptly and went. I had the feeling that she had meant something by her last remark that I did not quite understand.

CHAPTER XV

"YOUR ROOM'S READY," said Sophia.

She stood by my side looking out at the garden. It looked bleak and grey now with the half-denuded trees swaying in the wind.

Sophia echoed my thought as she said:

"How desolate it looks . . ."

As we watched, a figure, and then presently another came through the yew hedge from the rock garden. They both looked grey and unsubstantial in the fading light.

Brenda Leonides was the first. She was wrapped in a grey chinchilla coat and there was something catlike and stealthy in the way she moved. She slipped through the twilight with a kind of eerie grace.

I saw her face as she passed the window. There was a half-smile on it, the curving, crooked smile I had noticed upstairs. A few minutes later Laurence Brown, looking slender and shrunken, also slipped through the twilight. I can only put it that way. They did not seem like two people walking, two people who had been out for a stroll. There was something furtive and unsubstantial about them like two ghosts.

I wondered if it was under Brenda's or Laurence's foot that a twig had snapped.

By a natural association of ideas, I asked:

"Where's Josephine?"

"Probably with Eustace up in the schoolroom." She frowned. "I'm worried about Eustace, Charles."

"Why?"

"He's so moody and odd. He's been so different ever since that wretched paralysis. I can't make out what's going on in his mind. Sometimes he seems to hate us all."

"He'll probably grow out of all that. It's just a phase."

"Yes, I suppose so. But I do get worried, Charles."

"Why, dear heart?"

"Really, I suppose, because mother and father never worry. They're not like a mother and father."

"That may be all for the best. More children suffer from interference than from non-interference."

"That's true. You know, I never thought about it until I came back from abroad, but they really are a queer couple. Father living determinedly in a world of obscure historical bypaths and mother having a lovely time creating scenes. That tomfoolery this evening was all mother. There was no need for it. She just wanted to play a family conclave scene. She gets bored, you know, down here and has to try and work up a drama."

For the moment I had a fantastic vision of Sophia's mother poisoning her elderly father-in-law in a light-hearted manner in order to observe a murder drama at first-hand with herself in the leading role.

An amusing thought! I dismissed it as such—but it left me a little uneasy.

"Mother," said Sophia, "has to be looked after the whole time. You never know *what* she's up to!"

"Forget your family, Sophia," I said firmly.

"I shall be only too delighted to, but it's a little difficult at the present moment. But I *was* happy out in Cairo when I had forgotten them all."

I remembered how Sophia had never mentioned her home or her people.

"Is that why you never talked about them?" I asked. "Because you wanted to forget them?"

"I think so. We've always, all of us, lived too much in each other's pockets. We're—we're all too fond of each other. We're not like some families where they all hate each other like poison. That must be pretty bad, but it's almost worse to live all tangled up in conflicting affections."

She added:

"I think that's what I meant when I said we all lived together in a little crooked house. I didn't mean that it was crooked in the dishonest sense. I think what I meant was that we hadn't been able to grow up independent, standing by ourselves, upright. We're all a bit twisted and twining."

I saw Edith de Haviland's heel grinding a weed into the path as Sophia added:

"Like bindweed . . ."

And then suddenly Magda was with us—flinging open the door—crying out:

"Darlings, why don't you have the lights on? It's almost dark."

And she pressed the switches and the lights sprang up on the walls and on the tables, and she and Sophia and I pulled the heavy rose curtains, and there we were in the flower-scented interior, and Magda, flinging herself on the sofa, cried:

"What an incredible scene it was, wasn't it? How cross Eustace was! He told me he thought it was all positively indecent. How funny boys are!"

She sighed.

"Roger's rather a pet. I love him when he rumples his

hair and starts knocking things over. Wasn't it sweet of Edith to offer her legacy to him? She really meant it, you know, it wasn't just a gesture. But it was terribly stupid—it might have made Philip think he ought to do it too! Of course Edith would do *anything* for the family! There's something very pathetic in the love of a spinster for her sister's children. Some day I shall play one of those devoted spinster aunts. Inquisitive and obstinate and devoted."

"It must have been hard for her after her sister died," I said, refusing to be side-tracked into discussion of another of Magda's roles. "I mean if she disliked old Leonides so much."

Magda interrupted me.

"Disliked him? Who told you that? Nonsense. She was in love with him."

"Mother!" said Sophia.

"Now don't try and contradict me, Sophia. Naturally at your age, you think love is all two good-looking young people in the moonlight."

"She told me," I said, "that she had always disliked him."

"Probably she did when she first came. She'd been angry with her sister for marrying him. I dare say there was always some antagonism—but she was in love with him all right! Darlings, I do know what I'm talking about! Of course, with deceased wife's sister and all that, he couldn't have married her, and I dare say he never thought of it—and quite probably she didn't either. She was quite happy mothering the children, and having fights with him. But she didn't like it when he married Brenda. She didn't like it a *bit*!"

"No more did you and father," said Sophia.

"No, of course we hated it! Naturally! But Edith hated

it most. Darling, the way I've seen her *look* at Brenda!"

"Now, mother," said Sophia.

Magda threw her an affectionate and half-guilty glance, the glance of a mischievous, spoilt child.

She went on, with no apparent realisation of any lack of continuity:

"I've decided Josephine really must go to school."

"Josephine? To school?"

"Yes. To Switzerland. I'm going to see about it to-morrow. I really think we might get her off *at once*. It's so bad for her to be mixed up in a horrid business like this. She's getting quite morbid about it. What she needs is other children of her own age. School life. I've always thought so."

"Grandfather didn't want her to go to school," said Sophia slowly. "He was very much against it."

"Darling old Sweetie Pie liked us all here under his eye. Very old people are often selfish in that way. A child ought to be amongst other children. And Switzerland is so healthy—all the winter sports, and the air, and such—much, much better food than we get here!"

"It will be difficult to arrange for Switzerland now with all the currency regulations, won't it?" I asked.

"Nonsense, Charles. There's some kind of educational racket—or you exchange with a Swiss child—there are all sorts of ways. Rudolph Alstir's in Lausanne. I shall wire him to-morrow to arrange *everything*. We can get her off by the end of the week!"

Magda punched a cushion, smiled at us, went to the door, stood a moment looking back at us in a quite enchanting fashion.

"It's only the young who count," she said. As she said it, it was a lovely line. "They must always come first.

And, darlings—think of the flowers—the blue gentians, the narcissus . . ."

"In October?" asked Sophia, but Magda had gone.

Sophia heaved an exasperated sigh.

"Really," she said. "Mother is too trying! She gets these sudden ideas, and she sends thousands of telegrams and everything has to be arranged at a moment's notice. Why should Josephine be hustled off to Switzerland all in a flurry?"

"There's probably something in the idea of school. I think children of her own age would be a good thing for Josephine."

"Grandfather didn't think so," said Sophia obstinately.

I felt slightly irritated.

"My dear Sophia, do you really think an old gentleman of over eighty is the best judge of a child's welfare?"

"He was about the best judge of anybody in this house," said Sophia.

"Better than your Aunt Edith?"

"No, perhaps not. She did rather favour school. I admit Josephine's got into rather difficult ways—she's got a horrible habit of snooping. But I really think it's just because she's playing detectives."

Was it only the concern for Josephine's welfare which had occasioned Magda's sudden decision? I wondered. Josephine was remarkably well-informed about all sorts of things that had happened prior to the murder and which had been certainly no business of hers. A healthy school life with plenty of games would probably do her a world of good. But I did rather wonder at the suddenness and urgency of Magda's decision—Switzerland was a long way off.

CHAPTER XVI

THE OLD MAN had said:

"Let them talk to you."

As I shaved the following morning, I considered just how far that had taken me.

Edith de Haviland had talked to me—she had sought me out for that especial purpose. Clemency had talked to me (or had I talked to her?). Magda had talked to me in a sense—that is, I had formed part of the audience to one of her broadcasts. Sophia naturally had talked to me. Even Nannie had talked to me. Was I any the wiser for what I had learned from them all? Was there any significant word or phrase? More, was there any evidence of that abnormal vanity on which my father had laid stress? I couldn't see that there was.

The only person who had shown absolutely no desire to talk to me in any way, or on any subject, was Philip. Was not that, in a way, rather abnormal? He must know by now that I wanted to marry his daughter. Yet he continued to act as though I was not in the house at all. Presumably he resented my presence there. Edith de Haviland had apologised for him. She had said it was just "manner." She had shown herself concerned about Philip. Why?

I considered Sophia's father. He was in every sense a repressed individual. He had been an unhappy jealous child. He had been forced back into himself. He had taken refuge in the world of books—in the historical past. That studied coldness and reserve of his might conceal a good deal of passionate feeling. The inadequate motive of financial gain by his father's death was unconvincing—I did not think for a moment that Philip Leonides would kill his father because he himself had not quite as much money as he would like to have. But there might be some deep psychological reason for his desiring his father's death. Philip had come back to his father's house to live, and later, as a result of the Blitz Roger had come—and Philip had been obliged to see day by day that Roger was his father's favourite . . . Might things have come to such a pass in his tortured mind that the only relief possible was his father's death? And supposing that that death should incriminate his elder brother? Roger was short of money—on the verge of a crash. Knowing nothing of that last interview between Roger and his father and the latter's offer of assistance, might not Philip have believed that the motive would seem so powerful that Roger would be at once suspected? Was Philip's mental balance sufficiently disturbed to lead him to do murder?

I cut my chin with the razor and swore.

What the hell was I trying to do? Fasten murder on Sophia's father? That was a nice thing to try and do! That wasn't what Sophia had wanted me to come down here for.

Or—was it? There was something, had been something all along, behind Sophia's appeal. If there was any lingering suspicion in her mind that her father was the killer, then she would never consent to marry me—in case that suspicion might be true. And since she was Sophia, clear-eyed and brave, she wanted the truth, since uncertainty would be an eternal and perpetual barrier between us. Hadn't she been in effect saying to me, "Prove that this dreadful thing I am imagining is not true—but if it *is* true, then prove its truth to me—so that I can know the worst and face it!"

Did Edith de Haviland know, or suspect, that Philip was guilty. What had she meant by " this side idolatry "?

And what had Clemency meant by that peculiar look she had thrown at me when I had asked her who she suspected and she had answered: " Laurence and Brenda are the obvious suspects, aren't they?"

The whole family wanted it to be Brenda and Laurence, hoped it might be Brenda and Laurence, but didn't really believe it was Brenda and Laurence . . .

And of course, the whole family might be wrong, and it might really be Laurence and Brenda after all.

Or, it might be Laurence, and not Brenda . . .

That would be a much better solution.

I finished dabbing my cut chin and went down to breakfast filled with the determination to have an interview with Laurence Brown as soon as possible.

It was only as I drank my second cup of coffee that it occurred to me that the Crooked House was having its effect on me also. I, too, wanted to find, not the true solution, but the solution that suited *me* best.

After breakfast I went out through the hall and up the stairs. Sophia had told me that I should find Laurence giving instruction to Eustace and Josephine in the schoolroom.

I hesitated on the landing outside Brenda's front door. Did I ring and knock, or did I walk right in? I decided to treat the house as an integral Leonides home and not as Brenda's private residence.

I opened the door and passed inside. Everything was quiet, there seemed no one about. On my left the door into the big drawing-room was closed. On my right two open doors showed a bedroom and adjoining bathroom. This I knew was the bathroom adjoining Aristide Leonides' bedroom where the eserine and the insulin had been kept.

The police had finished with it now. I pushed the door open and slipped inside. I realised then how easy it would have been for anyone in the house (or from outside the house for the matter of that!) to come up here and into the bathroom unseen.

I stood in the bathroom looking round. It was sumptuously appointed with gleaming tiles and a sunk bath. At one side were various electric appliances; a hot plate and grill under, an electric kettle—a small electric saucepan, a toaster—everything that a valet attendant to an old gentleman might need. On the wall was a white enamelled cupboard. I opened it. Inside were medical appliances, two medicine glasses, eyebath, eye dropper and a few labelled bottles. Aspirin, boracic powder, iodine. Elastoplast bandages, etc. On a separate shelf were the stacked supply of insulin, two hypodermic needles, and a bottle of surgical spirit. On a third shelf was a bottle marked The Tablets—one or two to be taken at night as ordered. On this shelf, no doubt, had stood the bottle of eyedrops. It was all clear, well arranged, easy for anyone to get at if needed, and equally easy to get at for murder.

I could do what I liked with the bottles and then go softly out and downstairs again and nobody would ever know I had been there. All this was, of course, nothing new, but it brought home to me how difficult the task of the police was.

Only from the guilty party or parties could one find out what one needed.

"Rattle 'em," Taverner had said to me. "Get 'em on

the run. Make 'em think we're on to something. Keep ourselves well in the limelight. Sooner or later, if we do, our criminal will stop leaving well alone and try to be smarter still—and then—we've got him."

Well, the criminal hadn't reacted to this treatment so far.

I came out of the bathroom. Still no one about. I went on along the corridor. I passed the dining-room on the left, and Brenda's bedroom and bathroom on the right. In the latter, one of the maids was moving about. The dining-room door was closed. From a room beyond that, I heard Edith de Haviland's voice telephoning to the inevitable fishmonger. A spiral flight of stairs led to the floor above. I went up them. Edith's bedroom and sitting-room were here, I knew, and two more bathrooms and Laurence Brown's room. Beyond that again the short flight of steps down to the big room built out over the servants' quarters at the back which was used as a schoolroom.

Outside the door I paused. Laurence Brown's voice could be heard, slightly raised, from inside.

I think Josephine's habit of snooping must have been catching. Quite unashamedly I leaned against the door jamb and listened.

It was a history lesson that was in progress, and the period in question was the French *directoire*.

As I listened astonishment opened my eyes. It was a considerable surprise to me to discover that Laurence Brown was a magnificent teacher.

I don't know why it should have surprised me so much. After all, Aristide Leonides had always been a good picker of men. For all his mouselike exterior, Laurence had that supreme gift of being able to arouse enthusiasm and imagination in his pupils. The drama of Thermidor, the decree of Outlawry against the Robespierrists, the magnificence of Barras, the cunning of Fouché—Napoleon the half starved young gunner lieutenant—all these were real and living.

Suddenly Laurence stopped, he asked Eustace and Josephine a question, he made them put themselves in the places of first one and then another figure in the drama. Though he did not get much result from Josephine, whose voice sounded as though she had a cold in the head, Eustace sounded quite different from his usual moody self. He showed brains and intelligence and the keen historical sense which he had doubtless inherited from his father.

Then I heard the chairs being pushed back and scraped across the floor. I retreated up the steps and was apparently just coming down them when the door opened.

Eustace and Josephine came out.

" Hallo," I said.

Eustace looked surprised to see me.

" Do you want anything?" he asked politely.

Josephine, taking no interest in my presence, slipped past me.

" I just wanted to see the schoolroom," I said rather feebly.

" You saw it the other day, didn't you? It's just a kid's place really. Used to be the nursery. It's still got a lot of toys in it."

He held open the door for me and I went in.

Laurence Brown stood by the table. He looked up, flushed, murmured something in answer to my good morning and went hurriedly out.

" You've scared him," said Eustace. " He's very easily scared."

" Do you like him, Eustace?"

"Oh! he's all right. An awful ass, of course."

"But not a bad teacher?"

"No, as a matter of fact he's quite interesting. He knows an awful lot. He makes you see things from a different angle. I never knew that Henry the Eighth wrote poetry—to Anne Boleyn, of course—jolly decent poetry."

We talked for a few moments on such subjects as *The Ancient Mariner*, Chaucer, the political implications behind the Crusades, the Medieval approach to life, and the, to Eustace, surprising fact that Oliver Cromwell had prohibited the celebration of Christmas Day. Behind Eustace's scornful and rather ill-tempered manner there was, I perceived, an inquiring and able mind.

Very soon, I began to realise the source of his ill humour. His illness had not only been a frightening ordeal, it had also been a frustration and a setback, just at a moment when he had been enjoying life.

"I was to have been in the eleven next term—and I'd got my house colours. It's pretty thick to have to stop at home and do lessons with a rotten kid like Josephine. Why, she's only twelve."

"Yes, but you don't have the same studies, do you?"

"No, of course she doesn't do advanced maths—or Latin. But you don't want to have to share a tutor with a *girl*."

I tried to soothe his injured male pride by remarking that Josephine was quite an intelligent girl for her age.

"D'you think so? I think she's awfully wet. She's mad keen on this detecting stuff—goes round poking her nose in everywhere and writing things down in a little black book and pretending that she's finding out a lot. Just a silly kid, that's all she is," said Eustace loftily.

"Anyway," he added, "girls can't be detectives. I told

her so. I think mother's quite right and the sooner Jo's packed off to Switzerland the better."

"Wouldn't you miss her?"

"Miss a kid of that age?" said Eustace haughtily. "Of course not. My goodness, this house is the absolute limit! Mother always haring up and down to London and bullying tame dramatists to rewrite plays for her, and making frightful fusses about nothing at all. And father shut up with his books and sometimes not hearing you if you speak to him. I don't see why I should have to be burdened with such peculiar parents. Then there's Uncle Roger—always so hearty that it makes you shudder. Aunt Clemency's all right, she doesn't bother you, but I sometimes think she's a bit batty. Aunt Edith's not too bad, but she's old. Things have been a bit more cheerful since Sophia came back—though she can be pretty sharp sometimes. But it is a queer household, don't you think so? Having a step-grandmother young enough to be your aunt or your older sister. I mean, it makes you feel an awful ass!"

I had some comprehension of his feelings. I remembered (very dimly) my own supersensitiveness at Eustace's age. My horror of appearing in any way unusual or of my near relatives departing from the normal.

"What about your grandfather?" I said. "Were you fond of him?"

A curious expression flitted across Eustace's face.

"Grandfather," he said, "was definitely anti-social!"

"In what way?"

"He thought of nothing but the profit motive. Laurence says that's completely wrong. And he was a great individualist. All that sort of thing has got to go, don't you think so?"

"Well," I said, rather brutally, "he has gone."

" A good thing, really," said Eustace. " I don't want to be callous, but you can't really *enjoy* life at that age!"

" Didn't he?"

" He couldn't have. Anyway, it was time he went. He——"

Eustace broke off as Laurence Brown came back into the schoolroom.

Laurence began fussing about with some books, but I thought that he was watching me out of the corner of his eye.

He looked at his wrist-watch and said:

" Please be back here sharp at eleven, Eustace. We've wasted too much time the last few days."

" O.K., sir."

Eustace lounged towards the door and went out whistling.

Laurence Brown darted another sharp glance at me. He moistened his lips once or twice. I was convinced that he had come back into the schoolroom solely in order to talk to me.

Presently, after a little aimless stacking and unstacking of books and a pretence of looking for a book that was missing, he spoke:

" Er—How are they getting on?" he said.

" They?"

" The police."

His nose twitched. A mouse in a trap, I thought, a mouse in a trap.

" They don't take me into their confidence," I said.

" Oh. I thought your father was the Assistant Commissioner."

" He is," I said. " But naturally he would not betray official secrets."

I made my voice purposely pompous.

"Then you don't know how—what—if——" His voice trailed off. "They're not going to make an arrest, are they?"

"Not so far as I know. But then, as I say, I mightn't know."

Get 'em on the run, Inspector Taverner had said. Get 'em rattled. Well, Laurence Brown was rattled all right.

He began talking quickly and nervously.

"You don't know what it's like . . . The strain . . . Not knowing what—I mean, they just come and go—Asking questions . . . Questions that don't seem to have anything to do with the case . . ."

He broke off. I waited. He wanted to talk—well, then, let him talk.

"You were there when the chief-inspector made that monstrous suggestion the other day? About Mrs. Leonides and myself . . . It *was* monstrous. It makes one feel so helpless. One is powerless to prevent people *thinking* things! And it is all so wickedly untrue. Just because she is—was—so many years younger than her husband. People have dreadful minds—dreadful minds. I feel—I can't help feeling, that it is all a *plot*."

"A plot? That's interesting."

It was interesting, though not quite in the way he took it.

"The family, you know; Mr. Leonides' family have never been sympathetic to me. They were always aloof. I always felt that they despised me."

His hands had begun to shake.

"Just because they have always been rich and—powerful. They looked down on me. What was I to them? Only the tutor. Only a wretched conscientious objector. And my objections *were* conscientious. They were indeed!"

I said nothing.

" All right then," he burst out. " What if I was—afraid? Afraid I'd make a mess of it. Afraid that when I had to pull a trigger—I mightn't be able to bring myself to do it. How can you be sure it's a Nazi you're going to kill? It might be some decent lad—some village boy—with no political leanings, just called up for his country's service. I believe war is *wrong*, do you understand? I believe it is *wrong*."

I was still silent. I believed that my silence was achieving more than any arguments or agreements could do. Laurence Brown was arguing with himself, and in so doing was revealing a good deal of himself.

" Everyone's always laughed at me." His voice shook. " I seem to have a knack of making myself ridiculous. It isn't that I really lack courage—but I always do the thing wrong. I went into a burning house to rescue a woman they said was trapped there. But I lost the way at once, and the smoke made me unconscious, and it gave a lot of trouble to the firemen finding me. I heard them say, ' Why couldn't the silly chump leave it to us?' It's no good my trying, everyone's against me. Whoever killed Mr. Leonides arranged it so that I would be suspected. Someone killed him so as to ruin *me*."

" What about Mrs. Leonides?" I asked.

He flushed. He became less of a mouse and more like a man.

" Mrs. Leonides is an angel," he said, " an angel. Her sweetness, her kindness to her elderly husband were wonderful. To think of her in connection with poison is laughable—laughable! And that thick-headed inspector can't see it!"

" He's prejudiced," I said, " by the number of cases on

his files where elderly husbands have been poisoned by sweet young wives."

"The insufferable dolt," said Laurence Brown angrily.

He went over to a bookcase in the corner and began rummaging the books in it. I didn't think I should get anything more out of him. I went slowly out of the room.

As I was going along the passage, a door on my left opened and Josephine almost fell on top of me. Her appearance had the suddenness of a demon in an old-fashioned pantomime.

Her face and hands were filthy and a large cobweb floated from one ear.

"Where have you been, Josephine?"

I peered through the half open door. A couple of steps led up into an attic-like rectangular space in the gloom of which several large tanks could be seen.

"In the cistern room."

"Why in the cistern room?"

Josephine replied in a brief businesslike way:

"Detecting."

"What on earth is there to detect among the cisterns?"

To this, Josephine merely replied:

"I must wash."

"I should say most decidedly."

Josephine disappeared through the nearest bathroom door. She looked back to say:

"I should say it's about time for the next murder, wouldn't you?"

"What do you mean—the next murder?"

"Well, in books there's always a second murder about now. Someone who knows something is bumped off before they can tell what they know."

"You read too many detective stories, Josephine. Real

life isn't like that. And if anybody in this house knows something the last thing they seem to want to do is to talk about it."

Josephine's reply came to me rather obscured by the gushing of water from a tap.

"Sometimes it's something that they don't know that they do know."

I blinked as I tried to think this out. Then, leaving Josephine to her ablutions, I went down to the floor below.

Just as I was going out through the front door to the staircase, Brenda came with a soft rush through the drawing-room door.

She came close to me and laid her hand on my arm, looking up in my face.

"Well?" she asked.

It was the same demand for information that Laurence had made, only it was phrased differently. And her one word far more effective.

I shook my head.

"Nothing," I said.

She gave a long sigh.

"I'm so frightened," she said. "Charles, I'm so frightened . . ."

Her fear was very real. It communicated itself to me there in that narrow space. I wanted to reassure her, to help her. I had once more that poignant sense of her as terribly alone in hostile surroundings.

She might well have cried out: "*Who is on my side?*"

And what would the answer have been? Laurence Brown? And what, after all, was Laurence Brown? No tower of strength in a time of trouble. One of the weaker vessels. I remembered the two of them drifting in from the garden the night before.

I wanted to help her. I badly wanted to help her. But there was nothing much I could say or do. And I had at the bottom of my mind an embarrassed guilty feeling, as though Sophia's scornful eyes were watching me. I remembered Sophia's voice saying : " So she got you."

And Sophia did not see, did not want to see, Brenda's side of it. Alone, suspected of murder, with no one to stand by her.

" The inquest's to-morrow," Brenda said. " What—what will happen?"

There I could reassure her.

" Nothing," I said. " You needn't worry about that. It will be adjourned for the police to make inquiries. It will probably set the Press loose, though. So far, there's been no indication in the papers that it wasn't a natural death. The Leonideses have got a good deal of influence. But with an adjourned inquest—well, the fun will start."

(What extraordinary things one said! The *fun*! Why must I choose that particular word?)

" Will—will they be very dreadful?"

" I shouldn't give any interviews if I were you. You know, Brenda, you ought to have a lawyer——" She recoiled with a terrific gasp of dismay. " No—no—not the way you mean. But someone to look after your interests and advise you as to procedure, and what to say and do, and what not to say and do.

" You see," I added, " you're very much alone."

Her hand pressed my arm more closely.

" Yes," she said. " You do understand that. You've helped, Charles, you have helped . . ."

I went down the stairs with a feeling of warmth, of satisfaction . . . Then I saw Sophia standing by the front door. Her voice was cold and rather dry.

"What a long time you've been," she said. "They rang up for you from London. Your father wants you."

"At the Yard?"

"Yes."

"I wonder what they want me for. They didn't say?"

Sophia shook her head. Her eyes were anxious. I drew her to me.

"Don't worry, darling," I said, "I'll soon be back."

CHAPTER XVII

THERE WAS something strained in the atmosphere of my father's room. The Old Man sat behind his table, Chief-Inspector Taverner leaned against the window frame. In the visitor's chair sat Mr. Gaitskill, looking ruffled.

"—extraordinary want of confidence," he was saying acidly.

"Of course, of course." My father spoke soothingly. "Ah, hallo, Charles, you've made good time. Rather a surprising development has occurred."

"Unprecedented," Mr. Gaitskill said.

Something had clearly ruffled the little lawyer to the core. Behind him, Chief-Inspector Taverner grinned at me.

"If I may recapitulate?" my father said. "Mr. Gaitskill received a somewhat surprising communication this morning, Charles. It was from a Mr. Agrodopolous, proprietor of the Delphos Restaurant. He is a very old man, a Greek by birth, and when he was a young man he was helped and befriended by Aristide Leonides. He has always remained deeply grateful to his friend and benefactor and it seems that Aristide Leonides placed great reliance and trust in him."

"I would never have believed Leonides was of such a suspicious and secretive nature," said Mr. Gaitskill. "Of course, he was of advanced years—practically in his dotage, one might say."

"Nationality tells," said my father gently. "You see, Gaitskill, when you are very old your mind dwells a good deal on the days of your youth and the friends of your youth."

"But Leonides' affairs had been in my hands for well over forty years," said Mr. Gaitskill. "Forty-three years and six months to be precise."

Taverner grinned again.

"What happened?" I asked.

Mr. Gaitskill opened his mouth, but my father forestalled him.

"Mr. Agrodopolous stated in his communication that he was obeying certain instructions given him by his friend Aristide Leonides. Briefly, about a year ago he had been entrusted by Mr. Leonides with a sealed envelope which Mr. Agrodopolous was to forward to Mr. Gaitskill immediately after Mr. Leonides' death. In the event of Mr. Agrodopolous dying first, his son, a godson of Mr. Leonides, was to carry out the same instructions. Mr. Agrodopolous apologises for the delay, but explains that he has been ill with pneumonia and only learned of his old friend's death yesterday afternoon."

"The whole business is most unprofessional," said Mr. Gaitskill.

"When Mr. Gaitskill had opened the sealed envelope and made himself acquainted with its contents, he decided that it was his duty——"

"Under the circumstances," said Mr. Gaitskill.

"To let us see the enclosures. They consist of a will, duly signed and attested, and a covering letter."

"So the will has turned up at last?" I said.

Mr. Gaitskill turned a bright purple.

"It is not the same will," he barked. "This is not the

document I drew up at Mr. Leonides' request. This has been written out in his own hand, a most dangerous thing for any layman to do. It seems to have been Mr. Leonides' intention to make me look a complete fool."

Chief-Inspector Taverner endeavoured to inject a little balm into the prevailing bitterness.

"He was a very old gentleman, Mr. Gaitskill," he said. "They're inclined to be cranky when they get old, you know—not barmy, of course, but just a little eccentric."

Mr. Gaitskill sniffed.

"Mr. Gaitskill rang us up," my father said, "and apprised us of the main contents of the will and I asked him to come round and bring the two documents with him. I also rang you up, Charles."

I did not quite see why I had been rung up. It seemed to me singularly unorthodox procedure on both my father's and Taverner's part. I should have learnt about the will in due course, and it was really not my business at all how old Leonides had left his money.

"Is it a different will?" I asked. "I mean, does it dispose of his estate in a different way?"

"It does indeed," said Mr. Gaitskill.

My father was looking at me. Chief-Inspector Taverner was very carefully not looking at me. In some way, I felt vaguely uneasy . . .

Something was going on in both their minds—and it was a something to which I had no clue.

I looked inquiringly at Gaitskill.

"It's none of my business," I said. "But——"

He responded.

"Mr. Leonides' testamentary dispositions are not, of course, a secret," he said. "I conceived it to be my duty to lay the facts before the police authorities first, and to be guided by them in my subsequent procedure. I understand," he paused, " that there is an—understanding, shall we say—between you and Miss Sophia Leonides?"

" I hope to marry her," I said, " but she will not consent to an engagement at the present time."

" Very proper," said Mr. Gaitskill.

I disagreed with him. But this was no time for argument.

" By this will," said Mr. Gaitskill, " dated November the 29th of last year Mr. Leonides, after a bequest to his wife of one hundred thousand pounds, leaves his entire estate, real and personal, to his granddaughter, Sophia Katherine Leonides absolutely."

I gasped. Whatever I had expected, it was not this.

" He left the whole caboodle to Sophia," I said. " What an extraordinary thing. Any reason?"

" He set out his reasons very clearly in the covering letter," said my father. He picked up a sheet of paper from the desk in front of him. " You have no objection to Charles reading this, Mr. Gaitskill?"

" I am in your hands," said Mr. Gaitskill coldly. " The letter does at least offer an explanation—and possibly (though I am doubtful as to this) an excuse for Mr. Leonides' extraordinary conduct."

The Old Man handed me the letter. It was written in a small crabbed handwriting in very black ink. The handwriting showed character and individuality. It was not at all like the handwriting of an old man—except perhaps for the careful forming of the letters, more characteristic of a bygone period, when literacy was something painstakingly acquired and correspondingly valued.

Dear Gaitskill (*it ran*),

You will be astonished to get this, and probably

offended. But I have my own reasons for behaving in what may seem to you an unnecessarily secretive manner. I have long been a believer in the individual. In a family (this I have observed in my boyhood and never forgotten) there is always one strong character and it usually falls to this one person to care for, and bear the burden, of the rest of the family. In my family I was that person. I came to London, established myself there, supported my mother and my aged grandparents in Smyrna, extricated one of my brothers from the grip of the law, secured the freedom of my sister from an unhappy marriage and so on. God has been pleased to grant me a long life, and I have been able to watch over and care for my own children and their children. Many have been taken from me by death; the rest, I am happy to say, are under my roof. When I die, the burden I have carried must descend on someone else. I have debated whether to divide my fortune as equally as possible amongst my dear ones —but to do so would not eventually result in a proper equality. Men are not born equal—to offset the natural inequality of Nature one must redress the balance. In other words, someone must be my successor, must take upon him or herself the burden of responsibility for the rest of the family. After close observation I do not consider either of my sons fit for this responsibility. My dearly loved son Roger has no business sense, and though of a lovable nature is too impulsive to have good judgment. My son Philip is too unsure of himself to do anything but retreat from life. Eustace, my grandson, is very young and I do not think he has the qualities of sense and judgment necessary. He is indolent and very easily influenced by the ideas of anyone whom he meets. Only my granddaughter Sophia seems to me to have the positive qualities required. She has brains, judgment, courage, a fair and unbiassed mind and, I think, generosity of spirit. To her I commit the family welfare—and the welfare of my kind sister-in-law Edith de Haviland, for whose lifelong devotion to the family I am deeply grateful.

This explains the enclosed document. What will be harder to explain—or rather to explain to you, my old friend—is the deception that I have employed. I thought it wise not to raise speculation about the disposal of my money, and I have no intention of letting my family know that Sophia is to be my heir. Since my two sons have already had considerable fortunes settled upon them, I do not feel that my testamentary dispositions will place them in a humiliating position.

To stifle curiosity and surmise, I asked you to draw me up a will. This will I read aloud to my assembled family. I laid it on my desk, placed a sheet of blotting paper over it and asked for two servants to be summoned. When they came I slid the blotting paper up a little, exposing the bottom of a document, signed my name and caused them to sign theirs. I need hardly say that what I and they signed was the will which I now enclose and *not* the one drafted by you which I had read aloud.

I cannot hope that you will understand what prompted me to execute this trick. I will merely ask you to forgive me for keeping you in the dark. A very old man likes to keep his little secrets.

Thank you, my dear friend, for the assiduity with which you have always attended to my affairs. Give

Sophia my dear love. Ask her to watch over the family well and shield them from harm.

Yours very sincerely,

Aristide Leonides

I read this very remarkable document with intense interest.

"Extraordinary," I said.

"Most extraordinary," said Mr. Gaitskill, rising. "I repeat, I think my old friend Mr. Leonides might have trusted *me*."

"No, Gaitskill," said my father. "He was a natural twister. He liked, if I may put it so, doing things the crooked way."

"That's right, sir," said Chief-Inspector Taverner. "He was a twister if there ever was one!"

He spoke with feeling.

Gaitskill stalked out unmolified. He had been wounded to the depths of his professional nature.

"It's hit him hard," said Taverner. "Very respectable firm, Gaitskill, Callum & Gaitskill. No hanky panky with them. When old Leonides put through a doubtful deal, he never put it through with Gaitskill, Callum & Gaitskill. He had half a dozen different firms of solicitors who acted for him. Oh, he was a twister!"

"And never more so than when making his will," said my father.

"We were fools," said Taverner. "When you come to think of it, the only person who *could* have played tricks with that will was the old boy himself. It just never occurred to us that he could want to!"

I remembered Josephine's superior smile as she had said:

"Aren't the police *stupid*?"

But Josephine had not been present on the occasion of the will. And even if she had been listening outside the door (which I was fully prepared to believe!) she could hardly have guessed what her grandfather was doing. Why, then, the superior air? What did she know that made her say the police were stupid? Or was it, again, just showing off?

Struck by the silence in the room I looked up sharply—both my father and Taverner were watching me. I don't know what there was in their manner that compelled me to blurt out defiantly:

"Sophia knew nothing about this! Nothing at all."

"No?" said my father.

I didn't quite know whether it was an agreement or a question.

"She'll be absolutely astounded!"

"Yes?"

"Astounded!"

There was a pause. Then, with what seemed sudden harshness, the telephone on my father's desk rang.

"Yes?" He lifted the receiver—listened and then said: "Put her through."

He looked at me.

"It's your young woman," he said. "She wants to speak to us. It's urgent."

I took the receiver from him.

"Sophia?"

"Charles? Is that you? It's—Josephine!" Her voice broke slightly.

"What about Josephine?"

"She's been hit on the head. Concussion. She's—she's pretty bad . . . They say she may not recover . . ."

I turned to the other two.

"Josephine's been knocked out," I said.

My father took the receiver from me. He said sharply as he did so:

"I told you to keep an eye on that child . . ."

CHAPTER XVIII

IN next to no time Taverner and I were racing in a fast police car in the direction of Swinly Dean.

I remembered Josephine emerging from among the cisterns, and her airy remark that it was "about time for the second murder." The poor child had had no idea that she herself was likely to be the victim of the "second murder."

I accepted fully the blame that my father had tacitly ascribed to me. Of course I ought to have kept an eye on Josephine. Though neither Taverner nor I had any real clue to the poisoner of old Leonides, it was highly possible that Josephine had. What I had taken for childish nonsense and "showing off" might very well have been something quite different. Josephine, in her favourite sports of snooping and prying, might have become aware of some piece of information that she herself could not assess at its proper value.

I remembered the twig that had cracked in the garden.

I had had an inkling then that danger was about. I had acted upon it at the moment, and afterwards it had seemed to me that my suspicions had been melodramatic and unreal. On the contrary. I should have realised that this was murder, that whoever had committed murder had endangered their neck, and that consequently that same person would not hesitate to repeat the crime if by that way safety could be assured.

Perhaps Magda, by some obscure maternal instinct, had recognised that Josephine was in peril, and that may have been what occasioned her sudden feverish haste to get the child sent to Switzerland.

Sophia came out to meet us as we arrived. Josephine, she said, had been taken by ambulance to Market Basing General Hospital. Dr. Gray would let them know as soon as possible the result of the X-ray.

"How did it happen?" asked Taverner.

Sophia led the way round to the back of the house and through a door into a small disused yard. In one corner a door stood ajar.

"It's a kind of wash house," Sophia explained. "There's a cat hole in the bottom of the door, and Josephine used to stand on it and swing to and fro."

I remembered swinging on doors in my own youth.

The wash house was small and rather dark. There were wooden boxes in it, some old hose pipe, a few derelict garden implements and some broken furniture. Just inside the door was a marble lion door stop.

"It's the door stopper from the front door," Sophia explained. "It must have been balanced on the top of the door."

Taverner reached up a hand to the top of the door. It was a low door, the top of it only about a foot above his head.

"A booby trap," he said.

He swung the door experimentally to and fro. Then he stooped to the block of marble but he did not touch it.

"Has anyone handled this?"

"No," said Sophia. "I wouldn't let anyone touch it."

"Quite right. Who found her?"

"I did. She didn't come in for her dinner at one o'clock.

Nannie was calling her. She'd passed through the kitchen and out into the stable yard about a quarter of an hour before. Nannie said, 'She'll be bouncing her ball or swinging on that door again.' I said I'd fetch her in."

Sophia paused.

"She had a habit of playing in that way, you said? Who knew about that?"

Sophia shrugged her shoulders.

"Pretty well everybody in the house, I should think."

"Who else used the wash house? Gardeners?"

Sophia shook her head.

"Hardly anyone ever goes into it."

"And this little yard isn't overlooked from the house?" Taverner summed it up. "Anyone could have slipped out from the house or round the front and fixed up that trap ready, but it would be chancy . . ."

He broke off, looking at the door, and swinging it gently to and fro.

"Nothing certain about it. Hit or miss. And likelier miss than hit. But she was unlucky. With her it was hit."

Sophia shivered.

He peered at the floor. There were various dents on it.

"Looks as though someone experimented first . . . to see just how it would fall . . . The sound wouldn't carry to the house."

"No, we didn't hear anything. We'd no idea anything was wrong until I came out and found her lying face down —all sprawled out." Sophia's voice broke a little. "There was blood on her hair."

"That her scarf?" Taverner pointed to a checked woollen muffler lying on the floor.

"Yes."

Using the scarf he picked up the block of marble carefully.

"There may be fingerprints," he said, but he spoke without much hope. "But I rather think whoever did it was—careful." He said to me: "What are you looking at?"

I was looking at a broken-backed wooden kitchen chair which was among the derelicts. On the seat of it were a few fragments of earth.

"Curious," said Taverner. "Someone stood on that chair with muddy feet. Now why was that?"

He shook his head.

"What time was it when you found her, Miss Leonides?"

"It must have been five minutes past one."

"And your Nannie saw her going out about twenty minutes earlier. Who was the last person before that known to have been in the wash house?"

"I've no idea. Probably Josephine herself. Josephine was swinging on the door this morning after breakfast, I know."

Taverner nodded.

"So between then and a quarter to one *someone set the trap*. You say that bit of marble is the door stop you use for the front door? Any idea when that was missing?"

Sophia shook her head.

"The door hasn't been propped open at all to-day. It's been too cold."

"Any idea where everyone was all the morning?"

"I went out for a walk. Eustace and Josephine did lessons until half-past twelve—with a break at half-past ten Father, I think, has been in the library all the morning."

"Your mother?"

"She was just coming out of her bedroom when I came

in from my walk—that was about a quarter-past twelve. She doesn't get up very early."

We re-entered the house. I followed Sophia to the library. Philip, looking white and haggard, sat in his usual chair. Magda crouched against his knees, crying quietly. Sophia asked:

"Have they telephoned yet from the hospital?"

Philip shook his head.

Magda sobbed.

"Why wouldn't they let me go with her? My baby—my funny ugly baby. And I used to call her a changeling and make her so angry. How could I be so cruel? And now she'll die. I know she'll die."

"Hush, my dear," said Philip. "Hush."

I felt that I had no place in this family scene of anxiety and grief. I withdrew quietly and went to find Nannie. She was sitting in the kitchen crying quietly.

"It's a judgment on me, Mr. Charles, for the hard things I've been thinking. A judgment, that's what it is."

I did not try and fathom her meaning.

"There's wickedness in this house. That's what there is. I didn't wish to see it or believe it. But seeing's believing. Somebody killed the master and the same somebody must have tried to kill Josephine."

"Why should they try and kill Josephine?"

Nannie removed a corner of her handkerchief from her eye and gave me a shrewd glance.

"You know well enough what she was like, Mr. Charles. She liked to know things. She was always like that, even as a tiny thing. Used to hide under the dinner table and listen to the maids talking and then she'd hold it over them. Made her feel important. You see, she was passed over, as it were, by the mistress. She wasn't a handsome child, like the other two. She was always a plain little thing. A changeling, the mistress used to call her. I blame the mistress for that, for it's my belief it turned the child sour. But in a funny sort of way she got her own back by finding out things about people and letting them know she knew them. But it isn't safe to do that when there's a poisoner about!"

No, it hadn't been safe. And that brought something else to my mind. I asked Nannie: "Do you know where she kept a little black book—a notebook of some kind where she used to write down things?"

"I know what you mean, Mr. Charles. Very sly about it, she was. I've seen her sucking her pencil and writing in the book and sucking her pencil again. And 'don't do that,' I'd say, 'you'll get lead poisoning' and 'oh no, I shan't,' she said, 'because it isn't really lead in a pencil. It's carbon,' though I don't see how *that* could be so, for if you call a thing a lead pencil it stands to reason that that's because there's lead in it."

"You'd think so," I agreed. "But as a matter of fact she was right." (Josephine was always right!) "What about this notebook? Do you know where she kept it?"

"I've no idea at all, sir. It was one of the things she was sly about."

"She hadn't got it with her when she was found?"

"Oh no, Mr. Charles, there was no notebook."

Had someone taken the notebook? Or had she hidden it in her own room? The idea came to me to look and see. I was not sure which Josephine's room was, but as I stood hesitating in the passage Taverner's voice called me:

"Come in here," he said. "I'm in the kid's room. Did you ever see such a sight?"

I stepped over the threshold and stopped dead.

The small room looked as though it had been visited by a tornado. The drawers of the chest of drawers were pulled out and their contents scattered on the floor. The mattress and bedding had been pulled from the small bed. The rugs were tossed into heaps. The chairs had been turned upside down, the pictures taken down from the wall, the photographs wrenched out of their frames.

"Good Lord," I exclaimed. "What was the big idea?"

"What do you think?"

"Someone was looking for something."

"Exactly."

I looked round and whistled.

"But who on earth—surely nobody could come in here and do all this and not be heard—or seen?"

"Why not? Mrs. Leonides spends the morning in her bedroom doing her nails and ringing up her friends on the telephone and playing with her clothes. Philip sits in the library browsing over books. The nurse woman is in the kitchen peeling potatoes and stringing beans. In a family that knows each other's habits it would be easy enough. And I'll tell you this. Anyone in the house could have done our little job—could have set the trap for the child and wrecked her room. But it was someone in a hurry, someone who hadn't the time to search quietly."

"Anyone in the house, you say?"

"Yes, I've checked up. Everyone has some time or other unaccounted for. Philip, Magda, the nurse, your girl. The same upstairs. Brenda spent most of the morning alone. Laurence and Eustace had a half hour break—from ten-thirty to eleven—you were with them part of that time—but not all of it. Miss de Haviland was in the garden alone. Roger was in his study."

"Only Clemency was in London at her job."

" No, even she isn't out of it. She stayed at home to-day with a headache—she was alone in her room having that headache. Any of them—any blinking one of them! And I don't know which! I've no idea. If I knew what they were looking for in here——"

His eyes went round the wrecked room . . .

" And if I knew whether they'd found it . . ."

Something stirred in my brain—a memory . . .

Taverner clinched it by asking me :

" What was the kid doing when you last saw her?'

" Wait," I said.

I dashed out of the room and up the stairs. I passed through the left hand door and went up to the top floor. I pushed open the door of the cistern room, mounted the two steps and bending my head, since the ceiling was low and sloping, I looked round me.

Josephine had said when I asked her what she was doing there that she was " detecting."

I didn't see what there could be to detect in a cobwebby attic full of water tanks. But such an attic would make a good hiding-place. I considered it probable that Josephine had been hiding something there, something that she knew quite well she had no business to have. If so, it oughtn't to take long to find it.

It took me just three minutes. Tucked away behind the largest tank, from the interior of which a sibilant hissing added an eerie note to the atmosphere, I found a packet of letters wrapped in a torn piece of brown paper.

I read the first letter.

Oh Laurence—my darling, my own dear love . . . It was wonderful last night when you quoted that verse of poetry. I knew it was meant for me, though you didn't look at me. Aristide said, " You read verse well." He didn't guess what we were both feeling. My darling, I feel convinced that soon everything will come right. We shall be glad that he never knew, that he died happy. He's been good to me. I don't want him to suffer. But I don't really think that it can be any pleasure to live after you're eighty. *I* shouldn't want to! Soon we shall be together for always. How wonderful it will be when I can say to you: "My dear dear husband . . ." Dearest, we were made for each other. I love you, love you, love you—I can see no end to our love, I——

There was a good deal more, but I had no wish to go on.

Grimly I went downstairs and thrust my parcel into Taverner's hands.

"It's possible," I said, "that that's what our unknown friend was looking for."

Taverner read a few passages, whistled and shuffled through the various letters.

Then he looked at me with the expression of a cat who has been fed with the best cream.

"Well," he said softly. "This pretty well cooks Mrs. Brenda Leonides' goose. *And* Mr. Laurence Brown's. So it *was* them, all the time . . ."

CHAPTER XIX

IT SEEMS odd to me, looking back, how suddenly and completely my pity and sympathy for Brenda Leonides vanished with the discovery of her letters, the letters she had written to Laurence Brown. Was my vanity unable to stand up to the revelation that she loved Laurence Brown with a doting and sugary infatuation and had deliberately lied to me? I don't know. I'm not a psychologist. I prefer to believe that it was the thought of the child Josephine, struck down in ruthless self preservation, that dried up the springs of my sympathy.

"Brown fixed that booby trap, if you ask me," said Taverner, "and it explains what puzzled me about it."

"What did puzzle you?"

"Well, it was such a sappy thing to do. Look here, say the kid's got hold of these letters—letters that are absolutely damning! The first thing to do is to try and get them back (after all, if the kid talks about them, but has got nothing to show, it can be put down as mere romancing), but you can't get them back because you can't find them. Then the only thing to do is to put the kid out of action for good. You've done one murder and you're not squeamish about doing another. You know she's fond of swinging on a door in a disused yard. The ideal thing to do is wait behind the door and lay her out as she comes through, with a poker, or an iron bar, or a nice bit of hose-pipe. They're all there ready to hand. Why fiddle about with a marble lion perched on top of a door which is as likely as not to miss her altogether and which even if it *does* fall on her may not do the job properly (which actually is how it turns out). I ask you—*why*?"

"Well," I said, "what's the answer?"

"The only idea I got to begin with was that it was intended to tie in with someone's alibi. Somebody would have a nice fat alibi for the time when Josephine was being slugged. But that doesn't wash because, to begin with, nobody seems to have any kind of alibi, and secondly, someone's bound to look for the child at lunch time, and they'll find the booby trap and the marble block, the whole *modus operandi* will be quite plain to see. Of course, *if* the murderer had removed the block before the child was found, then we might have been puzzled. But as it is the whole thing just doesn't make sense."

He stretched out his hands.

"And what's your present explanation?"

"The personal element. Personal idiosyncrasy. Laurence Brown's idiosyncrasy. *He doesn't like violence—he can't force himself to do physical violence.* He literally *couldn't* have stood behind the door and socked the kid on the head. He *could* rig up a booby trap and go away and not see it happen."

"Yes, I see," I said slowly. "It's the eserine in the insulin bottle all over again?"

"Exactly."

"Do you think he did that without Brenda's knowing?"

"It would explain why she didn't throw away the insulin bottle. Of course, they may have fixed it up between them—or she may have thought up the poison trick all by herself—a nice easy death for her tired old husband and all for the best in the best of possible worlds! But I bet she didn't fix the booby trap. Women never have any faith in mechanical things working properly. And are they right. I think myself the eserine was her idea, but that she made her besotted slave do the switch. She's the kind that usually manages to avoid doing anything equivocable themselves. Then they keep a nice happy conscience."

He paused then went on:

"With these letters I think the D.P.P. will say we have a case. They'll take a bit of explaining away! Then, if the kid gets through all right everything in the garden will be lovely." He gave me a sideways glance. "How does it feel to be engaged to about a million pounds sterling?"

I winced. In the excitement of the last few hours, I had forgotten the developments about the will.

"Sophia doesn't know yet," I said. "Do you want me to tell her?"

"I understand Gaitskill is going to break the sad (or glad) news after the inquest to-morrow." Taverner paused and looked at me thoughtfully.

"I wonder," he said, "what the reactions will be from the family?"

CHAPTER XX

THE INQUEST went off much as I had prophesied. It was adjourned at the request of the police.

We were in good spirits, for news had come through the night before from the hospital that Josephine's injuries were much less serious than had been feared and that her recovery would be rapid. For the moment, Dr. Gray said, she was to be allowed no visitors—not even her mother.

"Particularly not her mother," Sophia murmured to me. "I made that quite clear to Dr. Gray. Anyway, he knows mother."

I must have looked rather doubtful for Sophia said sharply:

"Why the disapproving look?"

"Well—surely a mother——"

"I'm glad you've got a few nice old-fashioned ideas, Charles. But you don't quite know what my mother is capable of yet. The darling can't help it, but there would simply have to be a grand dramatic scene. And dramatic scenes aren't the best things for anyone recovering from head injuries."

"You do think of everything, don't you, my sweet."

"Well, somebody's got to do the thinking now that grandfather's gone."

I looked at her speculatively. I saw that old Leonides' acumen had not deserted him. The mantle of his responsibilities was already on Sophia's shoulders.

After the inquest, Gaitskill accompanied us back to Three Gables. He cleared his throat and said pontifically:

" There is an announcement it is my duty to make to you all."

For this purpose the family assembled in Magda's drawing-room. I had on this occasion the rather pleasurable sensations of the man behind the scenes. I knew in advance what Gaitskill had to say.

I prepared myself to observe the reactions of everyone.

Gaitskill was brief and dry. Any signs of personal feeling and annoyance were well held in check. He read first Aristide Leonides' letter and then the will itself.

It was very interesting to watch. I only wished my eyes could be everywhere at once.

I did not pay much attention to Brenda and Laurence. The provision for Brenda in this will was the same. I watched primarily Roger and Philip, and after them Magda and Clemency.

My first impression was that they all behaved very well.

Philip's lips were pressed closely together, his handsome head was thrown back against the tall chair in which he was sitting. He did not speak.

Magda, on the contrary, burst into speech as soon as Mr. Gaitskill finished, her rich voice surging over his thin tones like an incoming tide drowning a rivulet.

" Darling Sophia—how extraordinary—how *romantic*. Fancy old Sweetie Pie being so cunning and deceitful—just like a dear old baby. Didn't he trust us? Did he think we'd be cross? He never seemed to be fonder of Sophia than of the rest of us. But really, it's most dramatic."

Suddenly Magda jumped lightly to her feet, danced over to Sophia and swept her a very grand court curtsey.

" Madame Sophia, your penniless and broken-down old

mother begs you for alms." Her voice took on a Cockney whine. "Spare us a copper, old dear. Your ma wants to go to the pictures."

Her hand, crooked into a claw, twitched urgently at Sophia.

Philip, without moving, said through stiff lips:

"Please, Magda, there's no call for any unnecessary clowning."

"Oh, but Roger," cried Magda, suddenly turning to Roger. "Poor darling Roger. Sweetie was going to come to the rescue and then, before he could do it, he died. And now Roger doesn't get *anything*. Sophia," she turned imperiously, "you simply must do something about Roger."

"No," said Clemency. She had moved forward a step. Her face was defiant. "Nothing. Nothing at all."

Roger came shambling over to Sophia like a large amiable bear.

He took her hands affectionately.

"I don't want a penny, my dear girl. As soon as this business is cleared up—or has died down, which is more what it looks like—then Clemency and I are off to the West Indies and the simple life. If I'm ever in extremis I'll apply to the head of the family"—he grinned at her engagingly—"but until then I don't want a penny. I'm a very simple person really, my dear—you ask Clemency if I'm not."

An unexpected voice broke in. It was Edith de Haviland's.

"That's all very well," she said. "But you've to pay some attention to the look of the thing. If you go bankrupt, Roger, and then slink off to the ends of the earth without Sophia's holding out a helping hand, there will be a good deal of ill-natured talk that will not be pleasant for Sophia."

"What does public opinion matter?" asked Clemency scornfully.

"We know it doesn't to you, Clemency," said Edith de Haviland sharply, "but Sophia lives in *this* world. She's a girl with good brains and a good heart, and I've no doubt that Aristide was quite right in his selection of her to hold the family fortunes—though to pass over your two sons in their lifetime seems odd to our English ideas—but I think it would be very unfortunate if it got about that she behaved greedily over this—and had let Roger crash without trying to help him."

Roger went over to his aunt. He put his arms round her and hugged her.

"Aunt Edith," he said. "You are a darling—and a stubborn fighter, but you don't begin to understand. Clemency and I know what we want—and what we don't want!"

Clemency, a sudden spot of colour showing in each thin cheek, stood defiantly facing them.

"None of you," she said, "understand Roger. You never have! I don't suppose you ever will! Come on, Roger."

They left the room as Mr. Gaitskill began clearing his throat and arranging his papers. His countenance was one of deep disapprobation. He had disliked the foregoing scenes very much. That was clear.

My eyes came at last to Sophia herself. She stood straight and handsome by the fireplace, her chin up, her eyes steady. She had just been left an immense fortune, but my principal thought was how alone she had suddenly become. Between her and her family a barrier had been erected. Henceforth she was divided from them, and I fancied that she already knew and faced that fact. Old Leonides had laid a burden upon her shoulders—he had been aware of that and she knew it herself. He had believed that her shoulders were strong enough to bear it, but just at this moment I felt unutterably sorry for her.

So far she had not spoken—indeed she had been given no chance, but very soon now speech would be forced from her. Already, beneath the affection of her family, I could sense latent hostility. Even in Magda's graceful playacting there had been, I fancied, a subtle malice. And there were other darker undercurrents that had not yet come to the surface.

Mr. Gaitskill's throat clearings gave way to precise and measured speech.

"Allow me to congratulate you, Sophia," he said. "You are a very wealthy woman. I should not advise any—er—precipitate action. I can advance you what ready money is needed for current expenses. If you wish to discuss future arrangements I shall be happy to give you the best advice in my power. Make an appointment with me at Lincoln's Inn when you have had plenty of time to think things over."

"Roger," began Edith de Haviland obstinately.

Mr. Gaitskill snapped in quickly.

"Roger," he said, "must fend for himself. He's a grown man—er, fifty-four, I believe. And Aristide Leonides was quite right, you know. He isn't a businessman. Never will be." He looked at Sophia. "If you put Associated Catering on its legs again, don't be under any illusions that Roger can run it successfully."

"I shouldn't dream of putting Associated Catering on its legs again," said Sophia.

It was the first time she had spoken. Her voice was crisp and businesslike.

" It would be an idiotic thing to do," she added.

Gaitskill shot a glance at her from under his brows, and smiled to himself. Then he wished everyone good-bye and went out.

There were a few moments of silence, a realisation that the family circle was alone with itself.

Then Philip got up stiffly.

" I must get back to the library," he said. " I have lost a lot of time."

" Father——" Sophia spoke uncertainly, almost pleadingly.

I felt her quiver and draw back as Philip turned cold hostile eyes on her.

" You must forgive me not congratulating you," he said. " But this has been rather a shock to me. I would not have believed that my father would have so humiliated me—that he would have disregarded my lifetime's devotion—yes—devotion."

For the first time, the natural man broke through the crust of icy restraint.

" My God," he cried. " How could he do this to me? He was always unfair to me—always."

" Oh no, Philip, no, you mustn't think that," cried Edith de Haviland. " Don't regard this as another slight. It isn't. When people get old, they turn naturally to a younger generation . . . I assure you it's only that . . . and besides, Aristide had a very keen business sense. I've often heard him say that two lots of death duties——"

" He never cared for me," said Philip. His voice was low and hoarse. " It was always Roger—Roger. Well, at least "—an extraordinary expression of spite suddenly marred his handsome features—" father realised that Roger was a fool and a failure. He cut Roger out, too."

" What about me?" said Eustace.

I had hardly noticed Eustace until now, but I perceived that he was trembling with some violent emotion. His face was crimson, there were, I thought, tears in his eyes. His voice shook as it rose hysterically.

" It's a shame!" said Eustace. " It's a damned shame! How dare grandfather do this to me? How dare he? I was his only grandson. How dare he pass me over for Sophia? It's not fair. I hate him. I hate him. I'll never forgive him as long as I live. Beastly tyrannical old man. I wanted him to die. I wanted to get out of this house. I wanted to be my own master. And now I've got to be bullied and messed around by Sophia, and be made to look a fool. I wish I was dead . . ."

His voice broke and he rushed out of the room.

Edith de Haviland gave a sharp click of her tongue.

" No self control," she murmured.

" I know just how he feels," cried Magda.

" I'm sure you do," said Edith with acidity in her tone.

" The poor sweet! I must go after him."

" Now, Magda——" Edith hurried after her.

Their voices died away. Sophia remained looking at Philip. There was, I think, a certain pleading in her glance. If so, it got no response. He looked at her coldly, quite in control of himself once more.

" You played your cards very well, Sophia," he said and went out of the room.

" That was a cruel thing to say," I cried. " Sophia——"

She stretched out her hands to me. I took her in my arms.

" This is too much for you, my sweet."

" I know just how they feel," said Sophia.

" That old devil, your grandfather, shouldn't have let you in for this."

She straightened her shoulders.

" He believed I could take it. And so I can. I wish—I wish Eustace didn't mind so much."

" He'll get over it."

" Will he? I wonder. He's the kind that broods terribly. And I hate father being hurt."

" Your mother's all right."

" She minds a bit. It goes against the grain to have to come and ask your daughter for money to put on plays. She'll be after me to put on the Edith Thompson one before you can turn round."

" And what will you say? If it keeps her happy . . ."

Sophia pulled herself right out of my arms; her head went back.

" I shall say *No!* It's a rotten play and mother couldn't play the part. It would be throwing the money away."

I laughed softly. I couldn't help it.

" What is it?" Sophia demanded suspiciously.

" I'm beginning to understand why your grandfather left you his money. You're a chip off the old block, Sophia."

CHAPTER XXI

MY ONE feeling of regret at this time was that Josephine was out of it all. She would have enjoyed it all so much.

Her recovery was rapid and she was expected to be back any day now, but nevertheless she missed another event of importance.

I was in the rock garden one morning with Sophia and Brenda when a car drew up to the front door. Taverner and Sergeant Lamb got out of it. They went up the steps and into the house.

Brenda stood still, staring at the car.

"It's those men," she said. "They've come back, and I thought they'd given up—I thought it was all over."

I saw her shiver.

She had joined us about ten minutes before. Wrapped in her chinchilla coat, she had said: "If I don't get some air and exercise, I shall go mad. If I go outside the gate there's always a reporter waiting to pounce on me. It's like being besieged. Will it go on for ever?"

Sophia said that she supposed the reporters would soon get tired of it.

"You can go out in the car," she added.

"I tell you I want to get some exercise."

Then she said abruptly:

"You've given Laurence the sack, Sophia. Why?"

Sophia answered quietly:

"We're making other arrangements for Eustace. And Josephine is going to Switzerland."

"Well, you've upset Laurence very much. He feels you don't trust him."

Sophia did not reply and it was at that moment that Taverner's car had arrived.

Standing there, shivering in the moist autumn air, Brenda muttered: "What do they want? Why have they come?"

I thought I knew why they had come. I had said nothing to Sophia of the letters I had found by the cistern, but I knew that they had gone to the Director of Public Prosecutions.

Taverner came out of the house again. He walked across the drive and the lawn towards us. Brenda shivered more violently.

"What does he want?" she repeated nervously. "What does he want?"

Then Taverner was with us. He spoke curtly in his official voice using the official phrases.

"I have a warrant here for your arrest—you are charged with administering eserine to Aristide Leonides on September 19th last. I must warn you that anything you say may be used in evidence at your trial."

And then Brenda went to pieces. She screamed. She clung to me. She cried out, "No, no, no, it isn't true! Charles, tell them it isn't true! I didn't do it. I didn't know anything about it. It's all a plot. Don't let them take me away. It isn't true, I tell you . . . It *isn't true* . . . I haven't done anything . . ."

It was horrible—unbelievably horrible. I tried to soothe her, I unfastened her fingers from my arm. I told her that I would arrange for a lawyer for her—that she was to keep calm—that a lawyer would arrange everything——

Taverner took her gently under the elbow.

" Come along, Mrs. Leonides," he said. " You don't want a hat, do you? No? Then we'll go off right away."

She pulled back, staring at him with enormous cat's eyes.

" Laurence," she said. " What have you done to Laurence?"

" Mr. Laurence Brown is also under arrest," said Taverner.

She wilted then. Her body seemed to collapse and shrink. The tears poured down her face. She went away quietly with Taverner across the lawn to the car. I saw Laurence Brown and Sergeant Lamb come out of the house. They all got into the car. The car drove away.

I drew a deep breath and turned to Sophia. She was very pale and there was a look of distress on her face.

" It's horrible, Charles," she said. " It's quite horrible."

" I know."

" You must get her a really first-class solicitor—the best there is. She—she must have all the help possible."

" One doesn't realise," I said, " what these things are like. I've never seen anyone arrested before."

" I know. One has no idea."

We were both silent. I was thinking of the desperate terror on Brenda's face. It had seemed familiar to me and suddenly I realised why. It was the same expression that I had seen on Magda Leonides' face the first day I had come to the Crooked House when she had been talking about the Edith Thompson play.

" *And then*," she had said, " *sheer terror*, don't you think so?"

Sheer terror—that was what had been on Brenda's face. Brenda was not a fighter. I wondered that she had ever had the nerve to do murder. But possibly she had not. Possibly it had been Laurence Brown, with his persecution mania, his unstable personality who had put the contents of one little bottle into another little bottle—a simple easy act—to free the woman he loved.

"So it's over," said Sophia.

She sighed deeply, then asked:

"But why arrest them now? I thought there wasn't enough evidence."

"A certain amount of evidence has come to light. Letters."

"You mean love letters between them?"

"Yes."

"What fools people are to keep these things!"

Yes, indeed. Fools. The kind of folly which never seemed to profit by the experience of others. You couldn't open a daily newspaper without coming across some instance of that folly—the passion to keep the written word, the written assurance of love.

"It's quite beastly, Sophia," I said. "But it's no good minding about it. After all, it's what we've been hoping all along, isn't it? It's what you said that first night at Mario's. You said it would be all right if the right person had killed your grandfather. Brenda was the right person, wasn't she? Brenda or Laurence?"

"Don't, Charles, you make me feel awful."

"But we must be sensible. We can marry now, Sophia. You can't hold me off any longer. The Leonides family are out of it."

She stared at me. I had never realised before the vivid blue of her eyes.

"Yes," she said. "I suppose we're out of it now. We *are* out of it, aren't we? You're sure?"

" My dear girl, none of you ever really had a shadow of motive."

Her face went suddenly white.

" Except me, Charles. *I* had a motive."

" Yes, of course——" I was taken aback. " But not really. You didn't know, you see, about the will."

" But I did, Charles," she whispered.

" What?" I stared at her. I felt suddenly cold.

" I knew all the time that grandfather had left his money to me."

" But how?"

" He told me. About a fortnight before he was killed. He said to me quite suddenly: ' I've left all my money to you, Sophia. You must look after the family when I've gone.' "

I stared.

" You never told me."

" No. You see, when they all explained about the will and his signing it, I thought perhaps he had made a mistake —that he was just imagining that he left it to me. Or that if he had made a will leaving it to me, then it had got lost and would never turn up. I didn't want it to turn up—I was afraid."

" Afraid? Why?"

" I suppose—because of murder."

I remembered the look of terror on Brenda's face—the wild unreasoning panic. I remembered the sheer panic that Magda had conjured up at will when she considered playing the part of a murderess. There would be no panic in Sophia's mind, but she was a realist, and she could see clearly enough that Leonides' will made her a suspect. I understood better now (or thought I did) her refusal to become engaged to me and her insistence that I should find out the truth. Nothing but the truth, she had said, was any good to her. I remembered the passion, the earnestness with which she had said it.

We had turned to walk towards the house and suddenly, at a certain spot, I remembered something else she had said.

She had said that she supposed she could murder someone, but if so, she had added, it must be for something really worthwhile.

CHAPTER XXII

ROUND a turn of the rock garden Roger and Clemency came walking briskly towards us. Roger's flapping tweeds suited him better than his City clothes. He looked eager and excited. Clemency was frowning.

"Hallo, you two," said Roger. "At last! I thought they were never going to arrest that foul woman. What they've been waiting for, I don't know. Well, they've pinched her now, and her miserable boy friend—and I hope they hang them both."

Clemency's frown increased. She said:

"Don't be so uncivilised, Roger."

"Uncivilised? Bosh! Deliberate cold-blooded poisoning of a helpless trusting old man—and when I'm glad the murderers are caught and will pay the penalty you say I'm uncivilised! I tell you I'd willingly strangle that woman myself."

He added:

"She was with you, wasn't she, when the police came for her? How did she take it?"

"It was horrible," said Sophia in a low voice. "She was scared out of her wits."

"Serve her right."

"Don't be vindictive," said Clemency.

"Oh, I know, dearest, but you can't understand. It wasn't your father. I *loved* my father. Don't you understand? I *loved* him!"

"I should understand by now," said Clemency.

Roger said to her, half-jokingly:

"You've no imagination, Clemency. Suppose it had been I who had been poisoned——?"

I saw the quick droop of her lids, her half-clenched hands. She said sharply: "Don't say things like that even in fun."

"Never mind, darling, we'll soon be away from all this."

We moved towards the house. Roger and Sophia walked ahead and Clemency and I brought up the rear. She said:

"I suppose now—they'll let us go?"

"Are you so anxious to get off?" I asked.

"It's wearing me out."

I looked at her in surprise. She met my glance with a faint desperate smile and a nod of the head.

"Haven't you seen, Charles, that I'm fighting all the time? Fighting for my happiness. For Roger's. I've been so afraid the family would persuade him to stop in England. That we'd go on tangled up in the midst of them, stifled with family ties. I was afraid Sophia would offer him an income and that he'd stay in England because it would mean greater comfort and amenities for me. The trouble with Roger is that he will *not* listen. He gets ideas in his head—and they're never the right ideas. He doesn't know *anything*. And he's enough of a Leonides to think that happiness for a woman is bound up with comfort and money. But I will fight for my happiness—I will. I will get Roger away and give him the life that suits him where he won't feel a failure. I want him to myself—away from them all—right away——"

She had spoken in a low hurried voice with a kind of desperation that startled me. I had not realised how much on edge she was. I had not realised, either, quite how desperate and possessive was her feeling for Roger.

It brought back to my mind that odd quotation of Edith de Haviland's. She had quoted the line " this side idolatry " with a peculiar intonation. I wondered if she had been thinking of Clemency.

Roger, I thought, had loved his father better than he would ever love anyone else, better even than his wife, devoted though he was to her. I realised for the first time how urgent was Clemency's desire to get her husband to herself. Love for Roger, I saw, made up her entire existence. He was her child, as well as her husband and her lover.

A car drove up to the front door.

" Hallo," I said. " Here's Josephine back."

Josephine and Magda got out of the car. Josephine had a bandage round her head but otherwise looked remarkably well.

She said at once :

" I want to see my goldfish," and started towards us and the pond.

" Darling," cried Magda, " you'd better come in first and lie down a little, and perhaps have a little nourishing soup."

" Don't fuss, mother," said Josephine. " I'm quite all right, and I hate nourishing soup."

Magda looked irresolute. I knew that Josephine had really been fit to depart from the hospital for some days, and that it was only a hint from Taverner that had kept her there. He was taking no chances on Josephine's safety until his suspects were safe under lock and key.

I said to Magda :

" I dare say fresh air will do her good. I'll go and keep an eye on her."

I caught Josephine up before she got to the pond.

" All sorts of things have been happening while you've been away," I said.

Josephine did not reply. She peered with her short-sighted eyes into the pond.

" I don't see Ferdinand," she said.

" Which is Ferdinand?"

" The one with four tails."

" That kind is rather amusing. I like that bright gold one."

" It's quite a common one."

" I don't much care for that moth-eaten white one."

Josephine cast me a scornful glance.

" That's a chubunkin. They cost a lot—far more than goldfish."

" Don't you want to hear what's been happening, Josephine?"

" I expect I know about it."

" Did you know that another will has been found and that your grandfather left all his money to Sophia?"

Josephine nodded in a bored kind of way.

" Mother told me. Anyway, I knew it already."

" Do you mean you heard it in hospital?"

" No, I mean I knew that grandfather had left his money to Sophia. I heard him tell her so."

" Were you listening again?"

" Yes. I like listening."

" It's a disgraceful thing to do, and remember this, listeners hear no good of themselves."

Josephine gave me a peculiar glance.

" I heard what he said about me to her, if that's what you mean."

She added:

"Nannie gets wild if she catches me listening at doors. She says it's not the sort of thing a little lady does."

"She's quite right."

"Pooh," said Josephine. "Nobody's a lady nowadays. They said so on the Brains Trust. They said it was—ob-so-lete." She pronounced the word carefully.

I changed the subject.

"You've got home a bit late for the big event," I said. "Chief-Inspector Taverner has arrested Brenda and Laurence."

I expected that Josephine, in her character of young detective, would be thrilled by this information, but she merely repeated in her maddening bored fashion:

"Yes, I know."

"You can't know. It's only just happened."

"The car passed us on the road. Inspector Taverner and the detective with the suède shoes were inside with Brenda and Laurence, so of course I knew they must have been arrested. I hope he gave them the proper caution. You have to, you know."

I assured her that Taverner had acted strictly according to etiquette.

"I had to tell him about the letters," I said apologetically. "I found them behind the cistern. I'd have let you tell him only you were knocked out."

Josephine's hand went gingerly to her head.

"I ought to have been killed," she said with complacency. "I told you it was about the time for the second murder. The cistern was a rotten place to hide those letters. I guessed at once when I saw Laurence coming out of there one day. I mean he's not a useful kind of man who does things with ball taps, or pipes or fuses, so I knew he must have been hiding something."

"But I thought——" I broke off as Edith de Haviland's voice called authoritatively:

"Josephine. Josephine, come here at once."

Josephine sighed.

"More fuss," she said. "But I'd better go. You have to, if it's Aunt Edith."

She ran across the lawn. I followed more slowly.

After a brief interchange of words Josephine went into the house. I joined Edith de Haviland on the terrace.

This morning she looked fully her age. I was startled by the lines of weariness and suffering on her face. She looked exhausted and defeated. She saw the concern in my face and tried to smile.

"That child seems none the worse for her adventure," she said. "We must look after her better in future. Still—I suppose now it won't be necessary?"

She sighed and said:

"I'm glad it's over. But what an exhibition! If you *are* arrested for murder, you might at least have some dignity. I've no patience with people like Brenda who go to pieces and squeal. No guts, these people. Laurence Brown looked like a cornered rabbit."

An obscure instinct of pity rose in me.

"Poor devils," I said.

"Yes—poor devils. She'll have the sense to look after herself, I suppose? I mean the right lawyers—all that sort of thing."

It was queer, I thought, the dislike they all had for Brenda, and their scrupulous care for her to have all the advantages for defence.

Edith de Haviland went on:

"How long will it be? How long will the whole thing take?"

I said I didn't know exactly. They would be charged at the police court and presumably sent for trial. Three or four months, I estimated—and if convicted, there would be the appeal.

"Do you think they will be convicted?" she asked.

"I don't know. I don't know exactly how much evidence the police have. There are letters."

"Love letters? They *were* lovers then?"

"They were in love with each other."

Her face grew grimmer.

"I'm not happy about this, Charles. I don't like Brenda. In the past, I've disliked her very much. I've said sharp things about her. But now—I do feel that I want her to have every chance—every possible chance. Aristide would have wished that. I feel it's up to me to see that—that Brenda gets a square deal."

"And Laurence?"

"Oh, Laurence!" She shrugged her shoulders impatiently. "Men must look after themselves. But Aristide would never forgive us if——" She left the sentence unfinished.

Then she said:

"It must be almost lunch time. We'd better go in."

I explained that I was going up to London.

"In your car?"

"Yes."

"H'm. I wonder if you'd take me with you. I gather we're allowed off the lead now."

"Of course I will, but I believe Magda and Sophia are going up after lunch. You'll be more comfortable with them than in my two seater."

"I don't want to go with them. Take me with you, and don't say much about it."

I was surprised, but I did as she asked. We did not speak much on the way to town. I asked her where I should put her down.

" Harley Street."

I felt some faint apprehension, but I didn't like to say anything. She continued :

" No, it's too early. Drop me at Debenhams. I can have some lunch there and go to Harley Street afterwards."

" I hope——" I began and stopped.

" That's why I didn't want to go up with Magda. She dramatises things. Lot of fuss."

" I'm very sorry," I said.

" You needn't be. I've had a good life. A very good life." She gave a sudden grin. " And it's not over yet."

CHAPTER XXIII

I HAD NOT seen my father for some days. I found him busy with things other than the Leonides case, and I went in search of Taverner.

Taverner was enjoying a short spell of leisure and was willing to come out and have a drink with me. I congratulated him on having cleared up the case and he accepted my congratulations, but his manner remained far from jubilant.

"Well, that's over," he said. "We've got a case. Nobody can deny we've got a case."

"Do you think you'll get a conviction?"

"Impossible to say. The evidence is circumstantial—it nearly always is in a murder case—bound to be. A lot depends on the impression they make on the jury."

"How far do the letters go?"

"At first sight, Charles, they're pretty damning. There are references to their life together when her husband's dead. Phrases like—'it won't be long now.' Mind you, defence counsel will try and twist it the other way—the husband was so old that of course they could reasonably expect him to die. There's no actual mention of poisoning —not down in black or white—but there are some passages that could mean that. It depends what judge we get. If it's old Carberry he'll be down on them all through. He's always very righteous about illicit love. I suppose they'll have Eagles or Humphrey Kerr for the defence—Humphrey is magnificent in these cases—but he likes a gallant war record or something of that kind to help him do his stuff. A conscientious objector is going to cramp his style. The question is going to be will the jury like them? You can never tell with juries. You know, Charles, those two are not really sympathetic characters. She's a good-looking woman who married a very old man for his money, and Brown is a neurotic conscientious objector. The crime is so familiar—so according to pattern that you can't really believe they didn't do it. Of course, they may decide that he did it and she knew nothing about it—or alternatively that she did it, and he didn't know about it—or they may decide that they were both in it together."

"And what do you yourself think?" I asked.

He looked at me with a wooden expressionless face.

"I don't think anything. I've turned in the facts and they went to the D.P.P. and it was decided that there was a case. That's all. I've done my duty and I'm out of it. So now you know, Charles."

But I didn't know. I saw that for some reason Taverner was unhappy.

It was not until three days later that I unburdened myself to my father. He himself had never mentioned the case to me. There had been a kind of restraint between us —and I thought I knew the reason for it. But I had to break down that barrier.

"We've got to have this out," I said. "Taverner's not satisfied that those two did it—and you're not satisfied either."

My father shook his head. He said what Taverner had said:

"It's out of our hands. There is a case to answer. No question about that."

"But you don't—Taverner doesn't—think that they're guilty?"

"That's for a jury to decide."

"For God's sake," I said, "don't put me off with technical terms. What do you think—both of you—*personally*?"

"My personal opinion is no better than yours, Charles."

"Yes, it is. You've more experience."

"Then I'll be honest with you. I just—don't know!"

"They *could* be guilty?"

"Oh yes."

"But you don't feel sure that they are?"

My father shrugged his shoulders.

"How can one be sure?"

"Don't fence with me, Dad. You've been sure other times, haven't you? Dead sure? No doubt in your mind at all?"

"Sometimes, yes. Not always."

"I wish to God you were sure this time."

"So do I."

We were silent. I was thinking of those two figures drifting in from the garden in the dusk. Lonely and haunted and afraid. They had been afraid from the start. Didn't that show a guilty conscience?

But I answered myself: "Not necessarily." Both Brenda and Laurence were afraid of life—they had no confidence in themselves, in their ability to avoid danger and defeat, and they could see, only too clearly, the pattern of illicit love leading to murder which might involve them at any moment.

My father spoke, and his voice was grave and kind:

"Come, Charles," he said, "let's face it. You've still got it in your mind, haven't you, that one of the Leonides family is the real culprit?"

" Not really. I only wonder——"

" You do think so. You may be wrong, but you do think so."

" Yes," I said.

" Why?"

" Because "—I thought about it, trying to see clearly—to bring my wits to bear—" because " (yes, that was it), " because they think so themselves."

" They think so themselves? That's interesting. That's very interesting. Do you mean that they all suspect each other, or that they know, actually, who did it?"

" I'm not sure," I said. " It's all very nebulous and confused. I think—on the whole—that they try to cover up the knowledge from themselves."

My father nodded.

" Not Roger," I said. "Roger wholeheartedly believes it was Brenda and he wholeheartedly wants her hanged. It's—it's a relief to be with Roger, because he's simple and positive, and hasn't any reservations in the back of his mind.

" But the others are apologetic, they're uneasy—they urge me to be sure that Brenda has the best defence—that every possible advantage is given her—why?"

My father answered :

" Because they don't really, in their hearts, believe she is guilty . . . Yes, that's sound."

Then he asked quietly :

" Who *could* have done it? You've talked to them all? Who's the best bet?"

" I don't know," I said. " And it's driving me frantic. None of them fits your ' sketch of a murderer ' and yet I feel—I do feel—that one of them *is* a murderer."

" Sophia?"

" No. Good God, no!"

" The possibility's in your mind, Charles—yes, it is, don't deny it. All the more potently because you won't acknowledge it. What about the others? Philip?"

" Only for the most fantastic motive."

" Motives can be fantastic—or they can be absurdly slight. What's his motive?"

" He is bitterly jealous of Roger—always has been all his life. His father's preference for Roger drove Philip in upon himself. Roger was about to crash, then the old man heard of it. He promised to put Roger on his feet again. Supposing Philip learnt that. If the old man died that night there would be no assistance for Roger. Roger would be down and out. Oh! I know it's absurd——"

" Oh no, it isn't. It's abnormal, but it happens. It's human. What about Magda?"

" She's rather childish. She—she gets things out of proportion. But I would never have thought twice about her being involved if it hadn't been for the sudden way she wanted to pack Josephine off to Switzerland. I couldn't help feeling she was afraid of something that Josephine knew or might say——"

" And then Josephine was conked on the head?"

" Well, that couldn't be her mother!"

" Why not?"

" But, Dad, a mother wouldn't——"

" Charles, Charles, don't you ever read the police news. Again and again a mother takes a dislike to one of her children. Only one—she may be devoted to the others. There's some association, some reason, but it's often hard to get at. But when it exists, it's an unreasoning aversion, and it's very strong."

" She called Josephine a changeling," I admitted unwillingly.

"Did the child mind?"

"I don't think so."

"Who else is there? Roger?"

"Roger didn't kill his father. I'm quite sure of that."

"Wash out Roger then. His wife—what's her name—Clemency?"

"Yes," I said. "If she killed old Leonides it was for a very odd reason."

I told him of my conversation with Clemency. I said I thought it possible that in her passion to get Roger away from England she might have deliberately poisoned the old man.

"She'd persuaded Roger to go without telling his father. Then the old man found out. He was going to back up Associated Catering. All Clemency's hopes and plans were frustrated. And she really does care desperately for Roger—beyond idolatry."

"You're repeating what Edith de Haviland said!"

"Yes. And Edith's another whom I think—might have done it. But I don't know why. I can only believe that for what she considered a good and sufficient reason she might take the law into her own hand. She's that kind of person."

"And she also was very anxious that Brenda should be adequately defended?"

"Yes. That, I suppose, might be conscience. I don't think for a moment that if she did do it, she intended them to be accused of the crime."

"Probably not. But would she knock out the child, Josephine?"

"No," I said slowly, "I can't believe that. Which reminds me that there's something that Josephine said to me that keeps nagging at my mind, and I can't remember what it is. It's slipped my memory. But it's something that doesn't fit in where it should. If only I could remember——"

"Never mind. It will come back. Anything or anyone else on your mind?"

"Yes," I said. "Very much so. How much do you know about infantile paralysis. Its after-effects on character, I mean?"

"Eustace?"

"Yes. The more I think about it, the more it seems to me that Eustace might fit the bill. His dislike and resentment against his grandfather. His queerness and moodiness. He's not normal.

"He's the only one of the family whom I can see knocking out Josephine quite callously if she knew something about him—and she's quite likely to know. That child knows everything. She writes it down in a little book——"

I stopped.

"Good Lord," I said. "What a fool I am."

"What's the matter?"

"I know now what was wrong. We assumed, Taverner and I, that the wrecking of Josephine's room, the frantic search, was for those letters. I thought that she'd got hold of them and that she'd hidden them up in the cistern room. But when she was talking to me the other day she made it quite clear that it was *Laurence* who had hidden them there. She saw him coming out of the cistern room and went snooping around and found the letters. Then, of course, she read them. She would! But she left them where they were."

"Well?"

"Don't you see? *It couldn't have been the letters someone was looking for in Josephine's room.* It must have been something else."

"And that something——"

"Was the little black book she writes down her 'detection' in. That's what someone was looking for! I think, too, that whoever it was didn't find it. I think Josephine still has it. But if so——"

I half rose.

"If so," said my father, "she still isn't safe. Is that what you were going to say?"

"Yes. She won't be out of danger until she's actually started for Switzerland. They're planning to send her there, you know."

"Does she want to go?"

I considered.

"I don't think she does."

"Then she probably hasn't gone," said my father, dryly. "But I think you're right about the danger. You'd better go down there."

"Eustace?" I cried desperately. "Clemency?"

My father said gently:

"To my mind the facts point clearly in one direction . . . I wonder you don't see it yourself. I . . ."

Glover opened the door.

"Beg pardon, Mr. Charles, the telephone. Miss Leonides speaking from Swinly Dean. It's urgent."

It seemed like a horrible repetition. Had Josephine again fallen a victim. And had the murderer this time made no mistake . . . ?

I hurried to the telephone.

"Sophia? It's Charles here."

Sophia's voice came with a kind of hard desperation in it. "Charles, it isn't all over. The murderer is still here."

"What on earth do you mean? What's wrong? Is it—Josephine?"

" It's not Josephine. It's Nannie."

" *Nannie?*"

" Yes, there was some cocoa—Josephine's cocoa, she didn't drink it. She left it on the table. Nannie thought it was a pity to waste it. So she drank it."

" Poor Nannie. Is she very bad?"

Sophia's voice broke.

" Oh, Charles, she's *dead*."

CHAPTER XXIV

WE WERE back again in the nightmare.

That is what I thought as Taverner and I drove out of London. It was a repetition of our former journey.

At intervals, Taverner swore.

As for me, I repeated from time to time, stupidly, unprofitably:

" So it wasn't Brenda and Laurence. It wasn't Brenda and Laurence."

Had I ever really thought it was? I had been so glad to think it. So glad to escape from other, more sinister, possibilities . . .

They had fallen in love with each other. They had written silly sentimental romantic letters to each other. They had indulged in hopes that Brenda's old husband might soon die peacefully and happily—but I wondered really if they had even acutely desired his death. I had a feeling that the despairs and longings of an unhappy love affair suited them as well or better than commonplace married life together. I didn't think Brenda was really passionate. She was too anæmic, too apathetic. It was romance she craved for. And I thought Laurence, too, was the type to enjoy frustration and vague future dreams of bliss rather than the concrete satisfactions of the flesh.

They had been caught in a trap and, terrified, they had not had the wit to find their way out. Laurence with incredible stupidity, had not even destroyed Brenda's letters

Presumably Brenda had destroyed his, since they had not been found. And it was not Laurence who had balanced the marble door-stop on the wash house door. It was someone else whose face was still hidden behind a mask.

We drove up to the door. Taverner got out and I followed him. There was a plain clothes man in the hall whom I didn't know. He saluted Taverner and Taverner drew him aside.

My attention was taken by a pile of luggage in the hall. It was labelled and ready for departure. As I looked at it Clemency came down the stairs and through the open door at the bottom. She was dressed in her same red dress with a tweed coat over it and a red felt hat.

"You're in time to say good-bye, Charles," she said.

"You're leaving?"

"We go to London to-night. Our plane goes early to-morrow morning."

She was quiet and smiling, but I thought her eyes were watchful.

"But surely you can't go now?"

"Why not?" Her voice was hard.

"With this death——"

"Nannie's death has nothing to do with us."

"Perhaps not. But all the same——"

"Why do you say 'perhaps not?' It *has* nothing to do with us? Roger and I have been upstairs, finishing packing up. We did not come down at all during the time that the cocoa was left on the hall table."

"Can you prove that?"

"I can answer for Roger. And Roger can answer for me."

"No more than that . . . You're man and wife, remember."

Her anger flamed out.

"You're impossible, Charles! Roger and I are going away—to lead our own life. Why on earth should we want to poison a nice stupid old woman who had never done us any harm?"

"It mightn't have been her you meant to poison."

"Still less are we likely to poison a child."

"It depends rather on the child, doesn't it?"

"What do you mean?"

"Josephine isn't quite the ordinary child. She knows a good deal about people. She——"

I broke off. Josephine had emerged from the door leading to the drawing-room. She was eating the inevitable apple, and over its round rosiness her eyes sparkled with a kind of ghoulish enjoyment.

"Nannie's been poisoned," she said. "Just like grandfather. It's awfully exciting, isn't it?"

"Aren't you at all upset about it?" I demanded severely. "You were fond of her, weren't you?"

"Not particularly. She was always scolding me about something or other. She fussed."

"Are you fond of anybody, Josephine?" asked Clemency.

Josephine turned her ghoulish eyes towards Clemency.

"I love Aunt Edith," she said. "I love Aunt Edith very much. And I could love Eustace, only he's always such a beast to me and won't be interested in finding out who did all this."

"You'd better stop finding things out, Josephine," I said. "It isn't very safe."

"I don't need to find out any more," said Josephine. "I know."

There was a moment's silence. Josephine's eyes, solemn and unwinking, were fixed on Clemency. A sound like a long sigh reached my ears. I swung sharply round. Edith de Haviland stood half-way down the staircase—but I did not think it was she who had sighed. The sound had come from behind the door through which Josephine had just come.

I stepped sharply across to it and yanked it open. There was no one to be seen.

Nevertheless I was seriously disturbed. Someone had stood just within that door and had heard those words of Josephine's. I went back and took Josephine by the arm. She was eating her apple and staring stolidly at Clemency. Behind the solemnity there was, I thought, a certain malignant satisfaction.

"Come on, Josephine," I said. "We're going to have a little talk."

I think Josephine might have protested, but I was not standing any nonsense. I ran her along forcibly into her own part of the house. There was a small unused morning room where we could be reasonably sure of being undisturbed. I took her in there, closed the door firmly, and made her sit on a chair. I took another chair and drew it forward so that I faced her.

"Now, Josephine," I said, "we're going to have a showdown. What exactly do you know?"

"Lots of things."

"That I have no doubt about. That noddle of yours is probably crammed to overflowing with relevant and irrelevant information. But you know perfectly what I mean. Don't you?"

"Of course I do. *I*'m not stupid."

I didn't know whether the disparagement was for me or the police, but I paid no attention to it and went on:

"You know who put something in your cocoa?"

Josephine nodded.

" You know who poisoned your grandfather?"

Josephine nodded again.

" And who knocked you on the head?"

Again Josephine nodded.

" Then you're going to come across with what you know. You're going to tell me all about it—now."

" Shan't."

" You've got to. Every bit of information you've got or ferret out has got to be given to the police."

" I won't tell the police anything. They're stupid. They thought Brenda had done it—or Laurence. I wasn't stupid like that. I knew jolly well they hadn't done it. I've had an idea who it was all along, and then I made a kind of test—and now I know I'm right."

She finished on a triumphant note.

I prayed to Heaven for patience and started again.

" Listen, Josephine, I dare say you're extremely clever ——" Josephine looked gratified. " But it won't be much good to you to be clever if you're not alive to enjoy the fact. Don't you see, you little fool, that as long as you keep your secrets in this silly way you're in imminent danger?"

Josephine nodded approvingly.

" Of course I am."

" Already you've had two very narrow escapes. One attempt nearly did for you. The other has cost somebody else their life. Don't you see if you go on strutting about the house and proclaiming at the top of your voice that you know who the killer is, there will be more attempts made—and that either you'll die or somebody else will?"

" In some books person after person is killed," Josephine informed me with gusto. " You end by spotting the murderer because he or she is practically the only person left."

"This isn't a detective story. This is Three Gables, Swinly Dean, and you're a silly little girl who's read more than is good for her. I'll make you tell me what you know if I have to shake you till your teeth rattle."

"I could always tell you something that wasn't true."

"You could, but you won't. What are you waiting for, anyway?"

"You don't understand," said Josephine. "Perhaps I may never tell, you see, I might—be fond of the person."

She paused as though to let this sink in.

"And if I do tell," she went on, "I shall do it properly. I shall have everybody sitting round, and then I'll go over it all—with the clues, and then I shall say, quite suddenly:

"And it was *you* . . ."

She thrust out a dramatic forefinger just as Edith de Haviland entered the room.

"Put that core in the waste-paper basket, Josephine," said Edith. "Have you got a handkerchief? Your fingers are sticky. I'm taking you out in the car." Her eyes met mine with significance as she said: "She'll be safer out of here for the next hour or so." As Josephine looked mutinous, Edith added: "We'll go into Longbridge and have an ice cream soda."

Josephine's eyes brightened and she said: "Two."

"Perhaps," said Edith. "Now go and get your hat and coat on and your dark blue scarf. It's cold out to-day. Charles, you had better go with her while she gets them. Don't leave her. I have just a couple of notes to write."

She sat down at the desk, and I escorted Josephine out of the room. Even without Edith's warning, I would have stuck to Josephine like a leech.

I was convinced that there was danger to the child very near at hand.

As I finished superintending Josephine's toilet, Sophia came into the room. She seemed rather astonished to see me.

" Why, Charles, have you turned nursemaid? I didn't know you were here."

" I'm going into Longbridge with Aunt Edith," said Josephine importantly. " We're going to have ice creams."

" Brrrr, on a day like this?"

" Ice cream sodas are always lovely," said Josephine. " When you're cold inside, it makes you feel hotter outside."

Sophia frowned. She looked worried, and I was shocked by her pallor and the circles under her eyes.

We went back to the morning room. Edith was just blotting a couple of envelopes. She got up briskly.

" We'll start now," she said. " I told Evans to bring round the Ford."

She swept out to the hall. We followed her.

My eye was again caught by the suitcases and their blue labels. For some reason they aroused in me a vague disquietude.

" It's quite a nice day," said Edith de Haviland, pulling on her gloves and glancing up at the sky. The Ford 10 was waiting in front of the house. " Cold—but bracing. A real English autumn day. How beautiful trees look with their bare branches against the sky—and just a golden leaf or two still hanging . . ."

She was silent a moment or two, then she turned and kissed Sophia.

" Good-bye, dear," she said. " Don't worry too much Certain things have to be faced and endured."

Then she said, " Come on, Josephine," and got into the car. Josephine climbed in beside her.

They both waved as the car drove off.

" I suppose she's right, and it's better to keep Josephine out of this for a while. But we've got to make that child tell what she knows, Sophia."

" She probably doesn't know anything. She's just showing off. Josephine likes to make herself look important, you know."

" It's more than that. Do they know what poison it was in the cocoa?"

" They think it's digitalin. Aunt Edith takes digitalin for her heart. She has a whole bottle full of little tablets up in her room. Now the bottle's empty."

" She ought to keep things like that locked up."

" She did. I suppose it wouldn't be difficult for someone to find out where she hid the key."

" Someone? Who?" I looked again at the pile of luggage. I said suddenly and loudly :

" They can't go away. They mustn't be allowed to."

Sophia looked surprised.

" Roger and Clemency? Charles, you don't think——"

" Well, what do *you* think?"

Sophia stretched out her hands in a helpless gesture.

" I don't know, Charles," she whispered. " I only know that I'm back—back in the nightmare——"

" I know. Those were the very words I used to myself as I drove down with Taverner."

" Because this is just what a nightmare is. Walking about among people you know, looking in their faces—and suddenly the faces change—and it's not someone you know any longer—it's a stranger—a cruel stranger . . ."

She cried :

" Come outside, Charles—come outside. It's safer outside . . . I'm afraid to stay in this house. . . ."

CHAPTER XXV

WE STAYED in the garden a long time. By a kind c
tacit consent, we did not discuss the horror that was weigh
ing upon us. Instead Sophia talked affectionately of th
dead woman, of things they had done, and games they ha
played as children with Nannie—and tales that the ol
woman used to tell them about Roger and their father an
the other brothers and sisters.

"They were her real children, you see. She only cam
back to us to help during the war when Josephine was
baby and Eustace was a funny little boy."

There was a certain balm for Sophia in these memorie
and I encouraged her to talk.

I wondered what Taverner was doing. Questioning th
household, I supposed. A car drove away with the polic
photographer and two other men, and presently an ambu
lance drove up.

Sophia shivered a little. Presently the ambulance lef
and we knew that Nannie's body had been taken away i
preparation for an autopsy.

And still we sat or walked in the garden and talked—
our words becoming more and more of a cloak for our rea
thoughts.

Finally, with a shiver, Sophia said:

"It must be very late—it's almost dark. We've got to g
in. Aunt Edith and Josephine haven't come back . .
Surely they ought to be back by now?"

A vague uneasiness woke in me. What had happened? Was Edith deliberately keeping the child away from the Crooked House?

We went in. Sophia drew all the curtains. The fire was lit and the big drawing-room looked harmonious with an unreal air of bygone luxury. Great bowls of bronze chrysanthemums stood on the tables.

Sophia rang and a maid whom I recognised as having been formerly upstairs brought in tea. She had red eyes and sniffed continuously. Also I noticed that she had a frightened way of glancing quickly over her shoulder.

Magda joined us, but Philip's tea was sent in to him in the library. Magda's role was a stiff frozen image of grief. She spoke little or not at all. She said once:

"Where are Edith and Josephine? They're out very late."

But she said it in a preoccupied kind of way.

But I myself was becoming increasingly uneasy. I asked if Taverner were still in the house and Magda replied that she thought so. I went in search of him. I told him that I was worried about Miss de Haviland and the child.

He went immediately to the telephone and gave certain instructions.

"I'll let you know when I have news," he said.

I thanked him and went back to the drawing-room. Sophia was there with Eustace. Magda had gone.

"He'll let us know if he hears anything," I said to Sophia.

She said in a low voice:

"Something's happened, Charles, something *must* have happened."

"My dear Sophia, it's not really late yet."

"What are you bothering about?" said Eustace. "They've probably gone to the cinema."

He lounged out of the room. I said to Sophia: "She may have taken Josephine to a hotel—or up to London. I think she fully realised that the child was in danger—perhaps she realised it better than we did."

Sophia replied with a sombre look that I could not quite fathom.

"She kissed me good-bye . . ."

I did not see quite what she meant by that disconnected remark, or what it was supposed to show. I asked if Magda was worried.

"Mother? No, she's all right. She's no sense of time. She's reading a new play of Vavasour Jones called *The Woman Disposes*. It's a funny play about murder—a female Bluebeard—cribbed from *Arsenic and Old Lace* if you ask me, but it's got a good woman's part, a woman who's got a mania for being a widow."

I said no more. We sat, pretending to read.

It was half-past six when Taverner opened the door and came in. His face prepared us for what he had to say.

Sophia got up.

"Yes?" she said.

"I'm sorry. I've got bad news for you. I sent out a general alarm for the car. A motorist reported having seen a Ford car with a number something like that turning off the main road at Flackspur Heath—through the woods."

"Not—the track to the Flackspur Quarry?"

"Yes, Miss Leonides." He paused and went on: "The car's been found in the quarry. Both the occupants were dead. You'll be glad to know they were killed outright."

"Josephine!" It was Magda standing in the doorway. Her voice rose in a wail. "Josephine . . . My baby."

Sophia went to her and put her arms round her. I said: "Wait a minute."

I had remembered something! Edith de Haviland writing a couple of letters at the desk, going out into the hall with them in her hand.

But they had not been in her hand when she got into the car.

I dashed out into the hall and went to the long oak chest. I found the letters—pushed inconspicuously to the back behind a brass tea-urn.

The uppermost was addressed to Chief-Inspector Taverner.

Taverner had followed me. I handed the letter to him and he tore it open. Standing beside him I read its brief contents.

> My expectation is that this will be opened after my death. I wish to enter into no details, but I accept full responsibility for the deaths of my brother-in-law, Aristide Leonides, and Janet Rowe (Nannie). I hereby solemnly declare that Brenda Leonides and Laurence Brown are innocent of the murder of Aristide Leonides. Inquiry of Dr. Michael Chavasse, 783 Harley Street, will confirm that my life could only have been prolonged for a few months. I prefer to take this way out and to spare two innocent people the ordeal of being charged with a murder they did not commit. I am of sound mind and fully conscious of what I write.
>
> *Edith Elfrida de Haviland.*

As I finished the letter I was aware that Sophia, too, had read it—whether with Taverner's concurrence or not, I don't know.

"*Aunt Edith . . .*" murmured Sophia.

I remembered Edith de Haviland's ruthless foot grinding bindweed into the earth. I remembered my early, almost fanciful, suspicions of her. But why——

Sophia spoke the thought in my mind before I came to it.

" But why Josephine? Why did she take Josephine with her?"

" Why did she do it at all?" I demanded. " What was her motive?"

But even as I said that, I knew the truth. I saw the whole thing clearly. I realised that I was still holding her second letter in my hand. I looked down and saw my own name on it.

It was thicker and harder than the other one. I think I knew what was in it before I opened it. I tore the envelope along and Josephine's little black notebook fell out. I picked it up off the floor—it came open in my hand and I saw the entry on the first page . . .

Sounding from a long way away, I heard Sophia's voice, clear and self-controlled.

" We've got it all wrong," she said. " Edith didn't do it."

" No," I said.

Sophia came closer to me—she whispered :

" It was—Josephine—wasn't it? That was it, Josephine."

Together we looked down on the first entry in the little black book, written in an unformed childish hand.

To-day I killed grandfather.

CHAPTER XXVI

I WAS to wonder afterwards that I could have been so blind. The truth had stuck out so clearly all along. Josephine and only Josephine fitted in with all the necessary qualifications. Her vanity, her persistent self importance, her delight in talking, her reiteration on how clever *she* was, and how stupid the police were.

I had never considered her because she was a child. But children have committed murders, and this particular murder had been well within a child's compass. Her grandfather himself had indicated the precise method—he had practically handed her a blueprint. All she had to do was to avoid leaving fingerprints and the slightest knowledge of detective fiction would teach her that. And everything else had been a mere hotch potch, culled at random from stock mystery stories. The notebook—the sleuthing—her pretended suspicions, her insistence that she was not going to tell till she was sure. . . .

And finally the attack on herself. An almost incredible performance considering that she might easily have killed herself. But then, childlike, she had never considered such a possibility. She was the heroine. The heroine isn't killed. Yet there had been a clue there—the traces of earth on the seat of the old chair in the wash house. Josephine was the only person who would have had to climb up on a chair to balance the block of marble on the top of the door. Obviously it had missed her more than once (the dints in the floor) and patiently she had climbed up again and replaced it, handling it with her scarf to avoid fingerprints. And then it had fallen—and she had a near escape from death.

It had been the perfect set up—the impression she was aiming for! She was in danger, she " knew something," she had been attacked!

I saw how that had deliberately drawn my attention to her presence in the cistern room. And she had completed the artistic disorder of her room before going out to the wash house.

But when she had returned from hospital, when she had found Brenda and Laurence arrested, she must have become dissatisfied. The case was over—and she—Josephine, was out of the limelight.

So she stole the digitalin from Edith's room and put it in her own cup of cocoa and left the cup untouched on the hall table.

Did she know that Nannie would drink it? Possibly. From her words that morning, she had resented Nannie's criticisms of her. Did Nannie, perhaps, wise from a lifetime of experience with children, suspect? I think that Nannie knew, had always known, that Josephine was not normal. With her precocious mental development had gone a retarded moral sense. Perhaps, too, the various factors of heredity—what Sophia had called the " ruthlessness " of the family had met together.

She had had an authoritarian ruthlessness of her grandmother's family, and the ruthless egoism of Magda, seeing only her own point of view. She had also presumably suffered, sensitive like Philip, from the stigma of being the unattractive—the changeling child—of the family. Finally, in her very marrow had run the essential crooked strain of old Leonides. She had been Leonides' grandchild, she had resembled him in brain and in cunning—but where his love had gone outwards to family and friends, hers had turned inward to herself.

I thought that old Leonides had realised what none of the rest of the family had realised, that Josephine might be a source of danger to others and to herself. He had kept her from school life because he was afraid of what she might do. He had shielded her, and guarded her in the home, and I understood now his urgency to Sophia to look after Josephine.

Magda's sudden decision to send Josephine abroad had that, too, been due to a fear for the child? Not, perhaps, a conscious fear, but some vague maternal instinct.

And Edith de Haviland? Had she first suspected, then feared—and finally known?

I looked down at the letter in my hand.

Dear Charles. This is in confidence for you—and for Sophia if you so decide. It is imperative that someone should know the truth. I found the enclosed in the disused dog kennel outside the back door. She kept it there. It confirms what I already suspected. The action I am about to take may be right or wrong—I do not know. But my life, in any case, is close to its end, and I do not want the child to suffer as I believe she would suffer if called to earthly account for what she has done.

There is often one of the litter who is "not quite right."

If I do wrong, God forgive me—but I do it out of love. God bless you both.

Edith de Haviland.

I hesitated for only a moment, then I handed the letter to Sophia. Together we again opened Josephine's little black book.

To-day I killed grandfather.

We turned the pages. It was an amazing production. Interesting, I should imagine, to a psychologist. It set out, with such terrible clarity, the fury of thwarted egoism. The motive for the crime was set down, pitifully childish and inadequate.

Grandfather wouldn't let me do bally dancing so I made up my mind I would kill him. Then we would go to London and live and mother wouldn't mind me doing bally.

I give only a few entries. They are all significant.

I don't want to go to Switzerland—I won't go. If mother makes me I will kill her too—only I can't get any poison. Perhaps I could make it with youberries. They are poisonous, the book says so.

Eustace has made me very cross to-day. He says I am only a girl and no use and that its silly my detecting. He wouldn't think me silly if he knew it was me did the murder.

I like Charles—but he is rather stupid. I have not decided yet who I shall make have done the crime. Perhaps Brenda and Laurence—Brenda is nasty to me—she says I am not all there but I like Laurence—he told me about Charlot Korday—she killed someone in his bath. She was not very clever about it.

The last entry was revealing.

I hate Nannie . . . I hate her . . . I hate her . . . She says I am only a little girl. She says I show off. She's making mother send me abroad . . . I'm going to kill her too—I think Aunt Edith's medicine would do it.

> If there is another murder, then the police will come back and it will all be exciting again.
>
> Nannie's dead. I am glad. I haven't decided yet where I'll hide the bottle with the little pill things. Perhaps in Aunt Clemency's room—or else Eustace's. When I am dead as an old woman I shall leave this behind me addressed to the Chief of the Police and they will see what a really great criminal I was.

I closed the book. Sophia's tears were flowing fast.

"Oh, Charles—oh Charles—it's so dreadful. She's such a little monster—and yet—and yet it's so terribly pathetic."

I had felt the same.

I had liked Josephine . . . I still felt a fondness for her . . . You do not like anyone less because they have tuberculosis or some other fatal disease. Josephine was, as Sophia had said, a little monster, but she was a pathetic little monster. She had been born with a kink—the crooked child of the little Crooked House.

Sophia asked:

"If—she had lived—what would have happened?"

"I suppose she would have been sent to a reformatory or a special school. Later she would have been released—or possibly certified, I don't know."

Sophia shuddered.

"It's better the way it is. But Aunt Edith—I don't like to think of her taking the blame."

"She chose to do so. I don't suppose it will be made public. I imagine that when Brenda and Laurence come to trial, no case will be brought against them and they will be discharged.

"And you, Sophia," I said, this time on a different note and taking both her hands in mine, "will marry me. I've just heard I'm appointed to Persia. We will go out there together, and you will forget the little Crooked House. Your mother can put on plays and your father can buy more books and Eustace will soon go to a university. Don't worry about them any more. Think of me."

Sophia looked at me, straight in the eyes.

"Aren't you afraid, Charles, to marry me?"

"Why should I be? In poor little Josephine all the worst of the family came together. In you, Sophia, I fully believe that all that is bravest and best in the Leonides family has been handed down to you. Your grandfather thought highly of you and he seems to have been a man who was usually right. Hold up your head, my darling. The future is ours."

"I will, Charles. I love you and I'll marry you and make you happy." She looked down at the notebook. "Poor Josephine."

"Poor Josephine," I said.

"What's the truth of it, Charles?" said my father.

I never lie to the Old Man.

"It wasn't Edith de Haviland, sir," I said. "It was Josephine."

My father nodded his head gently.

"Yes," he said. "I've thought so for some time. Poor child. . . ."

Passenger to Frankfurt

TO
MARGARET GUILLAUME

'Leadership, besides being a
great creative force, can be
diabolical. . . '

JAN SMUTS

CONTENTS

INTRODUCTION

The Author speaks:

The first question put to an author, personally, or through the post, is:

'Where do you get your ideas from?'

The temptation is great to reply: 'I always go to Harrods,' or 'I get them mostly at the Army & Navy Stores,' or, snappily, 'Try Marks and Spencer.'

The universal opinion seems firmly established that there is a magic source of ideas which authors have discovered how to tap.

One can hardly send one's questioners back to Elizabethan times, with Shakespeare's:

> *Tell me, where is fancy bred,*
> *Or in the heart or in the head,*
> *How begot, how nourished?*
> *Reply, reply.*

You merely say firmly: 'My own head.'

That, of course, is no help to anybody. If you like the look of your questioner you relent and go a little further.

'If one idea in particular seems attractive, and you feel you could do something with it, then you toss it around, play tricks with it, work it up, tone it down, and gradually get it into shape. Then, of course, you have to start writing it. That's not nearly such fun – it becomes hard work. Alternatively, you can tuck it carefully away, in storage, for perhaps using in a year or two years' time.'

A second question – or rather a statement – is then likely to be:

'I suppose you take most of your characters from real life?'

An indignant denial to that monstrous suggestion.

'No, I don't. I invent them. They are *mine.* They've got to be *my* characters – doing what I want them to do, being what I want them to be – coming alive for me, having their own ideas sometimes, but only because I've made them become *real.*'

So the author has produced the ideas, and the characters – but now comes the third necessity – the setting. The first two come from inside sources, but the third is outside – it must be there – waiting – in existence already. You don't invent that – it's there – it's real.

You have been perhaps for a cruise on the Nile – you remember it all – just the setting you want for this particular story. You have had a meal at a Chelsea café. A quarrel was going on – one girl pulled out a handful of another girl's hair. An excellent start for the book you are going to write next. You travel on the Orient Express. What fun to make it the scene for a plot you are considering. You go to tea with a friend. As you arrive her brother closes a book he is reading – throws it aside, says: 'Not bad, but why on earth didn't they ask Evans?'

So you decide immediately a book of yours shortly to be written will bear the title, *Why Didn't They Ask Evans?*

You don't know yet who Evans is going to be. Never mind. Evans will come in due course – the title is fixed.

So, in a sense, you don't invent your settings. They are outside you, all around you, in existence – you have only to stretch out your hand and pick and choose. A railway train, a hospital, a London hotel, a Caribbean beach, a country village, a cocktail party, a girls' school.

But one thing only applies – they must be there – in existence. Real people, real places. A definite place in time and space. If here and now – how shall you get full information – apart from the evidence of your own eyes and ears? The answer is frighteningly simple.

It is what the Press brings to you every day, served up in your morning paper under the general heading of News. Collect it from the front page. What is going on in the world today? What is everyone saying, thinking, doing? Hold up a mirror to 1970 in England.

Look at that front page every day for a month, make notes, consider and classify.

Every day there is a killing.

A girl strangled.

Elderly woman attacked and robbed of her meagre savings.

Young men or boys – attacking or attacked.

Buildings and telephone kiosks smashed and gutted.

Drug smuggling.

Robbery and assault.

Children missing and children's murdered bodies found not far from their homes.

Can this be England? Is England *really* like this? One feels – no – not yet, *but it could be.*

Fear is awakening – fear of what may be. Not so much because of actual happenings but because of the possible causes behind them. Some known, some unknown, but *felt.* And not only in our own country. There are smaller paragraphs on other pages – giving news from Europe – from Asia – from the Americas – Worldwide News.

Hi-jacking of planes.

Kidnapping.

Violence.

Riots.

Hate.

Anarchy – all growing stronger.

All seeming to lead to worship of destruction, pleasure in cruelty.

What does it all mean? An Elizabethan phrase echoes from the past, speaking of Life:

> *. . . it is a tale*
> *Told by an idiot, full of sound and fury,*
> *Signifying nothing.*

And yet one knows – of one's own knowledge – how much goodness there is in this world of ours – the kindnesses done, the goodness of heart, the acts of compassion, the kindness of neighbour to neighbour, the helpful actions of girls and boys.

Then why this fantastic atmosphere of daily news – of things that happen – that are actual *facts*?

To write a story in this year of Our Lord 1970 – you must come to terms with your background. If the background is fantastic, then the story must accept its background. It, too, must be a fantasy – an extravaganza. The setting must include the fantastic facts of daily life.

Can one envisage a fantastic cause? A secret Campaign for Power? Can a maniacal desire for destruction create a new world? Can one go a step further and suggest deliverance by fantastic and impossible-sounding means?

Nothing is impossible, science has taught us that.

This story is in essence a fantasy. It pretends to be nothing more.

But most of the things that happen in it are happening, or giving promise of happening in the world of today.

It is not an impossible story – it is only a fantastic one.

BOOK 1

INTERRUPTED JOURNEY

1. PASSENGER TO FRANKFURT

'Fasten your seat-belts, please.' The diverse passengers in the plane were slow to obey. There was a general feeling that they couldn't possibly be arriving at Geneva yet. The drowsy groaned and yawned. The more than drowsy had to be gently roused by an authoritative stewardess.

'Your seat-belts, please.'

The dry voice came authoritatively over the Tannoy. It explained in German, in French, and in English that a short period of rough weather would shortly be experienced. Sir Stafford Nye opened his mouth to its full extent, yawned and pulled himself upright in his seat. He had been dreaming very happily of fishing an English river.

He was a man of forty-five, of medium height, with a smooth, olive, clean-shaven face. In dress he rather liked to affect the bizarre. A man of excellent family, he felt fully at ease indulging any such sartorial whims. If it made the more conventionally dressed of his colleagues wince occasionally, that was merely a source of malicious pleasure to him. There was something about him of the eighteenth-century buck. He liked to be noticed.

His particular kind of affectation when travelling was a kind of bandit's cloak which he had once purchased in Corsica. It was of a very dark purply-blue, had a scarlet lining and had a kind of burnous hanging down behind which he could draw up over his head when he wished to, so as to obviate draughts.

Sir Stafford Nye had been a disappointment in diplomatic circles. Marked out in early youth by his gifts for great things, he had singularly failed to fulfil his early promise. A peculiar and diabolical sense of humour was wont to afflict him in what should have been his most serious moments. When it came to the point, he found that he always preferred to indulge his delicate Puckish malice to boring himself. He was a well-known figure in public life without ever having reached eminence. It was felt that Stafford Nye, though definitely brilliant, was not – and presumably never would be – a safe man. In these days of tangled politics and tangled foreign relations, safety, especially if one were to reach ambassadorial rank, was preferable to brilliance. Sir Stafford Nye was relegated to the shelf, though he was occasionally entrusted with such missions as needed the art of intrigue, but were not of too important or public a nature. Journalists sometimes referred to him as the dark horse of diplomacy.

Whether Sir Stafford himself was disappointed with his own career, nobody ever knew. Probably not even Sir Stafford himself. He was a man of a certain vanity, but he was also a man who very much enjoyed indulging his own proclivities for mischief.

He was returning now from a commission of inquiry in Malaya. He had found it singularly lacking in interest. His colleagues had, in his opinion, made up their minds beforehand what their findings were going to be. They saw and they listened, but their preconceived views were not affected. Sir Stafford had thrown a few spanners into the works, more for the hell of it than from any pronounced convictions. At all events, he thought, it had livened things up. He wished there were more possibilities of doing that sort of thing. His fellow members of the commission had been sound, dependable fellows, and remarkably dull. Even the well-known Mrs Nathaniel Edge, the only woman member, well known as having bees in her bonnet, was no fool when it came down to plain facts. She saw, she listened and she played safe.

He had met her before on the occasion of a problem to be solved in one of the Balkan capitals. It was there that Sir Stafford Nye had not been able to refrain from embarking on a few interesting suggestions. In that scandal-loving periodical *Inside News* it was insinuated that Sir Stafford Nye's presence in that Balkan capital was intimately connected with Balkan problems, and that his mission was a secret one of the greatest delicacy. A kind friend had sent Sir Stafford a copy of this with the relevant passage marked. Sir Stafford was not taken aback. He read it with a delighted grin. It amused him very much to reflect how ludicrously far from the truth the journalists were on this occasion. His presence in Sofiagrad had been due entirely to a blameless interest in the rarer wild flowers and to the urgencies of an elderly friend of his, Lady Lucy Cleghorn, who was indefatigable in her quest for these shy floral rarities, and who at any moment would scale a rock cliff or leap joyously into a bog at the sight of some flowerlet, the length of whose Latin name was in inverse proportion to its size.

A small band of enthusiasts had been pursuing this botanical search on the slopes of mountains for about ten days when it occurred to Sir Stafford that it was a pity the paragraph was not true. He was a little – just a little – tired of wild flowers and, fond as he was of dear Lucy, her ability despite her sixty-odd years to race up hills at top speed, easily outpacing him, sometimes annoyed him. Always just in front of him he saw the seat of those bright royal blue trousers and Lucy, though scraggy enough elsewhere, goodness knows, was decidedly too broad in the beam to wear royal blue corduroy trousers. A nice little international pie, he had thought, in which to dip his fingers, in which to play about . . .

In the aeroplane the metallic Tannoy voice spoke again.

It told the passengers that owing to heavy fog at Geneva, the plane would be diverted to Frankfurt airport and proceed from there to London. Passengers to Geneva would be re-routed from Frankfurt as soon as possible. It made no difference to Sir Stafford Nye. If there was fog in London, he supposed they would re-route the plane to Prestwick. He hoped that would not happen. He had been to Prestwick once or twice too often. Life, he thought, and journeys by air, were really excessively boring. If only – he didn't know – if only – *what*?

It was warm in the Transit Passenger Lounge at Frankfurt, so Sir Stafford Nye slipped back his cloak, allowing its crimson lining to drape itself spectacularly round his shoulders. He was drinking a glass of beer and listening with half an ear to the various announcements as they were made.

'Flight 4387. Flying to Moscow. Flight 2381 bound for Egypt and Calcutta.'

Journeys all over the globe. How romantic it ought to be. But there was something about the atmosphere of a Passengers' Lounge in an airport that chilled romance. It was too full of people, too full of things to buy, too full of similarly coloured seats, too full of plastic, too full of human beings, too full of crying children. He tried to remember who had said:

I wish I loved the Human Race;
I wish I loved its silly face

Chesterton perhaps? It was undoubtedly true. Put enough people together and they looked so painfully alike that one could hardly bear it. An interesting face now, thought Sir Stafford. What a difference it would make. He looked disparagingly at two young women, splendidly made up, dressed in the national uniform of their country – England he presumed – of shorter and shorter miniskirts, and another young woman, even better made up – in fact quite good-looking – who was wearing what he believed to be called a culotte suit. She had gone a little further along the road of fashion.

He wasn't very interested in nice-looking girls who looked like all the other nice-looking girls. He would like someone to be different. Someone sat down beside him on the plastic-covered artificial leather settee on which he was sitting. Her face attracted his attention at once. Not precisely because it was different, in fact he almost seemed to recognize it as a face he knew. Here was someone he had seen before. He couldn't remember where or when but it was certainly familiar. Twenty-five or six, he thought, possibly, as to age. A delicate high-bridged aquiline nose, a black heavy bush of hair reaching to her shoulders. She had a magazine in front of her but she was not paying attention to it. She was, in fact, looking with something that was almost eagerness at him. Quite suddenly she spoke. It was a deep contralto voice, almost as deep as a man's. It had a very faint foreign accent. She said,

'Can I speak to you?'

He studied her for a moment before replying. No – not what one might have thought – this wasn't a pick-up. This was something else.

'I see no reason,' he said, 'why you should not do so. We have time to waste here, it seems.'

'Fog,' said the woman, 'fog in Geneva, fog in London, perhaps. Fog everywhere. I don't know what to do.'

'Oh, you mustn't worry,' he said reassuringly, 'they'll land you somewhere all right. They're quite efficient, you know. Where are you going?'

'I was going to Geneva.'

'Well, I expect you'll get there in the end.'

'I have to get there *now*. If I can get to Geneva, it will be all right. There is someone who will meet me there. I can be safe.'

'Safe?' He smiled a little.

She said, 'Safe is a four-letter word but not the kind of four-letter word that people are interested in nowadays. And yet it can mean a lot. It means a lot to me.' Then she said, 'You see, if I can't get to Geneva, if I have to leave this plane here, or go on in this plane to London with no arrangements made, I shall be killed.' She looked at him sharply. 'I suppose you don't believe that.'

'I'm afraid I don't.'

'It's quite true. People can be. They are, every day.'

'Who wants to kill you?'

'Does it matter?'

'Not to me.'

'You can believe me if you wish to believe me. I am speaking the truth. I want help. Help to get to London safely.'

'And why should you select me to help you?'

'Because I think that you know something about death. You have known of death, perhaps seen death happen.'

He looked sharply at her and then away again.

'Any other reason?' he said.

'Yes. This.' She stretched out her narrow olive-skinned hand and touched the folds of the voluminous cloak. 'This,' she said.

For the first time his interest was aroused.

'Now what do you mean by that?'

'It's unusual – characteristic. It's not what everyone wears.'

'True enough. It's one of my affectations, shall we say?'

'It's an affectation that could be useful to me.'

'What do you mean?'

'I am asking you something. Probably you will refuse but you might not refuse because I think you are a man who is ready to take risks. Just as I am a woman who takes risks.'

'I'll listen to your project,' he said, with a faint smile.

'I want your cloak to wear. I want your passport. I want your boarding ticket for the plane. Presently, in twenty minutes or so, say, the flight for London will be called. I shall have your passport, I shall wear your cloak. And so I shall travel to London and arrive safely.'

'You mean you'll pass yourself off as me? My dear girl.'

She opened a handbag. From it she took a small square mirror.

'Look there,' she said. 'Look at me and then look at your own face.'

He saw then, saw what had been vaguely nagging at his mind. His sister, Pamela, who had died about twenty years ago. They had always been very alike, he and Pamela. A strong family resemblance. She had had a slightly masculine type of face. His face, perhaps, had been, certainly in early life, of a slightly effeminate type. They had both had the high-bridged nose, the tilt of eyebrows, the slightly sideways smile of the lips. Pamela had been tall, five foot eight, he himself five foot ten. He looked at the woman who had tendered him the mirror.

'There is a facial likeness between us, that's what you mean, isn't it? But my dear girl, it wouldn't deceive anyone who knew me or knew you.'

'Of course it wouldn't. Don't you understand? It doesn't need to. I am travelling wearing slacks. You have been travelling with the hood of your cloak drawn up round your face. All I have to do is to cut off my hair, wrap it up in a twist of newspaper, throw it in one of the litter-baskets here. Then I put on your burnous, I have your boarding card, ticket, and passport. Unless there is someone who knows you well on this plane, and I presume there is not or they would have spoken to you already, then I can safely travel as you. Showing your passport when it's necessary, keeping the burnous and cloak drawn up so that my nose and eyes and mouth are about all that are seen. I can walk out safely when the plane reaches its destination because no one will know I have travelled by it. Walk out safely and disappear into the crowds of the city of London.'

'And what do I do?' asked Sir Stafford, with a slight smile.

'I can make a suggestion if you have the nerve to face it.'

'Suggest,' he said. 'I always like to hear suggestions.'

'You get up from here, you go away and buy a magazine or a newspaper, or a gift at the gift counter. You leave your cloak hanging here on the seat. When you come back with whatever it is, you sit down somewhere else – say at the end of that bench opposite here. There will be a glass in front of you, this glass still. In it there will be something that will send you to sleep. Sleep in a quiet corner.'

'What happens next?'

'You will have been presumably the victim of a robbery,' she said. 'Somebody will have added a few knock-out drops to your drink, and will have stolen your wallet from you. Something of that kind. You declare your identity, say that your passport and things are stolen. You can easily establish your identity.'

'You know who I am? My name, I mean?'

'Not yet,' she said. 'I haven't seen your passport yet. I've no idea who you are.'

'And yet you say I can establish my identity easily.'

'I am a good judge of people. I know who is important or who isn't. You are an important person.'

'And why should I do all this?'

'Perhaps to save the life of a fellow human being.'

'Isn't that rather a highly coloured story?'

'Oh yes. Quite easily not believed. Do you believe it?'

He looked at her thoughtfully. 'You know what you're talking like? A beautiful spy in a thriller.'

'Yes, perhaps. But I am not beautiful.'

'And you're not a spy?'

'I might be so described, perhaps. I have certain information. Information I want to preserve. You will have to take my word for it, it is information that would be valuable to your country.'

'Don't you think you're being rather absurd?'

'Yes I do. If this was written down it would look absurd. But so many absurd things are true, aren't they?'

He looked at her again. She was very like Pamela. Her voice, although foreign in intonation, was like Pamela's. What she proposed was ridiculous, absurd, quite impossible, and probably dangerous. Dangerous to him. Unfortunately, though, that was what attracted him. To have the nerve to suggest such a thing to him! What would come of it all? It would be interesting, certainly, to find out.

'What do I get out of it?' he said. 'That's what I'd like to know.'

She looked at him consideringly. 'Diversion,' she said. 'Something out of the everyday happenings? An antidote to boredom, perhaps. We've not got very long. It's up to you.'

'And what happens to *your* passport? Do I have to buy myself a wig, if they sell such a thing, at the counter? Do I have to impersonate a female?'

'No. There's no question of exchanging places. You have been robbed and drugged but you remain yourself. Make up your mind. There isn't long. Time is passing very quickly. I have got to do my own transformation.'

'You win,' he said. 'One mustn't refuse the unusual, if it is offered to one.'

'I hoped you might feel that way, but it was a toss-up.'

From his pocket Stafford Nye took out his passport. He slipped it into the outer pocket of the cloak he had been wearing. He rose to his feet, yawned, looked round him, looked at his watch, and strolled over to the counter where various goods were displayed for sale. He did not even look back. He bought a paperback book and fingered some small woolly animals, a suitable gift for some child. Finally he chose a panda. He looked round the lounge, came back to where he had been sitting. The cloak was gone and so had the girl. A half glass of beer was on the table still. Here, he thought, is where I take the risk. He picked up the glass, moved away a little, and drank it. Not quickly. Quite slowly. It tasted much the same as it had tasted before.

'Now I wonder,' said Sir Stafford. 'Now I wonder.'

He walked across the lounge to a far corner. There was a somewhat noisy family sitting there, laughing and talking together. He sat down near them, yawned, let his head fall back on the edge of the cushion. A flight was announced leaving for Teheran. A large number of passengers got up and went to queue by the requisite numbered gate. The lounge still remained half full. He opened his paperback book. He yawned again. He was really sleepy now, yes, he was very sleepy . . . He must just think out where it was best for him to go off to sleep. Somewhere where he could remain . . .

Trans-European Airways announced the departure of their plane, Flight 309 for London.

Quite a good sprinkling of passengers rose to their feet to obey the summons. By this time though, more passengers had entered the transit lounge waiting for other planes. Announcements followed as to fog at Geneva and other disabilities of travel. A slim man of middle height wearing a dark blue cloak with its red lining showing and with a hood drawn up over a close-cropped head, not noticeably more untidy than many of the heads of young men nowadays, walked across the floor to take his place in the queue for the plane. Showing a boarding ticket, he passed out through gate No. 9.

More announcements followed. Swissair flying to Zürich. BEA to Athens and Cyprus – And then a different type of announcement.

'Will Miss Daphne Theodofanous, passenger to Geneva, kindly come to the flight desk. Plane to Geneva is delayed owing to fog. Passengers will travel by way of Athens. The aeroplane is now ready to leave.'

Other announcements followed dealing with passengers to Japan, to Egypt, to South Africa, air lines spanning the world. Mr Sidney Cook, passenger to South Africa, was urged to come to the flight desk where there was a message for him. Daphne Theodofanous was called for again.

'This is the last call before the departure of Flight 309.'

In a corner of the lounge a little girl was looking up at a man in a dark suit who was fast asleep, his head resting against the cushion of the red settee. In his hand he held a small woolly panda.

The little girl's hand stretched out towards the panda. Her mother said:

'Now, Joan, don't touch that. The poor gentleman's asleep.'

'Where is he going?'

'Perhaps he's going to Australia too,' said her mother, 'like we are.'

'Has he got a little girl like me?'

'I think he must have,' said her mother.

The little girl sighed and looked at the panda again. Sir Stafford Nye continued to sleep. He was dreaming that he was trying to shoot a leopard. A very dangerous animal, he was saying to the safari guide who was accompanying him. 'A very dangerous animal, so I've always heard. You can't trust a leopard.'

The dream switched at that moment, as dreams have a habit of doing, and he was having tea with his Great-Aunt Matilda, and trying to make her hear. She was deafer than ever! He had not heard any of the announcements except the first one for Miss Daphne Theodofanous. The little girl's mother said:

'I've always wondered, you know, about a passenger that's missing. Nearly always, whenever you go anywhere by air, you hear it. Somebody they can't find. Somebody who hasn't heard the call or isn't on the plane or something like that. I always wonder who it is and what they're doing, and *why* they haven't come. I suppose this Miss What's-a-name or whatever it is will just have missed her plane. What will they do with her then?'

Nobody was able to answer her question because nobody had the proper information.

11. LONDON

Sir Stafford Nye's flat was a very pleasant one. It looked out upon Green Park. He switched on the coffee percolator and went to see what the post had left him this morning. It did not appear to have left him anything very interesting. He sorted through the letters, a bill or two, a receipt and letters with rather uninteresting postmarks. He shuffled them together and placed them on the table where some mail was already lying, accumulating from the last two days. He'd have to get down to things soon, he supposed. His secretary would be coming in some time or other this afternoon.

He went back to the kitchen, poured coffee into a cup and brought it to the table. He picked up the two or three letters that he had opened late last night when he arrived. One of them he referred to, and smiled a little as he read it.

'Eleven-thirty,' he said. 'Quite a suitable time. I wonder now. I expect I'd better just think things over, and get prepared for Chetwynd.'

Somebody pushed something through the letter-box. He went out into the hall and got the morning paper. There was very little news in the paper. A political crisis, an item of foreign news which might have been disquieting, but he didn't think it was. It was merely a journalist letting off steam and trying to make things rather more important than they were. Must give the people something to read. A girl had been strangled in the park. Girls were always being strangled. One a day, he thought callously. No child had been kidnapped or raped this morning. That was a nice surprise. He made himself a piece of toast and drank his coffee.

Later, he went out of the building, down into the street, and walked through the park in the direction of Whitehall. He was smiling to himself. Life, he felt, was rather good this morning. He began to think about Chetwynd. Chetwynd was a silly fool if there ever was one. A good façade, important-seeming, and a nicely suspicious mind. He'd rather enjoy talking to Chetwynd.

He reached Whitehall a comfortable seven minutes late. That was only due to his own importance compared with that of Chetwynd, he thought. He walked into the room. Chetwynd was sitting behind his desk and had a lot of papers on it and a secretary there. He was looking properly important, as he always did when he could make it.

'Hullo, Nye,' said Chetwynd, smiling all over his impressively handsome face. 'Glad to be back? How was Malaya?'

'Hot,' said Stafford Nye.

'Yes. Well, I suppose it always is. You meant atmospherically, I suppose, not politically?'

'Oh, purely atmospherically,' said Stafford Nye.

He accepted a cigarette and sat down.

'Get any results to speak of?'

'Oh, hardly. Not what you'd call results. I've sent in my report. All a lot of talky-talky as usual. How's Lazenby?'

'Oh, a nuisance as he always is. He'll never change,' said Chetwynd.

'No, that would seem too much to hope for. I haven't served on anything with Bascombe before. He can be quite fun when he likes.'

'Can he? I don't know him very well. Yes. I suppose he can.'

'Well, well, well. No other news, I suppose?'

'No, nothing. Nothing I think that would interest you.'

'You didn't mention in your letter quite why you wanted to see me.'

'Oh, just to go over a few things, that's all. You know, in case you'd brought any special dope home with you. Anything we ought to be prepared for, you know. Questions in the House. Anything like that.'

'Yes, of course.'

'Came home by air, didn't you? Had a bit of trouble, I gather.'

Stafford Nye put on the face he had been determined to put on beforehand. It was slightly rueful, with a faint tinge of annoyance.

'Oh, so you heard about that, did you?' he said. 'Silly business.'

'Yes. Yes, must have been.'

'Extraordinary,' said Stafford Nye, 'how things always get into the press. There was a paragraph in the stop press this morning.'

'You'd rather they wouldn't have, I suppose?'

'Well, makes me look a bit of an ass, doesn't it?' said Stafford Nye. 'Got to admit it. At my age too!'

'What happened exactly? I wondered if the report in the paper had been exaggerating.'

'Well, I suppose they made the most of it, that's all. You know what these journeys are. Damn boring. There was fog at Geneva so they had to re-route the plane. Then there was two hours' delay at Frankfurt.'

'Is that when it happened?'

'Yes. One's bored stiff in these airports. Planes coming, planes going. Tannoy going full steam ahead. Flight 302 leaving for Hong Kong, Flight 109 going to Ireland. This that and the other. People getting up, people leaving. And you just sit there yawning.'

'What happened exactly?' said Chetwynd.

'Well, I'd got a drink in front of me, Pilsner as a matter of fact, then I thought I'd got to get something else to read. I'd read everything I'd got with me so I went over to the counter and bought some wretched paperback or other. Detective story, I think it was, and I bought a woolly animal for one of my nieces. Then I came back, finished my drink, opened my paperback and then I went to sleep.'

'Yes, I see. You went to sleep.'

'Well, a very natural thing to do, isn't it? I suppose they called my flight but if they did I didn't hear it. I didn't hear it apparently for the best of reasons. I'm capable of going to sleep in an airport any time but I'm also capable of hearing an announcement that concerns me. This time I didn't. When I woke up, or came to, however you like to put it, I was having a bit of medical attention. Somebody apparently had dropped a Mickey Finn or something or other in my drink. Must have done it when I was away getting the paperback.'

'Rather an extraordinary thing to happen, wasn't it?' said Chetwynd.

'Well, it's never happened to me before,' said Stafford Nye. 'I hope it never will again. It makes you feel an awful fool, you know. Besides having a hangover. There was a doctor and some nurse creature, or something. Anyway, there was no great harm done apparently. My wallet had been pinched with some money in it and my passport. It was awkward of course. Fortunately, I hadn't got much money. My travellers' cheques were in an inner pocket. There always has to be a bit of red tape and all that if you lose your passport. Anyway, I had letters and things and identification was not difficult. And in due course things were squared up and I resumed my flight.'

'Still, very annoying for you,' said Chetwynd. 'A person of your status, I mean.' His tone was disapproving.

'Yes,' said Stafford Nye. 'It doesn't show me in a very good light, does it? I mean, not as bright as a fellow of my – er – status ought to be.' The idea seemed to amuse him.

'Does this often happen, did you find out?'

'I don't think it's a matter of general occurrence. It could be. I suppose any person with a pick-pocket trend could notice a fellow asleep and slip a hand into a pocket, and if he's accomplished in his profession, get hold of a wallet or a pocket-book or something like that, and hope for some luck.'

'Pretty awkward to lose a passport.'

'Yes, I shall have to put in for another one now. Make a lot of explanations, I suppose. As I say, the whole thing's a damn silly business. And let's face it, Chetwynd, it doesn't show me in a very favourable light, does it?'

'Oh, not your fault, my dear boy, not your fault. It could happen to anybody, anybody at all.'

'Very nice of you to say so,' said Stafford Nye, smiling at him agreeably. 'Teach me a sharp lesson, won't it?'

'You don't think anyone wanted *your* passport specially?'

'I shouldn't think so,' said Stafford Nye. 'Why should they want my passport. Unless it was a matter of someone who wished to annoy me and that hardly seems likely. Or somebody who took a fancy to my passport photo – and that seems even less likely!'

'Did you see anyone you knew at this – where did you say you were – Frankfurt?'

'No, no. Nobody at all.'

'Talk to anyone?'

'Not particularly. Said something to a nice fat woman who'd got a small child she was trying to amuse. Came from Wigan, I think. Going to Australia. Don't remember anybody else.'

'You're sure?'

'There was some woman or other who wanted to know what she did if she wanted to study archaeology in Egypt. Said I didn't know anything about that. I told her she'd better go and ask the British Museum. And I had a word or two with a man who I think was an anti-vivisectionist. Very passionate about it.'

'One always feels,' said Chetwynd, 'that there might be something *behind* things like this.'

'Things like what?'

'Well, things like what happened to you.'

'I don't see what can be behind this,' said Sir Stafford. 'I daresay journalists could make up some story, they're so clever at that sort of thing. Still, it's a silly business. For goodness' sake, let's forget it. I suppose now it's been mentioned in the press, all my friends will start asking me about it. How's old Leyland? What's he up to nowadays? I heard one or two things about him out there. Leyland always talks a bit too much.'

The two men talked amiable shop for ten minutes or so, then Sir Stafford got up and went out.

'I've got a lot of things to do this morning,' he said. 'Presents to buy for my relations. The trouble is that if one goes to Malaya, all one's relations expect you to bring exotic presents to them. I'll go round to Liberty's, I think. They have a nice stock of Eastern goods there.'

He went out cheerfully, nodding to a couple of men he knew in the corridor outside. After he had gone, Chetwynd spoke through the telephone to his secretary.

'Ask Colonel Munro if he can come to me.'

Colonel Munro came in, bringing another tall middle-aged man with him.

'Don't know whether you know Horsham,' he said, 'in Security.'

'Think I've met you,' said Chetwynd.

'Nye's just left you, hasn't he?' said Colonel Munro. 'Anything in this story about Frankfurt? Anything, I mean, that we ought to take any notice of?'

'Doesn't seem so,' said Chetwynd. 'He's a bit put out about it. Thinks it makes him look a silly ass. Which it does, of course.'

The man called Horsham nodded his head. 'That's the way he takes it, is it?'

'Well, he tried to put a good face upon it,' said Chetwynd.

'All the same, you know,' said Horsham, 'he's not really a silly ass, is he?'

Chetwynd shrugged his shoulders. 'These things happen,' he said.

'I know,' said Colonel Munro, 'yes, yes, I know. All the same, well, I've always felt in some ways that Nye is a bit unpredictable. That in some ways, you know, he mightn't be really *sound* in his views.'

The man called Horsham spoke. 'Nothing against him,' he said. 'Nothing at all as far as *we* know.'

'Oh, I didn't mean there was. I didn't mean that at all,' said Chetwynd. 'It's just – how shall I put it? – he's not always very serious about things.'

Mr Horsham had a moustache. He found it useful to have a moustache. It concealed moments when he found it difficult to avoid smiling.

'He's not a stupid man,' said Munro. 'Got brains, you know. You don't think that – well, I mean you don't think there could be anything at all doubtful about this?'

'On his part? It doesn't seem so.'

'You've been into it all, Horsham?'

'Well, we haven't had very much time yet. But as far as it goes it's all right. But his passport *was* used.'

'Used? In what way?'

'It passed through Heathrow.'

'You mean someone represented himself as Sir Stafford Nye?'

'No, no,' said Horsham, 'not in so many words. We could hardly hope for that. It went through with other passports. There was no alarm out, you know. He hadn't even woken up, I gather, at that time, from the dope or whatever it was he was given. He was still at Frankfurt.'

'But someone could have stolen that passport and come on the plane and so got into England?'

'Yes,' said Munro, 'that's the presumption. Either someone took a wallet which had money in it and a passport, or else someone wanted a passport and settled on Sir Stafford Nye as a convenient person to take it from. A drink was waiting on a table, put a pinch in that, wait till the man went off to sleep, take the passport and chance it.'

'But after all, they look at a passport. Must have seen it wasn't the right man,' said Chetwynd.

'Well, there must have been a certain resemblance, certainly,' said Horsham. 'But it isn't as though there was any notice of his being missing, any special attention drawn to that particular passport in any way. A large crowd comes through on a plane that's overdue. A man looks reasonably like the photograph in his passport. That's all. Brief glance, handed back, pass it on. Anyway what they're looking for usually is the *foreigners* that are coming in, not the British lot. Dark hair, dark blue eyes, clean shaven, five foot ten or whatever it is. That's about all you want to see. Not on a list of undesirable aliens or anything like that.'

'I know, I know. Still, you'd say if anybody wanted merely to pinch a wallet or some money or that, they wouldn't use the passport, would they. Too much risk.'

'Yes,' said Horsham. 'Yes, that is the interesting part of it. Of course,' he said, 'we're making investigations, asking a few questions here and there.'

'And what's your own opinion?'

'I wouldn't like to say yet,' said Horsham. 'It takes a little time, you know. One can't hurry things.'

'They're all the same,' said Colonel Munro, when Horsham had left the room. 'They never will tell you anything, those damned security people. If they think they're on the trail of anything, they won't admit it.'

'Well, that's natural,' said Chetwynd, 'because they might be wrong.'

It seemed a typically political view.

'Horsham's a pretty good man,' said Munro. 'They think very highly of him at headquarters. He's not likely to be wrong.'

111. THE MAN FROM THE CLEANERS

Sir Stafford Nye returned to his flat. A large woman bounced out of the small kitchen with welcoming words.

'See you got back all right, sir. Those nasty planes. You never know, do you?'

'Quite true, Mrs Worrit,' said Sir Stafford Nye. 'Two hours late, the plane was.'

'Same as cars, aren't they,' said Mrs Worrit. 'I mean, you never know, do you, what's going to go wrong with *them*. Only it's more worrying, so to speak, being up in the air, isn't it? Can't just draw up to the kerb, not the same way, can you? I mean, there you are. I wouldn't go by one myself, not if it was ever so.' She went on, 'I've ordered in a few things. I hope that's all right. Eggs, butter, coffee, tea – ' She ran off the words with the loquacity of a Near Eastern guide showing a Pharaoh's palace. 'There,' said Mrs Worrit, pausing to take breath, 'I think that's all as you're likely to want. I've ordered the French mustard.'

'Not Dijon, is it? They always try and give you Dijon.'

'I don't know who *he* was, but it's Esther Dragon, the one you like, isn't it?'

'Quite right,' said Sir Stafford, 'you're a wonder.'

Mrs Worrit looked pleased. She retired into the kitchen again, as Sir Stafford Nye put his hand on his bedroom door handle preparatory to going into the bedroom.

'All right to give your clothes to the gentleman what called for them, I suppose, sir? You hadn't said or left word or anything like that.'

'What clothes?' said Sir Stafford Nye, pausing.

'Two suits, it was, the gentleman said as called for them. Twiss and Bonywork it was, think that's the same name as called before. We'd had a bit of a dispute with the White Swan Laundry if I remember rightly.'

'Two suits?' said Sir Stafford Nye. 'Which suits?'

'Well, there was the one you travelled home in, sir. I made out that would be one of them. I wasn't quite so sure about the other, but there was the blue pinstripe that you didn't leave no orders about when you went away. It could do with cleaning, and there was a repair wanted doing to the right-hand cuff, but I didn't like to take it on myself while you were away. I never likes to do that,' said Mrs Worrit with an air of palpable virtue.

'So the chap, whoever he was, took those suits away?'

'I hope I didn't do wrong, sir.' Mrs Worrit became worried.

'I don't mind the blue pinstripe. I daresay it's all for the best. The suit I came home in, well – '

'It's a bit thin, that suit, sir, for this time of year, you know, sir. All right for those parts as you've been in where it's hot. And it could do with a clean. He said as you'd rung up about them. That's what the gentleman said as called for them.'

'Did he go into my room and pick them out himself?'

'Yes, sir. I thought that was best.'

'Very interesting,' said Sir Stafford. 'Yes, very interesting.'

He went into his bedroom and looked round it. It was neat and tidy. The bed was made, the hand of Mrs Worrit was apparent, his electric razor was on charge, the things on the dressing-table were neatly arranged.

He went to the wardrobe and looked inside. He looked in the drawers of the tallboy that stood against the wall near the window. It was all quite tidy. It was tidier indeed than it should have been. He had done a little unpacking last night and what little he had done had been of a cursory nature. He had thrown underclothing and various odds and ends in the appropriate drawer but he had not arranged them neatly. He would have done that himself either today or tomorrow. He would not have expected Mrs Worrit to do it for him. He expected her merely to keep things as she found them. Then, when he came back from abroad, there would be a time for rearrangements and readjustments because of climate and other matters. So someone had looked round here, someone had taken out drawers, looked through them quickly, hurriedly, had replaced things, partly because of his hurry, more tidily and neatly than he should have done. A quick careful job and he had gone away with two suits and a plausible explanation. One suit obviously worn by Sir Stafford when travelling and a suit of thin material which might have been one taken abroad and brought home. So why?

'Because,' said Sir Stafford thoughtfully, to himself, 'because somebody was looking for something. But what? And who? And also perhaps why?' Yes, it was interesting.

He sat down in a chair and thought about it. Presently his eyes strayed to the table by the bed on which sat, rather pertly, a small furry panda. It started a train of thought. He went to the telephone and rang a number.

'That you, Aunt Matilda?' he said. 'Stafford here.'

'Ah, my dear boy, so you're back. I'm so glad. I read in the paper they'd got cholera in Malaya yesterday, at least I think it was Malaya. I always get so mixed up with those places. I hope you're coming to see me soon? Don't pretend you're busy. You can't be busy all the time. One really only accepts that sort of thing from tycoons, people in industry, you know, in the middle of mergers and take-overs. I never know what it all really means. It used to mean doing your work properly but now it means things all tied up with atom bombs and factories in concrete,' said Aunt Matilda, rather wildly. 'And those terrible computers that get all one's figures wrong, to say nothing of making them the wrong shape. Really, they have made life so difficult for us nowadays. You wouldn't believe the things they've done to my bank account. And to my postal address too. Well, I suppose I've lived too long.'

'Don't you believe it! All right if I come down next week?'

'Come down tomorrow if you like. I've got the vicar coming to dinner, but I can easily put him off.'

'Oh, look here, no need to do that.'

'Yes there is, every need. He's a most irritating man and he wants a new organ too. This one does quite well as it is. I mean the trouble is with the organist, really, not the organ. An absolutely abominable musician. The vicar's sorry for him because he lost his mother whom he was very fond of. But really, being fond of your mother doesn't make you play the organ any better, does it? I mean, one has to look at things as they are.'

'Quite right. It will have to be next week – I've got a few things to see to. How's Sybil?'

'Dear child! Very naughty but such fun.'

'I brought her home a woolly panda,' said Sir Stafford Nye.

'Well, that was very nice of you, dear.'

'I hope she'll like it,' said Sir Stafford, catching the panda's eye and feeling slightly nervous.

'Well, at any rate, she's got very good manners,' said Aunt Matilda, which seemed a somewhat doubtful answer, the meaning of which Sir Stafford did not quite appreciate.

Aunt Matilda suggested likely trains for next week with the warning that they very often did not run, or changed their plans, and also commanded that he should bring her down a Camembert cheese and half a Stilton.

'Impossible to get anything down here now. Our own grocer – such a nice man, so thoughtful and such good taste in what we all liked – turned suddenly into a supermarket, six times the size, all rebuilt, baskets and wire trays to carry round and try to fill up with things you don't want and mothers always losing their babies, and crying and having hysterics. Most exhausting. Well, I'll be expecting you, dear boy.' She rang off.

The telephone rang again at once.

'Hullo? Stafford? Eric Pugh here. Heard you were back from Malaya – what about dining tonight?'

'Like to very much.'

'Good – Limpits Club – eight-fifteen?'

Mrs Worrit panted into the room as Sir Stafford replaced the receiver.

'A gentleman downstairs wanting to see you, sir,' she

said. 'At least I mean, I suppose he's that. Anyway he said he was sure you wouldn't mind.'

'What's his name?'

'Horsham, sir, like the place on the way to Brighton.'

'Horsham.' Sir Stafford Nye was a little surprised.

He went out of his bedroom, down a half flight of stairs that led to the big sitting-room on the lower floor. Mrs Worrit had made no mistake. Horsham it was, looking as he had looked half an hour ago, stalwart, trustworthy, cleft chin, rubicund cheeks, bushy grey moustache and a general air of imperturbability.

'Hope you don't mind,' he said agreeably, rising to his feet.

'Hope I don't mind what?' said Sir Stafford Nye.

'Seeing me again so soon. We met in the passage outside Mr Gordon Chetwynd's door – if you remember?'

'No objections at all,' said Sir Stafford Nye.

He pushed a cigarette-box along the table.

'Sit down. Something forgotten, something left unsaid?'

'Very nice man, Mr Chetwynd,' said Horsham. 'We've got him quietened down, I think. He and Colonel Munro. They're a bit upset about it all, you know. About you, I mean.'

'Really?'

Sir Stafford Nye sat down too. He smiled, he smoked, and he looked thoughtfully at Henry Horsham. 'And where do we go from here?' he asked.

'I was just wondering if I might ask, without undue curiosity, where you're going from here?'

'Delighted to tell you,' said Sir Stafford Nye. 'I'm going to stay with an aunt of mine, Lady Matilda Cleckheaton. I'll give you the address if you like.'

'I know it,' said Henry Horsham. 'Well, I expect that's a very good idea. She'll be glad to see you've come home safely all right. Might have been a near thing, mightn't it?'

'Is that what Colonel Munro thinks and Mr Chetwynd?'

'Well, you know what it is, sir,' said Horsham. 'You know well enough. They're always in a state, gentlemen in that department. They're not sure whether they trust you or not.'

'Trust me?' said Sir Stafford Nye in an offended voice. 'What do you mean by that, Mr Horsham?'

Mr Horsham was not taken aback. He merely grinned.

'You see,' he said, 'you've got a reputation for not taking things seriously.'

'Oh. I thought you meant I was a fellow traveller or a convert to the wrong side. Something of that kind.'

'Oh no, sir, they just don't think you're serious. They think you like having a bit of a joke now and again.'

'One cannot go entirely through life taking oneself and other people seriously,' said Sir Stafford Nye, disapprovingly.

'No. But you took a pretty good risk, as I've said before, didn't you?'

'I wonder if I know in the least what you are talking about.'

'I'll tell you. Things go wrong, sir, sometimes, and they don't always go wrong because people have made them go wrong. What you might call the Almighty takes a hand, or the other gentleman – the one with the tail, I mean.'

Sir Stafford Nye was slightly diverted.

'Are you referring to fog at Geneva?' he said.

'Exactly, sir. There was fog at Geneva and that upset people's plans. Somebody was in a nasty hole.'

'Tell me all about it,' said Sir Stafford Nye. 'I really would like to know.'

'Well, a passenger was missing when that plane of yours left Frankfurt yesterday. You'd drunk your beer and you were sitting in a corner snoring nicely and comfortably by yourself. One passenger didn't report and they called her and they called her again. In the end, presumably, the plane left without her.'

'Ah. And what had happened to her?'

'It would be interesting to know. In any case, your passport arrived at Heathrow even if you didn't.'

'And where is it now? Am I supposed to have got it?'

'No. I don't think so. That would be rather too quick work. Good reliable stuff, that dope. Just right, if I may say so. It put you out and it didn't produce any particularly bad effects.'

'It gave me a very nasty hangover,' said Sir Stafford.

'Ah well, you can't avoid that. Not in the circumstances.'

'What would have happened,' Sir Stafford asked, 'since you seem to know all about everything, if I had refused to accept the proposition that may – I will only say may – have been put up to me?'

'It's quite possible that it would have been curtains for Mary Ann.'

'Mary Ann? Who's Mary Ann?'

'Miss Daphne Theodofanous.'

'That's the name I do seem to have heard – being summoned as a missing traveller?'

'Yes, that's the name she was travelling under. We call her Mary Ann.'

'Who is she – just as a matter of interest?'

'In her own line she's more or less the tops.'

'And what is her line? Is she ours or is she theirs, if you know who "theirs" is? I must say I find a little difficulty myself when making my mind up about that.'

'Yes, it's not so easy, is it? What with the Chinese and the Russkies and the rather queer crowd that's behind all the student troubles and the New Mafia and the rather odd lot in South America. And the nice little nest of financiers who seem to have got something funny up their sleeves. Yes, it's not easy to say.'

'Mary Ann,' said Sir Stafford Nye thoughtfully. 'It seems a curious name to have for her if her real one is Daphne Theodofanous.'

'Well, her mother's Greek, her father was an Englishman, and her grandfather was an Austrian subject.'

'What would have happened if I hadn't made her a – loan of a certain garment?'

'She might have been killed.'

'Come, come. Not really?'

'We're worried about the airport at Heathrow. Things have happened there lately, things that need a bit of explaining. If the plane had gone via Geneva as planned, it would have been all right. She'd have had full protection all arranged. But this other way – there wouldn't have been time to arrange anything and you don't know who's who always, nowadays. Everyone's playing a double game or a treble or a quadruple one.'

'You alarm me,' said Sir Stafford Nye. 'But she's all right, is she? Is that what you're telling me?'

'I hope she's all right. We haven't heard anything to the contrary.'

'If it's any help to you,' said Sir Stafford Nye, 'somebody called here this morning while I was out talking to my little pals in Whitehall. He represented that I telephoned a firm of cleaners and he removed the suit that I wore yesterday, and also another suit. Of course it may have been merely that he took a fancy to the other suit, or he may have made a practice of collecting various gentlemen's suitings who have recently returned from abroad. Or – well, perhaps you've got an "or" to add?'

'He might have been looking for something.'

'Yes, I think he was. Somebody's been looking for something. All very nice and tidily arranged again. Not the way I left it. All right, he was looking for something. What was he looking for?'

'I'm not sure myself,' said Horsham, slowly. 'I wish I was. There's something going on – somewhere. There are bits of it sticking out, you know, like a badly done up parcel. You get a peep here and a peep there. One moment you think it's going on at the Bayreuth Festival and the next minute you think it's tucking out of a South American estancia and then you get a bit of a lead in the USA. There's a lot of nasty business going on in different places, working up to something. Maybe politics, maybe something quite different from politics. It's probably money.' He added: 'You know Mr Robinson, don't you? Or rather Mr Robinson knows you, I think he said.'

'Robinson?' Sir Stafford Nye considered. 'Robinson. Nice English name.' He looked across to Horsham. 'Large, yellow face?' he said. 'Fat? Finger in financial pies generally?' He asked: 'Is he, too, on the side of the angels – is that what you're telling me?'

'I don't know about angels,' said Henry Horsham. 'He's pulled us out of a hole in this country more than once. People like Mr Chetwynd don't go for him much. Think he's too expensive, I suppose. Inclined to be a mean man, Mr Chetwynd. A great one for making economies in the wrong place.'

'One used to say "Poor but honest",' said Sir Stafford Nye thoughtfully. 'I take it that you would put it differently. You would describe our Mr Robinson as expensive but honest. Or shall we put it, honest but expensive.' He sighed. 'I wish you could tell me what all this is about,' he said plaintively. 'Here I seem to be mixed up in something and no idea what it is.' He looked at Henry Horsham hopefully, but Horsham shook his head.

'None of us knows. Not exactly,' he said.

'What am I supposed to have got hidden here that someone comes fiddling and looking for?'

'Frankly, I haven't the least idea, Sir Stafford.'

'Well, that's a pity because I haven't either.'

'As far as *you* know you haven't got anything. Nobody gave you anything to keep, to take anywhere, to look after?'

'Nothing whatsoever. If you mean Mary Ann, she said she wanted her life saved, that's all.'

'And unless there's a paragraph in the evening papers, you *have* saved her life.'

'It seems rather the end of the chapter, doesn't it? A pity. My curiosity is rising. I find I want to know very much what's going to happen next. All you people seem very pessimistic.'

'Frankly, we are. Things are going badly in this country. Can you wonder?'

'I know what you mean. I sometimes wonder myself –'

IV. DINNER WITH ERIC

'Do you mind if I tell you something, old man?' said Eric Pugh.

Sir Stafford Nye looked at him. He had known Eric Pugh for a good many years. They had not been close friends. Old Eric, or so Sir Stafford thought, was rather a boring friend. He was, on the other hand, faithful. And he was the type of man who, though not amusing, had a knack of knowing things. People said things to him and he remembered what they said and stored them up. Sometimes he could push out a useful bit of information.

'Come back from that Malay Conference, haven't you?'

'Yes,' said Sir Stafford.

'Anything particular turn up there?'

'Just the usual,' said Sir Stafford.

'Oh. I wondered if something had – well, you know what I mean. Anything had occurred to put the cat among the pigeons.'

'What, at the Conference? No, just painfully predictable. Everyone said just what you thought they'd say only they said it unfortunately at rather greater length than you could have imagined possible. I don't know why I go on these things.'

Eric Pugh made a rather tedious remark or two as to what the Chinese were really up to.

'I don't think they're really up to anything,' said Sir Stafford. 'All the usual rumours, you know, about the diseases poor old Mao has got and who's intriguing against him and why.'

'And what about the Arab-Israeli business?'

'That's proceeding according to plan also. Their plan, that is to say. And anyway, what's that got to do with Malaya?'

'Well, I didn't really mean so much Malaya.'

'You're looking rather like the Mock Turtle,' said Sir Stafford Nye. ' "Soup of the evening, beautiful soup." Wherefore this gloom?'

'Well, I just wondered if you'd – you'll forgive me, won't you? – I mean you haven't done anything to blot your copybook, have you, in any way?'

'Me?' said Sir Stafford, looking highly surprised.

'Well, you know what you're like, Staff. You like giving people a jolt sometimes, don't you?'

'I have behaved impeccably of late,' said Sir Stafford. 'What have you been hearing about me?'

'I hear there was some trouble about something that happened in a plane on your way home.'

'Oh? Who did you hear that from?'

'Well, you know, I saw old Cartison.'

'Terrible old bore. Always imagining things that haven't happened.'

'Yes, I know. I know he is like that. But he was just saying that somebody or other – Winterton, at least – seemed to think you'd been up to something.'

'Up to something? I wish I had,' said Sir Stafford Nye.

'There's some espionage racket going on somewhere and he got a bit worried about certain people.'

'What do they think I am – another Philby, something of that kind?'

'You know you're very unwise sometimes in the things you say, the things you make jokes about.'

'It's very hard to resist sometimes,' his friend told him. 'All these politicians and diplomats and the rest of them. They're so bloody solemn. You'd like to give them a bit of a stir up now and again.'

'Your sense of fun is very distorted, my boy. It really is. I worry about you sometimes. They wanted to ask you some questions about something that happened on the flight back and they seem to think that you didn't, well – that perhaps you didn't exactly speak the truth about it all.'

'Ah, that's what they think, is it? Interesting. I think I must work that up a bit.'

'Now don't do anything rash.'

'I must have my moments of fun sometimes.'

'Look here, old fellow, you don't want to go and ruin your career just by indulging your sense of humour.'

'I am quickly coming to the conclusion that there is nothing so boring as having a career.'

'I know, I know. You are always inclined to take that point of view, and you haven't got on as far as you ought to have, you know. You were in the running for Vienna at one time. I don't like to see you muck up things.'

'I am behaving with the utmost sobriety and virtue, I assure you,' said Sir Stafford Nye. He added, 'Cheer up, Eric. You're a good friend, but really, I'm not guilty of fun and games.'

Eric shook his head doubtfully.

It was a fine evening. Sir Stafford walked home across Green Park. As he crossed the road in Birdcage Walk, a car leaping down the street missed him by a few inches. Sir Stafford was an athletic man. His leap took him safely on to the pavement. The car disappeared down the street. He wondered. Just for a moment he could have sworn that that car had deliberately tried to run him down. An interesting thought. First his flat had been searched, and now he himself might have been marked down. Probably a mere coincidence. And yet, in the course of his life, some of which had been spent in wild neighbourhoods and places, Sir Stafford Nye had come in contact with danger. He knew, as it were, the touch and feel and smell of danger. He felt it now. Someone, somewhere was gunning for him. But why? For what reason? As far as he knew, he had not stuck his neck out in any way. He wondered.

He let himself into his flat and picked up the mail that lay on the floor inside. Nothing much. A couple of bills and copy of *Lifeboat* periodical. He threw the bills on to his desk and put a finger through the wrapper of *Lifeboat*.

It was a cause to which he occasionally contributed. He turned the pages without much attention because he was still absorbed in what he was thinking. Then he stopped the action of his fingers abruptly. Something was taped between two of the pages. Taped with adhesive tape. He looked at it closely. It was his passport returned to him unexpectedly in this fashion. He tore it free and looked at it. The last stamp on it was the arrival stamp at Heathrow the day before. She had used his passport, getting back here safely, and had chosen this way to return it to him. Where was she now? He would like to know.

He wondered if he would ever see her again. Who was she? Where had she gone, and why? It was like waiting for the second act of a play. Indeed, he felt the first act had hardly been played yet. What had he seen? An old-fashioned curtain-raiser, perhaps. A girl who had ridiculously wanted to dress herself up and pass herself off as of the male sex, who had passed the passport control oι Heathrow without attracting suspicion of any kind to herself and who had now disappeared through that gateway into London. No, he would probably never see her again. It annoyed him. But why, he thought, why do I want to? She wasn't particularly attractive, she wasn't anything. No, that wasn't quite true. She was something, or someone, or she could not have induced him, with no particular persuasion, with no overt sex stimulation, nothing except a plain demand for help, to do what she wanted. A demand from one human being to another human being because, or so she had intimated, not precisely in words, but nevertheless it was what she *had* intimated, she knew people and she recognized in him a man who was willing to take a risk to help another human being. And he had taken a risk, too, thought Sir Stafford Nye. She could have put anything in that beer glass of his. He could have been found, if she had so willed it, found as a dead body in a seat tucked away in the corner of a departure lounge in an airport. And if she had, as no doubt she must have had, a knowledgeable recourse to drugs, his death might have been passed off as an attack of heart trouble due to altitude or difficult pressurizing – something or other like that. Oh well, why think about it? He wasn't likely to see her again and he was annoyed.

Yes, he was annoyed, and he didn't like being annoyed. He considered the matter for some minutes. Then he wrote out an advertisement, to be repeated three times. '*Passenger to Frankfurt. November 3rd. Please communicate with fellow traveller to London.*' No more than that. Either she would or she wouldn't. If it ever came to her eyes she would know by whom that advertisement had been inserted. She had had his passport, she knew his name. She could look him up. He might hear from her. He might not. Probably not. If not, the curtain-raiser would remain a curtain-raiser, a silly little play that received late-comers to the theatre and diverted them until the real business of the evening began. Very useful in pre-war times. In all probability, though, he would not hear from her again and one of the reasons might be that she might have accomplished whatever it was she had come to do in London, and have now left the country once more, flying abroad to Geneva, or the Middle East, or to Russia or to China or to South America, or to the United States. And why, thought Sir Stafford, do I include South America? There must be a reason. She had not mentioned South America. Nobody had mentioned South America. Except Horsham, that was true. And even Horsham had only mentioned South America among a lot of other mentions.

On the following morning as he walked slowly homeward, after handing in his advertisement, along the pathway across St James's Park his eye picked out, half unseeing, the autumn flowers. The chrysanthemums looking by now stiff and leggy with their button tops of gold and bronze. Their smell came to him faintly, a rather goatlike smell, he had always thought, a smell that reminded him of hillsides in Greece. He must remember to keep his eye on the Personal Column. Not yet. Two or three days at least would have to pass before his own advertisement was put in and before there had been time for anyone to put in one in answer. He must not miss it if there was an answer because, after all, it was irritating not to know – not to have any idea what all this was about.

He tried to recall not the girl at the airport but his sister Pamela's face. A long time since her death. He remembered her. Of course he remembered her, but he could not somehow picture her face. It irritated him not to be able to do so. He had paused just when he was about to cross one of the roads. There was no traffic except for a car jigging slowly along with the solemn demeanour of a bored dowager. An elderly car, he thought. An old-fashioned Daimler limousine. He shook his shoulders. Why stand here in this idiotic way, lost in thought?

He took an abrupt step to cross the road and suddenly with surprising vigour the dowager limousine, as he had thought of it in his mind, accelerated. Accelerated with a sudden astonishing speed. It bore down on him with such swiftness that he only just had time to leap across on to the opposite pavement. It disappeared with a flash, turning round the curve of the road further on.

'I wonder,' said Sir Stafford to himself. 'Now I wonder. Could it be that there *is* someone that doesn't like me? Someone following me, perhaps, watching me take my way home, waiting for an opportunity?'

Colonel Pikeaway, his bulk sprawled out in his chair in the small room in Bloomsbury where he sat from ten to five with a short interval for lunch, was surrounded as usual by an atmosphere of thick cigar smoke; with his eyes closed, only an occasional blink showed that he was awake and not asleep. He seldom raised his head. Somebody had said that he looked like a cross between an ancient Buddha and a large blue frog, with perhaps, as some impudent youngster had added, just a touch of a bar sinister from a hippopotamus in his ancestry.

The gentle buzz of the intercom on his desk roused him. He blinked three times and opened his eyes. He stretched forth a rather weary-looking hand and picked up the receiver.

'Well?' he said.

His secretary's voice spoke.

'The Minister is here waiting to see you.'

'Is he now?' said Colonel Pikeaway. 'And what Minister is that? The Baptist minister from the church round the corner?'

'Oh no, Colonel Pikeaway, it's Sir George Packham.'

'Pity,' said Colonel Pikeaway, breathing asthmatically. 'Great pity. The Reverend McGill is far more amusing. There's a splendid touch of hell fire about him.'

'Shall I bring him in, Colonel Pikeaway?'

'I suppose he will expect to be brought in at once. Under Secretaries are far more touchy than Secretaries of State,' said Colonel Pikeaway gloomily. 'All these Ministers insist on coming in and having kittens all over the place.'

Sir George Packham was shown in. He coughed and wheezed. Most people did. The windows of the small room were tightly closed. Colonel Pikeaway reclined in his chair, completely smothered in cigar ash. The atmosphere was almost unbearable and the room was known in official circles as the 'small cat-house'.

'Ah, my dear fellow,' said Sir George, speaking briskly and cheerfully in a way that did not match his ascetic and sad appearance. 'Quite a long time since we've met, I think.'

'Sit down, sit down do,' said Pikeaway. 'Have a cigar?'

Sir George shuddered slightly.

'No, thank you,' he said, 'no, thanks very much.'

He looked hard at the windows. Colonel Pikeaway did not take the hint. Sir George cleared his throat and coughed again before saying:

'Er – I believe Horsham has been to see you.'

'Yes, Horsham's been and said his piece,' said Colonel Pikeaway, slowly allowing his eyes to close again.

'I thought it was the best way. I mean, that he should call upon you here. It's most important that things shouldn't get round anywhere.'

'Ah,' said Colonel Pikeaway, 'but they will, won't they?'

'I beg your pardon?'

'They will,' said Colonel Pikeaway.

'I don't know how much you – er – well, know about this last business.'

'We know everything here,' said Colonel Pikeaway. 'That's what we're for.'

'Oh – oh yes, yes certainly. About Sir S.N. – you know who I mean?'

'Recently a passenger from Frankfurt,' said Colonel Pikeaway.

'Most extraordinary business. Most extraordinary. One wonders – one really does not know, one can't begin to imagine . . .'

Colonel Pikeaway listened kindly.

'What is one to think?' pursued Sir George. 'Do you know him personally?'

'I've come across him once or twice,' said Colonel Pikeaway.

'One really cannot help wondering –'

Colonel Pikeaway subdued a yawn with some difficulty. He was rather tired of Sir George's thinking, wondering, and imagining. He had a poor opinion anyway of Sir George's process of thought. A cautious man, a man who could be relied upon to run his department in a cautious manner. Not a man of scintillating intellect. Perhaps, thought Colonel Pikeaway, all the better for that. At any rate, those who think and wonder and are not quite sure are reasonably safe in the place where God and the electors have put them.

'One cannot quite forget,' continued Sir George, 'the disillusionment we have suffered in the past.'

Colonel Pikeaway smiled kindly.

'Charleston, Conway and Courtauld,' he said. 'Fully trusted, vetted and approved of. All beginning with C, all crooked as sin.'

'Sometimes I wonder if we can trust anyone,' said Sir George unhappily.

'That's easy,' said Colonel Pikeaway, 'you can't.'

'Now take Stafford Nye,' said Sir George. 'Good family, excellent family, knew his father, his grandfather.'

'Often a slip-up in the third generation,' said Colonel Pikeaway.

The remark did not help Sir George.

'I cannot help doubting – I mean, sometimes he doesn't really seem serious.'

'Took my two nieces to see the châteaux of the Loire when I was a young man,' said Colonel Pikeaway unexpectedly. 'Man fishing on the bank. I had my fishing-rod with me, too. He said to me, "*Vous n'êtes pas un pecheur sérieux. Vous avez des femmes avec vous.*" '

'You mean you think Sir Stafford – ?'

'No, no, never been mixed up with women much. Irony's his trouble. Likes surprising people. He can't help liking to score off people.'

'Well, that's not very satisfactory, is it?'

'Why not?' said Colonel Pikeaway. 'Liking a private joke is much better than having some deal with a defector.'

'If one could feel that he was really sound. What would you say – your personal opinion?'

'Sound as a bell,' said Colonel Pikeaway. 'If a bell is sound. It makes a sound, but that's different, isn't it?' He smiled kindly. 'Shouldn't worry, if I were you,' he said.

Sir Stafford Nye pushed aside his cup of coffee. He picked up the newspaper, glancing over the headlines, then he turned it carefully to the page which gave Personal advertisements. He'd looked down that particular column for seven days now. It was disappointing but not surprising. Why on earth should he expect to find an answer? His eye went slowly down miscellaneous peculiarities which had always made that particular page rather fascinating in his eyes. They were not so strictly personal. Half of them or even more than half were disguised advertisements or offers of things for sale or wanted for sale. They should perhaps have been put under a different heading but they had found their way here considering that they were more likely to catch the eye that way. They included one or two of the hopeful variety.

> 'Young man who objects to hard work and who would like an easy life would be glad to undertake a job that would suit him.'

'Girl wants to travel to Cambodia. Refuses to look after children.'

'Firearm used at Waterloo. What offers.'

'Glorious fun-fur coat. Must be sold immediately. Owner going abroad.'

'Do you know Jenny Capstan? Her cakes are superb. Come to 14 Lizzard Street, S.W.3.'

For a moment Stafford Nye's finger came to a stop. Jenny Capstan. He liked the name. Was there any Lizzard Street? He supposed so. He had never heard of it. With a sigh, the finger went down the column and almost at once was arrested once more.

'Passenger from Frankfurt, Thursday Nov. 11, Hungerford Bridge 7.20.'

Thursday, November 11th. That was – yes, that was today. Sir Stafford Nye leaned back in his chair and drank more coffee. He was excited, stimulated. Hungerford. Hungerford Bridge. He got up and went into the kitchenette. Mrs Worrit was cutting potatoes into strips and throwing them into a large bowl of water. She looked up with some slight surprise.

'Anything you want, sir?'

'Yes,' said Sir Stafford Nye. 'If anyone said Hungerford Bridge to you, where would you go?'

'Where should I go?' Mrs Worrit considered. 'You mean if I wanted to go, do you?'

'We can proceed on that assumption.'

'Well, then, I suppose I'd go to Hungerford Bridge, wouldn't I?'

'You mean you would go to Hungerford in Berkshire?'

'Where is that?' said Mrs Worrit.

'Eight miles beyond Newbury.'

'I've heard of Newbury. My old man backed a horse there last year. Did well, too.'

'So you'd go to Hungerford near Newbury?'

'No, of course I wouldn't,' said Mrs Worrit. 'Go all that way – what for? I'd go to Hungerford Bridge, of course.'

'You mean – ?'

'Well, it's near Charing Cross. You know where it is. Over the Thames.'

'Yes,' said Sir Stafford Nye. 'Yes, I do know where it is quite well. Thank you, Mrs Worrit.'

It had been, he felt, rather like tossing a penny heads or tails. An advertisement in a morning paper in London meant Hungerford Railway Bridge in London. Presumably therefore that is what the advertiser meant, although about this particular advertiser Sir Stafford Nye was not at all sure. Her ideas, from the brief experience he had had of her, were original ideas. They were not the normal responses to be expected. But still, what else could one do. Besides, there were probably other Hungerfords, and possibly they would also have bridges, in various parts of England. But today, well, today he would see.

It was a cold windy evening with occasional bursts of thin misty rain. Sir Stafford Nye turned up the collar of his mackintosh and plodded on. It was not the first time he had gone across Hungerford Bridge, but it had never seemed to him a walk to take for pleasure. Beneath him was the river and crossing the bridge were large quantities of hurrying figures like himself. Their mackintoshes pulled round them, their hats pulled down and on the part of one and all of them an earnest desire to get home and out of the wind and rain as soon as possible. It would be, thought Sir Stafford Nye, very difficult to recognize anybody in this scurrying crowd. 7.20. Not a good moment to choose for a rendezvous of any kind. Perhaps it was

Hungerford Bridge in Berkshire. Anyway, it seemed very odd.

He plodded on. He kept an even pace, not overtaking those ahead of him, pushing past those coming the opposite way. He went fast enough not to be overtaken by the others behind him, though it would be possible for them to do so if they wanted to. A joke, perhaps, thought Stafford Nye. Not quite his kind of joke, but someone else's.

And yet – not her brand of humour either, he would have thought. Hurrying figures passed him again, pushing him slightly aside. A woman in a mackintosh was coming along, walking heavily. She collided with him, slipped, dropped to her knees. He assisted her up.

'All right?'

'Yes, thanks.'

She hurried on, but as she passed him, her wet hand, by which he had held her as he pulled her to her feet, slipped something into the palm of his hand, closing the fingers over it. Then she was gone, vanishing behind him, mingling with the crowd. Stafford Nye went on. He couldn't overtake her. She did not wish to be overtaken, either. He hurried on and his hand held something firmly. And so, at long last it seemed, he came to the end of the bridge on the Surrey side.

A few minutes later he had turned into a small café and sat there behind a table, ordering coffee. Then he looked at what was in his hand. It was a very thin oilskin envelope. Inside it was a cheap quality white envelope. That too he opened. What was inside surprised him. It was a ticket.

A ticket for the Festival Hall for the following evening.

V. WAGNERIAN MOTIF

Sir Stafford Nye adjusted himself more comfortably in his seat and listened to the persistent hammering of the Nibelungen, with which the programme began.

Though he enjoyed Wagnerian opera, *Siegfried* was by no means his favourite of the operas composing the Ring. *Rheingold* and *Götterdämmerung* were his two preferences. The music of the young Siegfried, listening to the songs of the birds, had always for some strange reason irritated him instead of filling him with melodic satisfaction. It might have been because he went to a performance in Munich in his young days which had displayed a magnificent tenor of unfortunately over-magnificent proportions, and he had been too young to divorce the joy of music from the visual joy of seeing a young Siegfried that looked even passably young. The fact of an outsized tenor rolling about on the ground in an access of boyishness had revolted him. He was also not particularly fond of birds and forest murmurs. No, give him the Rhine Maidens every time, although in Munich even the Rhine Maidens in those days had been of fairly solid proportions. But that mattered less. Carried away by the melodic flow of water and the joyous impersonal song, he had not allowed visual appreciation to matter.

From time to time he looked about him casually. He had taken his seat fairly early. It was a full house, as it usually was. The intermission came. Sir Stafford rose and looked about him. The seat beside his had remained empty. Someone who was supposed to have arrived had not arrived. Was that the answer, or was it merely a case of being excluded because someone had arrived late, which practice still held on the occasions when Wagnerian music was listened to.

He went out, strolled about, drank a cup of coffee, smoked a cigarette, and returned when the summons came. This time, as he drew near, he saw that the seat next to his was filled. Immediately his excitement returned. He regained his seat and sat down. Yes, it was the woman of the Frankfurt Air Lounge. She did not look at him, she was looking straight ahead. Her face in profile was as clean-cut and pure as he remembered it. Her head turned slightly, and her eyes passed over him but without recognition. So intent was that non-recognition that it was as good as a word spoken. This was a meeting that was not to be acknowledged. Not now, at any event. The lights began to dim. The woman beside him turned.

'Excuse me, could I look at your programme? I have dropped mine, I'm afraid, coming to my seat.'

'Of course,' he said.

He handed over the programme and she took it from him. She opened it, studied the items. The lights went lower. The second half of the programme began. It started with the overture to *Lohengrin*. At the end of it she handed back the programme to him with a few words of thanks.

'Thank you so much. It was very kind of you.'

The next item was the Siegfried forest murmur music. He consulted the programme she had returned to him. It was then that he noticed something faintly pencilled at the foot of a page. He did not attempt to read it now. Indeed, the light would have not been sufficient. He merely closed the programme and held it. He had not, he was quite sure, written anything there himself. Not, that is, in his own programme. She had, he thought, had her own programme ready, folded perhaps in her handbag and had already written some message ready to pass to him. Altogether, it seemed to him, there was still that atmosphere of secrecy, of danger. The meeting on Hungerford Bridge and the envelope with the ticket forced into his hand. And now the silent woman who sat beside him. He glanced at her once or twice with the quick, careless glance that one gives to a stranger sitting next to one. She lolled back in her seat; her high-necked dress was of dull black crêpe, an antique torque of gold encircled her neck. Her dark hair was cropped closely and shaped to her head. She did not glance at him or return any look. He wondered. Was there someone in the seats of the Festival Hall watching her – or watching him? Noting whether they looked or spoke to each other? Presumably there must be, or there must be at least the possibility of such a thing. She had answered his appeal in the newspaper advertisement. Let that be enough for him. His curiosity was unimpaired, but he did at least know now that Daphne Theodofanous – alias Mary Ann – was here in London. There were possibilities in the future of his learning more of what was afoot. But the plan of campaign must be left to her. He must follow her lead. As he had obeyed her in the airport, so he would obey her now and – let him admit it – life had become suddenly more interesting. This was better than the boring conferences of his political life. Had a car really tried to run him down the other night? He thought it had. Two attempts – not only one. It was easy enough to imagine that one was the target of assault, people drove so recklessly nowadays that you could easily fancy malice aforethought when it was not so. He folded his programme, did not look at it again. The music came to its end. The woman next to him spoke. She did not turn her head or appear to speak to him, but she spoke aloud, with a little sigh between the words as though she was communing with herself or possibly to her neighbour on the other side.

'The young Siegfried,' she said, and sighed again.

The programme ended with the March from *Die Meistersinger*. After enthusiastic applause, people began to leave their seats. He waited to see if she would give him any lead, but she did not. She gathered up her wrap, moved out of the row of chairs, and with a slightly accelerated step, moved along with other people and disappeared in the crowd.

Stafford Nye regained his car and drove home. Arrived there, he spread out the Festival Hall programme on his desk and examined it carefully, after putting the coffee to percolate.

The programme was disappointing to say the least of it. There did not appear to be any message inside. Only on one page above the list of the items, were the pencil marks that he had vaguely observed. But they were not words or letters or even figures. They appeared to be merely a musical notation. It was as though someone had scribbled a phrase of music with a somewhat inadequate pencil. For a moment it occurred to Stafford Nye there might perhaps be a secret message he could bring out by applying heat. Rather gingerly, and in a way rather ashamed of his melodramatic fancy, he held it towards the bar of the electric fire but nothing resulted. With a sigh he tossed the programme back on to the table. But he felt justifiably annoyed. All this rigmarole, a rendezvous on a windy and rainy bridge overlooking the river! Sitting through a concert by the side of a woman of whom he yearned to ask at least a dozen questions – and at the end of it? Nothing! No further on. Still, she *had* met him. But why? If she didn't want to speak to him, to make further arrangements with him, why had she come at all?

His eyes passed idly across the room to his bookcase which he reserved for various thrillers, works of detective fiction and an occasional volume of science fiction; he shook his head. Fiction, he thought, was infinitely superior to real life. Dead bodies, mysterious telephone calls, beautiful foreign spies in profusion! However, this particular elusive lady might not have done with him yet. Next time, he thought, he would make some arrangements of his own. Two could play at the game that she was playing.

He pushed aside the programme and drank another cup of coffee and went to the window. He had the programme still in his hand. As he looked out towards the street below his eyes fell back again on the open programme in his hand and he hummed to himself, almost unconsciously. He had a good ear for music and he could hum the notes that were scrawled there quite easily. Vaguely they sounded familiar as he hummed them. He increased his voice a little. What was it now? Tum, tum, tum tum ti-tum. Tum. Tum. Yes, definitely familiar.

He started opening his letters.

They were mostly uninteresting. A couple of invitations, one from the American Embassy, one from Lady Athelhampton, a Charity Variety performance which Royalty would attend and for which it was suggested five guineas would not be an exorbitant fee to obtain a seat. He threw them aside lightly. He doubted very much whether he wished to accept any of them. He decided that instead of remaining in London he would without more ado go and see his Aunt Matilda, as he had promised. He was fond of his Aunt Matilda though he did not visit her very often. She lived in a rehabilitated apartment consisting of a series of rooms in one wing of a large Georgian manor house in the country which she had inherited from his grandfather.

She had a large, beautifully proportioned sitting-room, a small oval dining-room, a new kitchen made from the old housekeeper's room, two bedrooms for guests, a large comfortable bedroom for herself with an adjoining bathroom, and adequate quarters for a patient companion who shared her daily life. The remains of a faithful domestic staff were well provided for and housed. The rest of the house remained under dust sheets with periodical cleaning. Stafford Nye was fond of the place, having spent holidays there as a boy. It had been a gay house then. His eldest uncle had lived there with his wife and their two children. Yes, it had been pleasant there then. There had been money and a sufficient staff to run it. He had not specially noticed in those days the portraits and pictures. There had been large-sized examples of Victorian art occupying pride of place – overcrowding the walls, but there had been other masters of an older age. Yes, there had been some good portraits there. A Raeburn, two Lawrences, a Gainsborough, a Lely, two rather dubious Vandykes. A couple of Turners, too. Some of them had had to be sold to provide the family with money. He still enjoyed when visiting there strolling about and studying the family pictures.

His Aunt Matilda was a great chatterbox but she always enjoyed his visits. He was fond of her in a desultory way, but he was not quite sure why it was that he had suddenly wanted to visit her now. And what it was that had brought family portraits into his mind? Could it have been because there was a portrait of his sister Pamela by one of the leading artists of the day twenty years ago. He would like to see that portrait of Pamela and look at it more closely. See how close the resemblance had been between the stranger who had disrupted his life in this really outrageous fashion and his sister.

He picked up the Festival Hall programme again with some irritation and began to hum the pencilled notes. Tum, tum, ti tum – Then it came to him and he knew what it was. It was the Siegfried motif. Siegfried's Horn. The Young Siegfried motif. That was what the woman had said last night. Not apparently to him, not apparently to anybody. But it had been the message, a message that would have meant nothing to anyone around since it would have seemed to refer to the music that had just been played. And the motif had been written on his programme also in musical terms. The Young Siegfried. It must have meant something. Well, perhaps further enlightenment would come. The Young Siegfried. What the hell *did* that mean? Why and how and when and what? Ridiculous! All those questioning words.

He rang the telephone and obtained Aunt Matilda's number.

'But of course, Staffy dear, it will be lovely to have you. Take the four-thirty train. It still runs, you know, but it gets here an hour and a half later. And it leaves Paddington later – five-fifteen. That's what they mean by improving the railways, I suppose. Stops at several most absurd stations on the way. All right. Horace will meet you at King's Marston.'

'He's still there then?'

'Of course he's still there.'

'I suppose he is,' said Sir Stafford Nye.

Horace, once a groom, then a coachman, had survived as a chauffeur, and apparently was still surviving. 'He must be at least eighty,' said Sir Stafford. He smiled to himself.

VI. PORTRAIT OF A LADY

'You look very nice and brown, dear,' said Aunt Matilda, surveying him appreciatively. 'That's Malaya, I suppose. If it *was* Malaya you went to? Or was it Siam or Thailand? They change the names of all these places and really it makes it very difficult. Anyway, it wasn't Vietnam, was it? You know, I don't like the sound of Vietnam *at all*. It's all very confusing, North Vietnam and South Vietnam and the Viet-Cong and the Viet – whatever the other thing is and all wanting to fight each other and nobody wanting to stop. They won't go to Paris or wherever it is and sit round tables and talk sensibly. Don't you think really, dear – I've been thinking it over and I thought it would be a very nice solution – couldn't you make a lot of football fields and then they could all go and fight each other there, but with less lethal weapons. Not that nasty palm burning stuff. You know. Just hit each other and punch each other and all that. They'd enjoy it, everyone would enjoy it and you could charge admission for people to go and see them do it. I do think really that we don't understand giving people the things they really want.'

'I think it's a very fine idea of yours, Aunt Matilda,' said Sir Stafford Nye as he kissed a pleasantly perfumed, pale pink wrinkled cheek. 'And how are you, my dear?'

'Well, I'm old,' said Lady Matilda Cleckheaton. 'Yes, I'm old. Of course you don't know what it is to be old. If it isn't one thing it's another. Rheumatism or arthritis or a nasty bit of asthma or a sore throat or an ankle you've turned. Always *something*, you know. Nothing very important. But there it is. Why have you come to see me, dear?'

Sir Stafford was slightly taken aback by the directness of the query.

'I usually come and see you when I return from a trip abroad.'

'You'll have to come one chair nearer,' said Aunt Matilda. 'I'm just that bit deafer since you saw me last. You look different . . . Why do you look different?'

'Because I'm more sunburnt. You said so.'

'Nonsense, that's not what I mean at all. Don't tell me it's a girl at last.'

'A girl?'

'Well, I've always felt it might be one some day. The trouble is you've got too much sense of humour.'

'Now why should you think that?'

'Well, it's what people do think about you. Oh yes, they do. Your sense of humour is in the way of your career, too. You know, you're all mixed up with all these people. Diplomatic and political. What they call younger statesmen and elder statesmen and middle statesmen too. And all those different Parties. Really I think it's too silly to have too many Parties. First of all those awful, awful Labour people.' She raised her Conservative nose into the air. 'Why, when I was a girl there wasn't such a thing as a *Labour* Party. Nobody would have known what you meant by it. They'd have said "nonsense". Pity it wasn't nonsense, too. And then there's the Liberals, of course, but they're terribly wet. And then there are the Tories, or the Conservatives as they call themselves again now.'

'And what's the matter with them?' asked Stafford Nye, smiling slightly.

'Too many earnest women. Makes them lack gaiety, you know.'

'Oh well, no political party goes in for gaiety much nowadays.'

'Just so,' said Aunt Matilda. 'And then of course that's where you go wrong. You want to cheer things up. You want to have a little gaiety and so you make a little gentle fun at people and of course they don't like it. They say "*Ce n'est pas un garçon serieux,*" like that man in the fishing.'

Sir Stafford Nye laughed. His eyes were wandering round the room.

'What are you looking at?' said Lady Matilda.

'Your pictures.'

'You don't want me to sell them, do you? Everyone seems to be selling their pictures nowadays. Old Lord Grampion, you know. He sold his Turners and he sold some of his ancestors as well. And Geoffrey Gouldman. All those lovely horses of his. By Stubbs, weren't they? Something like that. Really, the prices one gets!

'But I don't want to sell my pictures. I like them. Most of them in this room have a real interest because they're ancestors. I know nobody wants ancestors nowadays but then I'm old-fashioned. I like ancestors. My own ancestors, I mean. What are you looking at? Pamela?'

'Yes, I was. I was thinking about her the other day.'

'Astonishing how alike you two are. I mean, it's not even as though you were twins, though they say that different sex twins, even if they are twins, can't be identical, if you know what I mean.'

'So Shakespeare must have made rather a mistake over Viola and Sebastian.'

'Well, ordinary brothers and sisters can be alike, can't they? You and Pamela were always very alike – to look at, I mean.'

'Not in any other way? Don't you think we were alike in character?'

'No, not in the least. That's the funny part of it. But of course you and Pamela have what I call the family face. Not a Nye face. I mean the Baldwen-White face.'

Sir Stafford Nye had never quite been able to compete when it came down to talking on a question of genealogy with his great-aunt.

'I've always thought that you and Pamela both took after Alexa,' she went on.

'Which was Alexa?'

'Your great-great – I think one more great – grandmother. Hungarian. A Hungarian countess or baroness or something. Your great-great-great-grandfather fell in love with her when he was at Vienna in the Embassy. Yes. Hungarian. That's what she was. Very sporting too. They are sporting, you know, Hungarians. She rode to hounds, rode magnificently.'

'Is she in the picture gallery?'

'She's on the first landing. Just over the head of the stairs, a little to the right.'

'I must go and look at her when I go to bed.'

'Why don't you go and look at her now and then you can come back and talk about her.'

'I will if you like.' He smiled at her.

He ran out of the room and up the staircase. Yes, she had a sharp eye, old Matilda. That was the face. That was the face that he had seen and remembered. Remembered not for its likeness to himself, not even for its likeness to Pamela, but for a closer resemblance still to this picture here. A handsome girl brought home by his Ambassador great-great-great-grandfather if that was enough greats. Aunt Matilda was never satisfied with only a few. About twenty she had been. She had come here and been high-spirited and rode a horse magnificently and danced divinely and men had fallen in love with her. But she had been faithful, so it was always said, to great-great-great-grandfather, a very steady and sober member of the Diplomatic Service. She had gone with him to foreign Embassies and returned here and had had children – three or four children, he believed. Through one of those children the inheritance of her face, her nose, the turn of her neck had been passed down to him and to his sister, Pamela. He wondered if the young woman who had doped his beer and forced him to lend her his cloak and who had depicted herself as being in danger of death unless he did what she asked, had been possibly related as a fifth or sixth cousin removed, a descendant of the woman pictured on the wall at which he looked. Well, it could be. They had been of the same nationality, perhaps. Anyway their faces had resembled each other a good deal. How upright she'd sat at the opera, how straight that profile, the thin, slightly arched aquiline nose. And the atmosphere that hung about her.

'Find it?' asked Lady Matilda, when her nephew returned to the white drawing-room, as her sitting-room was usually called. 'Interesting face, isn't it?'

'Yes, quite handsome, too.'

'It's much better to be interesting than handsome. But you haven't been in Hungary or Austria, have you? You wouldn't meet anyone like her out in Malaya? She wouldn't be sitting round a table there making little notes or correcting speeches or things like that. She was a wild creature, by all accounts. Lovely manners and all the rest of it. But wild. Wild as a wild bird. She didn't know what danger was.'

'How do you know so much about her?'

'Oh, I agree I wasn't a contemporary of hers, I wasn't born until several years after she was dead. All the same,

I've always been interested in her. She was adventurous, you know. Very adventurous. Very queer stories were told about her, about things she was mixed up in.'

'And how did my great-great-great-grandfather react to that?'

'I expect it worried him to death,' said Lady Matilda. 'They say he was devoted to her, though. By the way, Staffy, did you ever read *The Prisoner of Zenda*?'

'Prisoner of Zenda? Sounds very familiar.'

'Well, of course it's familiar, it's a book.'

'Yes, yes, I realize it's a book.'

'You wouldn't know about it, I expect. After your time. But when I was a girl – that's about the first taste of romance we got. Not pop singers or Beatles. Just a romantic novel. We weren't allowed to read novels when I was young. Not in the morning anyway. You could read them in the afternoon.'

'What extraordinary rules,' said Sir Stafford. 'Why is it wrong to read novels in the morning and not in the afternoon?'

'Well, in the mornings, you see, girls were supposed to be doing something useful. You know, doing the flowers or cleaning the silver photograph frames. All the things we girls did. Doing a bit of studying with the governess – all that sort of thing. In the afternoon we were allowed to sit down and read a story book and *The Prisoner of Zenda* was usually one of the first ones that came our way.'

'A very nice, respectable story, was it? I seem to remember something about it. Perhaps I did read it. All very pure, I suppose. Not too sexy?'

'Certainly not. We didn't have sexy books. We had romance. *The Prisoner of Zenda* was very romantic. One fell in love, usually, with the hero, Rudolf Rassendyll.'

'I seem to remember that name too. Bit florid, isn't it?'

'Well, I still think it was rather a romantic name. Twelve years old, I must have been. It made me think of it, you know, your going up and looking at that portrait. Princess Flavia,' she added.

Stafford Nye was smiling at her.

'You look young and pink and very sentimental,' he said.

'Well, that's just what I'm feeling. Girls can't feel like that nowadays. They're swooning with love, or they're fainting when somebody plays the guitar or sings in a very loud voice, but they're not sentimental. But I wasn't in love with Rudolf Rassendyll. I was in love with the other one – his double.'

'Did he have a double?'

'Oh yes, a king. The King of Ruritania.'

'Ah, of course, now I know. That's where the word Ruritania comes from: one is always throwing it about. Yes, I think I did read it, you know. The King of Ruritania, and Rudolf Rassendyll was stand-in for the King and fell in love with Princess Flavia to whom the King was officially betrothed.'

Lady Matilda gave some more deep sighs.

'Yes. Rudolf Rassendyll had inherited his red hair from an ancestress, and somewhere in the book he bows to the portrait and says something about the – I can't remember the name now – the Countess Amelia or something like that from whom he inherited his looks and all the rest of it. So I looked at you and thought of you as Rudolf Rassendyll and you went out and looked at a picture of someone who might have been an ancestress of yours and saw whether she reminded you of someone. So you're mixed up in a romance of some kind, are you?'

'What on earth makes you say that?'

'Well, there aren't so many patterns in life, you know. One recognizes patterns as they come up. It's like a book on knitting. About sixty-five different fancy stitches. Well, you know a particular stitch when you see it. Your stitch, at the moment, I should say, is the romantic adventure.' She sighed. 'But you won't tell me about it, I suppose.'

'There's nothing to tell,' said Sir Stafford.

'You always were quite an accomplished liar. Well, never mind. You bring her to see me some time. That's all I'd like, before the doctors succeed in killing me with yet another type of antibiotic that they've just discovered. The different coloured pills I've had to take by this time! You wouldn't believe it.'

'I don't know why you say "she" and "her" –'

'Don't you? Oh, well, I know a she when I come across a she. There's a she somewhere dodging about in your life. What beats me is how you found her. In Malaya, at the conference table? Ambassador's daughter or minister's daughter? Good-looking secretary from the Embassy pool? No, none of it seems to fit. Ship coming home? No, you don't use ships nowadays. Plane, perhaps.'

'You are getting slightly nearer,' Sir Stafford Nye could not help saying.

'Ah!' She pounced. 'Air hostess?'

He shook his head.

'Ah well. Keep your secret. I shall find out, mind you. I've always had a good nose for things going on where you're concerned. Things generally as well. Of course I'm out of everything nowadays, but I meet my old cronies from time to time and it's quite easy, you know, to get a hint or two from them. People are worried. Everywhere – they're worried.'

'You mean there's a general kind of discontent – upset?'

'No, I didn't mean that at all. I mean the highups are worried. Our awful governments are worried. The dear old sleepy Foreign Office is worried. There are things going on, things that shouldn't be. Unrest.'

'Student unrest?'

'Oh, student unrest is just one flower on the tree. It's blossoming everywhere and in every country, or so it seems. I've got a nice girl who comes, you know, and reads the papers to me in the mornings. I can't read them properly myself. She's got a nice voice. Takes down my letters and she reads things from the papers and she's a good kind girl. She reads the things I want to know, not the things that she thinks are right for me to know. Yes, everyone's worried, as far as I can make out and this, mind you, came more or less from a very old friend of mine.'

'One of your old military cronies?'

'He's a major-general, if that's what you mean, retired a good many years ago but still in the know. Youth is what you might call the spearhead of it all. But that's not really what's so worrying. They – whoever *they* are – work through youth. Youth in every country. Youth urged on. Youth chanting slogans, slogans that sound exciting, though they don't always know what they mean. So easy to start a revolution. That's natural to youth. All youth has always rebelled. You rebel, you pull down, you want the world to be different from what it is. But you're blind, too. There are bandages over the eyes of youth. They can't see where things are taking them. What's going to come next? What's in front of them? And who it is behind them, urging them on? That's what's frightening about it. You know, someone holding out the carrot to get the donkey to come along and at the same time there is someone behind the donkey urging it on with a stick.'

'You've got some extraordinary fancies.'

'They're not only fancies, my dear boy. That's what people said about Hitler. Hitler and the Hitler Youth.

But it was a long careful preparation. It was a war that was worked out in detail. It was a fifth column being planted in different countries all ready for the supermen. The supermen were to be the flower of the German nation. That's what they thought and believed in passionately. Somebody else is perhaps believing something like that now. It's a creed that they'll be willing to accept – if it's offered cleverly enough.'

'Who are you talking about? Do you mean the Chinese or the Russians? What do you mean?'

'I don't know. I haven't the faintest idea. But there's something somewhere, and it's running on the same lines. Pattern again, you see. Pattern! The Russians? Bogged down by Communism, I should think they're considered old-fashioned. The Chinese? I think they've lost their way. Too much Chairman Mao, perhaps. I don't know who these people are who are doing the planning. As I said before, it's why and where and when and *who*.'

'Very interesting.'

'It's so frightening, this same idea that always recurs. History repeating itself. The young hero, the golden superman that all must follow.' She paused, then said, 'Same idea, you know. The young Siegfried.'

V11. ADVICE FROM GREAT AUNT MATILDA

Great-Aunt Matilda looked at him. She had a very sharp and shrewd eye. Stafford Nye had noticed that before. He noticed it particularly at this moment.

'So you've heard that term before,' she said. 'I see.'

'What does it mean?'

'You don't know?' She raised her eyebrows.

'Cross my heart and wish to die,' said Sir Stafford, in nursery language.

'Yes, we always used to say that, didn't we,' said Lady Matilda. 'Do you really mean what you're saying?'

'I don't know anything about it.'

'But you'd heard the term before.'

'Yes. Someone said it to me.'

'Anyone important?'

'It could be. I suppose it could be. What do you mean by "anyone important"?'

'Well, you've been involved in various Government missions lately, haven't you? You've represented this poor, miserable country as best you could, which I shouldn't wonder wasn't rather better than many others could do, sitting round a table and talking. I don't know whether anything's come of all that.'

'Probably not,' said Stafford Nye. 'After all, one isn't optimistic when one goes into these things.'

'One does one's best,' said Lady Matilda correctively.

'A very Christian principle. Nowadays if one does one's worst one often seems to get on a good deal better. What does all this mean, Aunt Matilda?'

'I don't suppose *I* know,' said his aunt.

'Well, you very often do know things.'

'Not exactly. I just pick up things here and there.'

'Yes?'

'I've got a few old friends left, you know. Friends who are in the know. Of course most of them are either practically stone deaf or half blind or a little bit gone in the top storey or unable to walk straight. But something still functions. Something, shall we say, up here.' She hit the top of her neatly arranged white head. 'There's a good deal of alarm and despondency about. More than usual. That's one of the things I've picked up.'

'Isn't there always?'

'Yes, yes, but this is a bit more than that. Active instead of passive, as you might say. For a long time, as I have noticed from the outside, and you, no doubt, from the inside, we have felt that things are in a mess. A rather bad mess. But now we've got to a point where we feel that perhaps something might have been done about the mess. There's an element of danger in it. Something is going on – something is brewing. Not just in one country. In quite a lot of countries. They've recruited a service of their own and the danger about that is that it's a service of young people. And the kind of people who will go anywhere, do anything, unfortunately believe anything, and so long as they are promised a certain amount of pulling down, wrecking, throwing spanners in the works, then they think the cause must be a good one and that the world will be a different place. They're not creative, that's the trouble – only destructive. The creative young write poems, write books, probably compose music, paint pictures just as they always have done. They'll be all right – But once people learn to love destruction for its own sake, evil leadership gets its chance.'

'You say "they" or "them". Who do you mean?'

'Wish I knew,' said Lady Matilda. 'Yes, I wish I knew. Very much indeed. If I hear anything useful, I'll tell you. Then you can do something about it.'

'Unfortunately, *I* haven't got anyone to tell, I mean to pass it on to.'

'Yes, don't pass it on to just anyone. You can't trust people. Don't pass it on to any one of those idiots in the Government, or connected with government or hoping to be participating in government after this lot runs out.

Politicians don't have time to look at the world they're living in. They see the country they're living in and they see it as one vast electoral platform. That's quite enough to put on their plates for the time being. They do things which they honestly believe will make things better and then they're surprised when they don't make things better because they're not the things that people want to have. And one can't help coming to the conclusion that politicians have a feeling that they have a kind of divine right to tell lies in a good cause. It's not really so very long ago since Mr Baldwin made his famous remark – "If I had spoken the truth, I should have lost the election." Prime Ministers still feel like that. Now and again we have a great man, thank God. But it's rare.'

'Well, what do you suggest ought to be done?'

'Are you asking my advice? Mine? Do you know how old I am?'

'Getting on for ninety,' suggested her nephew.

'Not quite as old as that,' said Lady Matilda, slightly affronted. 'Do I look it, my dear boy?'

'No, darling. You look a nice, comfortable sixty-six.'

'That's better,' said Lady Matilda. 'Quite untrue. But better. If I get a tip of any kind from one of my dear old admirals or an old general or even possibly an air marshal – they do hear things, you know – they've got cronies still and the old boys get together and talk. And so it gets around. There's always been the grapevine and there still is a grapevine, no matter how elderly the people are. The young Siegfried. We want a clue to just what that means – I don't know if he's a person or a password or the name of a Club or a new Messiah or a Pop singer. But that term covers *something*. There's the musical motif too. I've rather forgotten my Wagnerian days.' Her aged voice croaked out a partially recognizable melody. 'Siegfried's horn call isn't that it? Get a recorder, why don't you? Do I mean a recorder. I don't mean a record that you put on a gramophone – I mean the things that schoolchildren play. They have classes for them. Went to a talk the other day. Our vicar got it up. Quite interesting. You know, tracing the history of the recorder and the kind of recorders there were from the Elizabethan age onwards. Some big, some small, all different notes and sounds. Very interesting. Interesting hearing in two senses. The recorders themselves. Some of them give out lovely noises. And the history. Yes. Well, what was I saying?'

'You told me to get one of these instruments, I gather.'

'Yes. Get a recorder and learn to blow Siegfried's horn call on it. You're musical, you always were. You can manage that, I hope?'

'Well, it seems a very small part to play in the salvation of the world, but I daresay I could manage that.'

'And have the thing ready. Because, you see – ' she tapped on the table with her spectacle case – 'you might want it to impress the wrong people some time. Might come in useful. They'd welcome you with open arms and then you might learn a bit.'

'You certainly have ideas,' said Sir Stafford admiringly.

'What else can you have when you're my age?' said his great-aunt. 'You can't get about. You can't meddle with people much, you can't do any gardening. All you *can* do is sit in your chair and have ideas. Remember that when you're forty years older.'

'One remark you made interested me.'

'Only one?' said Lady Matilda. 'That's rather poor measure considering how much I've been talking. What was it?'

'You suggested that I might be capable of impressing the wrong people with my recorder – did you mean that?'

'Well, it's one way, isn't it? The right people don't matter. But the wrong people – well, you've got to find out things, haven't you? You've got to permeate things. Rather like a death-watch beetle,' she said thoughtfully.

'So I should make significant noises in the night?'

'Well, that sort of thing, yes. We had death-watch beetle in the east wing here once. Very expensive it was to put it right. I dare say it will be just as expensive to put the world right.'

'In fact a good deal more expensive,' said Stafford Nye.

'That won't matter,' said Lady Matilda. 'People never mind spending a great deal of money. It impresses them. It's when you want to do things economically, they won't play. We're the same people, you know. In this country, I mean. We're the same people we always were.'

'What do you mean by that?'

'We're capable of doing big things. We were good at running an empire. We weren't good at *keeping* an empire running, but then you see we didn't need an empire any more. And we recognized that. Too difficult to keep up. Robbie made me see that,' she added.

'Robbie?' It was faintly familiar.

'Robbie Shoreham. Robert Shoreham. He's a very old friend of mine. Paralysed down the left side. But he can talk still and he's got a moderately good hearing-aid.'

'Besides being one of the most famous physicists in the world,' said Stafford Nye. 'So he's another of your old cronies, is he?'

'Known him since he was a boy,' said Lady Matilda. 'I suppose it surprises you that we should be friends, have a lot in common and enjoy talking together?'

'Well, I shouldn't have thought that –'

'That we had much to talk about? It's true I could never do mathematics. Fortunately, when I was a girl one didn't even try. Mathematics came easily to Robbie when he was about four years old, I believe. They say nowadays that that's quite natural. He's got plenty to talk about. He liked me always because I was frivolous and made him laugh. And I'm a good listener, too. And really, he says some very interesting things sometimes.'

'So I suppose,' said Stafford Nye drily.

'Now don't be superior. Molière married his housemaid, didn't he, and made a great success of it – if it *is* Molière I mean. If a man's frantic with brains he doesn't really want a woman who's also frantic with brains to talk to. It would be exhausting. He'd much prefer a lovely nitwit who can make him laugh. I wasn't bad-looking when I was young,' said Lady Matilda complacently. 'I know I have no academic distinctions. I'm not in the least intellectual. But Robert has always said that I've got a great deal of common sense, of intelligence.'

'You're a lovely person,' said Sir Stafford Nye. 'I enjoy coming to see you and I shall go away remembering all the things you've said to me. There are a good many more things, I expect, that you could tell me but you're obviously not going to.'

'Not until the right moment comes,' said Lady Matilda, 'but I've got your interests at heart. Let me know what you're doing from time to time. You're dining at the American Embassy, aren't you, next week?'

'How did you know that? I've been asked.'

'And you've accepted, I understand.'

'Well, it's all in the course of duty.' He looked at her curiously. 'How do you manage to be so well informed?'

'Oh, Milly told me.'

'Milly?'

'Milly Jean Cortman. The American Ambassador's

wife. A most attractive creature, you know. Small and rather perfect-looking.'

'Oh, you mean Mildred Cortman.'

'She was christened Mildred but she preferred Milly Jean. I was talking to her on the telephone about some Charity Matinée or other – she's what we used to call a pocket Venus.'

'A most attractive term to use,' said Stafford Nye.

V111 AN EMBASSY DINNER

As Mrs Cortman came to meet him with outstretched hand, Stafford Nye recalled the term his great-aunt had used. Milly Jean Cortman was a woman of between thirty-five and forty. She had delicate features, big blue-grey eyes, a very perfectly shaped head with bluish-grey hair tinted to a particularly attractive shade which fitted her with a perfection of grooming. She was very popular in London. Her husband, Sam Cortman, was a big, heavy man, slightly ponderous. He was very proud of his wife. He himself was one of those slow, rather over-emphatic talkers. People found their attention occasionally straying when he was elucidating at some length a point which hardly needed making.

'Back from Malaya, aren't you, Sir Stafford? It must have been quite interesting to go out there, though it's not the time of year I'd have chosen. But I'm sure we're all glad to see you back. Let me see now. You know Lady Aldborough and Sir John, and Herr von Roken, Frau von Roken. Mr and Mrs Staggenham.'

They were all people known to Stafford Nye in more or

less degree. There was a Dutchman and his wife whom he had not met before, since they had only just taken up their appointment. The Staggenhams were the Minister of Social Security and his wife. A particularly uninteresting couple, he had always thought.

'And the Countess Renata Zerkowski. I think she said she'd met you before.'

'It must be about a year ago. When I was last in England,' said the Countess.

And there she was, the passenger from Frankfurt again. Self-possessed, at ease, beautifully turned out in faint grey-blue with a touch of chinchilla. Her hair dressed high (a wig ?) and a ruby cross of antique design round her neck.

'Signor Gasparo, Count Reitner, Mr and Mrs Arbuthnot.'

About twenty-six in all. At dinner Stafford Nye sat between the dreary Mrs Staggenham and Signora Gasparo on the other side of him. Renata Zerkowski sat exactly opposite him.

An Embassy dinner. A dinner such as he so often attended, holding much of the same type of guests. Various members of the Diplomatic Corps, junior ministers, one or two industrialists, a sprinkling of socialites usually included because they were good conversationalists, natural, pleasant people to meet, though one or two, thought Stafford Nye, one or two were maybe different. Even while he was busy sustaining his conversation with Signora Gasparo, a charming person to talk to, a chatterbox, slightly flirtatious; his mind was roving in the same way that his eye also roved, though the latter was not very noticeable. As it roved round the dinner table, you would not have said that he was summing up conclusions in his own mind. He had been asked here. Why? For any reason or for no reason in particular. Because his name had come up automatically on the list that the secretaries produced from time to time with checks against such members as were due for their turn. Or as the extra man or the extra woman required for the balancing of the table. He had always been in request when an extra was needed.

'Oh yes,' a diplomatic hostess would say, 'Stafford Nye will do beautifully. You will put him next to Madame So-and-so, or Lady Somebody else.'

He had been asked perhaps to fill in for no further reason than that. And yet, he wondered. He knew by experience that there were certain other reasons. And so his eye with its swift social amiability, its air of not looking really at anything in particular, was busy.

Amongst these guests there was someone perhaps who for some reason mattered, was important. Someone who had been asked – not to fill in – on the contrary – someone who had had a selection of other guests invited to fit in round him – or her. Someone who mattered. He wondered – he wondered which of them it might be.

Cortman knew, of course. Milly Jean, perhaps. One never really knew with wives. Some of them were better diplomats than their husbands. Some of them could be relied upon merely for their charm, for their adaptability, their readiness to please, their lack of curiosity. Some again, he thought ruefully to himself, were, as far as their husbands were concerned, disasters. Hostesses who, though they may have brought prestige or money to a diplomatic marriage, were yet capable at any moment of saying or doing the wrong thing, and creating an unfortunate situation. If that was to be guarded against, it would need one of the guests, or two or even three of the guests, to be what one might call professional smoothers-over.

Did this dinner party this evening mean anything but a

social event? His quick and noticing eye had by now been round the dinner table picking out one or two people whom so far he had not entirely taken in. An American business man. Pleasant, not socially brilliant. A professor from one of the universities of the Middle West. A married couple, the husband German, the wife predominantly, almost aggressively American. A very beautiful woman, too. Sexually, highly attractive, Sir Stafford thought. Was one of them important? Initials floated through his mind. FBI. CIA. The business man perhaps a CIA man, there for a purpose. Things were like that nowadays. Not as they used to be. How had the formula gone? Big brother is watching you. Yes, well it went further than that now. Transatlantic Cousin is watching you. High Finance for Middle Europe is watching you. A diplomatic difficulty has been asked here for *you* to watch *him*. Oh yes. There was often a lot behind things nowadays. But was that just another formula, just another fashion? Could it really mean more than that, something vital, something real? How did one talk of events in Europe nowadays? The Common Market. Well, that was fair enough, that dealt with trade, with economics, with the inter-relationships of countries.

That was the stage to set. But behind the stage. Backstage. Waiting for the cue. Ready to prompt if prompting were needed. What was going on? Going on in the big world and behind the big world. He wondered.

Some things he knew, some things he guessed at, some things, he thought to himself, I know nothing about and nobody wants me to know anything about them.

His eyes rested for a moment on his vis-à-vis, her chin tilted upward, her mouth just gently curved in a polite smile, and their eyes met. Those eyes told him nothing, the smile told him nothing. What was she doing here? She was in her element, she fitted in, she knew this world. Yes, she was at home here. He could find out, he thought, without much difficulty where she figured in the diplomatic world, but would that tell him where she really had her place?

The young woman in the slacks who had spoken to him suddenly at Frankfurt had had an eager intelligent face. Was that the real woman, or was this casual social acquaintance the real woman? Was one of those personalities a part being played? And if so, which one? And there might be more than just those two personalities. He wondered. He wanted to find out.

Or had the fact that he had been asked to meet her been pure coincidence? Milly Jean was rising to her feet. The other ladies rose with her. Then suddenly an unexpected clamour arose. A clamour from outside the house. Shouts. Yells. The crash of breaking glass in a window. Shouts. Sounds – surely pistol shots. Signora Gasparo spoke, clutching Stafford Nye's arm.

'What again!' she exclaimed. '*Dio*! – again it is those terrible students. It is the same in our country. Why do they attack Embassies? They fight, resist the police – go marching, shouting idiotic things, lie down in the streets. *Si*, *si*. We have them in Rome – in Milan – We have them like a pest everywhere in Europe. Why are they never happy, these young ones? What do they want?'

Stafford Nye sipped his brandy and listened to the heavy accents of Mr Charles Staggenham, who was being pontifical and taking his time about it. The commotion had subsided. It would seem that the police had marched off some of the hotheads. It was one of those occurrences which once would have been thought extraordinary and even alarming but which were now taken as a matter of course.

'A larger police force. That's what we need. A larger police force. It's more than these chaps can deal with. It's the same everywhere, they say. I was talking to Herr Lurwitz the other day. They have their troubles, so have the French. Not quite so much of it in the Scandinavian countries. What do they all want – just trouble? I tell you if I had my way –'

Stafford Nye removed his mind to another subject while keeping up a flattering pretence as Charles Staggenham explained just what his way would be, which in any case was easily to be anticipated beforehand.

'Shouting about Vietnam and all that. What do any of them know about Vietnam. None of them have ever been there, have they?'

'One would think it very unlikely,' said Sir Stafford Nye.

'Man was telling me earlier this evening, they've had a lot of trouble in California. In the universities – If we had a sensible policy . . .'

Presently the men joined the ladies in the drawing-room. Stafford Nye, moving with that leisurely grace, that air of complete lack of purpose he found so useful, sat down by a golden-haired, talkative woman whom he knew moderately well, and who could be guaranteed seldom to say anything worth listening to as regards ideas or wit, but who was excessively knowledgeable about all her fellow creatures within the bounds of her acquaintance. Stafford Nye asked no direct questions but presently, without the lady being even aware of the means by which he had guided the subject of conversation, he was hearing a few remarks about the Countess Renata Zerkowski.

'Still very good-looking, isn't she? She doesn't come over here very often nowadays. Mostly New York, you know, or that wonderful island place. You know the one

I mean. Not Minorca. One of the other ones in the Mediterranean. Her sister's married to that soap king, at least I think it's a soap king. Not the Greek one. He's Swedish, I think. Rolling in money. And then of course, she spends a lot of time in some castle place in the Dolomites – or near Munich – very musical, she always has been. She said you'd met before, didn't she?'

'Yes. A year or two years ago, I think.'

'Oh yes, I suppose when she was over in England before. They say she was mixed up in the Czechoslovakian business. Or do I mean the Polish trouble? Oh dear, it's so difficult, isn't it. All the names, I mean. They have so many z's and k's. Most peculiar, and so hard to spell. She's very literary. You know, gets up petitions for people to sign. To give writers asylum here, or whatever it is. Not that anyone really pays much attention. I mean, what else can one think of nowadays except how one can possibly pay one's own taxes. The travel allowance makes things a little better but not much. I mean, you've got to get the money, haven't you, before you can take it abroad. I don't know how anyone manages to have money now, but there's a lot of it about. Oh yes, there's a lot of it about.'

She looked down in a complacent fashion at her left hand, on which were two solitaire rings, one a diamond and one an emerald, which seemed to prove conclusively that a considerable amount of money had been spent upon her at least.

The evening drew on to its close. He knew very little more about his passenger from Frankfurt than he had known before. He knew that she had a façade, a façade it seemed to him, very highly faceted, if you could use those two alliterative words together. She was interested in music. Well, he had met her at the Festival Hall, had he not? Fond of outdoor sports. Rich relations who owned

Mediterranean islands. Given to supporting literary charities. Somebody in fact who had good connections, was well related, had entries to the social field. Not apparently highly political and yet, quietly perhaps, affiliated to some group. Someone who moved about from place to place and country to country. Moving among the rich, amongst the talented, about the literary world.

He thought of espionage for a moment or two. That seemed the most likely answer. And yet he was not wholly satisfied with it.

The evening drew on. It came at last to be his turn to be collected by his hostess. Milly Jean was very good at her job.

'I've been longing to talk to you for ages. I wanted to hear about Malaya. I'm so stupid about all these places in Asia, you know, I mix them up. Tell me, what happened out there? Anything interesting or was everything terribly boring?'

'I'm sure you can guess the answer to that one.'

'Well, I should guess it was very boring. But perhaps you're not allowed to say so.'

'Oh yes, I can think it, and I can say it. It wasn't really my cup of tea, you know.'

'Why did you go then?'

'Oh well, I'm always fond of travelling, I like seeing countries.'

'You're such an intriguing person in many ways. Really, of course, all diplomatic life is very boring, isn't it? *I* oughtn't to say so. I only say it to you.'

Very blue eyes. Blue like bluebells in a wood. They opened a little wider and the black brows above them came down gently at the outside corners while the inside corners went up a little. It made her face look like a rather beautiful Persian cat. He wondered what Milly Jean was really like. Her soft voice was that of a southerner. The beautifully shaped little head, her profile with the perfection of a coin – what was she really like? No fool, he thought. One who could use social weapons when needed, who could charm when she wished to, who could withdraw into being enigmatic. If she wanted anything from anyone she would be adroit in getting it. He noticed the intensity of the glance she was giving him now. Did she want something of him? He didn't know. He didn't think it could be likely. She said, 'Have you met Mr Staggenham?'

'Ah yes. I was talking to him at the dinner table. I hadn't met him before.'

'He is said to be very important,' said Milly Jean. 'He's the President of PBF as you know.'

'One should know all those things,' said Sir Stafford Nye. 'PBF and DCV. LYH. And all the world of initials.'

'Hateful,' said Milly Jean. 'Hateful. All these initials, no personalities, no *people* any more. Just initials. What a hateful world! That's what I sometimes think. What a hateful world. I want it to be different, quite, quite different –'

Did she mean that? He thought for one moment that perhaps she did. Interesting . . .

Grosvenor Square was quietness itself. There were traces of broken glass still on the pavements. There were even eggs, squashed tomatoes and fragments of gleaming metal. But above, the stars were peaceful. Car after car drove up to the Embassy door to collect the home-going guests. The police were there in the corners of the square but without ostentation. Everything was under control. One of the political guests leaving spoke to one of the police officers. He came back and murmured, 'Not too many arrests. Eight. They'll be up at Bow Street in the morning. More or less the usual lot. Petronella was here, of course, and Stephen and his crowd. Ah well. One would think they'd get tired of it one of these days.'

'You live not very far from here, don't you?' said a voice in Sir Stafford Nye's ear. A deep contralto voice. 'I can drop you on my way.'

'No, no. I can walk perfectly. It's only ten minutes or so.'

'It will be no trouble to me, I assure you,' said the Countess Zerkowski. She added, 'I'm staying at the St James's Tower.'

The St James's Tower was one of the newer hotels.

'You are very kind.'

It was a big, expensive-looking hire car that waited. The chauffeur opened the door, the Countess Renata got in and Sir Stafford Nye followed her. It was she who gave Sir Stafford Nye's address to the chauffeur. The car drove off.

'So you know where I live?' he said.

'Why not?'

He wondered just what that answer meant: Why not?

'Why not indeed,' he said. 'You know so much, don't you?' He added, 'It was kind of you to return my passport.'

'I thought it might save certain inconveniences. It might be simpler if you burnt it. You've been issued with a new one, I presume –'

'You presume correctly.'

'Your bandit's cloak you will find in the bottom drawer of your tallboy. It was put there tonight. I believed that perhaps to purchase another one would not satisfy you, and indeed that to find one similar might not be possible.'

'It will mean more to me now that it has been through

certain – adventures,' said Stafford Nye. He added, 'It has served its purpose.'

The car purred through the night.

The Countess Zerkowski said:

'Yes. It has served its purpose since I am here – alive . . .'

Sir Stafford Nye said nothing. He was assuming, rightly or not, that she wanted him to ask questions, to press her, to know more of what she had been doing, of what fate she had escaped. She wanted him to display curiosity, but Sir Stafford Nye was not going to display curiosity. He rather enjoyed not doing so. He heard her laugh very gently. Yet he fancied, rather surprisingly, that it was a pleased laugh, a laugh of satisfaction, not of stalemate.

'Did you enjoy your evening?' she said.

'A good party, I think, but Milly Jean always gives good parties.'

'You know her well then?'

'I knew her when she was a girl in New York before she married. A pocket Venus.'

She looked at him in faint surprise.

'Is that your term for her?'

'Actually, no. It was said to me by an elderly relative of mine.'

'Yes, it isn't a description that one hears given often of a woman nowadays. It fits her, I think, very well. Only –'

'Only what?'

'Venus is seductive, is she not? Is she also ambitious?'

'You think Milly Jean Cortman is ambitious?'

'Oh yes. That above all.'

'And you think to be the wife of the Ambassador to St James's is insufficient to satisfy ambition?'

'Oh no,' said the Countess. 'That is only the beginning.'

He did not answer. He was looking out through the car window. He began to speak, then stopped himself. He noted her quick glance at him, but she too was silent. It was not till they were going over a bridge with the Thames below them that he said:

'So you are not giving me a lift home and you are not going back to the St James's Tower. We are crossing the Thames. We met there once before, crossing a bridge. Where are you taking me?'

'Do you mind?'

'I think I do.'

'Yes, I can see you might.'

'Well of course you are quite in the mode. Hi-jacking is the fashion nowadays, isn't it? You have hi-jacked me. Why?'

'Because, like once before, I have need of you.' She added, 'And others have need of you.'

'Indeed.'

'And that does not please you.'

'It would please me better to be asked.'

'If I had asked, would you have come?'

'Perhaps yes, perhaps no.'

'I am sorry.'

'I wonder.'

They drove on through the night in silence. It was not a drive through lonely country, they were on a main road. Now and then the lights picked up a name or a signpost so that Stafford Nye saw quite clearly where their route lay. Through Surrey and through the first residential portions of Sussex. Occasionally he thought they took a detour or a side road which was not the most direct route, but even of this he could not be sure. He almost asked his companion whether this was being done because they might possibly have been followed from London. But he had determined rather firmly on his policy of silence. It was for her to speak, for her to give information. He found her, even with the additional information he had been able to get, an enigmatic character.

They were driving to the country after a dinner party in London. They were, he was pretty sure, in one of the more expensive types of hire car. This was something planned beforehand. Reasonable, nothing doubtful or unexpected about it. Soon, he imagined, he would find out where it was they were going. Unless, that is, they were going to drive as far as the coast. That also was possible, he thought. Haslemere, he saw on a signpost. Now they were skirting Godalming. All very plain and above board. The rich countryside of moneyed suburbia. Agreeable woods, handsome residences. They took a few side turns and then as the car finally slowed, they seemed to be arriving at their destination. Gates. A small white lodge by the gates. Up a drive, well-kept rhododendrons on either side of it. They turned round a bend and drew up before a house. 'Stockbroker Tudor,' murmured Sir Stafford Nye, under his breath. His companion turned her head inquiringly.

'Just a comment,' said Stafford Nye. 'Pay no attention. I take it we are now arriving at the destination of your choice?'

'And you don't admire the look of it very much.'

'The grounds seem well-kept up,' said Sir Stafford, following the beam of the headlights as the car rounded the bend. 'Takes money to keep these places up and in good order. I should say this was a comfortable house to live in.'

'Comfortable but not beautiful. The man who lives in it prefers comfort to beauty, I should say.'

'Perhaps wisely,' said Sir Stafford. 'And yet in some ways he is very appreciative of beauty, of some kinds of beauty.'

They drew up before the well-lighted porch. Sir Stafford got out and tendered an arm to help his companion. The chauffeur had mounted the steps and pressed the bell. He looked inquiringly at the woman as she ascended the steps.

'You won't be requiring me again tonight, m'lady?'

'No. That's all for now. We'll telephone down in the morning.'

'Good night. Good night, sir.'

There were footsteps inside and the door was flung open. Sir Stafford had expected some kind of butler, but instead there was a tall grenadier of a parlour-maid. Grey-haired, tight-lipped, eminently reliable and competent, he thought. An invaluable asset and hard to find nowadays. Trustworthy, capable of being fierce.

'I am afraid we are a little late,' said Renata.

'The master is in the library. He asked that you and the gentleman should come to him there when you arrived.'

IX. THE HOUSE NEAR GODALMING

She led the way up the broad staircase and the two of them followed her. Yes, thought Stafford Nye, a very comfortable house. Jacobean paper, a most unsightly carved oak staircase but pleasantly shallow treads. Pictures nicely chosen but of no particular artistic interest. A rich man's house, he thought. A man, not of bad taste, a man of conventional tastes. Good thick pile carpet of an agreeable plum-coloured texture.

On the first floor, the grenadier-like parlour-maid went to the first door along it. She opened it and stood back to let them go in but she made no announcement of names.

The Countess went in first and Sir Stafford Nye followed her. He heard the door shut quietly behind him.

There were four people in the room. Sitting behind a large desk which was well covered with papers, documents, an open map or two and presumably other papers which were in the course of discussion, was a large, fat man with a very yellow face. It was a face Sir Stafford Nye had seen before, though he could not for the moment attach the proper name to it. It was a man whom he had met only in a casual fashion, and yet the occasion had been an important one. He should know, yes, definitely he should know. But why – why wouldn't the name come?

With a slight struggle, the figure sitting at the desk rose to his feet. He took the Countess Renata's outstretched hand.

'You've arrived,' he said, 'splendid.'

'Yes. Let me introduce you, though I think you already know him. Sir Stafford Nye, Mr Robinson.'

Of course. In Sir Stafford Nye's brain something clicked like a camera. That fitted in, too, with another name. Pikeaway. To say that he knew all about Mr Robinson was not true. He knew about Mr Robinson all that Mr Robinson permitted to be known. His name, as far as anyone knew, *was* Robinson, though it might have been any name of foreign origin. No one had ever suggested anything of that kind. Recognition came also of his personal appearance. The high forehead, the melancholy dark eyes, the large generous mouth, and the impressive large white teeth – false teeth, presumably, but at any rate teeth of which it might have been said, like in Red Riding Hood, 'the better to eat you with, child!'

He knew, too, what Mr Robinson stood for. Just one simple word described it. Mr Robinson represented Money with a capital M. Money in its every aspect. International money, world-wide money, private home finances, banking, foreign governments. Industrial projects. He represented money not in the way that the average person looked at it. You never thought of him as a very rich man. Undoubtedly he was a very rich man but that wasn't the important thing. He was one of the arrangers of money, the great clan of bankers. His personal tastes might even have been simple, but Sir Stafford Nye doubted if they were. A reasonable standard of comfort, even luxury, would be Mr Robinson's way of life. But not more than that. So behind all this mysterious business there was the power of money.

'I heard of you just a day or two ago,' said Mr Robinson, as he shook hands, 'from our friend Pikeaway, you know.'

That fitted in, thought Stafford Nye, because now he remembered that on the solitary occasion before that he had met Mr Robinson, Colonel Pikeaway had been present. Horsham, he remembered, had spoken of Mr Robinson. So now there was Mary Ann (or the Countess Zerkowski?) and Colonel Pikeaway sitting in his own smoke-filled room with his eyes half closed either going to sleep or just waking up, and there was Mr Robinson with his large, yellow face, and so there was money at stake somewhere, and his glance shifted to the three other people in the room because he wanted to see if he knew who they were and what they represented, or if he could guess.

In two cases at least he didn't need to guess. The man who sat in the tall porter's chair by the fireplace, an elderly figure framed by the chair as a picture-frame might have framed him, was a face that had been well known all over England. Indeed, it still *was* well known, although it was very seldom seen nowadays. A sick man, an invalid, a man who made very brief appearances, and then it was said, at physical cost to himself in pain and difficulty. Lord Altamount. A thin emaciated face, outstanding nose, grey hair which receded just a little from the forehead, and then flowed back in a thick grey mane; somewhat prominent ears that cartoonists had used in their time, and a deep piercing glance that not so much observed as probed. Probed deeply into what it was looking at. At the moment it was looking at Sir Stafford Nye. He stretched out a hand as Stafford Nye went towards him.

'I don't get up,' said Lord Altamount. His voice was faint, an old man's voice, a far-away voice. 'My back doesn't allow me to. Just come back from Malaya, haven't you, Stafford Nye?'

'Yes.'

'Was it worth your going? I expect you think it wasn't. You're probably right, too. Still, we have to have these excrescences in life, these ornamental trimmings to adorn the better kind of diplomatic lies. I'm glad you could come here or were brought here tonight. Mary Ann's doing, I suppose?'

So that's what he calls her and thinks of her as, thought Stafford Nye to himself. It was what Horsham had called her. She was in with them then, without a doubt. As for Altamount, he stood for – what did he stand for nowadays? Stafford Nye thought to himself; He stands for England. He still stands for England until he's buried in Westminster Abbey or a country mausoleum, whatever he chooses. He has *been* England, and he knows England, and I should say he knows the value of every politician and government official in England pretty well, even if he's never spoken to them.

Lord Altamount said:

'This is our colleague, Sir James Kleek.'

Stafford Nye didn't know Kleek. He didn't think he'd

even heard of him. A restless, fidgety type. Sharp, suspicious glances that never rested anywhere for long. He had the contained eagerness of a sporting dog awaiting the word of command. Ready to start off at a glance from his master's eye.

But who was his master? Altamount or Robinson?

Stafford's eye went round to the fourth man. He had risen to his feet from the chair where he had been sitting close to the door. Bushy moustache, raised eyebrows, watchful, withdrawn, managing in some way to remain familiar yet almost unrecognizable.

'So it's you,' said Sir Stafford Nye, 'how are you, Horsham?'

'Very pleased to see you here, Sir Stafford.'

Quite a representative gathering, Stafford Nye thought, with a swift glance round.

They had set a chair for Renata not far from the fire and Lord Altamount. She had stretched out a hand – her left hand, he noticed – and he had taken it between his two hands, holding it for a minute, then dropping it. He said:

'You took risks, child, you take too many risks.'

Looking at him, she said, 'It was you who taught me that, and it's the only way of life.'

Lord Altamount turned his head towards Sir Stafford Nye.

'It wasn't I who taught you to choose your man. You've got a natural genius for that.' Looking at Stafford Nye, he said, 'I know your great-aunt, or your great-great-aunt, is she?'

'Great-Aunt Matilda,' said Stafford Nye immediately.

'Yes. That's the one. One of the Victorian *tours-de-force* of the 'nineties. She must be nearly ninety herself now.'

He went on:

'I don't see her very often. Once or twice a year perhaps. But it strikes me every time – that sheer vitality of hers that outlives her bodily strength. They have the secret of that, those indomitable Victorians and some of the Edwardians as well.'

Sir James Kleek said, 'Let me get you a drink, Nye? What will you have?'

'Gin and tonic, if I may.'

The Countess refused with a small shake of the head.

James Kleek brought Nye his drink and set it on the table near Mr Robinson. Stafford Nye was not going to speak first. The dark eyes behind the desk lost their melancholy for a moment. They had quite suddenly a twinkle in them.

'Any questions?' he said.

'Too many,' said Sir Stafford Nye. 'Wouldn't it be better to have explanations first, questions later?'

'Is that what you'd like?'

'It might simplify matters.'

'Well, we start with a few plain statements of facts. You may or you may not have been asked to come here. If not, that fact may rankle slightly.'

'He prefers to be asked always,' said the Countess. 'He said as much to me.'

'Naturally,' said Mr Robinson.

'I was hi-jacked,' said Stafford Nye. 'Very fashionable, I know. One of our more modern methods.'

He kept his tone one of light amusement.

'Which invites, surely, a question from you,' said Mr Robinson.

'Just one small word of three letters. Why?'

'Quite so. Why? I admire your economy of speech. This is a private committee – a committee of inquiry. An inquiry of world-wide significance.'

'Sounds interesting,' said Sir Stafford Nye.

'It is more than interesting. It is poignant and immediate. Four different ways of life are represented in this room tonight,' said Lord Altamount. 'We represent different branches. I have retired from active participation in the affairs of this country, but I am still a consulting authority. I have been consulted and asked to preside over this particular inquiry as to what is going on in the world in this particular year of our Lord, because something *is* going on. James, here, has his own special task. He is my right-hand man. He is also our spokesman. Explain the general set-out, if you will, Jamie, to Sir Stafford here.'

It seemed to Stafford Nye that the gun dog quivered. At last! his eagerness seemed to be saying. At last! At last I can speak and get on with it! He leaned forward a little in his chair.

'If things happen in the world, you have to look for a cause for them. The outward signs are always easy to see but they're not, or so the Chairman –' he bowed to Lord Altamount – 'and Mr Robinson and Mr Horsham believe, important. It's always been the same way. You take a natural force, a great fall of water that will give you turbine power. You take the discovery of uranium from pitchblende, and that will give you in due course nuclear power that had not been dreamt of or known. When you found coal and minerals, they gave you transport, power, energy. There are forces at work always that give you certain things. But behind each of them there is *someone who controls it.* You've got to find who's controlling the powers that are slowly gaining ascendancy in practically every country in Europe, further afield still in parts of Asia. Less, possibly, in Africa, but again in the American continents both north and south. You've got to get behind the things that are happening and find out the motive force that's making them happen. One thing that makes things happen is *money*.'

He nodded towards Mr Robinson.

'Mr Robinson, there, knows as much about money as anybody in the world, I suppose.'

'It's quite simple,' said Mr Robinson. 'There are big movements afoot. There has to be money behind them. We've got to find out where that money's coming from. Who's operating with it? Where do they get it from? Where are they sending it to? Why? It's quite true what James says: I know a lot about money! As much as any man alive knows today. Then there are what you might call trends. It's a word we use a good deal nowadays! Trends or tendencies – there are innumerable words one uses. They mean not quite the same thing, but they're in relationship with each other. A tendency, shall we say, to rebellion shows up. Look back through history. You'll find it coming again and again, repeating itself like a periodic table, repeating a pattern. A desire for rebellion. A feeling for rebellion, the means of rebellion, the form the rebellion takes. It's not a thing particular to any particular country. If it arises in one country, it will arise in other countries in less or more degrees. That's what you mean, sir, isn't it?' He half turned towards Lord Altamount. 'That's the way you more or less put it to me.'

'Yes, you're expressing things very well, James.'

'It's a pattern, a pattern that arises and seems inevitable. You can recognize it where you find it. There was a period when a yearning towards crusades swept countries. All over Europe people embarked in ships, they went off to deliver the Holy Land. All quite clear, a perfectly good pattern of determined behaviour. But *why* did they go? That's the interest of history, you know. Seeing why these desires and patterns arise. It's not always a materialistic answer either. All sorts of things can cause rebellion, a desire for freedom, freedom of speech, freedom of religious worship, again a series of closely related patterns. It led people to embrace emigration to other countries, to formation of new religions very often as full of tyranny as the forms of religion they had left behind. But in all this, if you look hard enough, if you make enough investigations, you can see what started the onset of these and many other – I'll use the same word – patterns. In some ways it's like a virus disease. The virus can be carried – round the world, across seas, up mountains. It can go and infect. It goes apparently without being set in motion. But one can't be sure, even now, that that was always really true. There could have been causes. Causes that made things happen. One can go a few steps further. There are *people*. One person – ten persons – a few hundred persons who are capable of being and setting in motion a cause. So it is not the *end process* that one has to look at. It is the first people who set the cause in motion. You have your crusaders, you have your religious enthusiasts, you have your desires for liberty, you have all the other patterns but you've got to go further back still. Further back to a hinterland. Behind the materialistic results, there are ideas. Visions, dreams. The prophet Joel knew it when he wrote "Your old men shall dream dreams, your young men shall see visions." And of those two, which are the more powerful? Dreams are not destructive. But visions can open new worlds to you – and visions can also destroy the worlds that already exist . . .'

James Kleek turned suddenly towards Lord Altamount. 'I don't know if it connects up, sir,' he said, 'but you told me a story once of somebody in the Embassy at Berlin. A woman.'

'Oh that? Yes, I found it interesting at the time. Yes,

it has a bearing on what we are talking about now. One of the Embassy wives, clever, intelligent woman, well educated. She was very anxious to go personally and hear the Führer speak. I am talking, of course, of a time immediately preceding the 1939 war. She was curious to know what oratory could do. Why was everyone so impressed? And so she went. She came back and said, "It's extraordinary. I wouldn't have believed it. Of course I don't understand German very well but I was carried away, too. And I see now why everyone is. I mean, his ideas were wonderful . . . They inflamed you. The things he said. I mean, you just felt there *was* no other way of thinking, that a whole new world would happen if only one followed him. Oh, I can't explain properly. I'm going to write down as much as I can remember, and then if I bring it to you to see, you'll see better than my just trying to tell you the effect it had."

'I told her that was a very good idea. She came to me the next day and she said, "I don't know if you'll believe this. I started to write down the things I'd heard, the things Hitler had said. What they'd *meant* – but – it was frightening – *there wasn't anything to write down at all, I didn't seem able to remember a single stimulating or exciting sentence.* I have some of the words, but it doesn't seem to mean the same things as when I wrote them down. They are just – oh, they are just *meaningless*. I don't understand."

'That shows you one of the great dangers one doesn't always remember, *but it exists*. There are people capable of communicating to others a wild enthusiasm, a kind of vision of life and of happening. They can do that though it is not really by what they *say*, it is not the *words* you *hear*, it is not even the idea described. It's something else. It's the magnetic power that a very few men have of starting something, of producing and creating a vision. By their personal magnetism perhaps, a tone of voice, perhaps some emanation that comes forth straight from the *flesh.* I don't know, *but it exists.*

'Such people have power. The great religious teachers had this power, and so has an evil spirit power also. Belief can be created in a certain movement, in certain things to be done, things that will result in a new heaven and a new earth, and people will believe it and work for it and fight for it and even die for it.'

He lowered his voice as he said: 'Jan Smuts put it in a phrase. He said Leadership, besides being a great creative force, can be *diabolical.*'

Stafford Nye moved in his chair.

'I understand what you mean. It is interesting what you say. I can see perhaps that it might be true.'

'But you think it's exaggerated, of course.'

'I don't know that I do,' said Stafford Nye. 'Things that sound exaggerated are very often not exaggerated at all. They are only things that you haven't heard said before or thought about before. And therefore they come to you as so unfamiliar that you can hardly do anything about them except accept them. By the way, may I ask a simple question? What *does* one do about them?'

'If you come across the suspicion that this sort of thing is going on, you must find out about them,' said Lord Altamount. 'You've got to go like Kipling's mongoose: Go and find out. Find out where the money comes from and where the ideas are coming from, and where, if I may say so, the *machinery* comes from. Who is directing the machinery? There's a chief of staff, you know, as well as a commander-in-chief. That's what we're trying to do. We'd like you to come and help us.'

It was one of the rare occasions in his life when Sir Stafford Nye was taken aback. Whatever he may have felt on some former occasions, he had always managed to conceal the fact. But this time it was different. He looked from one to the other of the men in the room. At Mr Robinson, impassively yellow-faced with his mouthful of teeth displayed; to Sir James Kleek, a somewhat brash talker, Sir Stafford Nye had considered him, but nevertheless he had obviously his uses; Master's dog, he called him in his own mind. He looked at Lord Altamount, the hood of the porter's chair framed round his head. The lighting was not strong in the room. It gave him the look of a saint in a niche in a cathedral somewhere. Ascetic. Fourteenth-century. A great man. Yes, Altamount had been one of the great men of the past. Stafford Nye had no doubt of that, but he was now a very old man. Hence, he supposed, the necessity for Sir James Kleek, and Lord Altamount's reliance on him. He looked past them to the enigmatic, cool creature who had brought him here, the Countess Renata Zerkowski alias Mary Ann, alias Daphne Theodofanous. Her face told him nothing. She was not even looking at him. His eyes came round last to Mr Henry Horsham of Security.

With faint surprise he observed that Henry Horsham was grinning at him.

'But look here,' said Stafford Nye, dropping all formal language, and speaking rather like the schoolboy of eighteen he had once been. 'Where on earth do I come in? What do *I* know? Quite frankly, I'm not distinguished in any way in my own profession, you know. They don't think very much of me at the FO. Never have.'

'We know that,' said Lord Altamount.

It was Sir James Kleek's turn to grin and he did so.

'All the better perhaps,' he remarked, and added apologetically as Lord Altamount frowned at him, 'Sorry, sir.'

'This is a committee of investigation,' said Mr Robinson. 'It is not a question of what you have done in the past, of what other people's opinion of you may be. What we are doing is to recruit a committee to investigate. There are not very many of us at the moment forming this committee. We ask you to join it because we think that you have certain qualities which may help in an investigation.'

Stafford Nye turned his head towards the Security man. 'What about it, Horsham?' he said. 'I can't believe you'd agree with that?'

'Why not?' said Henry Horsham.

'Indeed? What are my "qualities", as you call them? I can't, quite frankly, believe in them myself.'

'You're not a hero-worshipper,' said Horsham. 'That's why. You're the kind who sees through humbug. You don't take anyone at their own or the world's valuation. You take them at your own valuation.'

Ce n'est pas un garçon sérieux. The words floated through Sir Stafford Nye's mind. A curious reason for which to be chosen for a difficult and exacting job.

'I've got to warn you,' he said, 'that my principal fault, and one that's been frequently noticed about me and which has cost me several good jobs is, I think, fairly well known. I'm not, I should say, a sufficiently serious sort of chap for an important job like this.'

'Believe it or not,' said Mr Horsham, 'that's one of the reasons why they want you. I'm right, my lord, aren't I?' He looked towards Lord Altamount.

'Public service!' said Lord Altamount. 'Let me tell you that very often one of the most serious disadvantages in public life is when people in a public position take themselves too seriously. We feel that you won't. Anyway,' he said, 'Mary Ann thinks so.'

Sir Stafford Nye turned his head. So here she was, no longer a countess. She had become Mary Ann again.

'You don't mind my asking,' he said, 'but who are you really? I mean, are you a real countess.'

'Absolutely. *Geboren*, as the Germans say. My father was a man of pedigree, a good sportsman, a splendid shot, and had a very romantic but somewhat dilapidated castle in Bavaria. It's still there, the castle. As far as that goes, I have connections with that large portion of the European world which is still heavily snobbish as far as birth is concerned. A poor and shabby countess sits down first at the table whilst a rich American with a fabulous fortune in dollars in the bank is kept waiting.'

'What about Daphne Theodofanous? Where does she come in?'

'A useful name for a passport. My mother was Greek.'

'And Mary Ann?'

It was almost the first smile Stafford Nye had seen on her face. Her eyes went to Lord Altamount and from him to Mr Robinson.

'Perhaps,' she said, 'because I'm a kind of maid-of-all-work, going places, looking for things, taking things from one country to another, sweeping under the mat, do anything, go anywhere, clear up the mess.' She looked towards Lord Altamount again. 'Am I right, Uncle Ned?'

'Quite right, my dear. Mary Ann you are and always will be to us.'

'Were you taking something on that plane? I mean taking something important from one country to another?'

'Yes. It was known I was carrying it. If you hadn't come to my rescue, if you hadn't drunk possibly poisoned beer and handed over your bandit cloak of bright colours as a disguise, well, accidents happen sometimes. I shouldn't have got here.'

'What were you carrying – or mustn't I ask? Are there things I shall never know?'

'There are a lot of things you will never know. There are a lot of things you won't be allowed to ask. I think that question of yours I shall answer. A bare answer of fact. If I am allowed to do so.'

Again she looked at Lord Altamount.

'I trust your judgment,' said Lord Altamount. 'Go ahead.'

'Give him the dope,' said the irreverent James Kleek.

Mr Horsham said, 'I suppose you've got to know. *I* wouldn't tell you, but then I'm Security. Go ahead, Mary Ann.'

'One sentence. *I was bringing a birth certificate. That's all.* I don't tell you any more and it won't be any use your asking any more questions.'

Stafford Nye looked round the assembly.

'All right. I'll join. I'm flattered at your asking me. Where do we go from here?'

'You and I,' said Renata, 'leave here tomorrow. We go to the Continent. You may have read, or know, that there's a Musical Festival taking place in Bavaria. It is something quite new which has only come into being in the last two years. It has a rather formidable German name meaning "The Company of the Youthful Singers" and is supported by the Governments of several different countries. It is in opposition to the traditional festivals and productions of Bayreuth. Much of the music given is modern – new young composers are given the chance of their compositions being heard. Whilst thought of highly by some, it is utterly repudiated and held in contempt by others.'

'Yes,' said Sir Stafford, 'I have read about it. Are we going to attend it?'

'We have seats booked for two of the performances.'

'Has this festival any special significance in our investigation?'

'No,' said Renata. 'It is more in the nature of what you might call an exit and entry convenience. We go there for an ostensible and true reason, and we leave it for our next step in due course.'

He looked round. 'Instructions? Do I get any marching orders? Am I to be briefed?'

'Not in your meaning of those terms. You are going on a voyage of exploration. You will learn things as you go along. You will go as yourself, knowing only what you know at present. You go as a lover of music, as a slightly disappointed diplomat who had perhaps hoped for some post in his own country which he has not been given. Otherwise, you will know nothing. It is safer so.'

'But that is the sum of activities at present? Germany, Bavaria, Austria, the Tyrol – that part of the world?'

'It is one of the centres of interest.'

'It is not the only one?'

'Indeed, not even the principal one. There are other spots on the globe, all of varying importance and interest. How much importance each one holds is what we have to find out.'

'And I don't know, or am not to be told, anything about these other centres?'

'Only in cursory fashion. One of them, we think the most important one, has its headquarters in South America, there are two with headquarters in the United States of America, one in California, the other in Baltimore. There is one in Sweden, there is one in Italy. Things have become very active in the latter in the last six months.

Portugal and Spain also have smaller centres. Paris, of course. There are further interesting spots just "coming into production", you might say. As yet not fully developed.'

'You mean Malaya, or Vietnam?'

'No. No, all that lies rather in the past. It was a good rallying cry for violence and student indignation and for many other things.

'What is being promoted, you must understand, is the growing organization of youth everywhere against their mode of government; against their parental customs, against very often the religions in which they have been brought up. There is the insidious cult of permissiveness, there is the increasing cult of violence. Violence not as a means of gaining money, but violence for the love of violence. That particularly is stressed, and the reasons for it are to the people concerned one of the most important things and of the utmost significance.'

'Permissiveness, is that important?'

'It is a way of life, no more. It lends itself to certain abuses but not unduly.'

'What about drugs?'

'The cult of drugs has been deliberately advanced and fomented. Vast sums of money have been made that way, but it is not, or so we think, entirely activated for the money motive.'

All of them looked at Mr Robinson, who slowly shook his head.

'No,' he said, 'it *looks* that way. There are people who are being apprehended and brought to justice. Pushers of drugs will be followed up. But there is more than just the drug racket behind all this. The drug racket is a means, and an evil means, of making money. But there is more to it than that.'

'But who –' Stafford Nye stopped.

'Who and what and why and where? The four W's. That is your mission, Sir Stafford,' said Mr Robinson. 'That's what you've got to find out. You and Mary Ann. It won't be easy, and one of the hardest things in the world, remember, is to keep one's secrets.'

Stafford Nye looked with interest at the fat yellow face of Mr Robinson. Perhaps the secret of Mr Robinson's domination in the financial world was just that. His secret was that he kept his secret. Mr Robinson's mouth showed its smile again. The large teeth gleamed.

'If you know a thing,' he said, 'it is always a great temptation to show that you know it; to talk about it, in other words. It is not that you want to give information, it is not that you have been offered payment to give information. It is that you want to show how important you are. Yes, it's just as simple as that. In fact,' said Mr Robinson, and he half closed his eyes, 'everything in this world is so very, *very* simple. That's what people don't understand.'

The Countess got to her feet and Stafford Nye followed her example.

'I hope you will sleep well and be comfortable,' said Mr Robinson. 'This house is, I think, moderately comfortable.'

Stafford Nye murmured that he was quite sure of that, and on that point he was shortly to be proved to have been quite right. He laid his head on the pillow and went to sleep immediately.

BOOK 11

JOURNEY TO SIEGFRIED

X. THE WOMAN IN THE SCHLOSS

They came out of the Festival Youth Theatre to the refreshing night air. Below them in a sweep of the ground, was a lighted restaurant. On the side of the hill was another, smaller one. The restaurants varied slightly in price though neither of them was inexpensive. Renata was in evening dress of black velvet, Sir Stafford Nye was in white tie and full evening dress.

'A very distinguished audience,' murmured Stafford Nye to his companion. 'Plenty of money there. A young audience on the whole. You wouldn't think they could afford it.'

'Oh! that can be seen to – it *is* seen to.'

'A subsidy for the élite of youth? That kind of thing?'

'Yes.'

They walked towards the restaurant on the high side of the hill.

'They give you an hour for the meal. Is that right?'

'Technically an hour. Actually an hour and a quarter.'

'That audience,' said Sir Stafford Nye, 'most of them, nearly all of them, I should say, are real lovers of music.'

'Most of them, yes. It's important, you know.'

'What do you mean – important?'

'That the enthusiasm should be genuine. At both ends of the scale,' she added.

'What did you mean, exactly, by that?'

'Those who practise and organize violence must love violence, must want it, must yearn for it. The seal of ecstasy in every movement, of slashing, hurting, destroying. And the same thing with the music. The ears must appreciate every moment of the harmonies and beauties. There can be no pretending in this game.'

'Can you double the rôles – do you mean you can combine violence *and* a love of music or a love of art?'

'It is not always easy, I think, but yes. There are many who can. It is safer really, if they don't have to combine rôles.'

'It's better to keep it simple, as our fat friend Mr Robinson would say? Let the lovers of music love music, let the violent practitioners love violence. Is that what you mean?'

'I think so.'

'I am enjoying this very much. The two days that we have stayed here, the two nights of music that we have enjoyed. I have not enjoyed all the music because I am not perhaps sufficiently modern in my taste. I find the clothes very interesting.'

'Are you talking of the stage production?'

'No, no, I was talking of the audience, really. You and I, the squares, the old-fashioned. You, Countess, in your society gown, I in my white tie and tails. Not a comfortable get-up, it never has been. And then the others, the silks and the velvets, the ruffled shirts of the men, real lace, I noticed, several times – and the plush and the hair and the luxury of *avant garde*, the luxury of the eighteen-hundreds or you might almost say of the Elizabethan age or of Van Dyck pictures.'

'Yes, you are right.'

'I'm no nearer, though, to what it all *means*. I haven't *learnt* anything. I haven't found out anything.'

'You mustn't be impatient. This is a rich show, supported, asked for, demanded perhaps by youth and provided by –'

'By whom?'

'We don't know yet. We shall know.'

'I'm so glad you are sure of it.'

They went into the restaurant and sat down. The food was good though not in any way ornate or luxurious. Once or twice they were spoken to by an acquaintance or a friend. Two people who recognized Sir Stafford Nye expressed pleasure and surprise at seeing him. Renata had a bigger circle of acquaintances since she knew more foreigners – well-dressed women, a man or two, mostly German or Austrian, Stafford Nye thought, one or two, Americans. Just a few desultory words. Where people had come from or were going to, criticism or appreciation of the musical fare. Nobody wasted much time since the interval for eating had not been very long.

They returned to their seats for the two final musical offerings. A Symphonic Poem, 'Disintegration in Joy', by a new young composer, Solukonov, and then the solemn grandeur of the March of the Meistersingers.

They came out again into the night. The car which was at their disposal every day was waiting there to take them back to the small but exclusive hotel in the village street. Stafford Nye said good-night to Renata. She spoke to him in a lowered voice.

'Four a.m.,' she said. 'Be ready.'

She went straight into her room and shut the door and he went to his.

The faint scrape of fingers on his door came precisely at three minutes to four the next morning. He opened the door and stood ready.

'The car is waiting,' she said. 'Come.'

They lunched at a small mountain inn. The weather was good, the mountains beautiful. Occasionally Stafford Nye wondered what on earth he was doing here. He understood less and less of his travelling companion. She spoke little. He found himself watching her profile. Where was she taking him? What was her real reason? At last, as the sun was almost setting, he said:

'Where are we going? Can I ask?'

'You can ask, yes.'

'But you do not reply?'

'I could reply. I could tell you things, but would they mean anything? It seems to me that if you come to where we are going without my preparing you with explanations (which cannot in the nature of things mean anything), your first impressions will have more force and significance.'

He looked at her again thoughtfully. She was wearing a tweed coat trimmed with fur, smart travelling clothes, foreign in make and cut.

'Mary Ann,' he said thoughtfully.

There was a faint question in it.

'No,' she said, 'not at the moment.'

'Ah. You are still the Countess Zerkowski.'

'At the moment I am still the Countess Zerkowski.'

'Are you in your own part of the world?'

'More or less. I grew up as a child in this part of the world. For a good portion of each year we used to come here in the autumn to a Schloss not very many miles from here.'

He smiled and said thoughtfully, 'What a nice word it is. A Schloss. So solid-sounding.'

'Schlösser are not standing very solidly nowadays. They are mostly disintegrated.'

'This is Hitler's country, isn't it? We're not far, are we, from Berchtesgaden?'

'It lies over there to the north-east.'

'Did your relations, your friends – did they accept Hitler, believe in him? Perhaps I ought not to ask things like that.'

'They disliked him and all he stood for. But they said "Heil Hitler". They acquiesced in what had happened to their country. What else could they do? What else could anybody do at that date?'

'We are going towards the Dolomites, are we not?'

'Does it matter where we are, or which way we are going?'

'Well, this is a voyage of exploration, is it not?'

'Yes, but the exploration is not geographical. We are going to see a personality.'

'You make me feel –' Stafford Nye looked up at the landscape of swelling mountains reaching up to the sky – 'as though we were going to visit the famous Old Man of the Mountain.'

'The Master of the Assassins, you mean, who kept his followers under drugs so that they died for him wholeheartedly, so that they killed, knowing that they themselves would also be killed, but believing, too, that that would transfer them immediately to the Moslem Paradise – beautiful women, hashish and erotic dreams – perfect and unending happiness.'

She paused a minute and then said:

'Spell-binders! I suppose they've always been there throughout the ages. People who make you believe in them so that you are ready to die for them. Not only Assassins. The Christians died also.'

'The holy Martyrs? Lord Altamount?'

'Why do you say Lord Altamount?'

'I saw him that way – suddenly – that evening. Carved in stone – in a thirteenth-century cathedral, perhaps.'

'One of us may have to die. Perhaps more.'

She stopped what he was about to say.

'There is another thing I think of sometimes. A verse in the New Testament – Luke, I think. Christ at the Last

Supper saying to his followers: "You are my companions and my friends, *yet one of you is a devil.*" So in all probability one of *us* is a devil.'

'You think it possible?'

'Almost certain. Someone we trust and know, but who goes to sleep at night, not dreaming of martyrdom but of thirty pieces of silver, and who wakes with the feel of them in the palm of his hand.'

'The love of money?'

'Ambition covers it better. How does one recognize a devil? How would one *know*? A devil would stand out in a crowd, would be exciting – would advertise himself – would exercise leadership.'

She was silent a moment and then said in a thoughtful voice:

'I had a friend once in the Diplomatic Service who told me how she had said to a German woman how moved she herself had been at the performance of the Passion Play at Oberammergau. But the German woman said scornfully: "You do not understand. *We* Germans have no need of a Jesus Christ! We have our Adolf Hitler here with us. He is greater than any Jesus that ever lived." She was quite a nice ordinary woman. But that is how she felt. Masses of people felt it. Hitler was a spell-binder. He spoke and they listened – and accepted the sadism, the gas chambers, the tortures of the Gestapo.'

She shrugged her shoulders and then said in her normal voice, 'All the same, it's odd that you should have said what you did just now.'

'What was that?'

'About the Old Man of the Mountain. The head of the Assassins.'

'Are you telling me there *is* an Old Man of the Mountain here?'

'No. Not an Old Man of the Mountain, but there might be an Old Woman of the Mountain.'

'An Old Woman of the Mountain. What's she like?'

'You'll see this evening.'

'What are we doing this evening?'

'Going into society,' said Renata.

'It seems a long time since you've been Mary Ann.'

'You'll have to wait till we're doing some air travel again.'

'I suppose it's very bad for one's morale,' Stafford Nye said thoughtfully, 'living high up in the world.'

'Are you talking socially?'

'No. Geographically. If you live in a castle on a mountain peak overlooking the world below you, well, it makes you despise the ordinary folk, doesn't it? You're the top one, you're the grand one. That's what Hitler felt in Berchtesgaden, that's what many people feel perhaps who climb mountains and look down on their fellow creatures in valleys below.'

'You must be careful tonight,' Renata warned him. 'It's going to be ticklish.'

'Any instructions?'

'You're a disgruntled man. You're one that's against the Establishment, against the conventional world. You're a rebel, but a secret rebel. Can you do it?'

'I can try.'

The scenery had grown wilder. The big car twisted and turned up the roads, passing through mountain villages, sometimes looking down on a bewilderingly distant view where lights shone on a river, where the steeples of churches showed in the distance.

'Where are we going, Mary Ann?'

'To an Eagle's nest.'

The road took a final turn. It wound through a forest.

Stafford Nye thought he caught glimpses now and again of deer or of animals of some kind. Occasionally, too, there were leather-jacketed men with guns. Keepers, he thought. And then they came finally to a view of an enormous Schloss standing on a crag. Some of it, he thought, was partially ruined, though most of it had been restored and rebuilt. It was both massive and magnificent but there was nothing new about it or in the message it held. It was representative of past power, power held through bygone ages.

'This was originally the Grand Duchy of Liechtenstolz. The Schloss was built by the Grand Duke Ludwig in 1790,' said Renata.

'Who lives there now? The present Grand Duke?'

'No. They're all gone and done with. Swept away.'

'And who lives here now then?'

'Someone who has present-day power,' said Renata.

'Money?'

'Yes. Very much so.'

'Shall we meet Mr Robinson, flown on ahead by air to greet us?'

'The last person you'll meet here will be Mr Robinson, I can assure you.'

'A pity,' said Stafford Nye. 'I like Mr Robinson. He's quite something, isn't he? Who is he really – what nationality is he?'

'I don't think anybody has ever known. Everyone tells one something different. Some people say he's a Turk, some that he's an Armenian, some that he's Dutch, some that he's just plain English. Some say that his mother was a Circassian slave, a Russian Grand-Duchess, an Indian Begum and so on. Nobody knows. One person told me that his mother was a Miss McLellan from Scotland. I think that's as likely as anything.'

They had drawn up beneath a large portico. Two menservants in livery came down the steps. Their bows were ostentatious as they welcomed the guests. The luggage was removed; they had a good deal of luggage with them. Stafford Nye had wondered to begin with why he had been told to bring so much, but he was beginning to understand now that from time to time there was need for it. There would, he thought, be need for it this evening. A few questioning remarks and his companion told him that this was so.

They met before dinner, summoned by the sound of a great resounding gong. As he paused in the hall, he waited for her to join him coming down the stairs. She was in full elaborate evening dress tonight, wearing a dark red velvet gown, rubies round her neck and a ruby tiara on her head. A manservant stepped forward and conducted them. Flinging open the door, he announced:

'The Gräfin Zerkowski, Sir Stafford Nye.'

'Here we come, and I hope we look the part,' said Sir Stafford Nye to himself.

He looked down in a satisfied manner at the sapphire and diamond studs in the front of his shirt. A moment later he had drawn his breath in an astonished gasp. Whatever he had expected to see it had not been this. It was an enormous room, rococo in style, chairs and sofas and hangings of the finest brocades and velvets. On the walls there were pictures that he could not recognize all at once, but where he noted almost immediately – for he was fond of pictures – what was certainly a Cézanne, a Matisse, possibly a Renoir. Pictures of inestimable value.

Sitting on a vast chair, throne-like in its suggestion, was an enormous woman. A whale of a woman, Stafford Nye thought, there really was no other word to describe her. A great, big, cheesy-looking woman, wallowing in fat.

Double, treble, almost quadruple chins. She wore a dress of stiff orange satin. On her head was an elaborate crown-like tiara of precious stones. Her hands, which rested on the brocaded arms of her seat, were also enormous. Great, big, fat hands with great, big, fat, shapeless fingers. On each finger, he noticed, was a solitaire ring. And in each ring, he thought, was a genuine solitaire stone. A ruby, an emerald, a sapphire, a diamond, a pale green stone which he did not know, a chrysoprase, perhaps, a yellow stone which, if not a topaz, was a yellow diamond. She was horrible, he thought. She wallowed in her fat. A great, white, creased, slobbering mass of fat was her face. And set in it, rather like currants in a vast currant bun, were two small black eyes. Very shrewd eyes, looking on the world, appraising it, appraising him, not appraising Renata, he thought. Renata she knew. Renata was here by command, by appointment. However you liked to put it. Renata had been told to bring *him* here. He wondered why. He couldn't really think why, but he was quite sure of it. It was at him she was looking. She was appraising *him*, summing *him* up. Was he what she wanted? Was he, yes, he'd rather put it this way, was he what the customer had ordered?

I'll have to make quite sure that I know what it is she does want, he thought. I'll have to do my best, otherwise . . . Otherwise he could quite imagine that she might raise a fat ringed hand and say to one of the tall, muscular footmen: 'Take him and throw him over the battlements.' It's ridiculous, thought Stafford Nye. Such things can't happen nowadays. Where am I? What kind of a parade, a masquerade or a theatrical performance am I taking part in?

'You have come very punctual to time, child.'

It was a hoarse, asthmatic voice which had once had

an undertone, he thought, of strength, possibly even of beauty. That was over now. Renata came forward, made a slight curtsy. She picked up the fat hand and dropped a courtesy kiss upon it.

'Let me present to you Sir Stafford Nye. The Gräfin Charlotte von Waldsausen.'

The fat hand was extended towards him. He bent over it in the foreign style. Then she said something that surprised him.

'I know your great-aunt,' she said.

He looked astounded, and he saw immediately that she was amused by that, but he saw too, that she had expected him to be surprised by it. She laughed, a rather queer, grating laugh. Not attractive.

'Shall we say, I used to know her. It is many, many years since I have seen her. We were in Switzerland together, at Lausanne, as girls. Matilda. Lady Matilda Baldwen-White.'

'What a wonderful piece of news to take home with me,' said Stafford Nye.

'She is older than I am. She is in good health?'

'For her age, in very good health. She lives in the country quietly. She has arthritis, rheumatism.'

'Ah yes, all the ills of old age. She should have injections of procaine. That is what the doctors do here in this altitude. It is very satisfactory. Does she know that you are visiting me?'

'I imagine that she has not the least idea of it,' said Sir Stafford Nye. 'She knew only that I was going to this festival of modern music.'

'Which you enjoyed, I hope?'

'Oh, enormously. It is a fine Festival Opera Hall, is it not?'

'One of the finest. Pah! It makes the old Bayreuth

Festival Hall look like a comprehensive school! Do you know what it cost to build, that Opera House?'

She mentioned a sum in millions of marks. It quite took Stafford Nye's breath away, but he was under no necessity to conceal that. She was pleased with the effect it made upon him.

'With money,' she said, 'if one knows, if one has the ability, if one has the discrimination, what is there that money cannot do? It can give one the best.'

She said the last two words with a rich enjoyment, a kind of smacking of the lips which he found both unpleasant and at the same time slightly sinister.

'I see that here,' he said, as he looked round the walls.

'You are fond of art? Yes, I see you are. There, on the east wall is the finest Cézanne in the world today. Some say that the – ah, I forget the name of it at the moment, the one in the Metropolitan in New York – is finer. That is not true. The best Matisse, the best Cézanne, the best of all that great school of art are here. Here in my mountain eyrie.'

'It is wonderful,' said Sir Stafford. 'Quite wonderful.'

Drinks were being handed round. The Old Woman of the Mountain, Sir Stafford Nye noticed, did not drink anything. It was possible, he thought, that she feared to take any risks over her blood pressure with that vast weight.

'And where did you meet this child?' asked the mountainous Dragon.

Was it a trap? He did not know, but he made his decision.

'At the American Embassy, in London.'

'Ah yes, so I heard. And how is – ah, I forget her name now – ah yes, Milly Jean, our southern heiress? Attractive, did you think?'

'Most charming. She has a great success in London.'

'And poor dull Sam Cortman, the United States Ambassador?'

'A very sound man, I'm sure,' said Stafford Nye politely.

She chuckled.

'Aha, you're tactful, are you not? Ah well, he does well enough. He does what he is told as a good politician should. And it is enjoyable to be Ambassador in London. She could do that for him, Milly Jean. Ah, she could get him an Embassy anywhere in the world, with that well-stuffed purse of hers. Her father owns half the oil in Texas, he owns land, goldfields, everything. A coarse, singularly ugly man – But what does she look like? A gentle little aristocrat. Not blatant, not rich. That is very clever of her, is it not?'

'Sometimes it presents no difficulties,' said Sir Stafford Nye.

'And you? You are not rich?'

'I wish I was.'

'The Foreign Office nowadays, it is not, shall we say, very rewarding?'

'Oh well, I would not put it like that . . . After all, one goes places, one meets amusing people, one sees the world, one sees something of what goes on.'

'Something, yes. But not everything.'

'That would be very difficult.'

'Have you ever wished to see what – how shall I put it – what goes on behind the scenes in life?'

'One has an idea sometimes.' He made his voice noncommittal.

'I have heard it said that that is true of you, that you have sometimes ideas about things. Not perhaps the conventional ideas?'

'There have been times when I've been made to feel the bad boy of the family,' said Stafford Nye and laughed.

Old Charlotte chuckled.

'You don't mind admitting things now and again, do you?'

'Why pretend? People always know what you're concealing.'

She looked at him.

'What do you want out of life, young man?'

He shrugged his shoulders. Here again, he had to play things by ear.

'Nothing,' he said.

'Come now, come now, am I to believe that?'

'Yes, you can believe it. I am not ambitious. Do I look ambitious?'

'No, I will admit that.'

'I ask only to be amused, to live comfortably, to eat, to drink in moderation, to have friends who amuse me.'

The old woman leant forward. Her eyes snapped open and shut three or four times. Then she spoke in a rather different voice. It was like a whistling note.

'Can you hate? Are you capable of hating?'

'To hate is a waste of time.'

'I see. I see. There are no lines of discontent in your face. That is true enough. All the same, I think you are ready to take a certain path which will lead you to a certain place, and you will go along it smiling, as though you did not care, but all the same, in the end, if you find the right advisers, the right helpers, you might attain what you want, if you are capable of wanting.'

'As to that,' said Stafford Nye, 'who isn't?' He shook his head at her very gently. 'You see too much,' he said. 'Much too much.'

Footmen threw open a door.

'Dinner is served.'

The proceedings were properly formal. They had indeed

almost a royal tinge about them. The big doors at the far end of the room were flung open, showing through to a brightly lighted ceremonial dining-room, with a painted ceiling and three enormous chandeliers. Two middle-aged women approached the Gräfin, one on either side. They wore evening dress, their grey hair was carefully piled on their heads, each wore a diamond brooch. To Sir Stafford Nye, all the same, they brought a faint flavour of wardresses. They were, he thought, not so much security guards as perhaps high-class nursing attendants in charge of the health, the toilet and other intimate details of the Gräfin Charlotte's existence. After respectful bows, each one of them slipped an arm below the shoulder and elbow of the sitting woman. With the ease of long practice aided by the effort which was obviously as much as she could make, they raised her to her feet in a dignified fashion.

'We will go in to dinner now,' said Charlotte.

With her two female attendants, she led the way. On her feet she looked even more a mass of wobbling jelly, yet she was still formidable. You could not dispose of her in your mind as just a fat old woman. She was somebody, knew she was somebody, intended to be somebody. Behind the three of them he and Renata followed.

As they entered through the portals of the dining-room, he felt it was almost more a banquet hall than a dining-room. There was a bodyguard here. Tall, fair-haired, handsome young men. They wore some kind of uniform. As Charlotte entered there was a clash as one and all drew their swords. They crossed them overhead to make a passageway, and Charlotte, steadying herself passed along that passageway, released by her attendants and making her progress solo to a vast carved chair with gold fittings and upholstered in golden brocade at the head of the long table. It was rather like a wedding procession, Stafford

Nye thought. A naval or military one. In this case surely, military, strictly military – but lacking a bridegroom.

They were all young men of super physique. None of them, he thought, was older than thirty. They had good looks, their health was evident. They did not smile, they were entirely serious, they were – he thought of a word for it – yes, dedicated. Perhaps not so much a military procession as a religious one. The servitors appeared, old-fashioned servitors belonging, he thought, to the Schloss's past, to a time before the 1939 war. It was like a super production of a period historic play. And queening over it, sitting in the chair or the throne or whatever you liked to call it, at the head of the table, was not a queen or an empress but an old woman noticeable mainly for her avoirdupois weight and her extraordinary and intense ugliness. Who was she? What was she doing here? Why?

Why all this masquerade, why this bodyguard, a security bodyguard perhaps? Other diners came to the table. They bowed to the monstrosity on the presiding throne and took their places. They wore ordinary evening dress. No introductions were made.

Stafford Nye, after long years of sizing up people, assessed them. Different types. A great many different types. Lawyers, he was certain. Several lawyers. Possibly accountants or financiers; one or two army officers in plain clothes. They were of the Household, he thought, but they were also in the old-fashioned feudal sense of the term those who 'sat below the salt'.

Food came. A vast boar's head pickled in aspic, venison, a cool refreshing lemon sorbet, a magnificent edifice of pastry – a super millefeuille that seemed of unbelievable confectionery richness.

The vast woman ate, ate greedily, hungrily, enjoying her food. From outside came a new sound. The sound of the powerful engine of a super sports car. It passed the windows in a white flash. There came a cry inside the room from the bodyguard. A great cry of 'Heil! Heil! Heil Franz!'

The bodyguard of young men moved with the ease of a military manoeuvre known by heart. Everyone had risen to their feet. Only the old woman sat without moving, her head lifted high, on her dais. And, so Stafford Nye thought, a new excitement now permeated the room.

The other guests, or the other members of the household, whatever they were, disappeared in a way that somehow reminded Stafford of lizards disappearing into the cracks of a wall. The golden-haired boys formed a new figure, their swords flew out, they saluted their patroness, she bowed her head in acknowledgment, their swords were sheathed and they turned, permission given, to march out through the door of the room. Her eyes followed them, then went first to Renata, and then to Stafford Nye.

'What do you think of them?' she said. 'My boys, my youth corps, my children. Yes, my children. Have you a word that can describe them?'

'I think so,' said Stafford Nye. 'Magnificent.' He spoke to her as to Royalty. 'Magnificent, ma'am.'

'Ah!' She bowed her head. She smiled, the wrinkles multiplying all over her face. It made her look exactly like a crocodile.

A terrible woman, he thought, a terrible woman, impossible, dramatic. Was any of this happening? He couldn't believe it was. What could this be but yet another festival hall in which a production was being given.

The doors clashed open again. The yellow-haired band of the young supermen marched as before through it. This time they did not wield swords, instead they sang. Sang with unusual beauty of tone and voice.

After a good many years of pop music Stafford Nye felt an incredulous pleasure. Trained voices, these. Not raucous shouting. Trained by masters of the singing art. Not allowed to strain their vocal cords, to be off key. They might be the new Heroes of a New World, but what they sang was not new music. It was music he had heard before. An arrangement of the Preislied, there must be a concealed orchestra somewhere, he thought, in a gallery round the top of the room. It was an arrangement or adaptation of various Wagnerian themes. It passed from the Preislied to the distant echoes of the Rhine music.

The Élite Corps made once more a double lane where somebody was expected to make an entrance. It was not the old Empress this time. She sat on her dais awaiting whoever was coming.

And at last he came. The music changed as he came. It gave out that motif which by now Stafford Nye had got by heart. The melody of the Young Siegfried. Siegfried's horn call, rising up in its youth and its triumph, its mastery of a new world which the young Siegfried came to conquer.

Through the doorway, marching up between the lines of what were clearly his followers, came one of the handsomest young men Stafford Nye had ever seen. Golden-haired, blue-eyed, perfectly proportioned, conjured up as it were by the wave of a magician's wand, he came forth out of the world of myth. Myth, heroes, resurrection, rebirth, it was all there. His beauty, his strength, his incredible assurance and arrogance.

He strode through the double lines of his bodyguard, until he stood before the hideous mountain of womanhood that sat there on her throne; he knelt on one knee, raised her hand to his lips, and then rising to his feet, he threw up one arm in salutation and uttered the cry that Stafford

Nye had heard from the others. 'Heil!' His German was not very clear, but Stafford Nye thought he distinguished the syllables 'Heil to the great mother!'

Then the handsome young hero looked from one side to the other. There was some faint recognition, though an uninterested one, of Renata, but when his gaze turned to Stafford Nye, there was definite interest and appraisal. Caution, thought Stafford Nye. Caution! He must play his part right now. Play the part that was expected of him. Only – what the hell was that part? What was he doing here? What were he or the girl supposed to be doing here? Why had they come?

The hero spoke.

'So,' he said, 'we have guests!' And he added, smiling with the arrogance of a young man who knows that he is vastly superior to any other person in the world. 'Welcome, guests, welcome to you both.'

Somewhere in the depths of the Schloss a great bell began tolling. It had no funereal sound about it, but it had a disciplinary air. The feeling of a monastery summoned to some holy office.

'We must sleep now,' said old Charlotte. 'Sleep. We will meet again tomorrow morning at eleven o'clock.'

She looked towards Renata and Sir Stafford Nye.

'You will be shown to your rooms. I hope you will sleep well.'

It was the Royal dismissal.

Stafford Nye saw Renata's arm fly up in the Fascist salute, but it was addressed not to Charlotte, but to the golden-haired boy. He thought she said: 'Heil Franz Joseph.' He copied her gesture and he, too, said 'Heil!'

Charlotte spoke to them.

'Would it please you tomorrow morning to start the day with a ride through the forest?'

'I should like it of all things,' said Stafford Nye.

'And you, child?'

'Yes, I too.'

'Very good then. It shall be arranged. Good night to you both. I am glad to welcome you here. Franz Joseph – give me your arm. We will go into the Chinese Boudoir. We have much to discuss, and you will have to leave in good time tomorrow morning.'

The menservants escorted Renata and Stafford Nye to their apartments. Nye hesitated for a moment on the threshold. Would it be possible for them to have a word or two now? He decided against it. As long as the castle walls surrounded them it was well to be careful. One never knew – each room might be wired with microphones.

Sooner or later, though, he *had* to ask questions. Certain things aroused a new and sinister apprehension in his mind. He was being persuaded, inveigled into something. But what? And whose doing was it?

The bedrooms were handsome, yet oppressive. The rich hangings of satin and velvets, some of them antique, gave out a faint perfume of decay, tempered by spices. He wondered how often Renata had stayed here before.

XI. THE YOUNG AND THE LOVELY

After breakfasting on the following morning in a small breakfast-room downstairs, he found Renata waiting for him. The horses were at the door.

Both of them had brought riding clothes with them. Everything they could possibly require seemed to have been intelligently anticipated.

They mounted and rode away down the castle drive. Renata spoke with the groom at some length.

'He asked if we would like him to accompany us but I said no. I know the tracks round here fairly well.'

'I see. You have been here before?'

'Not very often of late years. Early in my life I knew this place very well.'

He gave her a sharp look. She did not return it. As she rode beside him, he watched her profile – the thin, aquiline nose, the head carried so proudly on the slender neck. She rode a horse well, he saw that.

All the same, there was a sense of ill ease in his mind this morning. He wasn't sure why . . .

His mind went back to the Airport Lounge. The woman who had come to stand beside him. The glass of Pilsner on the table . . . Nothing in it that there shouldn't have been – neither then, nor later. A risk he had accepted. Why, when all that was long over, should it rouse uneasiness in him now?

They had a brief canter following a ride through the trees. A beautiful property, beautiful woods. In the distance he saw horned animals. A paradise for a sportsman, a paradise for the old way of living, a paradise that contained – what? A serpent? As it was in the beginning – with Paradise went a serpent. He drew rein and the horses fell to a walk. He and Renata were alone – no microphones, no listening walls – The time had come for his questions.

'Who is she?' he said urgently. 'What is she?'

'It's easy to answer. So easy that it's hardly believable.'

'Well?' he said.

'She's oil. Copper. Goldmines in South Africa. Armaments in Sweden. Uranium deposits in the north. Nuclear development, vast stretches of cobalt. She's all those things.'

'And yet, I hadn't heard about her, I didn't know her name, I didn't know –'

'She has not wanted people to know.'

'Can one keep such things quiet?'

'Easily, if you have enough copper and oil and nuclear deposits and armaments and all the rest of it. Money can advertise, or money can keep secrets, can hush things up.'

'But who *actually* is she?'

'Her grandfather was American. He was mainly railways, I think. Possibly Chicago hogs in those times. It's like going back into history, finding out. He married a German woman. You've heard of her, I expect. Big Belinda, they used to christen her. Armaments, shipping, the whole industrial wealth of Europe. She was her father's heiress.'

'Between those two, unbelievable wealth,' said Sir Stafford Nye. 'And so – power. Is that what you're telling me?'

'Yes. She didn't just inherit things, you know. She made money as well. She'd inherited brains, she was a big financier in her own right. Everything she touched multiplied itself. Turned to incredible sums of money, and she invested them. Taking advice, taking other people's judgment, but in the end always using her own. And always prospering. Always adding to her wealth so that it was too fabulous to be believed. Money creates money.'

'Yes, I can understand that. Wealth *has* to increase if there's a superfluity of it. But – what did *she* want? What has *she* got?'

'You said it just now. Power.'

'And she lives here? Or does she –?'

'She visits America and Sweden. On yes, she visits

places, but not often. This is where she prefers to be, in the centre of a web like a vast spider controlling all the threads. The threads of finance. Other threads too.'

'When you say, other threads –'

'The arts. Music, pictures, writers. Human beings – young human beings.'

'Yes. One might know that. Those pictures, a wonderful collection.'

'There are galleries of them upstairs in the Schloss. There are Rembrandts and Giottos and Raphaels and there are cases of jewels – some of the most wonderful jewels in the world.'

'All belonging to one ugly, gross old woman. Is she satisfied?'

'Not yet, but well on the way to being.'

'Where is she going, what does she want?'

'She loves youth. That is her mode of power. To control youth. The world is full of rebellious youth at this moment. That's been helped on. Modern philosophy, modern thought, writers and others whom she finances and controls.'

'But how can –?' He stopped.

'I can't tell you because I don't know. It's an enormous ramification. She's behind it in one sense, supports rather curious charities, earnest philanthropists and idealists, raises innumerable grants for students and artists and writers.'

'And yet you say it's not –'

'No, it's not yet complete. It's a great upheaval that's being planned. It's believed in, it's the new heaven and the new earth. That's what's been promised by leaders for thousands of years. Promised by religions, promised by those who support Messiahs, promised by those who come back to teach the law, like the Buddha. Promised by politicians. The crude heaven of an easy attainment such as the Assassins believed in, and the Old Man of the Assassins promised his followers and, from their point of view, gave to them.'

'Is she behind drugs as well?'

'Yes. Without conviction, of course. Only a means of having people bent to her will. It's one way, too, of destroying people. The weak ones. The ones she thinks are no good, although they had once shown promise. She'd never take drugs herself – she's strong. But drugs destroy weak people more easily and naturally than anything else.'

'And force? What about force? You can't do everything by propaganda.'

'No, of course not. Propaganda is the first stage and behind it there are vast armaments piling up. Arms that go to deprived countries and then on elsewhere. Tanks and guns and nuclear weapons that go to Africa and the South Seas and South America. In South America there's a lot building up. Forces of young men and women drilling and training. Enormous arms dumps – means of chemical warfare –'

'It's a nightmare! How do you know all this, Renata?'

'Partly because I've been told it; from information received, partly because I have been instrumental in proving some of it.'

'But *you*. You and *she*?'

'There's always something idiotic behind all great and vast projects.' She laughed suddenly. 'Once, you see, she was in love with my grandfather. A foolish story. He lived in this part of the world. He had a castle a mile or two from here.'

'Was he a man of genius?'

'Not at all. He was just a very good sportsman. Handsome, dissolute and attractive to women. And so, because of that, she is in a sense my protectress. And I am one of her converts or slaves! I work for her. I find people for her. I carry out her commands in different parts of the world.'

'Do you?'

'What do you mean by that?'

'I wondered,' said Sir Stafford Nye.

He did wonder. He looked at Renata and he thought again of the airport. He was working *for* Renata, he was working *with* Renata. She had brought him to this Schloss. Who had told her to bring him here? Big, gross Charlotte in the middle of her spider's web? He had had a reputation, a reputation of being unsound in certain diplomatic quarters. He could be useful to these people perhaps, but useful in a small and rather humiliating way. And he thought suddenly, in a kind of fog of question marks: Renata??? I took a risk with her at Frankfurt airport. But I was right. It came off. Nothing happened to me. But all the same, he thought, who is she? *What* is she? I don't know. I can't be *sure*. One can't in the world today be sure of *anyone*. Anyone at all. She was told perhaps to get me. To get me into the hollow of her hand, so that business at Frankfurt might have been cleverly thought out. It fitted in with my sense of risk, and it would make me sure of her. It would make me trust her.

'Let's canter again,' she said. 'We've walked the horses too long.'

'I haven't asked you what *you* are in all this?'

'I take orders.'

'From whom?'

'There's an opposition. There's always an opposition. There are people who have a suspicion of what's going on, of how the world is going to be made to change, of how with money, wealth, armaments, idealism, great trumpeting words of power what's going to happen. There are people who say it shall *not* happen.'

'And you are with them?'

'I say so.'

'What do you mean by that, Renata?'

She said, '*I say so.*'

He said: 'That young man last night –'

'Franz Joseph?'

'Is that his name?'

'It is the name he is known by.'

'But he has another name, hasn't he?'

'Do you think so?'

'He is, isn't he, the young Siegfried?'

'You saw him like that? You realized that's what he was, what he stands for?'

'I think so. Youth. Heroic youth. Aryan youth, it has to be Aryan youth in this part of the world. There is still that point of view. A super race, the supermen. They must be of Aryan descent.'

'Oh yes, it's lasted on from the time of Hitler. It doesn't always come out into the open much and, in other places all over the world, it isn't stressed so much. South America, as I say, is one of the strongholds. And Peru and South Africa also.'

'What does the young Siegfried do? What does he do besides look handsome and kiss the hand of his protectress?'

'Oh, he's quite an orator. He speaks and his following would follow him to death.'

'Is that true?'

'He believes it.'

'And you?'

'I think I might believe it.' She added: 'Oratory is very frightening, you know. What a voice can do, what words can do, and not particularly convincing words at that. The *way* they are said. His voice rings like a bell, and women cry and scream and faint away when he addresses them – you'll see that for yourself.

'You saw Charlotte's Bodyguard last night all dressed up – people do love dressing up nowadays. You'll see them all over the world in their own chosen get-up, different in different places, some with their long hair and their beards, and girls in their streaming white nightgowns, talking of peace and beauty, and the wonderful world that is the world of the young which is to be theirs when they've destroyed enough of the old world. The original Country of the Young was west of the Irish Sea, wasn't it? A very simple place, a different Country of the Young from what we're planning now – It was silver sands, and sunshine and singing in the waves . . .

'But now we want Anarchy, and breaking down and destroying. Only Anarchy can benefit those who march behind it. It's frightening, it's also wonderful – because of its violence, because it's bought with pain and suffering –'

'So that is how you see the world today?'

'Sometimes.'

'And what am *I* to do next?'

'Come with your guide. I'm your guide. Like Virgil with Dante, I'll take you down into hell, I'll show you the sadistic films partly copied from the old SS, show you cruelty and pain and violence worshipped. And I'll show you the great dreams of paradise in peace and beauty. You won't know which is which and what is what. But you'll have to make up your mind.'

'Do I trust you, Renata?'

'That will be your choice. You can run away from me if you like, or you can stay with me and see the new world. The new world that's in the making.'

'Pasteboard,' said Sir Stafford Nye violently.

She looked at him inquiringly.

'Like Alice in Wonderland. The cards, the pasteboard cards all rising up in the air. Flying about. Kings and Queens and Knaves. All sorts of things.'

'You mean – what do you mean exactly?'

'I mean it isn't real. It's make-believe. The whole damn thing is make-believe.'

'In one sense, yes.'

'All dressed up playing parts, putting on a show. I'm getting nearer, aren't I, to the meaning of things?'

'In a way, yes, and in a way, no –'

'There's one thing I'd like to ask you because it puzzles me. Big Charlotte ordered you to bring me to see her – why? What did she know about me? What use did she think she could make of me?'

'I don't quite know – possibly a kind of *Éminence Grise* – working behind a façade. That would suit you rather well.'

'But she knows nothing whatever about me!'

'Oh, *that*!' Suddenly Renata went into peals of laughter. 'It's so ridiculous, really – the same old nonsense all over again.'

'I don't understand you, Renata.'

'No – because it's so simple. Mr Robinson would understand.'

'Would you kindly explain what you are talking about?'

'It's the same old business – "*It's not what you are. It's who you know*". Your Great-Aunt Matilda and Big Charlotte were at school together –'

'You actually mean –'

'Girls together.'

He stared at her. Then he threw his head back and roared with laughter.

XII. COURT JESTER

They left the Schloss at midday, saying goodbye to their hostess. Then they had driven down the winding road, leaving the Schloss high above them and they had come at last, after many hours of driving, to a stronghold in the Dolomites – an amphitheatre in the mountains where meetings, concerts and reunions of the various Youth Groups were held.

Renata had brought him there, his guide, and from his seat on the bare rock he had watched what went on and had listened. He understood a little more what she had been talking about earlier that day. This great mass gathering, animated as all mass gatherings can be whether they are called by an evangelistic religious leader in Madison Square, New York, or in the shadow of a Welsh church or in a football crowd or in the super demonstrations which marched to attack embassies and police and universities and all the rest of it.

She had brought him there to show him the meaning of that one phrase: 'The Young Siegfried.'

Franz Joseph, if that was really his name, had addressed the crowd. His voice, rising, falling, with its curious exciting quality, its emotional appeal, had held sway over that groaning, almost moaning crowd of young women and young men. Every word that he had uttered had seemed pregnant with meaning, had held incredible appeal. The crowd had responded like an orchestra. His voice had been the baton of the conductor. And yet, what had the boy said? What had been the young Siegfried's message? There were no words that he could remember when it came to an end, but he knew that he had been moved, promised things, roused to enthusiasm. And now it was over. The crowd had surged round the rocky platform, calling, crying out. Some of the girls had been screaming with enthusiasm. Some of them had fainted. What a world it was nowadays, he thought. Everything used the whole time to arouse emotion. Discipline? Restraint? None of those things counted for anything any more. Nothing mattered but to *feel*.

What sort of a world, thought Stafford Nye, could that make?

His guide had touched him on the arm and they had disentangled themselves from the crowd. They had found their car and the driver had taken them by roads with which he was evidently well acquainted, to a town and an inn on a mountain side where rooms had been reserved for them.

They walked out of the inn presently and up the side of a mountain by a well-trodden path until they came to a seat. They sat there for some moments in silence. It was then that Stafford Nye had said again, 'Pasteboard.'

For some five minutes or so they sat looking down the valley, then Renata said, 'Well?'

'What are you asking me?'

'What you think so far of what I have shown you?'

'I'm not convinced,' said Stafford Nye.

She gave a sigh, a deep, unexpected sigh.

'That's what I hoped you would say.'

'It's none of it true, is it? It's a gigantic show. A show put on by a producer – a complete group of producers, perhaps.

'That monstrous woman pays the producer, hires the producer. We've not seen the producer. What we've seen today is the star performer.'

'What do you think of him?'

'He's not real either,' said Stafford Nye. 'He's just an actor. A first-class actor, superbly produced.'

A sound surprised him. It was Renata laughing. She got up from her seat. She looked suddenly excited, happy, and at the same time faintly ironical.

'I knew it,' she said. 'I knew you'd see. I knew you'd have your feet on the ground. You've always known, haven't you, about everything you've met in life? You've known humbug, you've known everything and everyone for what they really are.

'No need to go to Stratford and see Shakespearian plays to know what part you are cast for – The Kings and the great men have to have a Jester – The King's Jester who tells the King the truth, and talks common sense, and makes fun of all the things that are taking in other people.'

'So that's what I am, is it? A Court Jester?'

'Can't you feel it yourself? That's what we want – That's what we need. "Pasteboard," you said. "Cardboard". A vast, well-produced, splendid *sham*! And how right you are. But people are taken in. They think something's wonderful, or they think something's devilish, or they think it's something terribly important. Of course it isn't – only – only one's got to find out just how to *show* people – that the whole thing, all of it, is just *silly*. Just damn *silly*. That's what you and I are going to do.'

'Is it your idea that in the end we debunk all this?'

'It seems wildly unlikely, I agree. But you know once people are shown that something isn't real, that it's just one enormous leg-pull, well –'

'Are you proposing to preach a gospel of common sense?'

'Of course not,' said Renata. 'Nobody'd listen to that, would they?'

'Not just at present.'

'No. We'll have to give them evidence – facts – truth –'

'Have we got such things?'

'Yes. What I brought back with me via Frankfurt – what you helped to bring safely into England –'

'I don't understand –'

'Not yet – You will know later. For now we've got a part to play. We're ready and willing, fairly panting to be indoctrinated. We worship youth. We're followers and believers in the young Siegfried.'

'*You* can put that over, no doubt. I'm not so sure about myself. I've never been very successful as a worshipper of anything. The King's Jester isn't. He's the great debunker. Nobody's going to appreciate that very much just now, are they?'

'Of course they're not. No. You don't let that side of yourself show. Except, of course, when talking about your masters and betters, politicians and diplomats, Foreign Office, the Establishment, all the other things. Then you can be embittered, malicious, witty, slightly cruel.'

'I still don't see my rôle in the world crusade.'

'That's a very ancient one, the one that everybody understands and appreciates. Something in it for you. That's your line. You haven't been appreciated in the past, but the young Siegfried and all he stands for will hold out the hope of reward to you. Because you give him all the inside dope he wants about your own country, he will promise you places of power in that country in the good times to come.'

'You insinuate that this is a world movement. Is that true?'

'Of course it is. Rather like one of those hurricanes, you know, that have names. Flora or Little Annie. They come up out of the south or the north or the east or the west, but they come up from nowhere and destroy everything. That's what everyone wants. In Europe and Asia and America. Perhaps Africa, though there won't be so much enthusiasm there. They're fairly new to power and graft and things. Oh yes, it's a world movement all right. Run by youth and all the intense vitality of youth. They haven't got knowledge and they haven't got experience, but they've got vision and vitality, and they're backed by money. Rivers and rivers of money pouring in. There's been too much materialism, so we've asked for something else, and we've got it. But as it's based on hate, it can't get anywhere. It can't move off the ground. Don't you remember in 1919 everyone going about with a rapt face saying Communism was the answer to everything. That Marxist doctrine would produce a new heaven brought down to a new earth. So many noble ideas flowing about. But then, you see, whom have you got to work out the ideas with? After all, only the same human beings you've always had. You can create a third world now, or so everyone thinks, but the third world will have the same people in it as the first world or the second world or whatever names you like to call things. And when you have the same human beings running things, they'll run them the same way. You've only got to look at history.'

'Does anybody care to look at history nowadays?'

'No. They'd much rather look forward to an unforeseeable future. Science was once going to be the answer to everything. Freudian beliefs and unrepressed sex would be the next answer to human misery. There'd be no more people with mental troubles. If anyone had said that mental homes would be even fuller as the result of shutting out repressions nobody would have believed him.'

Stafford Nye interrupted her:

'I want to know something,' said Sir Stafford Nye.

'What is it?'

'Where are we going next?'

'South America. Possibly Pakistan or India on the way. And we must certainly go to the USA. There's a lot going on there that's very interesting indeed. Especially in California –'

'Universities?' Sir Stafford sighed. 'One gets very tired of universities. They repeat themselves so much.'

They sat silent for some minutes. The light was failing, but a mountain peak showed softly red.

Stafford Nye said in a nostalgic tone:

'If we had some more music *now* – this moment – do you know what I'd order?'

'More Wagner? Or have you torn yourself free from Wagner?'

'No – you're quite right – more Wagner. I'd have Hans Sachs sitting under his elder tree, saying of the world: "Mad, mad, all mad" –'

'Yes – that expresses it. It's lovely music, too. But *we're* not mad. We're sane.'

'Eminently sane,' said Stafford Nye. 'That is going to be the difficulty. There's one more thing I want to know.'

'Well?'

'Perhaps you won't tell me. But I've *got* to know. Is there going to be any fun to be got out of this mad business that we're attempting?'

'Of course there is. Why not?'

'Mad, mad, all mad – but we'll enjoy it all very much. Will our lives be long, Mary Ann?'

'Probably not,' said Renata.

'That's the spirit. I'm with you, my comrade, and my guide. Shall we get a better world as a result of our efforts?'

'I shouldn't think so, but it might be a kinder one. It's full of beliefs without kindness at present.'

'Good enough,' said Stafford Nye. 'Onward!'

BOOK 111

AT HOME AND ABROAD

X111. CONFERENCE IN PARIS

In a room in Paris five men were sitting. It was a room that had seen historic meetings before. Quite a number of them. This meeting was in many ways a meeting of a different kind yet it promised to be no less historic.

Monsieur Grosjean was presiding. He was a worried man doing his best to slide over things with facility and a charm of manner that had often helped him in the past. He did not feel it was helping him so much today. Signor Vitelli had arrived from Italy by air an hour before. His gestures were feverish, his manner unbalanced.

'It is beyond anything,' he was saying, 'it is beyond anything one could have imagined.'

'These students,' said Monsieur Grosjean, 'do we not all suffer?'

'This is more than students. It is beyond students. What can one compare this to? A swarm of bees. A disaster of nature intensified. Intensified beyond anything one could have imagined. They march. They have machine-guns. Somewhere they have acquired planes. They propose to take over the whole of North Italy. But it is madness, that! They are children – nothing more. And yet they have bombs, explosives. In the city of Milan alone they outnumber the police. What can we do, I ask you? The military? The army too – it is in revolt. They say they are with *les jeunes*. They say there is no hope for the world except in anarchy. They talk of something they call the Third World, but this cannot just happen.'

Monsieur Grosjean sighed. 'It is very popular among the young,' he said, 'the anarchy. A belief in anarchy. We know that from the days of Algeria, from all the troubles from which our country and our colonial empire has suffered. And what can we do? The military? In the end they back the students.'

'The students, ah, the students,' said Monsieur Poissonier.

He was a member of the French government to whom the word 'student' was anathema. If he had been asked he would have admitted to a preference for Asian 'flu or even an outbreak of bubonic plague. Either was preferable in his mind to the activities of students. A world with no students in it! That was what Monsieur Poissonier sometimes dreamt about. They were good dreams, those. They did not occur often enough.

'As for magistrates,' said Monsieur Grosjean, 'what has happened to our judicial authorities? The police – yes, they are loyal still, but the judiciary, they will not impose sentences, not on young men who are brought before them, young men who have destroyed property, government property, private property – every kind of property. And why not, one would like to know? I have been making inquiries lately. The Préfecture have suggested certain things to me. An increase is needed, they say, in the standard of living among judiciary authorities, especially in the provincial areas.'

'Come, come,' said Monsieur Poissonier, 'you must be careful what you suggest.'

'*Ma foi*, why should I be careful? Things need bringing into the open. We have had frauds before, gigantic frauds and there is money now circulating around. Money, and we do not know where it comes from, but the Préfecture have said to me – and I believe it – that they begin to get an idea of where it is *going*. Do we contemplate, can we contemplate a corrupt state subsidized from some outside source?'

'In Italy too,' said Signor Vitelli, 'in Italy, ah, I could tell you things. Yes, I could tell you of what we suspect. But who, who is corrupting our world? A group of industrialists, a group of tycoons? How could such a thing be so.'

'This business has got to stop,' said Monsieur Grosjean. 'Action must be taken. Military action. Action from the Air Force. These anarchists, these marauders, they come from every class. It must be put down.'

'Control by tear gas has been fairly successful,' said Poissonier dubiously.

'Tear gas is not enough,' said Monsieur Grosjean. 'The same result could be got by setting students to peel bunches of onions. Tears would flow from their eyes. It needs more than that.'

Monsieur Poissonier said in a shocked voice:

'You are not suggesting the use of nuclear weapons?'

'Nuclear weapons? *Quel blague!* What can we do with nuclear weapons. What would become of the soil of France, of the air of France if we use nuclear weapons? We can destroy Russia, we know that. We also know that Russia can destroy us.'

'You're not suggesting that groups of marching and demonstrating students could destroy our authoritarian forces?'

'That is exactly what I am suggesting. I have had a warning of such things. Of stock-piling of arms, and various forms of chemical warfare and of other things. I have had reports from some of our eminent scientists. Secrets are known. Stores – held in secret – weapons of warfare have been stolen. What is to happen next, I ask you. What is to happen next?'

The question was answered unexpectedly and with more rapidity than Monsieur Grosjean could possibly have calculated. The door opened and his principal secretary approached his master, his face showing urgent concern. Monsieur Grosjean looked at him with displeasure.

'Did I not say I wanted no interruptions?'

'Yes indeed, Monsieur le Président, but this is somewhat unusual –' He bent towards his master's ear. 'The Marshal is here. He demands entrance.'

'The Marshal? You mean –'

The secretary nodded his head vigorously several times to show that he did mean. Monsieur Poissonier looked at his colleague in perplexity.

'He demands admission. He will not take refusal.'

The two other men in the room looked first at Grosjean and then at the agitated Italian.

'Would it not be better,' said Monsieur Coin, the Minister for Home Affairs, 'if –'

He paused at the 'if' as the door was once more flung open and a man strode in. A very well-known man. A man whose word had been not only law, but above law in the country of France for many past years. To see him at this moment was an unwelcome surprise for those sitting there.

'Ah, I welcome you, dear colleagues,' said the Marshal. 'I come to help you. Our country is in danger. Action must be taken, immediate action! I come to put myself at your service. I take over all responsibility for acting in this crisis. There may be danger. I know there is, but honour is above danger. The salvation of France is above danger. They march this way now. A vast herd of students, of criminals who have been released from jails, some of them who have committed the crime of homicide. Men who have committed incendiarism. They shout names. They sing songs. They call on the names of their teachers, of their philosophers, of those who have led them on this path of insurrection. Those who will bring about the doom of France unless something is done. You sit here, you talk, you deplore things. More than that must be done. I have sent for two regiments. I have alerted the air force, special coded wires have gone out to our neighbouring ally, to my friends in Germany, for she is our ally now in this crisis!

'Riot must be put down. Rebellion! Insurrection! The danger to men, women and children, to property. I go forth now to quell the insurrection, to speak to them as their father, their leader. These students, these criminals even, they are my children. They are the youth of France. I go to speak to them of that. They shall listen to me, governments will be revised, their studies can be resumed under their own auspices. Their grants have been insufficient, their lives have been deprived of beauty, of leadership. I come to promise all this. I speak in my own name. I shall speak also in your name, the name of the Government, you have done your best, you have acted as well as you know how. But it needs higher leadership. It needs *my* leadership. I go now. I have lists of further coded wires to be sent. Such nuclear deterrents as can be used in unfrequented spots can be put into action in such a modified form that though they may bring terror to the mob, we ourselves shall know that there is no real danger in them. I have thought out everything. My plan will go. Come, my loyal friends, accompany me.'

'Marshal, we cannot allow – you cannot imperil yourself. We must . . .'

'I listen to nothing you say. I embrace my doom, my destiny.'

The Marshal strode to the door.

'My staff is outside. My chosen bodyguard. I go now to speak to these young rebels, this young flower of beauty and terror, to tell them where their duty lies.'

He disappeared through the door with the grandeur of a leading actor playing his favourite part.

'*Bon dieu*, he means it!' said Monsieur Poissonier.

'He will risk his life,' said Signor Vitelli. 'Who knows? It is brave, he is a brave man. It is gallant, yes, but what will happen to him? In the mood *les jeunes* are in now, they might kill him.'

A pleasurable sigh fell from Monsieur Poissonier's lips. It might be true, he thought. Yes, it might be true.

'It is possible,' he said. 'Yes, they might kill him.'

'One cannot wish that, of course,' said Monsieur Grosjean carefully.

Monsieur Grosjean did wish it. He hoped for it, though a natural pessimism led him to have the second thought that things seldom fell out in the way you wanted them to. Indeed, a much more awful prospect confronted him. It was quite possible, it was within the traditions of the Marshal's past, that somehow or other he might induce a large pack of exhilarated and bloodthirsty students to listen to what he said, trust in his promises, and insist on restoring him to the power that he had once held. It was the sort of thing that had happened once or twice in the career of the Marshal. His personal magnetism was such that politicians had before now met their defeat when they least expected it.

'We must restrain him,' he cried.

'Yes, yes,' said Signor Vitelli, 'he cannot be lost to the world.'

'One fears,' said Monsieur Poissonier. 'He has too many friends in Germany, too many contacts, and you know they move very quickly in military matters in Germany. They might leap at the opportunity.'

'*Bon dieu, bon dieu*,' said Monsieur Grosjean, wiping his

brow. 'What shall we do? What can we do? What is that noise? I hear rifles, do I not?'

'No, no,' said Monsieur Poissonier consolingly. 'It is the canteen coffee trays you hear.'

'There is a quotation I could use,' said Monsieur Grosjean, who was a great lover of the drama, 'if I could only remember it. A quotation from Shakespeare. "Will nobody rid me of this –" '

' "turbulent priest," ' said Monsieur Poissonier. 'From the play, Becket.'

'A madman like the Marshal is worse than a priest. A priest should at least be harmless, though indeed even His Holiness the Pope received a delegation of students only yesterday. He *blessed* them. He called them his children.'

'A Christian gesture, though,' said Monsieur Coin dubiously.

'One can go too far even with Christian gestures,' said Monsieur Grosjean.

XIV. CONFERENCE IN LONDON

In the Cabinet Room at 10 Downing Street, Mr Cedric Lazenby, the Prime Minister, sat at the head of the table and looked at his assembled Cabinet without any noticeable pleasure. The expression on his face was definitely gloomy, which in a way afforded him a certain relief. He was beginning to think that it was only in the privacy of his Cabinet Meetings that he could relax his face into an unhappy expression, and could abandon that look which he presented usually to the world, of a wise and contented optimism which had served him so well in the various crises of political life.

He looked round at Gordon Chetwynd, who was frowning, at Sir George Packham who was obviously worrying, thinking, and wondering as usual, at the military imperturbability of Colonel Munro, at Air Marshal Kenwood, a tight-lipped man who did not trouble to conceal his profound distrust of politicians. There was also Admiral Blunt, a large formidable man, who tapped his fingers on the table and bided his time until his moment should come.

'It is not too good,' the Air Marshal was saying. 'One has to admit it. Four of our planes hi-jacked within the last week. Flew 'em to Milan. Turned the passengers out, and flew them on somewhere else. Actually Africa. Had pilots waiting there. Black men.'

'Black Power,' said Colonel Munro thoughtfully.

'Or Red Power?' suggested Lazenby. 'I feel, you know, that all our difficulties might stem from Russian indoctrination. If one could get into touch with the Russians – I really think a personal visit at top level –'

'You stick where you are, Prime Minister,' said Admiral Blunt. 'Don't you start arseing around with the Russkies again. All *they* want at present is to keep out of all this mess. They haven't had as much trouble there with their students as most of us have. All they mind about is keeping an eye on the Chinese to see what they'll be up to next.'

'I do think that personal influence –'

'You stay here and look after your own country,' said Admiral Blunt. True to his name, and as was his wont, he said it bluntly:

'Hadn't we better hear – have a proper report of what's actually been happening?' Gordon Chetwynd looked towards Colonel Munro.

'Want facts? Quite right. They're all pretty unpalatable. I presume you want, not particulars of what's been happening here so much, as the general world situation?'

'Quite so.'

'Well, in France the Marshal's in hospital still. Two bullets in his arm. Hell's going on in political circles. Large tracts of the country are held by what they call the Youth Power troops.'

'You mean they've got arms?' said Gordon Chetwynd in a horrified voice.

'They've got a hell of a lot,' said the Colonel. 'I don't know really where they've got them from. There are certain ideas as to that. A large consignment of arms was sent from Sweden to West Africa.'

'What's that got to do with it?' said Mr Lazenby. 'Who cares? Let them have all the arms they want in West Africa. They can go on shooting each other.'

'Well, there's something a little curious about it as far as our Intelligence reports go. Here is a list of the armaments that were sent to West Africa. The interesting thing is they were sent there, but they were sent out again. They were accepted, delivery was acknowledged, payment may or may not have been made, but they were sent out of the country again before five days had passed. They were sent out, re-routed elsewhere.'

'But what's the idea of that?'

'The idea seems to be,' said Munro, 'that they were never really intended for West Africa. Payments were made and they were sent on somewhere else. It seems possible that they went on from Africa to the Near East. To the Persian Gulf, to Greece and to Turkey. Also, a consignment of planes was sent to Egypt. From Egypt they were sent to India, from India they were sent to Russia.'

'I thought they were sent *from* Russia.'

'– And from Russia they went to Prague. The whole thing's mad.'

'I don't understand,' said Sir George, 'one wonders –'

'Somewhere there seems to be some central organization which is directing the supplies of various things. Planes, armaments, bombs, both explosive and those that are used in germ warfare. All these consignments are moving in unexpected directions. They are delivered by various cross-country routes to trouble-spots, and used by leaders and regiments – if you like to call them that – of the Youth Power. They mostly go to the leaders of young guerrilla movements, professed anarchists who preach anarchy, and accept – though one doubts if they ever pay for – some of the latest most up-to-date models.'

'Do you mean to say we're facing something like war on a world scale?' Cedric Lazenby was shocked.

The mild man with the Asiatic face who sat lower down at the table, and had not yet spoken, lifted up his face with the Mongolian smile, and said:

'That is what one is now forced to believe. Our observations tell us –'

Lazenby interrupted.

'You'll have to stop observing. UNO will have to take arms itself and put all this down.'

The quiet face remained unmoved.

'That would be against our principles,' he said.

Colonel Munro raised his voice and went on with his summing up.

'There's fighting in some parts of every country. South-East Asia claimed Independence long ago and there are four, five different divisions of power in South America, Cuba, Peru, Guatemala and so on. As for the United States, you know Washington was practically burnt out – the West is overrun with Youth Power Armed Forces –

Chicago is under Martial Law. You know about Sam Cortman? Shot last night on the steps of the American Embassy here.'

'He was to attend here today,' said Lazenby. 'He was going to have given us his views of the situation.'

'I don't suppose that would have helped much,' said Colonel Munro. 'Quite a nice chap – but hardly a live wire.'

'But who's *behind* all this?' Lazenby's voice rose fretfully.

'It could be the Russians, of course –' He looked hopeful. He still envisaged himself flying to Moscow.

Colonel Munro shook his head. 'Doubt it,' he said.

'A personal appeal,' said Lazenby. His face brightened with hope. 'An entirely new sphere of influence. The Chinese . . .?'

'Nor the Chinese,' said Colonel Munro. 'But you know there's been a big revival in Neo-Fascism in Germany.'

'You don't really think the Germans could possibly . . .'

'I don't think they're behind all this necessarily, but when you say possibly – yes, I think possibly they easily could. They've done it before, you know. Prepared things years before, planned them, everything ready, waiting for the word GO. Good planners, very good planners. Staff work excellent. I admire them, you know. Can't help it.'

'But Germany seemed to be so peaceful and well run.'

'Yes, of course it is up to a point. But do you realize, South America is practically alive with Germans, with young Neo-Fascists, and they've got a big Youth Federation there. Call themselves the Super-Aryans, or something of that kind. You know, a bit of the old stuff still, swastikas and salutes, and someone who's running it, called the Young Wotan or the Young Siegfried or something like that. Lot of Aryan nonsense.'

There was a knock on the door and the secretary entered.

'Professor Eckstein is here, sir.'

'We'd better have him in,' said Cedric Lazenby. 'After all, if anyone can tell us what our latest research weapons are, he's the man. We may have something up our sleeve that can soon put an end to all this nonsense.' Besides being a professional traveller to foreign parts in the rôle of peacemaker, Mr Lazenby had an incurable fund of optimism seldom justified by results.

'We could do with a good secret weapon,' said the Air Marshal hopefully.

Professor Eckstein, considered by many to be Britain's top scientist, when you first looked at him seemed supremely unimportant. He was a small man with old-fashioned mutton-chop whiskers and an asthmatic cough. He had the manner of one anxious to apologize for his existence. He made noises like 'ah,' 'hrrumph' 'mrrh', blew his nose, coughed asthmatically again and shook hands in a shy manner, as he was introduced to those present. A good many of them he already knew and these he greeted with nervous nods of the head. He sat down on the chair indicated and looked round him vaguely. He raised a hand to his mouth and began to bite his nails.

'The Heads of the Services are here,' said Sir George Packham. 'We are very anxious to have your opinion as to what can be done.'

'Oh,' said Professor Eckstein, 'done? Yes, yes, done?'

There was a silence.

'The world is fast passing into a state of anarchy,' said Sir George.

'Seems so, doesn't it? At least, from what I read in the paper. Not that I trust to that. Really, the things journalists think up. Never any accuracy in their statements.'

'I understand you've made some most important discoveries lately, Professor,' said Cedric Lazenby encouragingly.

'Ah yes, so we have. So we have.' Professor Eckstein cheered up a little. 'Got a lot of very nasty chemical warfare fixed up. If we ever wanted it. Germ warfare, you know, biological stuff, gas laid on through normal gas outlets, air pollution and poisoning of water supplies. Yes, if you wanted it, I suppose we could kill half the population of England given about three days to do it in.' He rubbed his hands. 'That what you want?'

'No, no indeed. Oh dear, of course not.' Mr Lazenby looked horrified.

'Well, that's what I mean, you know. It's not a question of not having enough lethal weapons. We've got too much. Everything we've got is *too* lethal. The difficulty would be in keeping anybody alive, even ourselves. Eh? All the people at the top, you know. Well – *us*, for instance.' He gave a wheezy, happy little chuckle.

'But that isn't what we *want*,' Mr Lazenby insisted.

'It's not a question of what you *want*, it's a question of what we've *got*. Everything we've got is terrifically lethal. If you want everybody under thirty wiped off the map, I expect you could do it. Mind you, you'd have to take a lot of the older ones as well. It's difficult to segregate one lot from the other, you know. Personally, I should be against that. We've got some very good young Research fellows. Bloody-minded, but clever.'

'What's gone wrong with the world?' asked Kenwood suddenly.

'That's the point,' said Professor Eckstein. 'We don't know. We don't know up at our place in spite of all we *do* know about this, that and the other. We know a bit more about the moon nowadays, we know a lot about biology, we can transplant hearts and livers; brains, too, soon, I expect, though I don't know how *that'll* work out. But we don't know who is doing *this*. Somebody is, you know. It's a sort of high-powered background stuff. Oh yes, we've got it cropping up in different ways. You know, crime rings, drug rings, all that sort of thing. A high-powered lot, directed by a few good, shrewd brains behind the scenes. We've had it going on in this country or that country, occasionally on a European scale. But it's going a bit further now, other side of the globe – Southern Hemisphere. Down to the Antarctic Circle before we've finished, I expect.' He appeared to be pleased with his diagnosis.

'People of ill-will –'

'Well, you could put it like that. Ill-will for ill-will's sake or ill-will for the sake of money or power. Difficult, you know, to get at the *point* of it all. The poor dogsbodies themselves don't know. They want violence and they like violence. They don't like the world, they don't like our materialistic attitude. They don't like a lot of our nasty ways of making money, they don't like a lot of the fiddles we do. They don't like seeing poverty. They want a better world. Well, you *could* make a better world, perhaps, if you thought about it long enough. But the trouble is, if you insist on taking away something first, you've got to put something back in its place. Nature won't have a vacuum – an old saying, but true. Dash it all, it's like a heart transplant. You take one heart away but you've got to put another one there. One that works. And you've got to arrange about the heart you're going to put there *before* you take away the faulty heart that somebody's got at present. Matter of fact, I think a lot of those things are better left alone altogether, but nobody would listen to me, I suppose. And anyway it's not my subject.'

'A gas?' suggested Colonel Munro.

Professor Eckstein brightened.

'Oh, we've got all sorts of *gases* in stock. Mind you, some of them are reasonably harmless. Mild deterrents, shall we say. We've got all *those*.' He beamed like a complacent hardware dealer.

'Nuclear weapons?' suggested Mr Lazenby.

'Don't you monkey with *that*! You don't want a radio-active England, do you, or a radio-active continent, for that matter?'

'So you can't help us,' said Colonel Munro.

'Not until somebody's found out a bit more about all this,' said Professor Eckstein. 'Well, I'm sorry. But I must impress upon you that most of the things we're working on nowadays are *dangerous*.' He stressed the word. '*Really* dangerous.'

He looked at them anxiously, as a nervous uncle might look at a group of children left with a box of matches to play with, and who might quite easily set the house on fire.

'Well, thank you, Professor Eckstein,' said Mr Lazenby. He did not sound particularly thankful.

The Professor gathering correctly that he was released, smiled all round and trotted out of the room.

Mr Lazenby hardly waited for the door to close before venting his feelings.

'All alike, these scientists,' he said bitterly. 'Never any practical good. Never come up with anything sensible. All they can do is split the atom – and then tell *us* not to mess about with it!'

'Just as well if we never had,' said Admiral Blunt, again bluntly. 'What *we* want is something homely and domestic like a kind of selective weedkiller which would –' He paused abruptly. 'Now what the devil –?'

'Yes, Admiral?' said the Prime Minister politely.

'Nothing – just reminded me of something. Can't remember what –'

The Prime Minister sighed.

'Any more scientific experts waiting on the mat?' asked Gordon Chetwynd, glancing hopefully at his wristwatch.

'Old Pikeaway is here, I believe,' said Lazenby. 'Got a picture – or a drawing – or a map or something or other he wants us to look at –'

'What's it all about?'

'I don't know. It seems to be all bubbles,' said Mr Lazenby vaguely.

'Bubbles? Why bubbles?'

'I've no idea. Well,' he sighed, 'we'd better have a look at it.'

'Horsham's here, too –'

'He may have something new to tell us,' said Chetwynd.

Colonel Pikeaway stumped in. He was supporting a rolled-up burden which with Horsham's aid was unrolled and which with some difficulty was propped up so that those sitting round the table could look at it.

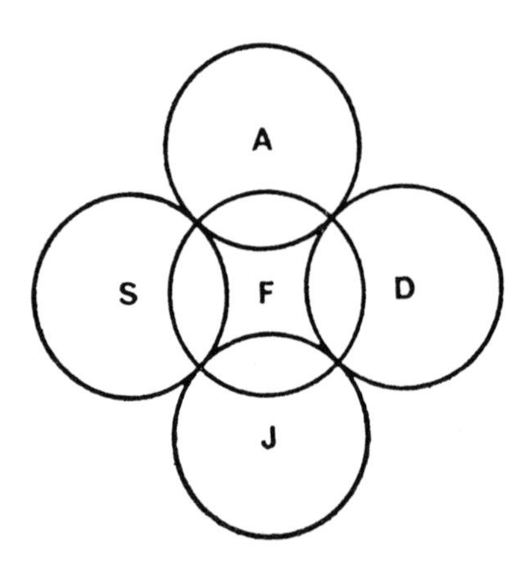

'Not exactly drawn to scale yet, but it gives you a rough idea,' said Colonel Pikeaway.

'What does it mean, if anything?'

'Bubbles?' murmured Sir George. An idea came to him. 'Is it a gas? A new gas?'

'You'd better deliver the lecture, Horsham,' said Pikeaway. 'You know the general idea.'

'I only know what I've been told. It's a rough diagram of an association of world control.'

'By whom?'

'By groups who own or control the sources of power – the raw materials of power.'

'And the letters of the alphabet?'

'Stand for a person or a code name for a special group. They are intersecting circles that by now cover the globe.

'That circle marked "A" stands for armaments. Someone, or some group is in control of armaments. All types of armaments. Explosives, guns, rifles. All over the world armaments are being produced according to plan, dispatched ostensibly to under-developed nations, backward nations, nations at war. But they don't remain where they are sent. They are re-routed almost immediately elsewhere. To guerrilla warfare in the South American Continent – to rioting and fighting in the USA – to Depots of Black Power – to various countries in Europe.

' "D" represents drugs – a network of suppliers run them from various depots and stockpiles. All kinds of drugs, from the more harmless varieties up to the true killers. The headquarters seem likely to be situated in the Levant, and to pass out through Turkey, Pakistan, India and Central Asia.'

'They make money out of it?'

'Enormous sums of money. But it's more than just an association of Pushers. It has a more sinister side to it. It's being used to finish off the weaklings amongst the young, shall we say, to make them complete slaves. Slaves so that they cannot live and exist or do jobs for their employers without a supply of drugs.'

Kenwood whistled.

'That's a bad show, isn't it? Don't you know at all who those Drug Pushers are?'

'Some of them, yes. But only the lesser fry. Not the real controllers. Drug headquarters are, so far as we can judge, in Central Asia and the Levant. They get delivered from there in the tyres of cars, in cement, in concrete, in all kinds of machinery and industrial goods. They're delivered all over the world and passed on as ordinary trade goods to where they are meant to go.

' "F" stands for finance. Money! A money spider's web in the centre of it all. You'll have to go to Mr Robinson to tell you about money. According to a memo here, money is coming very largely from America and there's also a headquarters in Bavaria. There's a vast reserve in South Africa, based on gold and diamonds. Most of the money is going to South America. One of the principal controllers, if I may so put it, of money, is a very powerful and talented woman. She's old now: must be near to death. But she is still strong and active. Her name was Charlotte Krapp. Her father owned the vast Krapp yards in Germany. She was a financial genius herself and operated in Wall Street. She accumulated fortune after fortune by investments in all parts of the world. She owns transport, she owns machinery, she owns industrial concerns. All these things. She lives in a vast castle in Bavaria – from there she directs a flow of money to different parts of the globe.

' "S" represents science – the new knowledge of chemical and biological warfare – Various young scientists have defected – There is a nucleus of them in the US, we believe, vowed and dedicated to the cause of anarchy.'

'Fighting for anarchy? A contradiction in terms. Can there be such a thing?'

'You believe in anarchy if you are young. You want a new world, and to begin with you must pull down the old one – just as you pull down a house before you build a new one to replace it. But if you don't know where you are going, if you don't know where you are being lured to go,' or even pushed to go, what will the new world be like, and where will the believers be when they get it? Some of them slaves, some of them blinded by hate, some by violence and sadism, both preached and practised. Some of them – and God help those – still idealistic, still believing as people did in France at the time of the French Revolution that that revolution would bring prosperity, peace, happiness, contentment to its people.'

'And what are *we* doing about all this? What are we proposing to do about it?' It was Admiral Blunt who spoke.

'What are we doing about it? All that we can. I assure you, all you who are here, we are doing all that we can. We have people working for us in every country. We have agents, inquirers, those who gather information, and bring it back here –'

'Which is very necessary,' said Colonel Pikeaway. 'First we've got to *know* – know who's who, who's with us and who's against us. And after that we've got to see what, if anything, can be done.'

'Our name for this diagram is The Ring. Here's a list of what we know about the Ring leaders. Those with a query mean that we know only the name they go by – or alternatively we only suspect that they are the ones we want.'

THE RING

F	Big Charlotte	– Bavaria
A	Eric Olafsson	– Sweden, Industrialist, Armaments
D	Said to go by the name of Demetrios	– Smyrna, Drugs
S	Dr Sarolensky	– Colorado, USA, Physicist-Chemist. Suspicion only
J		– A woman. Goes by Code name of Juanita. Said to be dangerous. No knowledge of her real name.

XV. AUNT MATILDA TAKES A CURE

1

'A cure of some kind, I thought?' Lady Matilda hazarded.

'A cure?' said Dr Donaldson. He looked faintly puzzled for a moment, losing his air of medical omniscience, which, of course, so Lady Matilda reflected, was one of the slight disadvantages attached to having a younger doctor attending one rather than the older specimen to whom one has been accustomed for several years.

'That's what we used to call them,' Lady Matilda explained. 'In my young days, you know, you went for the Cure. Marienbad, Carlsbad, Baden-Baden, all the rest of it. Just the other day I read about this new place in the paper. Quite new and up to date. Said to be all new ideas and things like that. Not that I'm really sold on new ideas, but I wouldn't really be afraid of them. I mean, they would probably be all the same things all over again.

Water tasting of bad eggs and the latest sort of diet and walking to take the Cure, or the Waters, or whatever they call them now, at a rather inconvenient hour in the morning. And I expect they give you massage or something. It used to be seaweed. But this place is somewhere in the mountains. Bavaria or Austria or somewhere like that. So I don't suppose it would be seaweed. Shaggy moss, perhaps – sounds like a dog. And perhaps quite a nice mineral water as well as the eggy sulphury one, I mean. Superb buildings, I understand. The only thing one is nervous about nowadays is that they never seem to put banisters in any up-to-date modern buildings. Flights of marble steps and all that, but nothing to hang on to.'

'I think I know the place you mean,' said Dr Donaldson. 'It's been publicized a good deal, in the press.'

'Well, you know what one is at my age,' said Lady Matilda. 'One likes trying new things. Really, I think it is just to amuse one. It doesn't really make one feel one's health would be any better. Still, you don't think it would be a bad idea, do you, Dr Donaldson?'

Dr Donaldson looked at her. He was not so young as Lady Matilda labelled him in her mind. He was just approaching forty and he was a tactful and kindly man and willing to indulge his elderly patients as far as he considered it desirable, without any actual danger of their attempting something obviously unsuitable.

'I'm sure it wouldn't do you any harm at all,' he said. 'Might be quite a good idea. Of course travel's a bit tiring though one flies to places very quickly and easily nowadays.'

'Quickly, yes. Easily, no,' said Lady Matilda. 'Ramps and moving staircases and in and out of buses from the airport to the plane, and the plane to another airport and from the airport to another bus. All that, you know.

But I understand one can have wheelchairs in the airports.'

'Of course you can. Excellent idea. If you promise to do that and not think you can walk everywhere . . .'

'I know, I know,' said his patient, interrupting him. 'You do understand. You're really a very understanding man. One has one's pride, you know, and while you can still hobble around with a stick or a little support, you don't really want to look absolutely a crock or bedridden or something. It'd be easier if I was a man,' she mused. 'I mean, one could tie up one's leg with one of those enormous bandages and padded things as though one had the gout. I mean, gout is all right for the male sex. Nobody thinks anything the worse of them. Some of their older friends think they've been tucking in to the port too much because that used to be the old idea, though I believe that is not really true at all. Port wine does *not* give you gout. Yes, a wheelchair, and I could fly to Munich or somewhere like that. One could arrange for a car or something at the other end.'

'You will take Miss Leatheran with you, of course.'

'Amy? Oh, of course. I couldn't do without her. Anyway, you think no harm would be done?'

'I think it might do you a world of good.'

'You really *are* a nice man.'

Lady Matilda gave him the twinkle from her eyes with which now he was becoming familiar.

'You think it'll amuse me and cheer me up to go somewhere new and see some new faces, and of course you're quite right. But I like to think that I'm taking a Cure, though really there's nothing for me to be cured of. Not really, is there? I mean, except old age. Unfortunately old age doesn't get cured, it only gets more so, doesn't it?'

'The point is really, will you enjoy yourself? Well, I think you will. When you get tired, by the way, when doing anything, stop doing it.'

'I shall still drink glasses of water if the water tastes of rotten eggs. Not because I like them or because frankly I think they do me any good. But it has a sort of mortifying feeling. It's like old women in our village always used to be. They always wanted a nice, strong medicine either coloured black or purple or deep pink, heavily flavoured with peppermint. They thought that did much more good than a nice little pill or a bottle that only appeared to be full of ordinary water without any exotic colouring.'

'You know too much about human nature,' said Dr Donaldson.

'You're very nice to me,' said Lady Matilda. 'I appreciate it. Amy!'

'Yes, Lady Matilda?'

'Get me an atlas, will you. I've lost track of Bavaria and the countries round it.'

'Let me see now. An atlas. There'll be one in the library, I suppose. There must be some old atlases about, dating back to about 1920 or thereabouts, I suppose.'

'I wondered if we had anything a little more modern.'

'Atlas,' said Amy, deep in reflection.

'If not, you can buy one and bring it along tomorrow morning. It's going to be very difficult because all the names are different, the countries are different, and I shan't know where I am. But you'll have to help me with that. Find a big magnifying glass, will you? I have an idea I was reading in bed with one the other day and it probably slipped down between the bed and the wall.'

Her requirements took a little time to satisfy but the atlas, the magnifying glass and an older atlas by which to check, were finally produced and Amy, nice woman that she was, Lady Matilda thought, was extremely helpful.

'Yes, here it is. It still seems to be called Monbrügge or something like that. It's either in the Tyrol or Bavaria. Everything seems to have changed places and got different names –'

II

Lady Matilda looked round her bedroom in the Gasthaus. It was well appointed. It was very expensive. It combined comfort with an appearance of such austerity as might lead the inhabitant to identify herself with an ascetic course of exercises, diet and possibly painful courses of massage. Its furnishings, she thought, were interesting. They provided for all tastes. There was a large framed Gothic script on the wall. Lady Matilda's German was not as good as it had been in her girlhood, but it dealt, she thought, with the golden and enchanting idea of a return to youth. Not only did youth hold the future in its hands but the old were being nicely indoctrinated to feel that they themselves might know such a second golden flowering.

Here there were gentle aids so as to enable one to pursue the doctrine of any of the many paths in life which attracted different classes of people. (Always presuming that they had enough money to pay for it.) Beside the bed was a Gideon Bible such as Lady Matilda when travelling in the United States had often found by her bedside. She picked it up approvingly, opened it at random and dropped a finger on one particular verse. She read it, nodding her head contentedly and made a brief note of it on a note pad that was lying on her bed table. She had often done that in the course of her life – it was her way of obtaining divine guidance at short notice.

I have been young and now am old, yet have I not seen the righteous forsaken.

She made further researches of the room. Handily placed but not too apparent was an *Almanach de Gotha*, modestly situated on a lower shelf of the bedside table. A most invaluable book for those who wished to familiarize themselves with the higher strata of society reaching back for several hundred years and which were still being observed and noted and checked by those of aristocratic lineage or interested in the same. It will come in handy, she thought, I can read up a good deal on that.

Near the desk, by the stove of period porcelain, were paperback editions of certain preachings and tenets by the modern prophets of the world. Those who were now or had recently been crying in the wilderness were here to be studied and approved by young followers with haloes of hair, strange raiment, and earnest hearts. Marcuse, Guevara, Lévi-Strauss, Fanon.

In case she was going to hold any conversations with golden youth she had better read up a little on that also.

At that moment there was a timid tap on the door. It opened slightly and the face of the faithful Amy came round the corner. Amy, Lady Matilda thought suddenly, would look exactly like a sheep when she was ten years older. A nice, faithful, kindly sheep. At the moment, Lady Matilda was glad to think, she looked still like a very agreeable plump lamb with nice curls of hair, thoughtful and kindly eyes, and able to give kindly baa's rather than to bleat.

'I do hope you slept well.'

'Yes, my dear, I did, excellently. Have you got that thing?'

Amy always knew what she meant. She handed it to her employer.

'Ah, my diet sheet. I see.' Lady Matilda perused it, then said, 'How incredibly unattractive! What's this water like one's supposed to drink?'

'It doesn't taste very nice.'

'No, I don't suppose it would. Come back in half an hour. I've got a letter I want you to post.'

Moving aside her breakfast tray, she moved over to the desk. She thought for a few minutes and then wrote her letter. 'It ought to do the trick,' she murmured.

'I beg your pardon, Lady Matilda, what did you say?'

'I was writing to the old friend I mentioned to you.'

'The one you said you haven't seen for about fifty or sixty years?'

Lady Matilda nodded.

'I do hope –' Amy was apologetic. 'I mean – I – it's such a long time. People have short memories nowadays. I do hope that she'll remember all about you and everything.'

'Of course she will,' said Lady Matilda. 'The people you don't forget are the people you knew when you were about ten to twenty. They stick in your mind for ever. You remember what hats they wore, and the way they laughed, and you remember their faults and their good qualities and everything about them. Now anyone I met twenty years ago, shall we say, I simply can't remember who they are. Not if they're mentioned to me, and not if I saw them even. Oh yes, she'll remember about *me*. And all about Lausanne. You get that letter posted. I've got to do a little homework.'

She picked up the *Almanach de Gotha* and returned to bed, where she made a serious study of such items as might come in useful. Some family relationships and various other kinships of the useful kind Who had married whom, who had lived where, what misfortunes had overtaken others. Not that the person whom she had in mind was herself likely to be found in the *Almanach de Gotha*. But she lived in a part of the world, had come there deliberately to live in a Schloss belonging to originally noble ancestors, and she had absorbed the local respect and adulation for those above all of good breeding. To good birth, even impaired with poverty, she herself, as Lady Matilda well knew, had no claim whatever. She had had to make do with money. Oceans of money. Incredible amounts of money.

Lady Matilda Cleckheaton had no doubt at all that she herself, the daughter of an eighth Duke, would be bidden to some kind of festivity. Coffee, perhaps, and delicious creamy cakes.

III

Lady Matilda Cleckheaton made her entrance into one of the grand reception rooms of the Schloss. It had been a fifteen-mile drive. She had dressed herself with some care, though somewhat to the disapproval of Amy. Amy seldom offered advice, but she was so anxious for her principal to succeed in whatever she was undertaking that she had ventured this time on a moderate remonstrance.

'You don't think your red dress is really a little *worn*, if you know what I mean. I mean just beneath the arms, and, well, there are two or three very shiny patches –'

'I know, my dear, I know. It is a shabby dress but it is nevertheless a Patou model. It is old but it was enormously expensive. I am not trying to look rich or extravagant. I am an impoverished member of an aristocratic family. Anyone of under fifty, no doubt, would despise me. But my hostess is living and has lived for some years in a part of the world where the rich will be kept waiting for their meal while the hostess will be willing to wait for a shabby, elderly woman of impeccable descent. Family traditions are things that one does not lose easily. One absorbs them, even, when one goes to a new neighbourhood. In my trunk, by the way, you will find a feather boa.'

'Are you going to put on a feather boa?'

'Yes, I am. An ostrich feather one.'

'Oh dear, that must be years old.'

'It is, but I've kept it very carefully. You'll see, Charlotte will recognize what it is. She will think one of the best families in England was reduced to wearing her old clothes that she had kept carefully for years. And I'll wear my sealskin coat, too. That's a little worn, but such a magnificent coat in its time.'

Thus arrayed, she set forth. Amy went with her as a well-dressed though only quietly smart attendant.

Matilda Cleckheaton had been prepared for what she saw. A whale, as Stafford had told her. A wallowing whale, a hideous old woman sitting in a room surrounded with pictures worth a fortune. Rising with some difficulty from a throne-like chair which could have figured on a stage representing the palace of some magnificent prince from any age from the Middle Ages down.

'Matilda!'

'Charlotte!'

'Ah! After all these years. How strange it seems!'

They exchanged words of greeting and pleasure, talking partly in German and partly in English. Lady Matilda's German was slightly faulty. Charlotte spoke excellent German, excellent English though with a strong guttural accent, and occasionally English with an American accent. She was really, Lady Matilda thought, quite splendidly hideous. For a moment she felt a fondness almost dating back to the past although, she reflected the next moment, Charlotte had been a most detestable girl.

Nobody had really liked her and she herself had certainly not done so. But there is a great bond, say what we will, in the memories of old schooldays. Whether Charlotte had liked her or not she did not know. But Charlotte, she remembered, had certainly – what used to be called in those days – sucked up to her. She had had visions, possibly, of staying in a ducal castle in England. Lady Matilda's father, though of most praiseworthy lineage, had been one of the most impecunious of English dukes. His estate had only been held together by the rich wife he had married whom he had treated with the utmost courtesy, and who had enjoyed bullying him whenever able to do so. Lady Matilda had been fortunate enough to be his daughter by a second marriage. Her own mother had been extremely agreeable and also a very successful actress, able to play the part of looking a duchess far more than any real duchess could do.

They exchanged reminiscences of past days, the tortures they had inflicted on some of their instructors, the fortunate and unfortunate marriages that had occurred to some of their schoolmates. Matilda made a few mentions of certain alliances and families culled from the pages of the *Almanach de Gotha* – 'but of course that must have been a terrible marriage for Elsa. One of the Bourbons de Parme, was it not? Yes, yes, well, one knows what that leads to. Most unfortunate.'

Coffee was brought, delicious coffee, plates of mille-feuille pastry and delicious cream cakes.

'I should not touch any of this,' cried Lady Matilda. 'No indeed! My doctor, he is most severe. He said that I must adhere strictly to the Cure while I was here. But after all, this is a day of holiday, is it not? Of renewal of youth. That is what interests me so much. My great-nephew who visited you not long ago – I forget who brought him here, the Countess – ah, it began with a Z, I cannot remember her name.'

'The Countess Renata Zerkowski –'

'Ah, that was the name, yes. A very charming young woman, I believe. And she brought him to visit you. It was most kind of her. He was so impressed. Impressed, too, with all your beautiful possessions. Your way of living, and indeed, the wonderful things which he had heard about you. How you have a whole movement of – oh, I do not know how to give the proper term. A Galaxy of Youth. Golden, beautiful youth. They flock round you. They worship you. What a wonderful life you must live. Not that I could support such a life. I have to live very quietly. Rheumatoid arthritis. And also the financial difficulties. Difficulty in keeping up the family house. Ah well, you know what it is for us in England – our taxation troubles.'

'I remember that nephew of yours, yes. He was agreeable, a very agreeable man. The Diplomatic Service, I understand?'

'Ah yes. But it is – well, you know, I cannot feel that his talents are being properly recognized. He does not say much. He does not complain, but he feels that he is – well, he feels that he has not been appreciated as he should. The powers that be, those who hold office at present, what are they?'

'*Canaille!*' said Big Charlotte.

'Intellectuals with no *savoir faire* in life. Fifty years ago it would have been different,' said Lady Matilda, 'but nowadays his promotion has been not advanced as it should. I will even tell you, in confidence, of course, that he has been distrusted. They suspect him, you know, of being in with – what shall I call it? – rebellious, revolutionary tendencies. And yet one must realize what the future could hold for a man who could embrace more advanced views.'

'You mean he is not, then, how do you say it in England, in sympathy with the Establishment, as they call it?'

'Hush, hush, we must not say these things. At least *I* must not,' said Lady Matilda.

'You interest me,' said Charlotte.

Matilda Cleckheaton sighed.

'Put it down, if you like, to the fondness of an elderly relative. Staffy has always been a favourite of mine. He has charm and wit. I think also he has ideas. He envisages the future, a future that should differ a good deal from what we have at present. Our country, alas, is politically in a very sad state. Stafford seems to be very much impressed by things you said to him or showed to him. You've done so much for music, I understand. What we need I cannot but feel is the ideal of the super race.'

'There should and could be a super race. Adolf Hitler had the right idea,' said Charlotte. 'A man of no importance in himself, but he had artistic elements in his character. And undoubtedly he had the power of leadership.'

'Ah yes. Leadership, that is what we need.'

'You had the wrong allies in the last war, my dear. If England and Germany now had arrayed themselves side by side, if they had had the same ideals, of youth, strength, two Aryan nations with the right ideals. Think where your country and mine might have arrived today? Yet perhaps even that is too narrow a view to take. In some ways the communists and the others have taught us a lesson. Workers of the world unite? But that is to set one's sights too low. Workers are only our material. It is "Leaders of the world unite!" Young men with the gift of leadership, of good blood. And we must start, not with the middle-aged men set in their ways, repeating themselves like a gramophone record that has stuck. We must seek among the student population, the young men with brave hearts, with great ideas, willing to march, willing to be killed but willing also to kill. To kill without any compunction – because it is certain that without aggressiveness, without violence, without attack – there can be no victory. I must show you something –'

With somewhat of a struggle she succeeded in rising to her feet. Lady Matilda followed suit, underlining a little her difficulty, which was not quite as much as she was making out.

'It was in May 1940,' said Charlotte, 'when Hitler Youth went on to its second stage. When Himmler obtained from Hitler a charter. The charter of the famous SS. It was formed for the destruction of the eastern peoples, the slaves, the appointed slaves of the world. It would make room for the German master race. The SS executive instrument came into being.' Her voice dropped a little. It held for a moment a kind of religious awe.

Lady Matilda nearly crossed herself by mistake.

'The Order of the Death's Head,' said Big Charlotte.

She walked slowly and painfully down the room and pointed to where on the wall hung, framed in gilt and surmounted with a skull, the Order of the Death's Head.

'See, it is my most cherished possession. It hangs here on my wall. My golden youth band, when they come here, salute it. And in our archives in the castle here are folios of its chronicles. Some of them are only reading for strong stomachs, but one must learn to accept these things. The deaths in gas chambers, the torture cells, the trials at Nuremberg speak venomously of all those things. But it was a great tradition. Strength through pain. They were trained young, the boys, so that they should not falter or turn back or suffer from any kind of softness. Even Lenin, preaching his Marxist doctrine, declared "Away with softness!" It was one of his first rules for creating a perfect State. But we were too narrow. We wished to confine our great dream only to the German master race. But there are other races. They too can attain masterhood through suffering and violence and through the considered practice of anarchy. We must pull down, pull down all the soft institutions. Pull down the more humiliating forms of religion. There is a religion of strength, the old religion of the Viking people. And we have a leader, young as yet, gaining in power every day. What did some great man say? Give me the tools and I will do the job. Something like that. Our leader has already the tools. He will have more tools. He will have the planes, the bombs, the means of chemical warfare. He will have the men to fight. He will have the transport. He will have shipping and oil. He will have what one might call the Aladdin's creation of genie. You rub the lamp and the genie appears. It is all in your hands. The means of production, the means of wealth and our young leader, a leader by birth as well as by character. He has all this.'

She wheezed and coughed.

'Let me help you.'

Lady Matilda supported her back to her seat Charlotte gasped a little as she sat down.

'It's sad to be old, but I shall last long enough. Long enough to see the triumph of a new world, a new creation. That is what you want for your nephew. I will see to it. Power in his own country, that is what he wants, is it not? You would be ready to encourage the spearhead there?'

'I had influence once. But now –' Lady Matilda shook her head sadly. 'All that is gone.'

'It will come again, dear,' said her friend. 'You were right to come to me. I have a certain influence.'

'It is a great cause,' said Lady Matilda. She sighed and murmured, 'The Young Siegfried.'

'I hope you enjoyed meeting your old friend,' said Amy as they drove back to the Gasthaus.

'If you could have heard all the nonsense I talked, you wouldn't believe it,' said Lady Matilda Cleckheaton.

XVI. PIKEAWAY TALKS

'The news from France is very bad,' said Colonel Pikeaway, brushing a cloud of cigar ash off his coat. 'I heard Winston Churchill say that in the last war. There was a man who could speak in plain words and no more than needed. It was very impressive. It told us what we needed to know. Well, it's a long time since then, but I say it again today. The news from France is very bad.'

He coughed, wheezed and brushed a little more ash off himself.

'The news from Italy is very bad,' he said. 'The news from Russia, I imagine, could be very bad if they let much out about it. They've got trouble there too. Marching bands of students in the street, shop windows smashed, Embassies attacked. News from Egypt is very bad. News from Jerusalem is very bad. News from Syria is very bad. That's all more or less normal, so we needn't worry too much. News from Argentine is what I'd call peculiar. Very peculiar indeed. Argentine, Brazil, Cuba, they've all got together. Call themselves the Golden Youth Federated

States, or something like that. It's got an army, too. Properly drilled, properly armed, properly commanded. They've got planes, they've got bombs, they've got God-knows-what. And most of them seem to know what to do with them, which makes it worse. There's a singing crowd as well, apparently. Pop songs, old local folk songs, and bygone battle hymns. They go along rather like the Salvation Army used to do – no blasphemy intended – I'm not crabbing the Salvation Army. Jolly good work they did always. And the girls – pretty as Punch in their bonnets.'

He went on:

'I've heard that something's going on in that line in the civilized countries, starting with *us*. Some of us can be called civilized still, I suppose? One of our politicians the other day, I remember, said we were a splendid nation, chiefly because we were permissive, we had demonstrations, we smashed things, we beat up anyone if we hadn't anything better to do, we got rid of our high spirits by showing violence, and our moral purity by taking most of our clothes off. I don't know what he thought he was talking about – politicians seldom do – but they can make it sound all right. That's why they are politicians.'

He paused and looked across at the man he was talking to.

'Distressing – sadly distressing,' said Sir George Packham. One can hardly believe – one worries – if one could only – Is that all the news you've got?' he asked plaintively.

'Isn't it enough? You're hard to satisfy. World anarchy well on its way – that's what we've got. A bit wobbly still – not fully established yet, but very near to it – very near indeed.'

'But action can surely be taken against all this?'

'Not so easy as you think. Tear gas puts a stop to rioting for a while and gives the police a break. And naturally we've got plenty of germ warfare and nuclear bombs and all the other pretty bags of tricks – What do you think would happen if we started using those? Mass massacre of all the marching girls and boys, and the housewife's shopping circle, and the old age pensioners at home, and a good quota of our pompous politicians as they tell us we've never had it so good, and in addition you and me – Ha, ha!

'And anyway,' added Colonel Pikeaway, 'if it's only news you're after, I understand you've got some hot news of your own arriving today. Top secret from Germany, Herr Heinrich Spiess himself.'

'How on earth did you hear that? It's supposed to be strictly – '

'We know everything here,' said Colonel Pikeaway, using his pet phrase – 'that's what we're for.'

'Bringing some tame doctor, too, I understand –' he added.

'Yes, a Dr Reichardt, a top scientist, I presume –'

'No. Medical doctor – Loony-bins –'

'Oh dear – a psychologist?'

'Probably. The ones that run loony-bins are mostly that. With any luck he'll have been brought over so that he can examine the heads of some of our young firebrands. Stuffed full they are of German philosophy, Black Power philosophy, dead French writers' philosophy, and so on and so forth. Possibly they'll let him examine some of the heads of our legal lights who preside over our judicial courts here saying we must be very careful not to do anything to damage a young man's ego because he *might* have to earn his living. We'd be a lot safer if they sent them all round to get plenty of National Assistance to live on and then they could go back to their rooms, not do any work, and enjoy themselves reading more philosophy. However, I'm out of date. I know that. You needn't tell me so.'

'One has to take into account the new modes of thought,' said Sir George Packham. 'One feels, I mean one hopes – well, it's difficult to say –'

'Must be very worrying for you,' said Colonel Pikeaway. 'Finding things so difficult to say.'

His telephone rang. He listened, then handed it to Sir George.

'Yes?' said Sir George. 'Yes? Oh yes. Yes. I agree. I suppose – No – no – not the Home Office. No. Privately, you mean. Well, I suppose we'd better use – er –' Sir George looked round him cautiously.

'This place isn't bugged,' said Colonel Pikeaway amiably.

'Code word Blue Danube,' said Sir George Packham in a loud, hoarse whisper. 'Yes, yes. I'll bring Pikeaway along with me. Oh yes, of course. Yes, yes. Get on to him. Yes, say you particularly want him to come, but to remember our meeting has got to be strictly private.'

'We can't take my car then,' said Pikeaway. 'It's too well known.'

'Henry Horsham's coming to fetch us in the Volkswagen.'

'Fine,' said Colonel Pikeaway. 'Interesting, you know, all this.'

'You don't think –' said Sir George and hesitated.

'I don't think what?'

'I meant just really – well, I – mean, if you wouldn't mind my suggesting – a clothes brush?'

'Oh, this.' Colonel Pikeaway hit himself lightly on the shoulder and a cloud of cigar ash flew up and made Sir George choke.

'Nanny,' Colonel Pikeaway shouted. He banged a buzzer on his desk.

A middle-aged woman came in with a clothes brush, appearing with the suddenness of a genie summoned by Aladdin's lamp.

'Hold your breath, please, Sir George,' she said. 'This may be a little pungent.'

She held the door open for him and he retired outside while she brushed Colonel Pikeaway, who coughed and complained:

'Damned nuisance these people are. Always wanting you to get fixed up like a barber's dummy.'

'I should not describe your appearance as quite like that, Colonel Pikeaway. You ought to be used to my cleaning you up nowadays. And you know the Home Secretary suffers from asthma.'

'Well, that's his fault. Not taking proper care to have pollution removed from the streets of London.

'Come on, Sir George, let's hear what our German friend has come over to say. Sounds as though it's a matter of some urgency.'

XV11. HERR HEINRICH SPIESS

Herr Heinrich Spiess was a worried man. He did not seek to conceal the fact. He acknowledged, indeed, without concealment, that the situation which these five men had come together to discuss was a serious situation. At the same time, he brought with him that sense of re-assurance which had been his principal asset in dealing with the recently difficult political life in Germany. He was a solid man, a thoughtful man, a man who could bring common sense to any assemblies he attended. He gave no sense of being a brilliant man, and that in itself was reassuring. Brilliant politicians had been responsible for about two-thirds of the national states of crisis in more countries than one. The other third of trouble had been caused by those politicians who were unable to conceal the fact that although duly elected by democratic governments, they had been unable to conceal their remarkably poor powers of judgment, common sense and, in fact, any noticeable brainy qualities.

'This is not in any sense an official visit, you understand,' said the Chancellor.

'Oh quite, quite.'

'A certain piece of knowledge has come to me which I thought is essential we should share. It throws a rather interesting light on certain happenings which have puzzled as well as distressed us. This is Dr Reichardt.'

Introductions were made. Dr Reichardt was a large and comfortable-looking man with the habit of saying 'Ach, so' from time to time.

'Dr Reichardt is in charge of a large establishment in the neighbourhood of Karlsruhe. He treats there mental patients. I think I am correct in saying that you treat there between five and six hundred patients, am I not right?'

'Ach, so,' said Dr Reichardt.

'I take it that you have several different forms of mental illness?'

'Ach, so. I have different forms of mental illness, but nevertheless, I have a special interest in, and treat almost exclusively one particular type of mental trouble.' He branched off into German and Herr Spiess presently rendered a brief translation in case some of his English colleagues should not understand. This was both necessary and tactful. Two of them did in part, one of them definitely did not, and the two others were truly puzzled.

'Dr Reichardt has had,' explained Herr Spiess, 'the greatest success in his treatment of what as a layman I describe as megalomania. The belief that you are someone other than you are. Ideas of being more important than you are. Ideas that if you have persecution mania –'

'Ach, no!' said Dr Reichardt. 'Persecution mania, *no*, that I do not treat. There is no persecution mania in my clinic. Not among the group with whom I am specially interested. On the contrary, they hold the delusions that they do because they wish to be happy. And they are happy, and I can keep them happy. But if I cure them, see you, they will not be happy. So I have to find a cure that will restore sanity to them, and yet they will be happy just the same. We call this particular state of mind –'

He uttered a long and ferociously sounding German word of at least eight syllables.

'For the purposes of our English friends, I shall still use my term of megalomania, though I know,' continued Herr Spiess, rather quickly, 'that that is not the term you use nowadays, Dr Reichardt. So, as I say, you have in your clinic six hundred patients.'

'And at one time, the time to which I am about to refer, I had eight hundred.'

'Eight hundred!'

'It was interesting – most interesting.'

'You have such persons – to start at the beginning –'

'We have God Almighty,' explained Dr Reichardt. 'You comprehend?'

Mr Lazenby looked slightly taken aback.

'Oh – er – yes – er – yes. Very interesting, I am sure.'

'There are one or two young men, of course, who think

they are Jesus Christ. But that is not so popular as the Almighty. And then there are the others. I had at the time I am about to mention twenty-four Adolf Hitlers. This you must understand was at the time when Hitler was alive. Yes, twenty-four or twenty-five Adolf Hitlers –' he consulted a small notebook which he took from his pocket – 'I have made some notes here, yes. Fifteen Napoleons. Napoleon, he is always popular, ten Mussolinis, five reincarnations of Julius Caesar, and many other cases, very curious and very interesting. But that I will not weary you with at this moment. Not being specially qualified in the medical sense, it would not be of any interest to you. We will come to the incident that matters.'

Dr Reichardt spoke again at rather shorter length, and Herr Spiess continued to translate.

'There came to him one day a government official. Highly thought of at that time – this was during the war, mind you – by the ruling government. I will call him for the moment Martin B. You will know who I mean. He brought with him his chief. In fact he brought with him – well, we will not beat about the bush – he brought the Führer himself.'

'Ach, so,' said Dr Reichardt.

'It was a great honour, you understand, that he should come to inspect,' went on the doctor. 'He was gracious, mein Führer. He told me that he had heard very good reports of my successes. He said that there had been trouble lately. Cases from the army. There, more than once there had been men believing they were Napoleon, sometimes believing they were some of Napoleon's Marshals and sometimes, you comprehend, behaving accordingly, giving out military orders and causing therefore military difficulties. I would have been happy to have give him any professional knowledge that might be useful to him, but Martin B. who accompanied him said that that would not be necessary. Our great Führer, however,' said Dr Reichardt, looking at Herr Spiess slightly uneasily, 'did not want to be bothered with such details. He said that no doubt it would be better if medically qualified men with some experience as neurologists should come and have a consultation. What he wanted was to – ach, well, he wanted to see round, and I soon found what he was really interested to see. It should not have surprised me. Oh no, because you see, it was a symptom that one recognizes. The strain of his life was already beginning to tell on the Führer.'

'I suppose he was beginning to think he was God Almighty himself at that time,' said Colonel Pikeaway unexpectedly, and he chuckled.

Dr Reichardt looked shocked.

'He asked me to let him know certain things. He said that Martin B. had told him that I actually had a large number of patients thinking, not to put too fine a point on it, that they were themselves Adolf Hitler. I explained to him that this was not uncommon, that naturally with the respect, the worship they paid to Hitler, it was only natural that the great wish to be like him should end eventually by them identifying themselves with him. I was a little anxious when I mentioned this but I was delighted to find that he expressed great signs of satisfaction. He took it, I am thankful to say, as a compliment, this passionate wish to find identity with himself. He next asked if he could meet a representative number of these patients with this particular affliction. We had a little consultation. Martin B. seemed doubtful, but he took me aside and assured me that Herr Hitler actually wished to have this experience. What he himself was anxious to ensure was that Herr Hitler did not meet – well, in short, that Herr Hitler was not to be allowed to run any risks. If any of these so-called Hitlers, believing passionately in themselves as such, were inclined to be a little violent or dangerous . . . I assured him that he need have no worry. I suggested that I should collect a group of the most amiable of our Führers and assemble them for him to meet. Herr B. insisted that the Führer was very anxious to interview and mingle with them without my accompanying him. The patients, he said, would not behave naturally if they saw the chief of the establishment there, and if there was no danger . . . I assured him again that there was no danger. I said, however, that I should be glad if Herr B. would wait upon him. There was no difficulty about that. It was arranged. Messages were sent to the Führers to assemble in a room for a very distinguished visitor who was anxious to compare notes with them.

'Ach, so. Martin B. and the Führer were introduced into the assembly. I retired, closing the door, and chatted with the two ADC's who had accompanied them. The Führer, I said, was looking in a particularly anxious state. He had no doubt had many troubles of late. This I may say was very shortly before the end of the war when things, quite frankly, were going badly. The Führer himself, they told me, had been greatly distressed of late but was convinced that he could bring the war to a successful close if the ideas which he was continually presenting to his general staff were acted upon, and accepted promptly.'

'The Führer, I presume,' said Sir George Packham, 'was at that time – I mean to say – no doubt he was in a state that –'

'We need not stress these points,' said Herr Spiess. 'He was completely beyond himself. Authority had to be taken for him on several points. But all that you will know well enough from the researches you have made in my country.'

'One remembers that at the Nuremberg trials –'

'There's no need to refer to the Nuremberg trials, I'm sure,' said Mr Lazenby decisively. 'All that is far behind us. We look forward to a great future in the Common Market with your Government's help, with the Government of Monsieur Grosjean and your other European colleagues. The past is the past.'

'Quite so,' said Herr Spiess, 'and it is of the past that we now talk. Martin B. and Herr Hitler remained for a very short time in the assembly room. They came out again after seven minutes. Herr B. expressed himself to Dr Reichardt as very well satisfied with their experience. Their car was waiting and he and Herr Hitler must proceed immediately to where they had another appointment. They left very hurriedly.'

There was a silence.

'And then?' asked Colonel Pikeaway. 'Something happened? Or had already happened?'

'The behaviour of one of our Hitler patients was unusual,' said Dr Reichardt. 'He was a man who had a particularly close resemblance to Herr Hitler, which had given him always a special confidence in his own portrayal. He insisted now more fiercely than ever that he *was* the Führer, that he must go immediately to Berlin, that he must preside over a Council of the General Staff. In fact, he behaved with no signs of the former slight amelioration which he had shown in his condition. He seemed so unlike himself that I really could not understand this change taking place so suddenly. I was relieved, indeed, when two days later, his relations called to take him home for future private treatment there.'

'And you let him go,' said Herr Spiess.

'Naturally I let him go. They had a responsible doctor with them, he was a voluntary patient, not certified, and therefore he was within his rights. So he left.'

'I don't see –' began Sir George Packham.

'Herr Spiess has a theory –'

'It's not a theory,' said Spiess. 'What I am telling you is fact. The Russians concealed it, we've concealed it. Plenty of evidence and proof has come in. Hitler, our Führer, *remained in the asylum by his own consent* that day and a man with the nearest resemblance to the real Hitler departed with Martin B. It was that patient's body which was subsequently found in the bunker. I will not beat about the bush. We need not go into unnecessary details.'

'We all have to know the truth,' said Lazenby.

'The real Führer was smuggled by a pre-arranged underground route to the Argentine and lived there for some years. He had a son there by a beautiful Aryan girl of good family. Some say she was an English girl. Hitler's mental condition worsened, and he died insane, believing himself to be commanding his armies in the field. It was the only plan possibly by which he could ever have escaped from Germany. He accepted it.'

'And you mean that for all these years nothing has leaked out about this, nothing has been known?'

'There have been rumours, there are always rumours. If you remember, one of the Czar's daughters in Russia was said to have escaped the general massacre of her family.'

'But that was –' George Packham stopped. 'False – quite false.'

'It was proved false by one set of people. It was accepted by another set of people, both of whom had known her. That Anastasia was indeed Anastasia, or that Anastasia, Grand Duchess of Russia, was really only a peasant girl. Which story was true? Rumours! The longer they go on, the less people believe them, except for those who have romantic minds, who go on believing them. It has often been rumoured that Hitler was alive, not dead. There is no one who has ever said with certainty that they have examined his dead body. The Russians declared so. They brought no proofs, though.'

'Do you really mean to say – Dr Reichardt, do *you* support this extraordinary story?'

'Ach,' said Dr Reichardt. 'You ask me, but I have told you my part. It was certainly Martin B. who came to my sanatorium. It was Martin B. who brought with him the Führer. It was Martin B. who treated him as the Führer, who spoke to him with the deference with which one speaks to the Führer. As for me, I lived already with some hundreds of Führers, of Napoleons, of Julius Caesars. You must understand that the Hitlers who lived in my sanatorium, they looked alike, they could have been, nearly all of them *could* have been, Adolf Hitler. They themselves could never have believed in themselves with the passion, the vehemence with which they knew that they were Hitler, unless they had had a basic resemblance, with make-up, clothing, continual acting, and playing of the part. I had had no personal meeting with Herr Adolf Hitler at any previous time. One saw pictures of him in the papers, one knew roughly what our great genius looked like, but one knew only the pictures that he wished shown. So he came, he was the Führer, Martin B. the man best to be believed on that subject said he was the Führer. No, I had no doubts. I obeyed orders. Herr Hitler wished to go alone into a room to meet a selection of his – what shall one say? – his plaster copies. He went in. He came out. An exchange of clothing could have been made, not very different clothing in any case. Was it he himself or one of the self-appointed Hitlers who came out? Rushed out quickly by Martin B. and driven away while the real man could have stayed behind, could have enjoyed playing his part, could have known that in this way and in this way only could he manage to escape from the country which at any moment might surrender. He was already disturbed in mind, mentally affected by rage and anger that the orders he gave, the wild fantastic messages sent to his staff, what they were to do, what they were to say, the impossible things they were to attempt, were not, as of old, immediately obeyed. He could feel already that he was no longer in supreme command. But he had a small faithful two or three and they had a plan for him, to get him out of this country, out of Europe, to a place where he could rally round him in a different continent his Nazi followers, the young ones who believed so passionately in him. The swastika would rise again there. He played his part. No doubt, he enjoyed it. Yes, that would be in keeping with a man whose reason was already tottering. He would show these others that he could play the part of Adolf Hitler better than they did. He laughed to himself occasionally, and my doctors, my nurses, they would look in, they would see some slight change. One patient who seemed unusually mentally disturbed, perhaps. Pah, there was nothing in that. It was always happening. With the Napoleons, with the Julius Caesars, with all of them. Some days, as one would say if one was a layman, they are madder than usual. That is the only way I can put it. So now it is for Herr Spiess to speak.'

'Fantastic!' said the Home Secretary.

'Yes, fantastic,' said Herr Spiess patiently, 'but fantastic things can happen, you know. In history, in real life, no matter how fantastic.'

'And nobody suspected, nobody knew?'

'It was very well planned. It was well planned, well thought out. The escape route was ready, the exact details of it are not clearly known, but one can make a pretty good recapitulation of them. Some of the people who were concerned, who passed a certain personage on from place to place under different disguises, under different names, some of those people, on our looking back and making inquiries, we find did not live as long as they might have done.'

'You mean in case they should give the secret away or should talk too much?'

'The SS saw to that. Rich rewards, praise, promises of high positions in the future and then – death is a much easier answer. And the SS were used to death. They knew the different ways of it, they knew means of disposing of bodies – Oh yes, I will tell you that, this has been inquired into for some time now. The knowledge has come little by little to us, and we have made inquiries, documents have been acquired and the truth has come out. Adolf Hitler certainly reached South America. It is said that a marriage ceremony was performed – that a child was born. The child was branded in the foot with the mark of the swastika. Branded as a baby. I have seen trusted agents whom I can believe. They have seen that branded foot in South America. There that child was brought up, carefully guarded, shielded, prepared – prepared as the Dalai Lama might have been prepared for his great destiny. For that was the idea behind the fanatical young, the idea was greater than the idea that they had started out with. This was not merely a revival of the new Nazis, the new German super race. It was that, yes, but it was many more things besides. It was the young of many other nations, the super race of the young men of nearly every country in Europe, to join together, to join the ranks of anarchy, to destroy the old world, the materialistic world, to usher in a great new band of killing, murdering, violent brothers. Bent first on destruction and then on rising to power. And they had now their leader. A leader with the right blood in his veins and a leader who, though he grew up with no great likeness to his dead father, was – no, *is* – a golden-haired fair Nordic boy, taking presumably after the looks of his mother. A golden boy. A boy whom the whole world could accept. The Germans and the Austrians first because it was the great article of their faith, of their music, the young Siegfried. So he grew up as the young Siegfried who would command them all, who would lead them into the promised land. Not the promised land of the Jews, whom they despised, where Moses led his followers. The Jews were dead under the ground, killed or murdered in the gas chambers. This was to be a land of their own, a land gained by their own prowess. The countries of Europe were to be banded together with the countries of South America. There already they had their spearhead, their anarchists, their prophets, their Guevaras, the Castros, the Guerrillas, their followers, a long arduous training in cruelty and torture and violence and death and after it, glorious life. Freedom! As Rulers of the New World State. The appointed conquerors.'

'Absurd nonsense,' said Mr Lazenby. 'Once all this is put a stop to -- the whole thing will collapse. This is all quite ridiculous. What *can* they do?' Cedric Lazenby sounded merely querulous.

Herr Spiess shook his heavy, wise head.

'You may ask. I tell you the answer, which is – *they do not know*. They don't know where they're going. They don't know what is going to be done with them.'

'You mean they're not the real leaders?'

'They are the young marching Heroes, treading their path to glory, on stepping-stones of violence, of pain, of hatred. They have now their following not only in South America and Europe. The cult has travelled north. In the United States, there too the young men riot, they march, they follow the banner of the Young Siegfried. They are taught his ways, they are taught to kill, to enjoy pain, they are taught the rules of the Death's Head, the rules of Himmler. They are being trained, you see. They are being secretly indoctrinated. They do not know what they're being trained for. But we do, some of us at least. And you? In this country?'

'Four or five of us, perhaps,' said Colonel Pikeaway.

'In Russia they know, in America they have begun to know. They know that there are the followers of the Young Hero, Siegfried, based on the Norse Legends, and that a young Siegfried is the leader. That that is their new religion. The religion of the glorious boy, the golden triumph of youth. In him the old Nordic Gods have risen again.

'But that, of course,' said Herr Spiess, dropping his voice to a commonplace tone, 'that of course is not the simple prosaic truth. There are some powerful personalities behind this. Evil men with first-class brains. A first-class financier, a great industrialist, someone who controls mines, oil, stores of uranium, who owns scientists of the top class, and those are the ones, a committee of men, who themselves do not look particularly interesting or extraordinary, but nevertheless have got control. They control the sources of power, and control through certain means of their own the young men who kill and the young men who are slaves. By control of drugs they acquire slaves. Slaves in every country who little by little progress from soft drugs to hard drugs and who are then completely subservient, completely dependent on men whom they do not even know but who secretly own them body and soul. Their craving need for a particular drug makes them slaves, and in due course, these slaves prove to be no good, because of their dependence on drugs, they will only be capable of sitting in apathy dreaming sweet dreams, and so they will be left to die, or even helped to die. They will not inherit that kingdom in which they believe. Strange religions are being deliberately introduced to them. The gods of the old days disguised.'

'And permissive sex also plays its part, I suppose?'

'Sex can destroy itself. In old Roman times the men who steeped themselves in vice, who were oversexed, who ran sex to death until they were bored and weary of sex, sometimes fled from it and went out into the desert and became Anchorites like St Simeon Stylites. Sex will exhaust itself. It does its work for the time being, but it cannot rule you as drugs rule you. Drugs and sadism and the love of power and hatred. A desire for pain for its own sake. The pleasures of inflicting it. They are teaching themselves the pleasures of evil. Once the pleasures of evil get a hold on you, you cannot draw back.'

'My dear Chancellor – I really can't believe you – I mean, well – I mean if there are these tendencies, they must be put down by adopting strong measures. I mean, really, one – one can't go on pandering to this sort of thing. One must take a firm stand – a firm stand.'

'Shut up, George.' Mr Lazenby pulled out his pipe, looked at it, put it back in his pocket again. 'The best plan, I think,' he said, his *idée fixe* reasserting itself, 'would be for me to fly to Russia. I understand that – well, that these facts are known to the Russians.'

'They know sufficient,' said Herr Spiess. 'How much they will admit they know –' he shrugged his shoulders –

'that is difficult to say. It is never easy to get the Russians to come out in the open. They have their own troubles on the Chinese border. They believe perhaps less in the far advanced stage, into which this movement has got, than we do.'

'I should make mine a special mission, I should.'

'I should stay here if I were you, Cedric.'

Lord Altamount's quiet voice spoke from where he leaned rather wearily back in his chair. 'We need you here, Cedric,' he said. There was gentle authority in his voice. 'You are the head of our Government – you must remain here. We have our trained agents – our own emissaries who are qualified for foreign missions.'

'Agents?' Sir George Packham dubiously demanded. 'What can agents do at this stage? We must have a report from – Ah, Horsham, there you are – I did not notice you before. Tell us – what agents have we got? And what can they possibly do?'

'We've got some very good agents,' said Henry Horsham quietly. 'Agents bring you information. Herr Spiess also has brought you information. Information which *his* agents have obtained for *him*. The trouble is – always has been – (you've only got to read about the last war) *nobody wishes to believe the news the agents bring.*'

'Surely – Intelligence –'

'Nobody wants to accept that the agents *are* intelligent! But they are, you know. They are highly trained and their reports, nine times out of ten, are *true*. What happens then? The High-Ups refuse to believe it, don't want to believe it, go further and refuse to act upon it in any way.'

'Really, my dear Horsham – I can't –'

Horsham turned to the German.

'Even in your country, sir, didn't that happen? True

reports were brought in, but they weren't always acted upon. *People don't want to know – if truth is unpalatable.*'

'I have to agree – that can and does happen – not often, of that I assure you – But yes – sometimes –'

Mr Lazenby was fidgeting again with his pipe.

'Let us not argue about information. It is a question of dealing – of acting upon the information we have got. This is not merely a national crisis – it is an international crisis. Decisions must be taken at top level – we must act. Munro, the police must be reinforced by the Army – military measures must be set in motion. Herr Spiess, you have always been a great military nation – rebellions must be put down by armed forces before they get out of hand. You would agree with that policy, I am sure –'

'The policy, yes. But these insurrections are already what you term "out of hand". They have tools, rifles, machine-guns, explosives, grenades, bombs, chemical and other gases –'

'But with our nuclear weapons – a mere threat of nuclear warfare – and –'

'These are not just disaffected schoolboys. With this Army of Youth there are scientists – young biologists, chemists, physicists. To start – or to engage in nuclear warfare in Europe –' Herr Spiess shook his head. 'Already we have had an attempt to poison the water supply at Cologne – Typhoid.'

'The whole position is incredible –' Cedric Lazenby looked round him hopefully – 'Chetwynd – Munro – Blunt?'

Admiral Blunt was, somewhat to Lazenby's surprise, the only one to respond.

'I don't know where the Admiralty comes in – not quite our pigeon. I'd advise you, Cedric, if you want to do the best thing for yourself, to take your pipe, and a big supply of tobacco, and get as far out of range of any nuclear warfare you are thinking of starting as you can. Go and camp in the Antarctic, or somewhere where radio-activity will take a long time catching up with you. Professor Eckstein warned us, you know, and he knows what he's talking about.'

XV111. PIKEAWAY'S POSTSCRIPT

The meeting broke up at this point. It split into a definite rearrangement.

The German Chancellor with the Prime Minister, Sir George Packham, Gordon Chetwynd and Dr Reichardt departed for lunch at Downing Street.

Admiral Blunt, Colonel Munro, Colonel Pikeaway and Henry Horsham remained to make their comments with more freedom of speech than they would have permitted themselves if the VIP's had remained.

The first remarks made were somewhat disjointed.

'Thank goodness they took George Packham with them,' said Colonel Pikeaway. 'Worry, fidget, wonder, surmise – gets me down sometimes.'

'You ought to have gone with them, Admiral,' said Colonel Munro. 'Can't see Gordon Chetwynd or George Packham being able to stop our Cedric from going off for a top-level consultation with the Russians, the Chinese, the Ethiopians, the Argentinians or anywhere else the fancy takes him.'

'I've got other kites to fly,' said the Admiral gruffly. 'Going to the country to see an old friend of mine.' He looked with some curiosity at Colonel Pikeaway.

'Was the Hitler business really a surprise to you, Pike-away?'

Colonel Pikeaway shook his head.

'Not really. We've known all about the rumours of our Adolf turning up in South America and keeping the swastika flying for years. Fifty-to-fifty chance of its being true. Whoever the chap was, madman, play-acting impostor, or the real thing, he passed in his checks quite soon. Nasty stories about that, too – he wasn't an asset to his supporters.'

'*Whose body was it in the Bunker?* is still a good talking point,' said Blunt. 'Never been any definite identification. Russians saw to that.'

He got up, nodded to the others and went towards the door.

Munro said thoughtfully, 'I suppose Dr Reichardt knows the truth – though he played it cagey.'

'What about the Chancellor?' said Munro.

'Sensible man,' grunted the Admiral, turning his head back from the doorway. 'He was getting his country the way he wanted it, when this youth business started playing fun and games with the civilized world – Pity!' He looked shrewdly at Colonel Munro.

'What about the Golden-Haired Wonder? Hitler's son? Know all about him?'

'No need to worry,' said Colonel Pikeaway unexpectedly.

The Admiral let go of the door-handle and came back and sat down.

'All my eye and Betty Martin,' said Colonel Pikeaway. 'Hitler never had a son.'

'You can't be sure of that.'

'We *are* sure – Franz Joseph, the Young Siegfried, the idolized Leader, is a common or garden fraud, a rank impostor. He's the son of an Argentinian carpenter and a good-looking blonde, a small-part German opera singer – inherited his looks and his singing voice from his mother. He was carefully chosen for the part he was to play, groomed for stardom. In his early youth he was a professional actor – he was branded in the foot with a swastika – a story made up for him full of romantic details. He was treated like a dedicated Dalai Lama.'

'And you've proof of this?'

'Full documentation,' Colonel Pikeaway grinned. 'One of my best agents got it. Affidavits, photostats, signed declaration, including one from the mother, and medical evidence as to the date of the scar, copy of the original birth certificate of Karl Aguileros – and signed evidence of his identity with the so-called Franz Joseph. The whole bag of tricks. My agent got away with it just in time. They were after her – might have got her if she hadn't had a bit of luck at Frankfurt.'

'And where are these documents now?'

'In a safe place. Waiting for the right moment for a spectacular debunking of a first-class impostor –'

'Do the Government know this? – the Prime Minister?'

'I never tell all I know to politicians – not until I can't avoid it, or until I'm quite sure they'll do the right thing.'

'You *are* an old devil, Pikeaway,' said Colonel Munro.

'Somebody has to be,' said Colonel Pikeaway, sadly.

X1X. SIR STAFFORD NYE HAS VISITORS

Sir Stafford Nye was entertaining guests. They were guests with whom he had previously been unacquainted except for one of them whom he knew fairly well by sight. They were good-looking young men, serious-minded and intelligent, or so he should judge. Their hair was controlled and stylish, their clothes were well cut though not unduly old-fashioned. Looking at them, Stafford Nye was unable to deny that he liked the look of them. At the same time he wondered what they wanted with him. One of them he knew was the son of an oil king. Another of them, since leaving the university, had interested himself in politics. He had an uncle who owned a chain of restaurants. The third one was a young man with beetle brows who frowned and to whom perpetual suspicion seemed to be second nature.

'It's very good of you to let us come and call upon you, Sir Stafford,' said the one who seemed to be the blond leader of the three.

His voice was very agreeable. His name was Clifford Bent.

'This is Roderick Ketelly and this is Jim Brewster. We're all anxious about the future. Shall I put it like that?'

'I suppose the answer to that is, aren't we all?' said Sir Stafford Nye.

'We don't like things the way they're going,' said Clifford Bent. 'Rebellion, anarchy, all that. Well, it's all right as a philosophy. Frankly I think we may say that we all seem to go through a phase of it but one does come out the other side. We want people to be able to pursue academic careers without their being interrupted. We want a good sufficiency of demonstrations but not demonstrations of hooliganism and violence. We want intelligent demonstrations. And what we want, quite frankly, or so I think, is a new political party. Jim Brewster here has been paying serious attention to entirely new ideas and plans concerning trade union matters. They've tried to shout him down and talk him out, but he's gone on talking, haven't you, Jim?'

'Muddle-headed old fools, most of them,' said Jim Brewster.

'We want a sensible and serious policy for youth, a more economical method of government. We want different ideas to obtain in education but nothing fantastic or highfalutin'. And we shall want, if we win seats, and if we are able finally to form a government – and I don't see why we shouldn't – to put these ideas into action. There are a lot of people in our movement. We stand for youth, you know, just as well as the violent ones do. We stand for moderation and we mean to have a sensible government, with a reduction in the number of MP's, and we're noting down, looking for the men already in politics no matter what their particular persuasion is, if we think they're men of sense. We've come here to see if we can interest you in our aims. At the moment they are still in a state of flux but we have got as far as knowing the men we want. I may say that we don't want the ones we've got at present and we don't want the ones who might be put in instead. As for the third party, it seems to have died out of the running, though there are one or two good people there who suffer now for being in a minority, but I think they would come over to our way of thinking. We want to interest you. We want, one of these days, perhaps not so far distant as you might think – we want someone who'd understand and put out a proper, successful foreign policy. The rest of the world's in a worse mess than we are now. Washington's razed to the ground, Europe has continual military actions, demonstrations, wrecking of airports. Oh well, I don't need to write you a news letter of the past six months, but our aim is not so much to put the world on its legs again as to put England on its legs again. To have the right men to do it. We want young men, a great many young men and we've got a great many young men who aren't revolutionary, who aren't anarchistic, who will be willing to try and make a country run profitably. And we want some of the older men – I don't mean men of sixty-odd, I mean men of forty or fifty – and we've come to you because, well, we've heard things about you. We know about you and you're the sort of man we want.'

'Do you think you are wise?' said Sir Stafford.

'Well, *we* think we are.'

The second young man laughed slightly.

'We hope you'll agree with us there.'

'I'm not sure that I do. You're talking in this room very freely.'

'It's your sitting-room.'

'Yes, yes, it's my flat and it's my sitting-room. But what you are saying, and in fact what you might be going to say, might be unwise. That means both for you as well as me.'

'Oh! I think I see what you're driving at.'

'You are offering me something. A way of life, a new career and you are suggesting a breaking of certain ties. You are suggesting a form of disloyalty.'

'We're not suggesting your becoming a defector to any other country, if that's what you mean.'

'No, no, this is not an invitation to Russia or an invitation to China or an invitation to other places mentioned in the past, but I think it is an invitation connected with some foreign interests.' He went on: 'I've recently come back from abroad. A very interesting journey. I have spent the last three weeks in South America. There is something I would like to tell you. I have been conscious since I returned to England that I have been followed.'

'Followed? You don't think you imagined it?'

'No, I don't think I've imagined it. Those are the sort of things I have learned to notice in the course of my career. I have been in some fairly far distant and – shall we say? – interesting parts of the world. You chose to call upon me to sound me as to a proposition. It might have been safer, though, if we had met elsewhere.'

He got up, opened the door into the bathroom and turned the tap.

'From the films I used to see some years ago,' he said, 'if you wished to disguise your conversation when a room was bugged, you turned on taps. I have no doubt that I am somewhat old-fashioned and that there are better methods of dealing with these things now. But at any rate perhaps we could speak a little more clearly now, though even then I still think we should be careful. South America,' he went on, 'is a very interesting part of the world. The Federation of South American countries (Spanish Gold has been one name for it), comprising by now Cuba, the Argentine, Brazil, Peru, one or two others not quite settled and fixed but coming into being. Yes. Very interesting.'

'And what are your views on the subject?' the suspicious-looking Jim Brewster asked. 'What have you got to say about things?'

'I shall continue to be careful,' said Sir Stafford. 'You will have more dependence on me if I do not talk unadvisedly. But I think that can be done quite well after I turn off the bath water.'

'Turn it off, Jim,' said Cliff Bent.

Jim grinned suddenly and obeyed.

Stafford Nye opened a drawer at the table and took out a recorder.

'Not a very practised player yet,' he said.

He put it to his lips and started a tune. Jim Brewster came back, scowling.

'What's this? A bloody concert we're going to put on?'

'Shut up,' said Cliff Bent. 'You ignoramus, you don't know anything about music.'

Stafford Nye smiled.

'You share my pleasure in Wagnerian music, I see,' he said. 'I was at the Youth Festival this year and enjoyed the concerts there very much.'

Again he repeated the tune.

'Not any tune I know,' said Jim Brewster. 'It might be the Internationale or the Red Flag or God Save the King or Yankee Doodle or the Star-Spangled Banner. What the devil is it?'

'It's a motif from an opera,' said Ketelly. 'And shut your mouth. We know all we want to know.'

'The horn call of a young Hero,' said Stafford Nye.

He brought his hand up in a quick gesture, the gesture from the past meaning 'Heil Hitler'. He murmured very gently,

'The new Siegfried.'

All three rose.

'You're quite right,' said Clifford Bent. 'We must all, I think, be very careful.'

He shook hands.

'We are glad to know that you will be with us. One of the things this country will need in its future – its great future, I hope – will be a first-class Foreign Minister.'

They went out of the room. Stafford Nye watched them

through the slightly open door go into the lift and descend.

He gave a curious smile, shut the door, glanced up at the clock on the wall and sat down in an easy chair – to wait . . .

His mind went back to the day, a week ago now, when he and Mary Ann had gone their separate ways from Kennedy Airport. They had stood there, both of them finding it difficult to speak. Stafford Nye had broken the silence first.

'Do you think we'll ever meet again? I wonder . . .'

'Is there any reason why we shouldn't?'

'Every reason, I should think.'

She looked at him, then quickly away again.

'These partings have to happen. It's – part of the job.'

'The job! It's always the job with you, isn't it?'

'It has to be.'

'You're a professional. I'm only an amateur. You're a –' he broke off. 'What are you? Who are you? I don't really know, do I?'

'No.'

He looked at her then. He saw sadness, he thought, in her face. Something that was almost pain.

'So I have to – wonder . . . You think I ought to trust you, I suppose?'

'No, not that. That is one of the things that I have learnt, that life has taught me. There is nobody that one can trust. Remember that – always.'

'So that is your world? A world of distrust, of fear, of danger.'

'I wish to stay alive. I am alive.'

'I know.'

'And I want *you* to stay alive.'

'*I* trusted you – in Frankfurt . . .'

'You took a risk.'

'It was a risk well worth taking. You know that as well as I do.'

'You mean because –?'

'Because we have been together. And now – That is my flight being called. Is this companionship of ours which started in an airport, to end here in another airport? You are going where? To do what?'

'To do what I have to do. To Baltimore, to Washington, to Texas. To do what I have been told to do.'

'And I? I have been told nothing. I am to go back to London – and do what there?'

'Wait.'

'Wait for what?'

'For the advances that almost certainly will be made to you.'

'And what am I to do then?'

She smiled at him, with the sudden gay smile that he knew so well.

'Then you play it by ear. You'll know how to do it, none better. You'll like the people who approach you. They'll be well chosen. It's important, very important, that we should know who they are.'

'I must go. Goodbye, Mary Ann.'

'*Auf Wiedersehen.*'

In the London flat, the telephone rang. At a singularly apposite moment, Stafford Nye thought, bringing him back from his past memories just at that moment of their farewell. '*Auf Wiedersehen,*' he murmured, as he rose to his feet crossed to take the receiver off, 'let it be so.'

A voice spoke whose wheezy accents were quite unmistakable.

'Stafford Nye?'

He gave the requisite answer: 'No smoke without fire.'

'My doctor says I should give up smoking. Poor fellow,'

said Colonel Pikeaway, 'he might as well give up hope of that. Any news?'

'Oh yes. Thirty pieces of silver. Promised, that is to say.'

'Damned swine!'

'Yes, yes, keep calm.'

'And what did you say?'

'I played them a tune. Siegfried's Horn motif. I was following an elderly aunt's advice. It went down very well.'

'Sounds crazy to me!'

'Do you know a song called Juanita? I must learn that too, in case I need it.'

'Do you know who Juanita is?'

'I think so.'

'H'm, I wonder – heard of in Baltimore last.'

'What about your Greek girl, Daphne Theodofanous? Where is she now, I wonder?'

'Sitting in an airport somewhere in Europe waiting for you, probably,' said Colonel Pikeaway.

'Most of the European airports seem to be closed down because they've been blown up or more or less damaged. High explosives, hi-jackers, high jinks.

> '*Boys and girls come out to play*
> *The moon doth shine as bright as day –*
> *Leave your supper and leave your sleep*
> *And shoot your playfellow in the street.*'

'The Children's Crusade à la mode.'

'Not that I really know much about it. I only know the one that Richard Coeur de Lion went to. But in a way this whole business is rather like the Children's Crusade.

Starting with idealism, starting with ideas of the Christian world delivering the holy city from pagans, and ending with death, death and again, death. Nearly all the children died. Or were sold into slavery. This will end the same way unless we can find some means of getting them out of it . . .'

XX. THE ADMIRAL VISITS AN OLD FRIEND

'Thought you must all be dead here,' said Admiral Blunt with a snort.

His remark was addressed not to the kind of butler which he would have liked to see opening this front door, but to the young woman whose surname he could never remember but whose Christian name was Amy.

'Rung you up at least four times in the last week. Gone abroad, that's what they said.'

'We have been abroad. We've only just come back.'

'Matilda oughtn't to go rampaging about abroad. Not at her time of life. She'll die of blood pressure or heart failure or something in one of these modern airplanes. Cavorting about, full of explosives put in them by the Arabs or the Israelis or somebody or other. Not safe at all any longer.'

'Her doctor recommended it to her.'

'Oh well, we all know what doctors are.'

'And she has really come back in very good spirits.'

'Where's she been, then?'

'Oh, taking a Cure. In Germany or – I never can quite remember whether it's Germany or Austria. That new place, you know, the Golden Gasthaus.'

'Ah yes, I know the place you mean. Costs the earth, doesn't it?'

'Well, it's said to produce very remarkable results.'

'Probably only a different way of killing you quicker,' said Admiral Blunt. 'How did *you* enjoy it?'

'Well, not really very much. The scenery was very nice, but –'

An imperious voice sounded from the floor above.

'Amy. Amy! What are you doing, talking in the hall all this time? Bring Admiral Blunt up here. I'm waiting for him.'

'Gallivanting about,' said Admiral Blunt, after he had greeted his old friend. 'That's how you'll kill yourself one of these days. You mark my words –'

'No, I shan't. There's no difficulty at all in travelling nowadays.'

'Running about all those airports, ramps, stairs, buses.'

'Not at all. I had a wheelchair.'

'A year or two ago when I saw you, you said you wouldn't hear of such a thing. You said you had too much pride to admit you needed one.'

'Well, I've had to give up some of my pride, nowadays, Philip. Come and sit down here and tell me why you wanted to come and see me so much all of a sudden. You've neglected me a great deal for the last year.'

'Well, I've not been so well myself. Besides, I've been looking into a few things. You know the sort of thing. Where they ask your advice but don't mean in the least to take it. They can't leave the Navy alone. Keep on wanting to fiddle about with it, drat them.'

'You look quite well to me,' said Lady Matilda.

'You don't look so bad yourself, my dear. You've got a nice sparkle in your eye.'

'I'm deafer than when you saw me last. You'll have to speak up more.'

'All right. I'll speak up.'

'What do you want, gin and tonic or whisky or rum?'

'You seem ready to dispense strong liquor of any kind. If it's all the same to you, I'll have a gin and tonic.'

Amy rose and left the room.

'And when she brings it,' said the Admiral, 'get rid of her again, will you? I want to talk to you. Talk to you particularly is what I mean.'

Refreshment brought, Lady Matilda made a dismissive wave of the hand and Amy departed with the air of one who is pleasing herself, not her employer. She was a tactful young woman.

'Nice girl,' said the Admiral, 'very nice.'

'Is that why you asked me to get rid of her and see she shut the door? So that she mightn't overhear you saying something nice about her?'

'No. I wanted to consult you.'

'What about? Your health or where to get some new servants or what to grow in the garden?'

'I want to consult you very seriously. I thought perhaps you might be able to remember something for me.'

'Dear Philip, how touching that you should think I can remember *anything*. Every year my memory gets worse. I've come to the conclusion one only remembers what's called the "friends of one's youth". Even horrid girls one was at school with one remembers, though one doesn't want to. That's where I've been now, as a matter of fact.'

'Where've you been now? Visiting schools?'

'No, no, no, I went to see an old school friend whom I haven't seen for thirty – forty – fifty – that sort of time.'

'What was she like?'

'Enormously fat and even nastier and horrider than I remembered her.'

'You've got very queer tastes, I must say, Matilda.'

'Well, go on, tell me. Tell me what it is you want me to remember?'

'I wondered if you remembered another friend of yours. Robert Shoreham.'

'Robbie Shoreham? Of course I do.'

'The scientist feller. Top scientist.'

'Of course. He wasn't the sort of man one would ever forget. I wonder what put him into your head.'

'Public need.'

'Funny you should say that,' said Lady Matilda. 'I thought the same myself the other day.'

'You thought what?'

'That he was needed. Or someone like him – if there is anyone like him.'

'There isn't. Now listen, Matilda. People talk to you a bit. They tell you things. I've told you things myself.'

'I've always wondered why, because you can't believe that I'll understand them or be able to describe them. And that was even more the case with Robbie than with you.'

'I don't tell you naval secrets.'

'Well, he didn't tell me scientific secrets. I mean, only in a very general way.'

'Yes, but he used to talk to you about them, didn't he?'

'Well, he liked saying things that would astonish me sometimes.'

'All right, then, here it comes. I want to know if he ever talked to you, in the days when he could talk properly, poor devil, about something called Project B.'

'Project B.' Matilda Cleckheaton considered thoughtfully. 'Sounds vaguely familiar,' she said. 'He used to talk about Project this or that sometimes, or Operation that or this. But you must realize that none of it ever made any kind of *sense* to me, and he knew it didn't. But he used to like – oh, how shall I put it? – astonishing me rather, you know. Sort of describing it the way that a conjuror might describe how he takes three rabbits out of a hat without your knowing how he did it. Project B? Yes, that was a good long time ago . . . He was wildly excited for a bit. I used to say to him sometimes "How's Project B going on?" '

'I know, I know, you've always been a tactful woman. You can always remember what people were doing or interested in. And even if you don't know the first thing about it you'd show an interest. I described a new kind of naval gun to you once and you must have been bored stiff. But you listened as brightly as though it was the thing you'd been wanting to hear about all your life.'

'As you tell me, I've been a tactful woman and a good listener, even if I've never had much in the way of brains.'

'Well, I want to hear a little more what Robbie said about Project B.'

'He said – well, it's very difficult to remember now. He mentioned it after talking about some operation that they used to do on people's brains. You know, the people who were terribly melancholic and who were thinking of suicide and who were so worried and neurasthenic that they had awful anxiety complexes. Stuff like that, the sort of thing people used to talk of in connection with Freud. And he said that the side effects were impossible. I mean, the people were quite happy and meek and docile and didn't worry any more, or want to kill themselves, but they – well I mean they didn't worry *enough* and therefore they used to get run over and all sorts of things like that because they weren't thinking of any danger and didn't notice it. I'm putting it badly but you do understand what I mean. And anyway, he said, that was going to be the trouble, he thought, with Project B.'

'Did he describe it at all more closely than that?'

'He said I'd put it into his head,' said Matilda Cleckheaton unexpectedly.

'What? Do you mean to say a scientist – a top-flight scientist like Robbie actually said to you that you had put something into his scientific brain? You don't know the first thing about science.'

'Of course not. But I used to try and put a little common sense into people's brains. The cleverer they are, the less common sense they have. I mean, really, the people who matter are the people who thought of simple things like perforations on postage stamps, or like somebody Adam, or whatever his name was – No – MacAdam in America who put black stuff on roads so that farmers could get all their crops from farms to the coast and make a better profit. I mean, they do much more good than all the high-powered scientists do. Scientists can only think of things for destroying you. Well, that's the sort of thing I said to Robbie. Quite nicely, of course, as a kind of joke. He'd been just telling me that some splendid things had been done in the scientific world about germ warfare and experiments with biology and what you can do to unborn babies if you get at them early enough. And also some peculiarly nasty and very unpleasant gases and saying how silly people were to protest against nuclear bombs because they were really a kindness compared to some of the other things that had been invented since then. And so I said it'd be much more to the point if Robbie, or someone clever like Robbie, could think of something really sensible. And he looked at me with that, you know, little twinkle he has in his eye sometimes and said, "Well what would you consider sensible?" And I said, "Well, instead of inventing all these germ warfares and these nasty gases, and all the rest of it, why don't you just invent something that makes people feel happy?" I said it oughtn't to be any more difficult to do. I said, "You've talked about this operation where, I think you said, they took out a bit of the front of your brain or maybe the back of your brain. But anyway it made a great difference in people's dispositions. They'd become quite different. They hadn't worried any more or they hadn't wanted to commit suicide. But," I said, "Well, if you can change people like that just by taking a little bit of bone or muscle or nerve or tinkering up a gland or taking out a gland or putting in more of a gland," I said, "if you can make all that difference in people's dispositions, why can't you invent something that will make people pleasant or just sleepy perhaps? Supposing you had something, not a sleeping draught, but just something that people sat down in a chair and had a nice dream. Twenty-four hours or so and just woke up to be fed now and again. I said it would be a much better idea".'

'And is that what Project B was?'

'Well, of course he never told me what it was exactly. But he was excited with an idea and he said I'd put it into his head, so it must have been something rather pleasant I'd put into his head, mustn't it? I mean, I hadn't suggested any ideas to him of any nastier ways for killing people and I didn't want people even – you know – to cry, like tear gas or anything like that. Perhaps laughing – yes, I believe I mentioned laughing gas. I said well if you have your teeth out, they give you three sniffs of it and you laugh, well, surely, surely you could invent something that's as useful as that but would last a little longer. Because I believe laughing gas only lasts about fifty seconds, doesn't it? I know my brother had some teeth out once. The dentist's chair was very near the window and my brother was laughing so much, when he was unconscious, I mean, that he stretched his leg right out and put it through the dentist's window and all the glass fell in the street, and the dentist was very cross about it.'

'Your stories always have such strange side-kicks,' said the Admiral. 'Anyway, this is what Robbie Shoreham had chosen to get on with, from your advice.'

'Well, I don't know what it was exactly. I mean, I don't think it was sleeping or laughing. At any rate, it was *something*. It wasn't really Project B. It had another name.'

'What sort of a name?'

'Well, he did mention it once I think, or twice. The name he'd given it. Rather like Benger's Food,' said Aunt Matilda, considering thoughtfully.

'Some soothing agent for the digestion?'

'I don't think it had anything to do with the digestion. I rather think it was something you sniffed or something, perhaps it was a gland. You know we talked of so many things that you never quite knew what he was talking about at the moment. Benger's Food. Ben – Ben – it did begin Ben. And there was a pleasant word associated with it.'

'Is that all you can remember about it?'

'I think so. I mean, this was just a talk we had once and then, quite a long time afterwards, he told me I'd put something into his head for Project Ben something. And after that, occasionally, if I remembered, I'd ask him if he was still working on Project Ben and then sometimes he'd be very exasperated and say no, he'd come up against a snag and he was putting it all aside now because it was in – in – well, I mean the next eight words were pure jargon and I couldn't remember them and you wouldn't understand them if I said them to you. But in the end, I think – oh dear, oh dear, this is all about eight or nine years ago – in the end he came one day and he said, "Do you remember Project Ben?" I said, "Of course I remember it. Are you still working on it?" And he said no, he was determined to lay it all aside. I said I was sorry. Sorry if he'd given it up and he said, "Well, it's not only that I can't get what I was trying for. I know now that it *could* be got. I know where I went wrong. I know just what the snag was, I know just how to put that snag right again. I've got Lisa working on it with me. Yes, it could work. It'd require experimenting on certain things but it could work." "Well," I said to him, "what are you worrying about?" And he said, "Because I don't know what it would really do to people." I said something about his being afraid it would kill people or maim them for life or something. "No," he said, "it's not like that." He said, it's a – oh, of course, now I remember. He called it Project Benvo. Yes. And that's because it had to do with *benevolence*.'

'Benevolence!' said the Admiral, highly surprised. 'Benevolence? Do you mean charity?'

'No, no, no. I think he meant simply that you could make people benevolent. *Feel* benevolent.'

'Peace and good will towards men?'

'Well, he didn't put it like that.'

'No, that's reserved for religious leaders. They preach that to you and if you did what they preach it'd be a very happy world. But Robbie, I gather, was not preaching. He proposed to do something in his laboratory to bring about this result by purely physical means.'

'That's the sort of thing. And he said you can never tell when things *are* beneficial to people or when they're not. They are in one way but they're not in another. And he said things about – oh, penicillin and sulphonamides and heart transplants and things like pills for women, though we hadn't got "The Pill" then. But you know, things that seem all right and they're wonder-drugs or wonder-gases or wonder-something or other, and then there's something about them that makes them go wrong as well as right, and then you wish they weren't there and had never been thought of. Well, that's the sort of thing that he seemed to be trying to get over to me. It was all rather difficult to understand. I said, "Do you mean you don't like to take the risk?" and he said; "You're quite right. I don't like to take the risk. That's the trouble because, you see, I don't know in the least what the risk will be. That's what happens to us poor devils of scientists. We take the risks and the risks are not in what we've discovered, it's the risks of what the people we'll have to tell about it will do with what we've discovered." I said; "Now you're talking about nuclear weapons again and atom bombs," and he said, "Oh, to Hell with nuclear weapons and atomic bombs. We've gone far beyond that."

' "But if you're going to make people nice-tempered and benevolent," I said, "what have you got to worry about?" And he said, "You don't *understand*, Matilda. You'll never understand. My fellow scientists in all probability would not understand either. And no politicians would ever understand. And so, you see, it's too big a risk to be taken. At any rate one would have to think for a long time."

' "But," I said, "you could bring people out of it again, just like laughing gas, couldn't you? I mean, you could make people benevolent just for a short time, and then they'd get all right again – or all wrong again – it depends which way you look at it, I should have thought." And he said, "No. This will be, you see, permanent. Quite permanent because it affects the –" and then he went into jargon again. You know, long words and numbers. Formulas, or molecular changes – something like that. I expect really it must be something like what they do to cretins. You know, to make them stop being cretins, like giving them thyroid or taking it away from them. I forget which it is. Something like that. Well, I expect there's some nice little gland somewhere and if you take it away or smoke it out, or do something rather drastic to it – but then, the people are permanently –'

'Permanently *benevolent*? You're sure that's the right word? Benevolence?'

'Yes, because that's why he nicknamed it *Benvo*.'

'But what did his colleagues think, I wonder, about his backing out?'

'I don't think he had many who knew. Lisa what's-her-name, the Austrian girl; she'd worked on it with him. And there was one young man called Leadenthal or some name like that, but he died of tuberculosis. And he rather spoke as though the other people who worked with him were merely assistants who didn't know exactly what he was doing or trying for. I see what you're getting at,' said Matilda suddenly. 'I don't think he ever told anybody, really. I mean, I think he destroyed his formulas or notes or whatever they were and gave up the whole idea. And then he had his stroke and got ill, and now, poor dear, he can't speak very well. He's paralysed one side. He can hear fairly well. He listens to music. That's his whole life now.'

'His life's work's ended, you think?'

'He doesn't even see friends. I think it's painful to him to see them. He always makes some excuse.'

'But he's alive,' said Admiral Blunt. 'He's alive still. Got his address?'

'It's in my address book somewhere. He's still in the same place. North Scotland somewhere. But – oh, do understand – he was such a wonderful man once. He isn't now. He's just – almost dead. For all intents and purposes.'

'There's always hope,' said Admiral Blunt. 'And belief,' he added. 'Faith.'

'And benevolence, I suppose,' said Lady Matilda.

XX1. PROJECT BENVO

Professor John Gottlieb sat in his chair looking very steadfastly at the handsome young woman sitting opposite him. He scratched his ear with a rather monkey-like gesture which was characteristic of him. He looked rather like a monkey anyway. A prognathous jaw, a high mathematical head which make a slight contrast in terms, and a small wizened frame.

'It's not every day,' said Professor Gottlieb, 'that a young lady brings me a letter from the President of the United States. However,' he said cheerfully, 'Presidents don't always know exactly what they're doing. What's this all about? I gather you're vouched for on the highest authority.'

'I've come to ask you what you know or what you can tell me about something called Project Benvo.'

'Are you really Countess Renata Zerkowski?'

'Technically, possibly, I am. I'm more often known as Mary Ann.'

'Yes, that's what they wrote me under separate cover. And you want to know about Project Benvo. Well, there was such a thing. Now it's dead and buried and the man who thought of it also, I expect.'

'You mean Professor Shoreham.'

'That's right. Robert Shoreham. One of the greatest geniuses of our age. Einstein, Niels Bohr and some others. But Robert Shoreham didn't last as long as he should. A great loss to science – what is it Shakespeare says of Lady Macbeth: "*She should have died hereafter.*" '

'He's not dead,' said Mary Ann.

'Oh. Sure of that? Nothing's been heard of him for a long time.'

'He's an invalid. He lives in the north of Scotland. He is paralysed, can't speak very well, can't walk very well. He sits most of the time listening to music.'

'Yes, I can imagine that. Well, I'm glad about that. If he can do that he won't be too unhappy. Otherwise it's a pretty fair hell for a brilliant man who isn't brilliant any more. Who's, as it were, dead in an invalid chair.'

'There *was* such a thing as Project Benvo?'

'Yes, he was very keen about it.'

'He talked to you about it?'

'He talked to some of us about it in the early days. You're not a scientist yourself, young woman, I suppose?'

'No, I'm –'

'You're just an agent, I suppose. I hope you're on the right side. We still have to hope for miracles these days, but I don't think you'll get anything out of Project Benvo.'

'Why not? You said he worked on it. It would have been a very great invention, wouldn't it? Or discovery, or whatever you call these things?'

'Yes, it would have been one of the greatest discoveries of the age. I don't know just what went wrong. It's happened before now. A thing goes along all right but in the last stages somehow, it doesn't click. Breaks down. Doesn't do what's expected of it and you give up in despair. Or else you do what Shoreham did.'

'What was that?'

'He destroyed it. Every damn bit of it. He told me so himself. Burnt all the formulas, all the papers concerning it, all the data. Three weeks later he had his stroke. I'm sorry. You see, I can't help you. I never knew any details about it, nothing but its main idea. I don't even remember that now, except for one thing. Benvo stood for Benevolence.'

XXII. JUANITA

Lord Altamount was dictating.

The voice that had once been ringing and dominant was now reduced to a gentleness that had still an unexpectedly special appeal. It seemed to come gently out of the shadows of the past, but to be emotionally moving in a way that a more dominant tone would not have been.

James Kleek was taking down the words as they came, pausing every now and then when a moment of hesitation came, allowing for it and waiting gently himself.

'Idealism,' said Lord Altamount, 'can arise and indeed usually does so when moved by a natural antagonism to injustice. That is a natural revulsion from crass materialism. The natural idealism of youth is fed more and more by a desire to destroy those two phases of modern life, injustice and crass materialism. That desire to destroy what is evil, sometimes leads to a love of destruction for its own sake. It can lead to a pleasure in violence and in the infliction of pain. All this can be fostered and strengthened from outside by those who are gifted by a natural power of leadership. This original idealism arises in a non-adult stage. It should and could lead on to a desire for a new world. It should lead also towards a love of all human beings, and of goodwill towards them. But those who have once learnt to love violence for its own sake will never become adult. They will be fixed in their own retarded development and will so remain for their lifetime.'

The buzzer went. Lord Altamount gestured and James Kleek lifted it up and listened.

'Mr Robinson is here.'

'Ah yes. Bring him in. We can go on with this later.'

James Kleek rose, laying aside his notebook and pencil.

Mr Robinson came in. James Kleek set a chair for him, one sufficiently widely proportioned to receive his form without discomfort. Mr Robinson smiled his thanks and arranged himself by Lord Altamount's side.

'Well,' said Lord Altamount. 'Got anything new for us? Diagrams? Circles? Bubbles?'

He seemed faintly amused.

'Not exactly,' said Mr Robinson imperturbably, 'it's more like plotting the course of a river –'

'River?' said Lord Altamount. 'What sort of a river?'

'A river of money,' said Mr Robinson, in the slightly apologetic voice he was wont to use when referring to his speciality. 'It's really just like a river, money is – coming from somewhere and definitely going to somewhere. Really very interesting – that is, if you are interested in these things – It tells its own story, you see –'

James Kleek looked as though he didn't see, but Altamount said, 'I understand. Go on.'

'It's flowing from Scandinavia – from Bavaria – from the USA – from South-east Asia – fed by lesser tributaries on the way –'

'And going – where?'

'Mainly to South America – meeting the demands of the now securely established Headquarters of Militant Youth –'

'And representing four of the five intertwined Circles you showed us – Armaments, Drugs, Scientific and Chemical Warfare Missiles as well as Finance?'

'Yes – we think we know now fairly accurately who controls these various groups –'

'What about Circle J – Juanita?' asked James Kleek.

'As yet we cannot be sure.'

'James has certain ideas as to that,' said Lord Altamount. 'I hope he may be wrong – yes, I hope so. The initial J is interesting. What does it stand for – Justice? Judgment?'

'A dedicated killer,' said James Kleek. 'The female of the species is more deadly than the male.'

'There are historical precedents,' admitted Altamount. 'Jael setting butter in a lordly dish before Sisera – and afterwards driving the nail through his head. Judith executing Holofernes, and applauded for it by her countrymen. Yes, you may have something there.'

'So you think you know who Juanita is, do you?' said Mr Robinson. 'That's interesting.'

'Well, perhaps I'm wrong, sir, but there have been things that made me think –'

'Yes,' said Mr Robinson, 'we have all had to think, haven't we? Better say who you think it is, James.'

'The Countess Renata Zerkowski.'

'What makes you pitch upon her?'

'The places she's been, the people she's been in contact with. There's been too much coincidence about the way she has been turning up in different places, and all that. She's been in Bavaria. She's been visiting Big Charlotte there. What's more, she took Stafford Nye with her. I think that's significant –'

'You think they're in this together?' asked Altamount.

'I wouldn't like to say that. I don't know enough about him, but . . .' He paused.

'Yes,' said Lord Altamount, 'there have been doubts about him. He was suspected from the beginning.'

'By Henry Horsham?'

'Henry Horsham for one, perhaps. Colonel Pikeaway isn't sure, I imagine. He's been under observation. Probably knows it too. He's not a fool.'

'Another of them,' said James Kleek savagely. 'Extraordinary, how we can breed them, how we trust them, tell 'em our secrets, let them know what we're doing, go on saying: "If there's one person I'm absolutely sure of it's – oh, Mclean, or Burgess, or Philby or any of the lot." And now – Stafford Nye.'

'Stafford Nye, indoctrinated by Renata alias Juanita,' said Mr Robinson.

'There was that curious business at Frankfurt airport,' said Kleek, 'and there was the visit to Charlotte. Stafford Nye, I gather, has since been in South America with her. As for she herself – do we know where she is now?'

'I dare say Mr Robinson does,' said Lord Altamount. 'Do you, Mr Robinson?'

'She's in the United States. I've heard that after staying with friends in Washington or near it, she was in Chicago, then in California and that she went from Austin to visit a top-flight scientist. That's the last I've heard.'

'What's she doing there?'

'One would presume,' said Mr Robinson, in his calm voice, 'that she is trying to obtain information.'

'What information?'

Mr Robinson sighed.

'That is what one wishes one knew. One presumes that it is the same information that *we* are anxious to obtain and that she is doing it on our behalf. But one never knows – it may be for the other side.'

He turned to look at Lord Altamount.

'Tonight, I understand, you are travelling to Scotland. Is that right?'

'Quite right.'

'I don't think he ought to, sir,' said James Kleek. He turned an anxious face to his employer. 'You've not been so well lately, sir. It'll be a very tiring journey whichever way you go. Air or train. Can't you leave it to Munro and Horsham?'

'At my age it's a waste of time to take care,' said Lord Altamount. 'If I can be useful I would like to die in harness, as the saying goes.'

He smiled at Mr Robinson.

'You'd better come with us, Robinson.'

XX111. JOURNEY TO SCOTLAND

The Squadron Leader wondered a little what it was all about. He was accustomed to being left only partly in the picture. That was Security's doing, he supposed. Taking no chances. He'd done this sort of thing before more than once. Flying a plane of people out to an unlikely spot, with unlikely passengers, being careful to ask no questions except such as were of an entirely factual nature. He knew some of his passengers on this flight but not all of them. Lord Altamount he recognized. An ill man, a very sick man, he thought, a man who, he judged, kept himself alive by sheer will-power. The keen hawk-faced man with him was his special guard dog, presumably. Seeing not so much to his safety as to his welfare. A faithful dog who never left his side. He would have with him restoratives, stimulants, all the medical box of tricks. The Squadron Leader wondered why there wasn't a doctor also in attendance. It would have been an extra precaution. Like a death's head, the old man looked. A noble death's head. Something made of marble in a museum. Henry Horsham the Squadron Leader knew quite well. He knew several of the Security lot. And Colonel Munro, looking slightly less fierce than usual, rather more worried. Not very happy on the whole. There was also a large, yellow-faced man. Foreigner, he might be. Asiatic? What was he doing, flying in a plane to the North of Scotland? The Squadron Leader said deferentially to Colonel Munro:

'Everything laid on, sir? The car is here waiting.'

'How far exactly is the distance?'

'Seventeen miles, sir, roughish road but not too bad. There are extra rugs in the car.'

'You have your orders? Repeat, please, if you will, Squadron Leader Andrews.'

The Squadron Leader repeated and the Colonel nodded satisfaction. As the car finally drove off, the Squadron Leader looked after it, wondering to himself why on earth those particular people were here on this drive over the lonely moor to a venerable old castle where a sick man lived as a recluse without friends or visitors in the general run of things. Horsham knew, he supposed. Horsham must know a lot of strange things. Oh well, Horsham wasn't likely to tell him anything.

The car was well and carefully driven. It drew up at last over a gravel driveway and came to a stop before the porch. It was a turreted building of heavy stone. Lights hung at either side of the big door. The door itself opened before there was any need to ring a bell or demand admittance.

An old Scottish woman of sixty-odd with a stern, dour face, stood in the doorway. The chauffeur helped the occupants out.

James Kleek and Horsham helped Lord Altamount to alight and supported him up the steps. The old Scottish woman stood aside and dropped a respectful curtsy to him. She said:

'Good evening, y'r lordship. The master's waiting for you. He knows you're arriving, we've got rooms prepared and fires for you in all of them.'

Another figure had arrived in the hall now. A tall lean woman between fifty and sixty, a woman who was still handsome. Her black hair was parted in the middle, she had a high forehead, an aquiline nose and a tanned skin.

'Here's Miss Neumann to look after you,' said the Scottish woman.

'Thank you, Janet,' said Miss Neumann. 'Be sure the fires are kept up in the bedrooms.'

'I will that.'

Lord Altamount shook hands with her.

'Good evening, Miss Neumann.'

'Good evening, Lord Altamount. I hope you are not too tired by your journey.'

'We had a very good flight. This is Colonel Munro, Miss Neumann. This is Mr Robinson, Sir James Kleek and Mr Horsham, of the Security Department.'

'I remember Mr Horsham from some years ago, I think.'

'I hadn't forgotten,' said Henry Horsham. 'It was at the Leveson Foundation. You were already, I think, Professor Shoreham's secretary at that time?'

'I was first his assistant in the laboratory, and afterwards his secretary. I am still, as far as he needs one, his secretary. He also has to have a hospital nurse living here more or less permanently. There have to be changes from time to time – Miss Ellis who is here now took over from Miss Bude only two days ago. I have suggested that she should stay near at hand to the room in which we ourselves shall be. I thought you would prefer privacy, but that she ought not to be out of call in case she was needed.'

'Is he in very bad health?' asked Colonel Munro.

'He doesn't actually suffer,' said Miss Neumann, 'but you must prepare yourself, if you have not seen him, that is, for a long time. He is only what is left of a man.'

'Just one moment before you take us to him. His mental processes are not too badly depleted? He can understand what one says to him?'

'Oh, yes, he can understand perfectly, but as he is semi-paralysed, he is unable to speak with much clarity, though that varies, and is unable to walk without help. His brain, in my opinion, is as good as ever it was. The only difference is that he tires very easily now. Now, would you like some refreshment first?'

'No,' said Lord Altamount. 'No, I don't want to wait. This is a rather urgent matter on which we have come, so if you will take us to him now – he expects us, I understand?'

'He expects you, yes,' said Lisa Neumann.

She led the way up some stairs, along a corridor and opened a room of medium size. It had tapestries on the wall, the heads of stags looked down on them, the place had been a one-time shooting-box. It had been little changed in its furnishing or arrangements. There was a big record-player on one side of the room.

The tall man sat in a chair by the fire. His head trembled a little, so did his left hand. The skin of his face was pulled down one side. Without beating about the bush, one could only describe him one way, as a wreck of a man. A man who had once been tall, sturdy, strong. He had a fine forehead, deep-set eyes, and a rugged, determined-looking chin. The eyes, below the heavy eyebrows, were intelligent. He said something. His voice was not weak, it made fairly clear sounds but not always recognizable ones. The faculty of speech had only partly gone from him, he was still understandable.

Lisa Neumann went to stand by him, watching his lips, so that she could interpret what he said if necessary.

'Professor Shoreham welcomes you. He is very pleased to see you here, Lord Altamount, Colonel Munro, Sir James Kleek, Mr Robinson and Mr Horsham. He would like me to tell you that his hearing is reasonably good. Anything you say to him he will be able to hear. If there is any difficulty I can assist. What he wants to say to you he will be able to transmit through me. If he gets too tired to articulate, I can lip-read and we also converse in a perfected sign language if there is any difficulty.'

'I shall try,' said Colonel Munro, 'not to waste your time and to tire you as little as possible, Professor Shoreham.'

The man in the chair bent his head in recognition of the words.

'Some questions I can ask of Miss Neumann.'

Shoreham's hand went out in a faint gesture towards the woman standing by his side. Sounds came from his lips, again not quite recognizable to them, but she translated quickly.

'He says he can depend on me to transcribe anything you wish to say to him or I to you.'

'You have, I think, already received a letter from me,' said Colonel Munro.

'That is so,' said Miss Neumann. 'Professor Shoreham received your letter and knows its contents.'

A hospital nurse opened the door just a crack – but she did not come in. She spoke in a low whisper:

'Is there anything I can get or do, Miss Neumann? For any of the guests or for Professor Shoreham?'

'I don't think there is anything, thank you, Miss Ellis. I should be glad, though, if you could stay in your sitting-room just along the passage, in case we should need anything.'

'Certainly – I quite understand.' She went away, closing the door softly.

'We don't want to lose time,' said Colonel Munro. 'No doubt Professor Shoreham is in tune with current affairs.'

'Entirely so,' said Miss Neumann, 'as far as he is interested.'

'Does he keep in touch with scientific advancements and such things?'

Robert Shoreham's head shook slightly from side to side. He himself answered.

'I have finished with all that.'

'But you know roughly the state the world is in? The success of what is called the Revolution of Youth. The seizing of power by youthful fully-equipped forces.'

Miss Neumann said, 'He is in touch entirely with everything that is going on – in a political sense, that is.'

'The world is now given over to violence, pain, revolutionary tenets, a strange and incredible philosophy of rule by an anarchic minority.'

A faint look of impatience went across the gaunt face.

'He knows all that,' said Mr Robinson, speaking unexpectedly. 'No need to go over a lot of things again. He's a man who knows everything.'

He said:

'Do you remember Admiral Blunt?'

Again the head bowed. Something like a smile showed on the twisted lips.

'Admiral Blunt remembered some scientific work you had done on a certain project – I think project is what you call these things? Project Benvo.'

They saw the alert look which came into the eyes.

'Project Benvo,' said Miss Neumann. 'You are going back quite a long time, Mr Robinson, to recall that.'

'It was *your* project, wasn't it?' said Mr Robinson.

'Yes, it was his project.' Miss Neumann now spoke more easily for him, as a matter of course.

'We cannot use nuclear weapons, we cannot use explosives or gas or chemistry, but *your* project, Project Benvo, we *could* use.'

There was silence and nobody spoke. And then again the queer distorted sounds came from Professor Shoreham's lips.

'He says, of course,' said Miss Neumann, 'Benvo *could* be used successfully in the circumstances in which we find ourselves –'

The man in the chair had turned to her and was saying something to her.

'He wants me to explain it to you,' said Miss Neumann. 'Project B, later called Project Benvo, was something that he worked upon for many years but which at last he laid aside for reasons of his own.'

'Because he had failed to make his project materialize?'

'No, he had not failed,' said Lisa Neumann. 'We had not failed. I worked with him on this project. He laid it aside for certain reasons, but he did not fail. He succeeded.

He was on the right track, he developed it, he tested it in various laboratory experiments, and it worked.' She turned to Professor Shoreham again, made a few gestures with her hand, touching her lips, ear, mouth in a strange kind of code signal.

'I am asking if he wants me to explain just what Benvo does.'

'We do want you to explain.'

'And he wants to know how you learnt about it.'

'We learnt about it,' said Colonel Munro, 'through an old friend of yours, Professor Shoreham. Not Admiral Blunt, he could not remember very much, but the other person to whom you had once spoken about it, Lady Matilda Cleckheaton.'

Again Miss Neumann turned to him and watched his lips. She smiled faintly.

'He says he thought Matilda was dead years ago.'

'She is very much alive. It is she who wanted us to know about this discovery of Professor Shoreham's.'

'Professor Shoreham will tell you the main points of what you want to know, though he has to warn you that this knowledge will be quite useless to you. Papers, formulae, accounts and proofs of this discovery were all destroyed. But since the only way to satisfy your questions is for you to learn the main outline of Project Benvo, I can tell you fairly clearly of what it consists. You know the uses and purpose of tear gas as used by the police in controlling riot crowds; violent demonstrations and so on. It induces a fit of weeping, painful tears and sinus inflammation.'

'And this is something of the same kind?'

'No, it is not in the least of the same kind but it can have the same purpose. It came into the heads of scientists that one can change not only men's principal reactions and feeling, but also mental characteristics. You can change a man's character. The qualities of an aphrodisiac are well known. They lead to a condition of sexual desire, there are various drugs or gases or glandular operations – any of these things can lead to a change in your mental vigour, increased energy as by alterations to the thyroid gland, and Professor Shoreham wishes to tell you that there is a certain process – he will not tell you now whether it is glandular, or a gas that can be manufactured, but there is something that can change a man in his outlook on life – his reaction to people and to life generally. He may be in a state of homicidal fury, he may be pathologically violent, and yet, by the influence of Project Benvo, he turns into something, or rather *someone*, quite different. He becomes – there is only one word for it, I believe, which is embodied in its name – he becomes *benevolent*. He wishes to benefit others. He exudes kindness. He has a horror of causing pain or inflicting violence. Benvo can be released over a big area, it can affect hundreds, thousands of people if manufactured in big enough quantities, and if distributed successfully.'

'How long does it last?' said Colonel Munro. 'Twenty-four hours? Longer?'

'You don't understand,' said Miss Neumann. 'It is *permanent*.'

'Permanent? You've changed a man's nature, you've altered a component, a physical component, of course, of his being which has produced the effect of a permanent change in his nature. And you cannot go back on that? You cannot put him back to where he was again. It has to be accepted as a permanent change?'

'Yes. It was, perhaps, a discovery more of medical interest at first, but Professor Shoreham had conceived of it as a deterrent to be used in war, in mass risings, riotings, revolutions, anarchy. He didn't think of it as merely medical. It does not produce happiness in the subject, only a great wish for others to be happy. That is an effect, he says, that everyone feels in their life at one time or another. They have a great wish to make someone, one person or many people – to make them comfortable, happy, in good health, all these things. And since people can and do feel these things, there is, we both believed, a component that controls that desire in their bodies, and if you once put that component in operation it can go on in perpetuity.'

'Wonderful,' said Mr Robinson.

He spoke thoughtfully rather than enthusiastically.

'Wonderful. What a thing to have discovered. What a thing to be able to put into action if – but why?'

The head resting towards the back of the chair turned slowly towards Mr Robinson. Miss Neumann said:

'He says you understand better than the others.'

'But it's the answer,' said James Kleek. 'It's the *exact* answer! It's wonderful.' His face was enthusiastically excited.

Miss Neumann was shaking her head.

'Project Benvo,' she said, 'is not for sale and not for a gift. It has been relinquished.'

'Are you telling us the answer is no?' said Colonel Munro incredulously.

'Yes. Professor Shoreham says the answer is no. He decided that it was against –' she paused a minute and turned to look at the man in the chair. He made quaint gestures with his head, with one hand, and a few guttural sounds came from his mouth. She waited and then she said, 'He will tell you himself, he was afraid. Afraid of what science has done in its time of triumph. The things it has found out and known, the things it has discovered and given to the world. The wonder drugs that have not always been wonder drugs, the penicillin that has saved lives and the penicillin that has taken lives, the heart transplants that have brought disillusion and the disappointment of a death not expected. He has lived in the period of nuclear fission; new weapons that have slain. The tragedies of radio-activity; the pollutions that new industrial discoveries have brought about. He has been afraid of what science could do, used indiscriminately.'

'But this is a benefit. A benefit to everyone,' cried Munro.

'So have many things been. Always greeted as great benefits to humanity, as great wonders. And then come the side effects, and worse than that, the fact that they have sometimes brought not benefit but disaster. And so he decided that he would give up. He says – she read from a paper she held, whilst beside her he nodded agreement from his chair – "*I am satisfied that I have done what I set out to do, that I made my discovery. But I decided not to put it into circulation. It must be destroyed. And so it* has *been destroyed. And so the answer to you is* no. *There is no benevolence on tap. There could have been once, but now all the formulae, all the know-how, my notes and my account of the necessary procedure are gone – burnt to ashes – I have destroyed my brain child*".'

Robert Shoreham struggled into raucous difficult speech.

'I have destroyed my brain child and nobody in the world knows how I arrived at it. One man helped me but he is dead. He died of tuberculosis a year after we had come to success. You must go away again. I cannot help you.'

'But this knowledge of yours means you could save the world!'

The man in the chair made a curious noise. It was laughter. Laughter of a crippled man.

'Save the world. Save the world! What a phrase! That's what your young people are doing, they think! They're going ahead in violence and hatred to save the world. But they don't know how! They will have to do it *themselves*, out of their own hearts, out of their own minds. We can't give them an artificial way of doing it. No. An artificial goodness? An artificial kindness? None of that. It wouldn't be *real*. It wouldn't *mean* anything. It would be against Nature.' He said slowly: '*Against God.*'

The last two words came out unexpectedly, clearly enunciated.

He looked round at his listeners. It was as though he pleaded with them for understanding, yet at the same time had no real hope of it.

'I had a right to destroy what I had created –'

'I doubt it very much,' said Mr Robinson, 'knowledge is knowledge. What you have given birth to – what you have made to come to life, you should not destroy.'

'You have a right to your opinion – but the fact you will have to accept.'

'No,' Mr Robinson brought the word out with force.

Lisa Neumann turned on him angrily.

'What do you mean by "No"?'

Her eyes were flashing. A handsome woman, Mr Robinson thought. A woman who had been in love with Robert Shoreham all her life probably. Had loved him, worked with him, and now lived beside him, ministering to him with her intellect, giving him devotion in its purest form without pity.

'There are things one gets to know in the course of one's lifetime,' said Mr Robinson. 'I don't suppose mine will be a long life. I carry too much weight to begin with.' He sighed as he looked down at his bulk. 'But I do know some things. I'm right, you know, Shoreham. You'll have to admit I'm right, too. You're an honest man. You wouldn't have destroyed your work. You couldn't have brought yourself to do it. You've got it somewhere still, locked away, hidden away, not in this house, probably. I'd guess, and I'm only making a guess, that you've got it somewhere in a safe deposit or a bank. She knows you've got it there, too. You trust her. She's the only person in the world you do trust.'

Shoreham said, and this time his voice was almost distinct:

'Who are *you*? Who the devil are you?'

'I'm just a man who knows about money,' said Mr Robinson, 'and the things that branch off from money, you know. People and their idiosyncrasies and their practices in life. If you liked to, you could lay your hand on the work that you've put away. I'm not saying that you could do the same work now, but I think it's all there somewhere. You've told us your views, and I wouldn't say they were all wrong,' said Mr Robinson.

'Possibly you're right. Benefits to humanity are tricky things to deal with. Poor old Beveridge, freedom from want, freedom from fear, freedom from whatever it was, he thought he was making a heaven on earth by saying that and planning for it and getting it done. But it hasn't made heaven on earth and I don't suppose your Benvo or whatever you call it (sounds like a patent food) will bring heaven on earth either. Benevolence has its dangers just like everything else. What it will do is save a lot of suffering, pain, anarchy, violence, slavery to drugs. Yes, it'll save quite a lot of bad things from happening, and it *might* save something that was important. It might – just *might* – make a difference to people. Young people. This Benvoleo of yours – now I've made it sound like a patent cleaner – is going to make people benevolent and I'll admit perhaps that it's also going to make them condescending, smug and pleased with themselves, but there's just a chance, too, that if you change people's natures by force and they have to go on using that particular kind of nature until they die, one or two of them – not many – might discover that they had a natural vocation, in humility, not pride, for what they were being forced to do. *Really* change themselves, I mean, before they died. Not be able to get out of a new habit they'd learnt.'

Colonel Munro said, 'I don't understand what the hell you're all talking about.'

Miss Neumann said, 'He's talking nonsense. You have to take Professor Shoreham's answer. He will do what he likes with his own discoveries. You can't coerce him.'

'No,' said Lord Altamount. 'We're not going to coerce you or torture you, Robert, or force you to reveal your hiding-places. You'll do what you think right. That's agreed.'

'Edward?' said Robert Shoreham. His speech failed him slightly again, his hands moved in gesture, and Miss Neumann translated quickly.

'Edward? He says you are Edward Altamount?'

Shoreham spoke again and she took the words from him.

'He asks you, Lord Altamount, if you are definitely, with your whole heart and mind, asking him to put Project Benvo in your jurisdiction. He says –' she paused, watching, listening – 'he says you are the only man in public life that he ever trusted. If it is *your* wish –'

James Kleek was suddenly on his feet. Anxious, quick to move like lightning, he stood by Lord Altamount's chair.

'Let me help you up, sir. You're ill. You're not well. Please stand back a little, Miss Neumann. I – I must get to him. I – I have his remedies here. I know what to do –'

His hand went into his pocket and came out again with a hypodermic syringe.

'Unless he gets this at once it'll be too late –' He had caught up Lord Altamount's arm, rolling up his sleeve, pinching up the flesh between his fingers, he held the hypodermic ready.

But someone else moved. Horsham was across the room, pushing Colonel Munro aside; his hand closed over James Kleek's as he wrenched the hypodermic away. Kleek struggled but Horsham was too strong for him. And Munro was now there, too.

'So it's been *you*, James Kleek,' he said. 'You who've been the traitor, a faithful disciple who wasn't a faithful disciple.'

Miss Neumann had gone to the door – had flung it open and was calling.

'Nurse! Come quickly. Come.'

The nurse appeared. She gave one quick glance to Professor Shoreham, but he waved her away and pointed across the room to where Horsham and Munro still held a struggling Kleek. Her hand went into the pocket of her uniform.

Shoreham stammered out, 'It's Altamount. A heart attack.'

'Heart attack, my foot,' roared Munro. 'It's attempted murder.' He stopped.

'Hold the chap,' he said to Horsham, and leapt across the room.

'Mrs Cortman? Since when have you entered the nursing profession? We'd rather lost sight of you since you gave us the slip in Baltimore.'

Milly Jean was still wrestling with her pocket. Now her hand came out with the small automatic in it. She glanced towards Shoreham but Munro blocked her, and Lisa Neumann was standing in front of Shoreham's chair.

James Kleek yelled, 'Get Altamount, Juanita – quick – get Altamount.'

Her arm flashed up and she fired.

James Kleek said,

'Damned good shot!'

Lord Altamount had had a classical education. He murmured faintly, looking at James Kleek,

'Jamie? *Et tu Brute?*' and collapsed against the back of his chair.

Dr McCulloch looked round him, a little uncertain of what he was going to do or say next. The evening had been a somewhat unusual experience for him.

Lisa Neumann came to him and set a glass by his side.

'A hot toddy,' she said.

'I always knew you were a woman in a thousand, Lisa.' He sipped appreciatively.

'I must say I'd like to know what all this has been about – but I gather it's the sort of thing that's so hush-hush that nobody's going to tell me anything.'

'The Professor – he's all right, isn't he?'

'The Professor?' He looked at her anxious face, kindly. 'He's fine. If you ask me, it's done him a world of good.'

'I thought perhaps the shock –'

'I'm quite all right,' said Shoreham. 'Shock treatment is what I needed. I feel – how shall I put it – *alive* again.' He looked surprised.

McCulloch said to Lisa, 'Notice how much stronger his voice is? It's apathy really that's the enemy in these cases – what *he* wants is to work again – the stimulation of some brain work. Music is all very well – it's kept him soothed and able to enjoy life in a mild way. But he's really a man of great intellectual power – and he misses the mental activity that was the essence of life to him. Get him started on it again if you can.'

He nodded encouragingly at her as she looked doubtfully at him.

'I think, Dr McCulloch,' said Colonel Munro, 'that we owe you a few explanations of what happened this evening, even though, as you surmise, the powers-that-be will demand a hush-hush policy. Lord Altamount's death –' He hesitated.

'The bullet didn't actually kill him,' said the doctor, 'death was due to shock. That hypodermic would have done the trick – strychnine. The young man –'

'I only just got it away from him in time,' said Horsham.

'Been the nigger in the woodpile all along?' asked the doctor.

'Yes – regarded with trust and affection for over seven years. The son of one of Lord Altamount's oldest friends –'

'It happens. And the lady – in it together, do I understand?'

'Yes. She got the post here by false credentials. She is also wanted by the police for murder.'

'Murder?'

'Yes. Murder of her husband, Sam Cortman, the American Ambassador. She shot him on the steps of the Embassy – and told a fine tale of young men, masked, attacking him.'

'Why did she have it in for him? Political or personal?'

'He found out about some of her activities, we think.'

'I'd say he suspected infidelity,' said Horsham. 'Instead he discovered a hornets' nest of espionage and conspiracy, and his wife running the show. He didn't know quite how to deal with it. Nice chap, but slow-thinking – and she had the sense to act quickly. Wonderful how she registered grief at the Memorial Service.'

'Memorial –' said Professor Shoreham.

Everyone, slightly startled, turned round to look at him.

'Difficult word to say, memorial – but I mean it. Lisa, you and I are going to have to start work again.'

'But, Robert –'

'I'm alive again. Ask the doctor if I ought to take things easy.'

Lisa turned her eyes inquiringly on McCulloch.

'If you do, you'll shorten your life and sink back into apathy –'

'There you are,' said Shoreham. 'Fash-fashion – medical fashion today. Make everyone, even if they're – at – death's door – go on working –'

Dr McCulloch laughed and got up.

'Not far wrong. I'll send you some pills along to help.'

'I shan't take them.'

'You'll do.'

At the door the doctor paused. 'Just want to know – how did you get the police along so quickly?'

'Squadron Leader Andrews,' said Munro, 'had it all in hand. Arrived on the dot. We knew the woman was around somewhere, but had no idea she was in the house already.'

'Well – I'll be off. Is all you've told me true? Feel I shall wake up any minute, having dropped off to sleep half way through the latest thriller. Spies, murders, traitors, espionage, scientists –'

He went out.

There was a silence.

Professor Shoreham said slowly and carefully:

'Back to work –'

Lisa said as women have always said:

'You must be *careful*, Robert –'

'Not – not careful. Time might be short.'

He said again:

'Memorial –'

'What *do* you mean? You said it before.'

'Memorial? Yes. To Edward. His Memorial! Always used to think he had the face of a martyr.'

Shoreham seemed lost in thought.

'I'd like to get hold of Gottlieb. May be dead. Good man to work with. With him and with you, Lisa – get the stuff out of the bank –'

'Professor Gottlieb is alive – in the Baker Foundation, Austin, Texas,' said Mr Robinson.

'What are you talking of doing?' said Lisa.

'Benvo, of course! Memorial to Edward Altamount. He died for it, didn't he? Nobody should die in vain.'

EPILOGUE

Sir Stafford Nye wrote out a telegraph message for the third time.

ZP 354XB 91 Dep S.Y.

HAVE ARRANGED FOR MARRIAGE CEREMONY TO BE PERFORMED ON THURSDAY OF NEXT WEEK AT ST CHRISTOPHERS IN THE VALE LOWER STAUNTON 2.30 PM STOP ORDINARY CHURCH OF ENGLAND SERVICE IF R.C. OR GREEK ORTHODOX DESIRED PLEASE WIRE INSTRUCTIONS STOP WHERE ARE YOU AND WHAT NAME DO YOU WISH TO USE FOR MARRIAGE CEREMONY STOP NAUGHTY NIECE OF MINE FIVE YEARS OLD AND HIGHLY DISOBEDIENT WISHES TO ATTEND AS BRIDESMAID RATHER SWEET REALLY NAME OF SYBIL STOP LOCAL HONEYMOON AS I THINK WE HAVE TRAVELLED ENOUGH LATELY STOP SIGNED PASSENGER TO FRANKFURT.

TO STAFFORD NYE BXY42698

ACCEPT SYBIL AS BRIDESMAID SUGGEST GREAT AUNT MATILDA AS MATRON OF HONOUR STOP ALSO ACCEPT PROPOSAL OF MARRIAGE THOUGH NOT OFFICIALLY MADE STOP C OF E QUITE SATISFACTORY ALSO HONEYMOON ARRANGEMENTS STOP INSIST PANDA SHOULD ALSO BE PRESENT STOP NO GOOD SAYING WHERE I AM AS I SHANT BE WHEN THIS REACHES YOU STOP SIGNED MARY ANN

'Do I look all right?' asked Stafford Nye nervously, twisting his head to look in the glass.

He was having a dress rehearsal of his wedding clothes.

'No worse than any other bridegroom,' said Lady

Matilda. 'They're always nervous. Not like brides who are usually quite blatantly exultant.'

'Suppose she doesn't come?'

'She'll come.'

'I feel – I feel – rather queer inside.'

'That's because you would have a second helping of pâté de foie gras. You've just got bridegroom's nerves. Don't fuss so much, Staffy. You'll be all right on the night – I mean you'll be all right when you get to the church –'

'That reminds me –'

'You haven't forgotten to buy the ring?'

'No, no – it's just I forgot to tell you that I've got a present for you, Aunt Matilda.'

'That's very nice of you, dear boy.'

'You said the organist had gone –'

'Yes, thank goodness.'

'I've brought you a new organist.'

'Really, Staffy, what an extraordinary idea! Where did you get him?'

'Bavaria – he sings like an angel –'

'We don't need him to sing. He'll have to play the organ.'

'He can do that too – he's a very talented musician.'

'Why does he want to leave Bavaria and come to England?'

'His mother died.'

'Oh dear, that's what happened to our organist. Organists' mothers seem to be very delicate. Will he require mothering? I'm not very good at it.'

'I dare say some grandmothering or great-grandmothering would do.'

The door was suddenly flung open and an angelic-looking child in pale pink pyjamas, powdered with rosebuds, made a dramatic entrance – and said in dulcet tones as of one expecting a rapturous welcome –

'It's me.'

'Sybil, why aren't you in bed?'

'Things aren't very pleasant in the nursery –'

'That means you've been a naughty girl, and Nannie isn't pleased with you. What did you do?'

Sybil looked at the ceiling and began to giggle.

'It was a caterpillar – a furry one. I put it on her and it went down *here*.'

Sybil's finger indicated a spot in the middle of her chest which in dressmaking parlance is referred to as 'the cleavage.'

'I don't wonder Nannie was cross – ugh,' said Lady Matilda.

Nannie entered at this moment, said that Miss Sybil was over-excited, wouldn't say her prayers, and wouldn't go to bed.

Sybil crept to Lady Matilda's side.

'I want to say my prayers with you, Tilda –'

'Very well – but then you go straight to bed.'

'Oh yes, Tilda.'

Sybil dropped on her knees, clasped her hands, and uttered various peculiar noises which seemed to be a necessary preliminary to approaching the Almighty in prayer. She sighed, groaned, grunted, gave a final catarrhal snort, and launched herself:

'Please God bless Daddy and Mummy in Singapore, and Aunt Tilda, and Uncle Staffy, and Amy and Cook and Ellen, and Thomas, and all the dogs, and my Pony Grizzle, and Margaret and Diana my best friends, and Joan, the last of my friends, and make me a good girl for Jesus' sake, Amen. And please God make Nannie nice.'

Sybil rose to her feet, exchanged glances with Nannie

with the assurance of having won a victory, said good-night and disappeared.

'Someone must have told her about Benvo,' said Lady Matilda. 'By the way, Staffy, who's going to be your best man?'

'Forgot all about it – Have I got to have one?'

'It's usual.'

Sir Stafford Nye picked up a small furry animal.

'Panda shall be my best man – please Sybil – please Mary Ann – And why not? Panda's been in it from the beginning – ever since Frankfurt. . .'